SCENE OF THE CRIME: MEANS AND MOTIVE

BY
CARLA CASSIDY

MILLS & BOON

First Published in Great Britain 2016
By Mills & Boon, an imprint of HarperCollins*Publishers*
1 London Bridge Street, London, SE1 9GF

© 2016 Carla Bracale

ISBN: 978-0-263-91923-3

46-1116

Our policy is to use papers that are natural, renewable and recyclable products and made from wood grown in sustainable forests. The logging and manufacturing processes conform to the legal environmental regulations of the country of origin.

Printed and bound in Spain
by CPI, Barcelona

Carla Cassidy is an award-winning, *New York Times* bestselling author who has written more than one hundred and twenty novels for Mills & Boon. In 1995, she won Best Silhouette Romance from *RT Book Reviews* for *Anything for Danny*. In 1998, she also won a Career Achievement Award for Best Innovative Series from *RT Book Reviews*. Carla believes the only thing better than curling up with a good book to read is sitting down at the computer with a good story to write.

To Bob and Jenny Offutt, thanks for the wonderful hospitality we received when we stayed with you at your beautiful resort, Crystal Cove Bed and Breakfast in Branson.

Chapter One

FBI Special Agent Jordon James hated two things—winter and murder—and she was about to be immersed in the middle of both. She frowned and stared out the small window of the helicopter that had carried her from Kansas City to the rousing tourist town of Branson, Missouri.

When they'd left Kansas City the ground had been winter brown and the temperature had been a balmy forty-five. Unfortunately, as they approached the Branson airport, the temperature had dropped into the teens and four inches of snow had fallen in the small vacation destination overnight.

As the helicopter circled for the landing, visions of a beach with a bright sun, a chaise lounge and a fruity alcoholic drink flirted in Jordon's head. She'd booked a long-awaited vacation in Florida for the end of next week. Hopefully, this mess in Branson could be cleaned up soon enough that she wouldn't have to postpone the long-awaited vacation.

She was here only in an advisory position as a favor between her FBI director and the Branson mayor. All she knew was that there had been three murders in as many months committed in a popular bed-and-breakfast. The latest murder victim had been stabbed to death and discovered by a maid in her room the day before.

Jordon played nice with others when it was absolutely necessary, but she preferred to work alone. She had a feeling that Director Tom Langford had tapped her for this job, knowing that she would have to try to work with a police chief who probably didn't want her here.

"It builds character to step out of your comfort zone." She wished she had a dime for every time Tom had said that to her in the last couple of years. "Don't be a cowboy, Jordon. That's what nearly got you killed a year ago," he'd reminded her right before she'd left.

The heart-shaped pattern of cigarette-burn scars on her left hip itched as memories of an old cellar and a serial killer named Ralph Hicks flashed in her head.

It had been nearly a year since she'd almost become the sixth victim of the man who had tortured and killed five other women over a six-month period in the Kansas City area. Thankfully, she had been the one who had walked out of that dank, terrifying cellar and Ralph Hicks had come out in a body bag.

The bump of the helicopter touching down snapped her back to the here and now. Jordon thanked the pilot, grabbed her two bags and climbed down to the tarmac, where a uniformed police officer greeted her.

"Agent James, I'm Lieutenant Mark Johnson." He shouted above the whoop whoop of the helicopter blades as the aircraft took off once again.

He grabbed her bags from her. "Good to have you here. My car is parked over here." He turned and headed for the parking lot in the distance. An icy gust of wind half stole her breath away as she quickly followed behind him.

Within minutes they were in his patrol car with a steady flow of heated air blowing in her face. "Have you been to Branson before?" he asked when they pulled away from the airport.

"Never, although I've certainly heard a lot about it from coworkers who have been here," she replied. She held her hands up to the air vents and squinted against the late-afternoon sunshine that glared off the snow cover.

At least the highway they traveled had been cleared, but as he turned onto a narrow snowpacked street that headed straight downhill, her breath caught in the back of her throat.

They had gone from city highway to thick woods and a precarious country road with a simple right-hand turn. "Diamond Cove is down this way," Mark said. "Chief of Police Gabriel Walters is waiting for you there." He eased up on the gas as the back end of the car slid ominously to the left.

Every muscle in Jordon's body tensed and didn't relax again until they had turned into a driveway in front of a cozy-looking log cabin. He parked next to a police car that was already there and shut off the engine.

"Welcome to Diamond Cove Bed-and-Breakfast," Mark said. "This is the main office and dining area." He pointed to the right. "As you can see through the trees up on the ridge there are four cabins that hold two suites each. The latest victim, Sandy Peters, was found in her bed in unit three yesterday morning by one of the housekeeping staff."

Jordon gazed at the four small log cabins with front porches. With the lack of leaves on the trees they were easily visible. Outside each doorway were two rocking chairs for the guests' pleasure.

In the spring and summer the thick woods that surrounded the cabins would hide them from view. The air would be filled with birdsong and squirrels would provide comic relief with their antics. Those rocking chairs would make perfect perches to nature-watch.

On the surface, the Diamond Cove resort appeared to be nestled on a secluded mountainside and promised peace and seclusion for the city-weary. But the peace had been shattered by three horrendous murders.

Mark opened his car door and Jordon did the same. A gust of frigid air greeted her and snow crunched underfoot as she got out of the car. Once again she thought of the beach and released a frosty, deep sigh.

"Follow me," he said after grabbing her bags from the backseat.

He bypassed the front door and instead led her around the building on a wraparound porch. They passed a beautiful waterfall that was obviously heated as the water trickled merrily over rocks and into a small pond despite the below-freezing temperature.

They entered the building and stepped into the main dining room. The air smelled of a hint of cinnamon, wood smoke and rich, freshly brewed coffee.

It was a small, cozy area with two long tables draped in elegant white cloths. Fat white candles and crystal salt and pepper shakers marked the center of each table. A bookcase holding preserves, jellies and cookbooks for sale was against one wall, and a fireplace with two chairs added to the homey atmosphere.

Jordon took all of this in with a single glance, for it was the man seated in one of the chairs by the fireplace that captured her full attention.

Chief of Police Gabriel Walters held a cup of coffee in his hand and stared into the flames of the crackling fire. He was apparently so deep in thought he hadn't even heard them come in.

His black hair was neatly cut and broad shoulders filled out the dark blue uniform shirt. His profile indicated a strong jawline and a perfectly straight nose.

"Chief?" Mark said hesitantly.

He shot up out of the chair and a touch of annoyance flashed across his handsome features. It was there only a moment and then covered by a smile that warmed Jordon right down to her frozen toes.

He might not mean the smile, but it didn't matter. He wore the gesture well even though it didn't quite light up the depths of his intense blue eyes.

"Special Agent James... I'm Chief Walters," he said and took her hand for a firm, no-nonsense shake.

"Please, make it Jordon," she replied.

He nodded and released her hand. "Jordon it is. Please, have a seat. Can I get you a cup of coffee?"

"That would be great," she replied. She unzipped her coat, shrugged it off and sat in the chair next to his in front of the fireplace.

He walked over to Mark and spoke so softly to the man that Jordon couldn't hear. Mark nodded a goodbye to Jordon and left the way they had come.

She watched as Gabriel moved over to a small table that held a coffeemaker and all the accoutrements for all tastes. "Cream? Sugar?" he asked.

"Black is fine," she replied. The man was definitely

hot. He boasted not only wonderfully broad shoulders, but also slim hips and a stomach that didn't appear to hold an ounce of body fat.

He hadn't offered her the choice of calling him by his given name and that alone told her he might not be happy to see her. She'd seen him for only a minute and already she had him pegged as intense and probably uptight and rigid.

His physical attractiveness definitely stirred a little fire of heat in the pit of her stomach, but if her suspicions about his personality were right, then she had a feeling it wouldn't be long before she might want to pinch his head off. Time would tell.

He held the coffee cup out to her and she took it with a murmured thanks. Then he returned to the chair next to her. "I don't know how much you know about what's going on here."

"No real specifics. I was only told that there have been three murders here, the most recent victim discovered yesterday morning."

He nodded. "Sandy Peters. She was thirty-four years old and a mystery writer. According to the owners of the resort, she came here every year in January to spend a couple of weeks holed up and writing."

"Married? Divorced?"

"Single, and according to everyone I spoke to yesterday who was close to her, she wasn't dating anyone," he replied. "Besides, she was killed in the same manner as the other two victims."

"Stabbed to death," Jordon said.

"That's right. My investigation hasn't turned up anything the three victims have in common other than they were all guests here at Diamond Cove at the time of their deaths. In fact, they were the only guests here at the time when they were killed."

Jordon took a sip of the coffee and leaned back in the chair. The warmth and scent of the fire combined with the deep smooth tone of his voice would make it easy to be lulled into a semicoma if they weren't talking about murder.

She leaned forward and caught a whiff of his pleasant, woodsy-scented cologne. "So, this doesn't sound like it's about any specific victimology, but tell me about the other victims anyway."

"The first one was twenty-five-year-old Samantha Kent. She and her husband had rented a suite just before Thanksgiving to celebrate their first wedding anniversary. She was stabbed to death on a trail near their cabin on a Tuesday morning."

He grimaced and then continued. "The second victim, Rick Sanders, booked a room a week before Christmas. He was found stabbed in the guest shed. Samantha was a schoolteacher from Kansas City. Rick was a restaurant owner from Dallas who had come here to check out some of the local food. Sandy was from St. Louis."

Jordon was impressed by how easily he rattled off the pertinent information of each victim without any notes. It meant he'd embraced the victims. They weren't just dead bodies to him… They were people. She liked that.

She took another sip of her coffee as he continued. "When Samantha was found on the trail, the first person we looked at hard was her husband, Eric. But he had a solid alibi. He'd been here having breakfast with the owners when she was killed and I could find no motive for him wanting her dead."

"What was she doing outside all alone?" Jordon asked, mentally taking notes of all the information he was giving to her.

"She was an amateur photographer...a nature buff, and according to her husband, she'd decided to skip breakfast on that particular morning to take some photographs. She had a quick cup of coffee here with the owners and her husband to start the day and then she left by herself."

"Who found her body?"

"Billy Bond, the groundskeeper. When he found her she was still breathing but unconscious and bleeding out. She died on the way to the hospital. According to the doctor, she had been attacked only minutes before she was discovered."

"So, the killer is probably local and you have no clue as to the motive," Jordon said.

Gabriel's lips thinned slightly. "No clue as to who or why. I guess that's why Mayor Stoddard thought it was important to bring in the big guns."

A small laugh escaped her despite the obvious displeasure on his face. "Don't worry, Chief Walters. This gun doesn't intend to get in your way. You're the big Uzi and I'm just a little backup handgun."

She held back a sigh. She'd been here only half an hour and already the very hot chief of police appeared to be attempting to engage her in a spitting match.

SHE DIDN'T INTEND to get in his way.

But something about FBI Special Agent Jordon James was already under his skin.

As Gabriel led her out of the main cabin and toward the smaller cabins so that she could see each of
the crime scenes, his gut twisted tight in frustration.

He hadn't been happy when the mayor had insisted
they get help from the FBI, even in just an advisory
position. He'd taken it as a vote of no confidence from
the man who was his boss.

Jordon James had said nothing out of line. She'd
been a complete professional so far, but while they'd
talked he'd had some very unprofessional thoughts
roll through his head.

She was strikingly pretty with her short curly dark
hair and green eyes that sparked not only a keen in-
telligence, but with what he sensed was also a glim-
mer of humor.

When she'd shrugged out of her coat it had been
impossible not to notice the length of her legs encased in the tight black slacks and the thrust of her
full breasts against the white cotton of her blouse.
Even the holster around her waist didn't detract from
her innate femininity.

He'd been living and breathing murder since the
first body had been found here almost three months
ago. His instant, sharp physical attraction to Jordon
had momentarily shaken him.

He now followed her up the wooden stairs that led
to the ridge where the cabins were located. At least
out here in the cold air he couldn't smell the enticing
flowery perfume that had permeated the air the moment she'd sat next to him in the dining room.

She reached the top of the ridge and turned back
to wait for him. When he joined her he pointed to a
small structure just to the right.

"That's the guest shed where Rick Sanders was found." She fell into step next to him as they approached the building where a cheerful hand-painted Welcome sign hung over the door.

They stepped inside to the tinkle of a little bell, and even though he'd been in the shed at least twenty times since the night that Rick's body had been found, his gaze took everything in as if it was the very first time he'd been inside the small building.

A bifold door to the left hid a stackable washer and dryer. A round table and chairs to the right invited the guests to sit and relax. Beyond that was another closed door that led to a small storage room.

A counter held a fancy coffeemaker with a carousel of little flavored coffees, and beneath the counter, a glass-doored refrigerator displayed a variety of sodas and bottled water for the guests to enjoy at no cost.

"What a nice idea for the people staying here," Jordon said.

Gabriel nodded, although his head filled with the vision of Rick Sanders dead on the floor, his back riddled with stab wounds. "He never saw what was coming. It appeared that he was standing in front of the coffeemaker waiting for a hot chocolate when he was attacked from behind."

She looked up at the bell hanging over the doorway. "He didn't hear it coming?"

"The bell wasn't hung there until after his murder," Gabriel explained. He watched Jordon closely as her narrowed gaze once again swept the room. He couldn't help but notice the long length of her dark eyelashes and the slightly pouty fullness of her lips.

She opened the door to the storage room, where

Gabriel knew the space held only cases of soda, boxes of the little coffee pods, paper napkins and other supplies.

"Okay," she said and gazed at him with eyes that gave away nothing.

"See anything me and my men might have missed?"

"Yes. In fact, I think I've solved the case. It was Colonel Mustard in the library with a wrench," she replied flippantly. He stared at her in stunned surprise. "Where to next?" she asked before he could even begin to formulate a response.

They exited the guest shed and he led her down a path that would eventually take them to the place where Samantha Kent's body had been found.

"There's about seven acres of trails here," he said.

"Good grief. I hope we aren't walking them all now." She pulled her coat collar closer around her slender neck. "I hate this weather. I've got a date with a beach in Florida at the end of next week and I can't wait to get in a bathing suit and enjoy a fruity, fun alcoholic beverage."

"Then I guess you'll need to hurry to solve this case in time to get to the beach," he replied. He took another couple of steps then halted when he realized she wasn't with him.

He turned around. She stood stock-still, her green eyes narrowed as if he was a puzzling crime scene she was analyzing. "Are you normally a jerk or are you just acting like one especially for me?"

Despite the cold air, a wave of warmth filled his cheeks. "No, I'm not normally a jerk," he replied. He drew in a deep breath and released it slowly. "But I guess I have been acting like one since you arrived and I apologize." He had to admit to himself that he'd been a bit antagonistic with her. It wasn't her fault she was here. She was just doing her job like he was trying to do his.

"Apology accepted," she said easily and grinned. "Can I expect more jerk from you or are you over it now?"

"I'm not sure," he admitted. He shoved his hands into his coat pockets. "It's not you personally."

Her grin widened. "Trust me, I didn't think it was about me personally. You haven't known me long enough to have attitude with me, although I'm sure if I'm here for a few more days that will eventually come."

He gazed at her curiously. "Why? Are you difficult to work with?"

"I'll let you draw your own conclusions." Her smile fell and she wrapped her arms around her chest. "Look, I get it that you probably aren't happy about FBI presence here. But I am here, and we might as well try to work together to solve these murders. Now, can we get on with this? I'm freezing my tush off."

And a fine tush it was, Gabriel thought as they continued walking on the narrow trail. Within minutes they were at the spot where Samantha Kent's body had been found.

"The trees were still fairly full of leaves when she was killed," he said. "Although you can see the cabins from here now, they weren't visible at the time of the murder."

Once again Jordon silently surveyed the scene. "She didn't scream or cry out for help? Nobody heard anything?"

"Nobody admitted to hearing anything. She was attacked from behind like Rick. She didn't have a single defensive wound and Billy didn't see or hear anyone else in the woods when he found her." The frustration of the cases burned in his stomach as once again his mind provided a memory of this particular crime scene.

Samantha had already been carried away to the hospital by the time Gabriel had arrived on scene, but her blood had stained the autumn leaves where she had fallen, transforming this piece of beautiful woods to a place of haunting, violent death.

"I've seen enough," Jordon said softly.

They were both silent as he led her to unit number three, where Sandy Peters had been found stabbed in her bed.

"Wow. Nice room," Jordon said after they'd stomped the snow off their boots and stepped inside. They both had donned gloves and bootees, as the room was still officially a crime scene.

"All the rooms are this nice," he replied. He stood by the door as Jordon wandered the area.

A king-size log bed was the center focal point, along with a stone fireplace and a sunken Jacuzzi tub for two. The bed had been stripped down to the mattress, but Sandy's suitcase was still open on one of the chairs in front of the fireplace, and a thick pink robe still hung on a coat tree next to the dresser.

He'd kept things intact in the room as much as possible for Jordon's perusal, although his men had already taken Sandy's cell phone and computer and the bedclothes into evidence. The room had been gone over with a fine-tooth comb and fingerprinted, so this evening he'd have some of his men clear the rest of Sandy's things from the room.

Jordon disappeared into the adjoining bathroom and then reappeared and stared at the tub, where a little basket held packets of bubble bath and two wineglasses with a bottle of white wine perched on the tile.

"There was obviously not a struggle." It was a statement of fact rather than a question.

"And the door wasn't forced," he replied. "It appears that she opened the door and was immediately stabbed. She fell backward to the bed and the attack continued there. She was stabbed a total of twelve times."

A frown danced across Jordon's features. "Overkill... That indicates a rage."

He nodded. "The same kind of rage was evident with the other two victims, as well."

"And the time of death?"

"The coroner placed it between around midnight and five in the morning," he replied. "Hannah, the owners' fifteen-year-old daughter, saw Sandy leaving the guest shed at around nine in the evening. She had a soda in her hand and told Hannah she planned on being up late working."

"What was Hannah doing out and about at that time of night in this weather?"

"One of her jobs here is to make sure the refrigerator is restocked each evening. She was later than usual that night." He looked toward the window where dusk had moved in. "I've arranged interviews with all the staff here to start in the morning at eight. In the meantime, we should get you settled in for the night.

I've made arrangements for you to stay at a motel not far from here."

She looked at him in surprise. "Why would I stay at another motel? I'm assuming there are vacant rooms here?"

"Yes, but there is also a killer using this bed-and-breakfast as his personal playground."

"All the more reason for me to stay here," she replied.

Gabriel frowned. "I really don't like the idea. I think it would be much better if you stayed somewhere else."

"I'll be fine here. I'm armed and I'm trained. Just get me a key and point me to a room."

The burn in his gut intensified. Even though he barely knew Jordon, he recognized the stubborn upward thrust of a chin, the resolute shine in her eyes.

The killer was savvy enough not to leave any evidence behind. In savagely murdering three people he hadn't made any mistakes that Gabriel had been able to find.

The last thing Gabriel wanted was for FBI Special Agent Jordon James to become the fourth victim.

Chapter Two

When they returned to the main dining room, two adults and two teenagers awaited them. Gabriel introduced them as owners Ted and Joan Overton and their two children, fifteen-year-old Hannah and seventeen-year-old Jason.

"I made fresh coffee and some sandwiches," Joan said as she and her husband jumped up from the table where they'd been seated. She hurried over to stand next to the table with the coffeemaker and twisted her hands together as if unsure what to do next.

"Thank you—I'd love a cup," Jordon said. "And the sandwiches look wonderful." Joan's pretty features lit up as if she was pleased to be able to serve somebody.

"We've canceled all of our reservations for the next two weeks," Ted said. Jordon took a seat across from him and Gabriel sat next to Jason.

"There weren't that many to cancel," Joan said as she set a cup of coffee in front of Jordon and then sat next to her husband. "This is our slowest time of year, but reservations had already fallen off because of the bad publicity we've received. Social media is destroying us."

"Your place is lovely," Jordon said. "How long have you all owned it?"

"We bought it a little over a year ago," Ted said. "We'd talked about leaving the rat race behind and doing something like this for years, and then this place came on the market as a foreclosure and so we bit the bullet and made the move."

"Made the move from where?" Jordon asked. She took half of one of the thick ham-and-cheese sandwiches that were on a platter and placed it on the small plate in front of her.

"Oklahoma City," Ted replied. He was a tall, thin man with dark hair and brown eyes, and his children took after him rather than their shorter, blond-haired, blue-eyed mother.

"Do we need to be here?" Jason asked. His cheeks colored slightly as Jordon turned her gaze on him. "I don't know anything about what's happened around here and I've got homework to finish."

Jordon shifted her gaze to Gabriel, who shrugged. She turned back to Jason. "I don't see any reason for you to hang around here while we talk to your mother and father." The young man was nearly out of his chair before Jordon had finished speaking.

"What about me?" Hannah asked. "I've already told Chief Walters everything I know."

"As long as it's okay with your parents, you both can be excused for tonight," Jordon replied. Hannah also flew out of her chair and pulled a cell phone from her pocket.

"Go directly to the house and no place else," Ted said.

"Where's the house?" Jordon asked as the two teenagers left the building.

"Across the street. It came with this property," Ted replied. "It's a nice three-bedroom with a lake view."

"And it has a huge detached garage that's far enough away from the house that I can't hear the banging and curses or noises that Ted makes when he's working on one of the cars or in the middle of a woodworking project," Joan added.

For the next hour Jordon questioned the couple about the murders, the victims and the daily operation of the bed-and-breakfast.

Gabriel was mostly silent during the conversation. She was grateful he allowed her to go over information she was certain he already knew.

The body language between the couple indicated a close, loving relationship, and Jordon sensed no underlying tension other than what would be deemed normal under the conditions.

By the time they'd finished up, night had fallen outside. "Agent James would like to stay here," Gabriel said when the interview had wound down. A deep frown cut across his forehead. "That wouldn't be a problem, would it?"

"Of course not," Joan replied with a touch of surprise.

"Are you sure you want to do that?" Ted asked.

"Positive," Jordon replied without hesitation. Gabriel's silent disapproval of the plan wafted in the air, but Jordon's mind was made up.

"We'll put you in unit seven," Ted said. They all got up from the table. "I'll just go get the key for you." He left the dining room through a door that Jordon assumed led into the main office.

"Breakfast is served from seven to nine. If that

doesn't work for you just let me know," Joan said. "We'll be glad to do whatever we can to accommodate you while you're here."

"I'd like you to keep things the way you would for any other guest," Jordon replied.

"And I'll be here around seven in the morning so that we can begin interviewing the staff at eight," Gabriel said. "I hope you don't mind me joining Agent James here for breakfast."

"You know you're always welcome here, Chief Walters," Joan said warmly.

Ted returned to the dining room and handed Jordon a room key. "I'll just grab my coat and show you to the room."

"Don't worry about it, Ted. I'll see her to the room," Gabriel replied. He pulled on his coat and Jordon did the same.

"Thank you for the sandwiches. It was very thoughtful of you," Jordon said to Joan.

"It was my pleasure," Joan replied.

"And I won't be needing daily maid service while I'm here. Once a week or so would be fine just for clean towels and sheets, and I can change my own bed."

Joan nodded. "If that's what you want. Hopefully the case will be solved soon and you won't even be here long enough for that."

"We'll see you in the morning." Gabriel picked up Jordon's suitcases.

Jordon took the smaller of the bags from him. "They seem like a nice couple," she said when they were out of the building and heading up the stairs to the cabins.

"They are. They have good kids, too. Both Jason and Hannah are excellent students and they work here for their parents after school." He shifted the suitcase he carried from one hand to the other. "But these murders are quickly destroying their livelihood."

"So, who would want to do that?" The cold air nearly stole her breath away as they trudged up the stairs to the row of cabins. She sighed in relief as they reached the unit she would call home for the duration of her stay.

"A few people come to mind."

She set the suitcase she carried down and retrieved the room key from her pocket. Although she was intrigued by any suspects he might have in mind, at the moment all she wanted to do was get out of the frigid night air.

She sighed in relief as she stepped into the warm room. Gabriel followed her just inside the door and set her suitcase on the floor. She shrugged out of her coat, flipped the switch that made the flames in the fireplace jump to life and then turned back to look at him. "So who are these people who come to mind?"

"Actually, I'd rather not get into all that tonight. It's getting late and I'll just let you get settled in. Why don't I meet you in the dining room at seven tomorrow morning and we can discuss it more then."

It was only eight o'clock, hardly a late night, but it was obvious by the rigid set of his shoulders and how close he stood to the door that he wasn't comfortable having a long conversation in the intimacy of the room.

Maybe he had a wife to get home to, she thought, although there was no wedding ring on his finger. She pegged him in his midthirties, certainly not only old enough to be married, but also to have some children running around.

"Okay, then I guess I'll see you in the morning," she said. "Oh, and one more thing. If it's possible, I'd like to have a car at my disposal while I'm here."

He gave a curt nod. "I'll see to it that you have one first thing in the morning. And we should exchange cell phone numbers." He pulled his phone from his pocket.

With her number in his phone and his in hers, Gabriel stared at her for a long moment. "You know I don't approve of you staying here. You need to call me immediately if you feel uncomfortable here or believe you're in any kind of danger."

The only danger at the moment was the possibility of getting lost in the simmering depths of his eyes. She'd watched those blue eyes through the course of the evening. She wondered if he had any idea how expressive they were.

As she'd spoken to the Overtons, his eyes had alternately radiated with a soft sympathy and a deep frustration. It was only when he gazed at her that they became utterly shuttered and unfathomable.

"Jordon?" he said, pulling her from her momentary contemplation.

"Don't worry about me. I'll be just fine." Her hand fell to the butt of her gun to emphasize her point. "Good night, Chief Walters. I'll see you in the morning."

He gave her a curt nod and then left the room. Jordon locked the door behind him. There was no dead bolt, only the simple lock in the doorknob. Apparently security had never been a real issue before the murders. She was vaguely surprised dead bolts hadn't been installed since then.

She sank down on the chair next to the fireplace, her thoughts consumed by the man who had just taken his bedroom eyes and his heady woodsy scent with him.

She had no idea how well they were going to work together. She wasn't sure yet how open he was to hearing anything she might have to say about the cases. But the bottom line was she had a job to do and she would do her best with or without his cooperation.

She pulled herself up off the chair and opened one of the suitcases on the bed. It took her only minutes to unpack and then place her toiletries in the bathroom.

She set up her laptop computer on the small coffee table in front of the fireplace and for the next half hour typed in notes and impressions while things were still fresh in her mind.

By the time she finished, she was still too wound up even to think about going to sleep. She should just pull her nightgown on and go to bed, but she had a feeling she would just stare at the dark ceiling while sleep remained elusive.

Although the idea of going outside in the cold night air was abhorrent, she pulled on her coat and snow boots with the intention of retrieving one of the flavored coffees that tasted like dessert from the guest shed.

The path to the shed was lit by small solar lights in the ground, and despite the frosty air, she kept her coat open and her hand on the butt of her gun. The night was soundless, the eerie quiet that thick snow cover always brought.

All of her senses went on high alert. There was no way she intended to be careless on her first night or any other night she stayed here.

A faint scent of pine lingered in the air and she noticed through the bare trees that the main building was dark. She was all alone on the Diamond Cove grounds.

When she reached the guest shed and stepped inside, a light blinked on and the bell tinkled overhead. She made sure the door was closed firmly behind her and then checked behind the door that hid the washer and dryer to make sure nobody was hiding there. She then moved to the storage room. With her gun in her hand, she threw open the door and breathed a small sigh of relief.

Assured that she was alone, she picked out a chocolate-flavored coffee, placed it in the coffee machine and then faced the door as she waited for the foam cup to fill.

This was what poor Rick Sanders had done. He'd come in here seeking a nice cup of hot chocolate and instead had ended up stabbed viciously in the back.

When the coffeemaker whooshed the last of the liquid into the foam cup, she turned and grabbed it and went back out into the quiet of the night.

She was halfway to her cabin when the center of her back began to burn and she had the wild sense that somebody was watching her.

She whirled around, her sudden movement sloshing hot coffee onto her hand as she gripped the butt of her gun with the other. Nobody. There was nobody on the path behind her.

There was no sound, no sign of anyone sharing the night with her. She hurried the rest of the way to her room, unlocked her door and went back inside. She set her coffee on the low table in front of the fireplace and then moved the curtain at the window aside to peer out.

Despite the fact that she saw nothing to cause her concern, she couldn't shake the feeling that somebody had been out there, somebody who had been watching her…waiting for the perfect opportunity to strike.

GABRIEL WAS UP before dawn, his thoughts shooting a hundred different directions and making any further sleep impossible. He got out of bed, pulled a thick black robe around him and then padded into the kitchen to make coffee.

As it began to brew he took a quick shower, dressed for the day and then sank down at the kitchen table with a cup of hot coffee before him.

He should be thinking about murder. He should be thinking about the interviews he'd set up for the day, but instead his head was filled with questions about the long-legged, green-eyed woman who had blown into his case…into his town on a gust of cold air.

Could she accomplish what he hadn't been able to do? Could she somehow identify the killer, who had remained elusive so far to him, and get him behind bars? If she could, then it would be worth whatever he had to put up with to work with her.

All he wanted was to get this murderer off his streets. He'd never dreamed when he'd left the Chicago Police Department behind three years ago to take this job that he'd be dealing with a serial killer in the town known as America's family destination.

He'd also never imagined he'd be working for a mayor who was contentious and petulant, a man who was also a pompous ass and passive-aggressive. It was no wonder the last chief of police had quit after only less than a year on the job. More than once throughout the past three years Gabriel had considered walking away from here and starting over someplace else.

Once again his thoughts went to Jordon. There was no question that he found her extremely attractive. He even admired the fact that she'd called him out on the jabs he'd shot at her. But that didn't mean he was going to like her and it certainly didn't mean he was going to work well with her.

She already had one strike against her. He hadn't approved of her decision to stay at Diamond Cove. She'd known he didn't like it and yet she'd done it anyway. She was placing herself in the eye of a storm, and as far as he was concerned, it was an unnecessary, foolish risk.

By the time he finished two cups of coffee and his scattered musings, the morning sun had peeked up over the horizon and it was almost six thirty.

He made a call to arrange for a patrol car to be taken to the bed-and-breakfast for Jordon to use and then pulled on his coat to head out.

It was going to be a long day. Diamond Cove employed four people full-time and he'd arranged for all of them to be interviewed today along with a few others away from the bed-and-breakfast, as well.

As he got into his car he swallowed a sigh of frustration. Everyone they would be interviewing about the latest murder were people he'd interviewed at least twice before with the first two homicides.

He was desperate for some new information that might lead to an arrest, but he really wasn't expecting to get any that day.

Thankfully, the road crews had handled the snowfall well and the streets had been cleared for both the locals and the tourists who braved the winter weather for a vacation.

There was another snowstorm forecast for early next week. Jordon better enjoy the next few days of sunshine because, according to the weather report, the approaching snowstorm was going to be a bad one.

Maybe they'd get lucky and solve the case before the storm hit. She could keep her date with the Florida beach and he could get back to dealing with the usual crimes that always occurred in a tourist town.

He arrived at the bed-and-breakfast at ten till seven and parked next to the patrol car that Jordon would use. He retrieved the keys from under the floor mat and then headed to the dining room.

Jordon was already seated at a table and he didn't like the way his adrenaline jumped up a bit at the sight of her. Once again she was dressed in the black slacks that hugged every curve and a white, tailored blouse— the unofficial uniform of FBI agents everywhere.

"Good morning," she said. Her eyes were bright and she exuded the energy of somebody who had slept well and was eager to face a new day.

"Morning," he replied. He took off his coat and slung it over the back of a chair and then got himself a cup of coffee and sat across from her. The scent of fresh spring flowers wafted from her.

"Are you a morning person, Chief Walters?" she asked.

He looked at her in surprise. "I've never thought about it before. Why?"

"My ex-husband wasn't a morning person and he found my cheerful morning chatter particularly irritating. If you need me to keep quiet until you've had a couple of cups of coffee, that's information I need to know."

"How long have you been divorced?" he asked curiously.

"Three years. What about you? Married? Divorced? In a relationship?"

"Single," he replied, although he'd always thought that by the time he reached thirty-five years old he'd be happily married with a couple of children. That birthday had passed two months ago and there was no special woman in his life, let alone any children.

"Here are the keys to a patrol car you can use while you're here." He slid the keys across the table.

"Thanks. I appreciate it," she replied.

"Good morning, Chief," Joan said as she came into the room carrying two plates. "We heard you come in and I figured you were both ready for some breakfast."

"Oh my gosh, this is too pretty to eat," Jordon said as she gazed at the huge waffle topped with plump strawberries and a generous dollop of whipped cream.

"Speak for yourself," Gabriel replied as he grabbed one of the pitchers of warm syrup from the center of the table. "As far as I'm concerned, Joan makes the best waffles in town."

"Appreciate it, Chief," Joan replied with a smile of pleasure. She poured herself a cup of coffee and then joined them at the table. Within minutes Ted also appeared to drink coffee while Gabriel and Jordon ate their meal.

For the next half hour the conversation remained light and pleasant. Ted and Joan told Jordon about the various shows and attractions offered at the many theaters and establishments along the main drag.

"If you have time to do anything, you should go to the Butterfly Palace," Joan said. "It's one of my favorite places here in Branson. It's like walking in an enchanted forest with different species of butterflies everywhere."

"That sounds nice, but I don't plan on having any downtime to enjoy the local flavor while I'm here," Jordon replied. "I've got a vacation planned in Florida next week so I can get away from the cold and the snow."

"So you think you'll be able to have this all solved by the end of next week?" Ted's voice was filled with hope as he looked first at Jordon and then at Gabriel.

The frustration that had been absent while Gabriel had eaten his waffle returned to burn in the pit of his belly. "Unfortunately, I can't promise to solve this case in a timeline that would accommodate Agent James's vacation plans."

"And certainly that isn't what I meant to imply," Jordon replied with a slight upward thrust to her chin. "Vacation plans can be postponed. I'm committed to being here as long as I need to be in order to be of assistance to Chief Walters." She gave him a decidedly chilly smile.

"And I appreciate any help that I can get," he replied, hoping to diffuse some of the tension that suddenly snapped in the air.

"Speaking of help…" Joan looked out the door where housekeeper Hilary Hollis and her daughter, Ann, stomped their boots before entering the building.

Joan cleared the table and then she and Ted disappeared into the office so Gabriel and Jordon could get down to work.

The interview with the two women didn't take long and Gabriel let Jordon take the lead. It had been twenty-one-year-old Ann who had found Sandy Peters's body when she'd entered the room to clean it.

The young woman's eyes still held the horror of the gruesome discovery as she recounted to Jordon the morning she would never forget.

Jordon took notes on a small pad and handled the interview like the pro she obviously was, not only gaining the information she needed from the two women, but also earning their trust, as well.

"Do you intend for me to conduct all the interviews?" she asked when the women had left and she and Gabriel were alone in the room.

"If you're comfortable with that. I've already spoken to these people several times before with the previous two homicides. Maybe you can get something out of one of them that I couldn't get."

She narrowed her eyes. "Are you being sarcastic?"

He smiled at her ruefully. "No, although I guess I shouldn't be surprised that you think I am." His smile fell into a frown as he continued to gaze at her. "I'm frustrated by these murders. I'm ticked off at the mayor, who has made me feel inadequate since the moment I took this job, and I guess I've been taking all that out on you."

The smile that curved her lips warmed some of the cold places that had resided inside him for months. "Apology accepted," she replied.

"That's twice you've easily accepted an apology from me. Are you always so forgiving?" he asked curiously.

"I try not to sweat the small stuff, although I have been known to have a temper. Now, who are we seeing next?"

Before he could reply, the outer door swung open and groundskeeper Billy Bond walked in. "I don't know why I've got to be here," Billy said after the introductions had been made and he'd thrown himself into a chair.

He looked at Gabriel, his dark eyes filled with his displeasure. "You've already talked to me a dozen times before when those other two people got killed. I don't know any more now about murder than I did then."

"But I don't know anything about you or anything you've told Chief Walters in the past, so you'll have to humor us and answer some questions for me." Jordon gave the surly man a charming smile. "Why don't we start with you telling me what your duties are around here?"

"I take care of the grounds."

"Can you be a little more specific?"

For the next forty-five minutes Jordon questioned the thirty-two-year-old man who had worked for the bed-and-breakfast since Joan and Ted had opened the doors for business.

Once again admiration for Jordon's interrogation skills filled him as he sipped coffee and listened. And as before as he watched Billy closely, as he heard what the man had to say, he couldn't help but believe the man was hiding something…but what?

"He's a charming guy," Jordon said wryly when Billy left.

"He definitely lacks some social skills," he replied.

She looked down at her notes. "He answered all of my questions fairly easily, but his posture and facial expressions indicated to me that he wasn't being completely truthful." She looked at Gabriel. "For most of the interview he refused to meet my gaze and I could smell his body sweat. He just seemed a bit shady to me."

"Billy is at the top of my potential suspect list because I have the same concerns about him, but I haven't been able to find anything to tie him to the murders and I can't figure out what he could be lying about."

"He would be on my suspect list simply because he's the one who found Samantha Kent in the woods," she replied. "He could have stabbed her and then waited until he knew she couldn't say anything to identify him and then played the hero in calling for help, knowing that she was going to die before she could say anything to anyone."

He nodded. The same thought had definitely been in his head. "But what's his motive? There's certainly no financial gain in him killing the guests and he doesn't seem to have an ax to grind with the Overtons."

"Crazy doesn't need a rational motive," Jordon replied. Her eyes simmered with what appeared to be a whisper of dark ghosts and Gabriel fought against a sudden dark foreboding of his own.

Chapter Three

It was just before noon when thirty-eight-year-old handyman Ed Rollings sat at the table for his interview. Ed had the face of a cherub, slightly plump and with the open friendliness of a man who'd never met a stranger in his life.

However, the pleasant man was another at the top of Gabriel's list of suspects. Before Ed had arrived, Gabriel had given Jordon just enough information to aid her in her questioning of Ed.

"I understand your brother Kevin owned this place before the Overtons bought it," Jordon now said.

Ed nodded and a strand of his blond hair fell across his broad forehead. "That's right. Kev had big dreams for Diamond Cove but he was short in the financial-planning area." Ed laughed and shook his head. "That's the story of Kevin's life… Big dreams and no smarts for the follow-through."

"And you weren't upset when the Overtons took over here?"

"Why would I be upset? I was just glad they hired me on. I'd been working here when my brother owned it and jobs aren't that easy to find around here. I don't have any hard feelings against Ted and Joan. They didn't screw things up for Kevin. He did that to himself."

"What about your brother? Does he have a grudge against the Overtons?" Jordon asked.

"Kevin has a grudge against the whole world. Most of the time he doesn't even like me or our brother Glen," Ed replied with another laugh.

Gabriel listened to the back and forth and thought about that moment when Jordon's eyes had darkened so much. Although he shouldn't be curious, he was.

He was intrigued about those dark shadows that had momentarily danced in the depths of her eyes. He wondered what had caused her divorce, if her curls were as soft as they looked and what her slightly plump lips might taste like.

He also wondered if the stress of these cases was making him lose his mind. Certainly his thoughts about Jordon were completely inappropriate.

As Jordon continued questioning Ed, Gabriel got up from the table and walked over to stare out the window. From this vantage point he could see not only the cabins up on the ridge, but also the guest shed.

The scene of each murder flashed in his head, along with all of the people he'd interviewed after each one had occurred. Had he interviewed the murderer twice before already? Had he sat across from the person who had viciously stabbed Samantha Kent, Rick Sanders and Sandy Peters and exchanged conversation? Had he somehow missed something vital? That was one of his biggest fears.

"So, where were you on Sunday night when Sandy Peters was killed?" Jordon asked Ed.

Gabriel turned from the window to gaze at the

man. "Where I usually am on most nights…at home with my wife."

"And she can corroborate that you didn't leave the house all night?"

Ed laughed yet again. "That woman knows if I turn over in my sleep. She'd definitely know if I left the house, which I didn't." His blue eyes shone with what appeared to be open honesty. "Look, I've got no reason to kill anyone and no reason to hurt Joan and Ted. Ted pays me a good wage for a day's work. Besides, I don't have it in me to murder somebody."

"I think that's it for now," Jordon said and looked at Gabriel to see if he had anything to add.

"I'm sure Ed will be available if we have any further questions for him," Gabriel said.

"You know where to find me. I'm either here or at home with Millie most of the time," Ed assured them as he got up from the table.

"How do burgers sound for lunch?" Gabriel asked when Ed had left the building.

"Sounds good to me. I'm starving." She got up from the table and reached for her coat slung across the back of her chair.

"I thought we'd grab some lunch and then head into the station. I figured you'd want to look at all the files of the other two murders."

"Definitely," she replied.

It took them only minutes to get into Gabriel's car and he headed for Benny's Burgers, a no-nonsense joint just off the main drag that didn't cater to the tourist trade.

"I seriously doubt that the two housekeepers had

anything to do with whatever is going on," she said once they were on their way.

"I agree." The warmth of the heater seemed to intensify the fresh floral scent of her that he found so appealing. He tightened his hands around the steering wheel.

"Tell me more about Ed Rollings and his brothers."

"They were all born and raised here. Ed and his wife have no children but he has two brothers who also live in the area. Glen is two years younger than Ed. He's single and works as a clerk in one of the souvenir shops. And as you now know, his older brother, Kevin, owned Diamond Cove but lost it in bankruptcy."

He pulled into Benny's Burgers' parking lot, pleased to see that the lunch crowd was already gone and only three cars were in the lot.

Within five minutes they had their burgers and were seated across from each other in a booth near the back of the place. At least in here the odors of fried onions and beef were heavy enough to overwhelm Jordon's evocative scent.

"I'm assuming you've interviewed Kevin Rollings," she said and then popped a French fry into her mouth.

"Several times, but not in relationship to Sandy's murder. He's on my list to speak with later this afternoon. He's another one who has been on my short list of suspects."

"You mentioned that Billy Bond was on your list, as well. Anyone else I need to know about?"

He shook his head. "My list is depressingly short and everyone on it has had some sort of an alibi for the first two murders. You can get a better idea of what we've done to investigate those murders when you read the files."

"I'm looking forward to that," she replied.

For the next few minutes they were silent and focused on their meals. The cheeseburger and onion rings were tasteless to Gabriel as thoughts of the three murdered people weighed heavily in his head.

Jordon's appetite didn't appear to suffer at all. She ate her burger and fries, and then, with an assenting nod from him, she pulled his plate closer to her and picked at the onion rings he'd left on his plate.

"This has got to be somebody who wants to hurt Ted and Joan personally," she said.

"I was hesitant to make that call until now." He leaned back against the red leather of the booth. "I've investigated their background thoroughly and so far haven't found anything or anybody that would send up a real red flag."

"What did they do back in Oklahoma City?"

"Ted sold home and vehicle insurance and Joan was a third-grade teacher. According to all their friends and relatives, they're solid people who didn't have enemies. Their coworkers also spoke highly of them. Kevin Rollings might want to destroy the business just for spite and I can't figure out if Billy Bond is hiding something or not."

"He definitely has a bit of a creep factor going on." She shoved his now-empty plate away.

"Unfortunately, I can't arrest Billy for being a creep and I can't arrest Kevin Rollings on just my suspicion alone. Why did you get a divorce?" The question was out of his mouth before he realized he intended to ask it.

Her eyes widened slightly in surprise and then she smiled. "I was madly in love and got married in an effort to play grown-up and be a traditional kind of woman. It took me two years to realize I wasn't a marriage kind of woman after all." She took a quick sip of her soda, her gaze curious. "What about you? Are you a marriage kind of man?"

"Definitely," he replied firmly.

"Then why aren't you already married? You're a hot-looking guy with a respectable job. Why hasn't some honey already snapped you up?"

"I'm cautious," he admitted. "I want to make sure that when I finally marry it's a one-shot, forever kind of deal. My parents just celebrated their fortieth anniversary together and I want that kind of a lasting relationship for myself."

"Footloose and fancy-free—that's the life for me," she replied.

The threat of his intense physical attraction to her eased in his mind. She was somebody he would never be interested in pursuing no matter how alluring he found her.

This brief conversation was enough to let him know that he and FBI Special Agent Jordon James wanted very different things in life. He wasn't sure why, but this fact gave him a bit of peace of mind.

For the first time since she'd arrived he relaxed. "I'm glad you're here, Jordon."

"Thanks, Chief Walters. Does that mean lunch is on you?"

He smiled at her. "Yes, lunch is on me, and please call me Gabriel."

The sexy smile she flashed him in return instantly surged an unwanted tension back in his belly.

JORDON STRETCHED WITH her arms overhead and got up from the table. She'd been seated in the small conference room alone for the last couple of hours reading all the information that had been gathered on the murders at the bed-and-breakfast.

She definitely admired how Gabriel and his team had conducted such thorough investigations following each of the crimes. She'd also been aware of the respect shown to Gabriel among everyone in the station.

Nobody had joked or been overly familiar with him, indicating to her that he ran a tight ship and kept himself somewhat distant from his staff. Despite that fact, she'd sensed that he was not only respected, but also well liked.

She paced the length of the table, and her brain whirled with all the information she'd gained in the past three hours of intense study. Still, as thorough as the investigations had been, it was all information that yielded no answer as to who was responsible for the three homicides.

Several times throughout the past couple of hours of being cooped up in the conference room, a female officer named Jane Albright had occasionally popped her head in to see if Jordon needed anything. Only once had Jordon requested a cup of coffee.

The murder crime photos had been utterly gruesome and had built up not only a surge of frustration, but also a rich anger inside her. She wanted this perp caught before another person was killed and before Joan and Ted Overton were forced to close their doors and lose their livelihood.

She opened the conference room door, stepped out into the short hallway and headed to Gabriel's office. She gave two quick raps on his door, and when she heard his deep voice respond, she walked in.

He looked ridiculously handsome seated behind a large wooden desk, a computer on one side and a stack of files at his right. He started to rise but she waved him back down and sat in a chair opposite the desk.

"Looks like a lot of work," she said and pointed to the files.

"The usual…break-ins, purse-snatchings, robberies and the occasional car theft." He leaned back in the leather chair, his blue eyes gazing at her expectantly.

"If you're waiting for me to give you the name of the killer, don't hold your breath. After reading the files I'm as aggravated as I'm sure you are. This guy is obviously smart and organized. He's not only managed to commit three hideous murders but he's also escaped each scene with nobody seeing him and leaving nothing behind."

He stood. "We can talk about it more on the drive to Mouse's Maze of Mirrors."

A knot spun tight in her chest. "Mouse's Maze of Mirrors?"

He nodded. "It's a fairly new attraction on the strip, and on most afternoons and evenings Kevin Rollings works the door."

She got up from her chair and fought against the unsteady shake of her legs. "I definitely think a chat with Kevin is in order."

Minutes later they were in Gabriel's car and headed to the popular 76 Country Boulevard, where, he explained, most of the theaters, eateries and attractions were located.

As he pointed out places of interest, she tried to still the faint simmer of panic inside her. *See how I got mirrors all set up so you can see yourself? You can watch yourself scream.* Ralph Hicks's gravelly voice filled her head.

The creep had placed three large mirrors in front of all of his victims so they could watch while he tortured them. It had been a horrid form of torture in and of itself.

Buck up, buttercup, she told herself firmly. She'd survived the mirrors and Ralph Hicks. She refused to let those long hours in the cellar affect her now or define who she was. She could deal with a silly maze of mirrors without freaking out.

"I definitely think Kevin Rollings looks good as a potential suspect. His alibis for the other murders weren't exactly stellar," she said, shoving away the haunting memories of her past to focus on the here and now.

"It's tough to break an alibi substantiated by another family member. His brother Glen swore Kevin was at his house drinking and then passed out on his sofa at the time of both the previous murders."

"And of course Glen would have a motive to lie to save his brother's hide," she replied.

"I turned up the heat when I questioned Glen, but he stuck with the story." Gabriel turned into a parking lot in front of a large brown building with a huge picture of a demented-looking mouse painted on the siding. "We'll see what kind of alibi Kevin comes up with for the time of Sandy's murder."

As they got out of the car and approached the building, the sun broke out of the layer of clouds and gleamed on the rich darkness of Gabriel's hair.

He walked with confidence, as if he owned the space around him. Salt of the earth…a traditional man with traditional values and three murders that he was desperate to solve.

He seemed to have taken these crimes personally, otherwise she'd be working with somebody else rather than the chief himself. She hoped together they could get this killer behind bars, where he belonged.

There were no other cars in the lot. There had been few cars on the road. Obviously mid-January after a snowfall was a slow time for the entire town.

They entered into a small lobby with a turnstile and a counter behind which Kevin Rollings sat. Although considerably older than Ed, Kevin had the same blond hair, the same round face as his brother, but that was where the similarities ended.

"I figured you'd be coming to talk to me," he said with a deep scowl that transformed his pleasant features into something mean and ugly.

"You figured right," Gabriel said and then introduced Jordon.

"Got the feds involved in local business." Kevin shook his head and sniffed as if he smelled something dirty.

"Nice to meet you, Kevin. We had a nice chat with your brother Ed early this morning and he had so many wonderful things to say about you." Jordon beamed a smile at the man.

"Ed's a damn fool," Kevin replied. "He's nothing more than a glorified lawn boy."

"What I'd really like to know is where you were on Sunday night," Jordon replied, cutting to the chase.

Kevin smiled, a tight slash of lips that didn't begin to reach his eyes. "That's easy. I met up with a couple of buddies for beers at Hillbilly Harry's. We were there until about midnight and then I went home and crashed out. I've got to admit I was pretty trashed. I could barely stumble from my car to the front door."

"Good thing I didn't meet you on the road. You'd have been looking at a little jail time and a DUI," Gabriel said.

"Kevin, do you live by yourself?" Jordon asked, not wanting the conversation to get off track.

"Yeah. My wife left me two months after the Diamond Cove went into bankruptcy. And yeah, I hold a grudge about the whole thing. If the damned bank would have just given me a little more time, things would have been fine."

His nostrils flared as he continued. "Now I'm working a minimum-wage crap job and barely making ends meet. I don't have anything to do with the Overtons. It's bad enough their kids hang out here with their snot-nosed friends all the time. Do I wish Diamond Cove would fall off the face of the earth? Damn straight. Did I kill those people? Hell, no." He drew in a deep breath and stood from the stool.

"We'll need the names of the men you were with on Sunday night," Jordon said. She was shocked by the venom Kevin hadn't even attempted to hide. He certainly had said enough to keep him high on the suspect list.

"Names?" Gabriel said and pulled a small notebook and pen from his coat pocket.

Kevin heaved a deep, audible sigh. "Glen was there and so was Wesley Mayfield, Tom Richmond, Dave Hampton and Neil Davies. You can check with all of them. They'll tell you I was with them on Sunday night and I wasn't anywhere near Diamond Cove."

"Don't worry. We will check it out." Gabriel tucked the pen and notepad back into his pocket.

"Maybe while you're here do the two of you want to go through the maze? I get a percentage of the till each night and today has definitely been a slow day." The anger that had gripped Kevin's features transformed to a mask of mock pleasantry. "Go see the mouse inside."

"It might be the only fun you'll have while you're here," Gabriel said to Jordon as he pulled his wallet from his pocket.

He paid for their admission and Jordon swallowed against the faint simmer of alarm that attempted to grip her. *It's just a silly tourist attraction*, she told herself. She went through the turnstile with Gabriel just behind her. *Don't freak out. Mirrors can't hurt you.*

A dark corridor led into the maze, where she stepped into a space with five reflections of herself staring back at her. Gabriel was right behind her, a calming presence as the back of her throat threatened to close up.

"This way," he said and led her into a corridor of mirrors to the right.

"Have you been in here before?" she asked.

"No, it's my first time, too." They both jumped as one of the mirrors lit up and displayed an image of the demented mouse and a loud, wicked cackle sounded from overhead.

"If I find you, Mouse, I'll tie your tail into knots," Jordon said as the mirror returned to normal.

"Come on. Let's find our way out of here."

She followed Gabriel's lead through the disorienting corridors as she fought against dark flashbacks. The scars on her hip burned and the phantom scent of cigarette smoke and sizzling flesh filled her nose.

Mouse suddenly appeared behind another mirror. "Beware. If you aren't fast enough I'll pull you into my mouse hole and nobody will ever find you again," a deep voice whispered over the speaker.

Jordon stared at the fat mouse with the oversize teeth and she was back in the cellar clad only in her bra and panties, her arms above her head with her wrists in shackles connected to chains that hung from the low ceiling.

Nobody will ever find you here. You're mine to play with until I get tired of you. Ralph Hicks's voice exploded in her head. *I'm going to take my time and have lots of fun with you, and you get to watch.*

She closed her eyes to dispel the memory and when she opened them again Gabriel was nowhere to be seen. She was alone…with the mirrors, and a deep, gripping panic froze her in place.

Help! Somebody please help me. The pleas filled her head. *Don't let him burn me again. Don't let him do all the things to me that he did to the other women. I don't want to die this way. Please help me!*

"Gabriel?" His name croaked out of the back of her throat, which had become far too narrow. "Gabriel!" This time the cry was a half scream.

"I'm right here." He appeared next to her.

She grabbed on to his hand and forced a bright smile. "Whew, I thought you were lost." She hoped her voice betrayed none of the sheer panic that had momentarily suffused her.

"I think I found the exit—follow me."

She dropped his hand and practically walked in the backs of his shoes and cracked several bad jokes in an effort to relieve her own tension. After several twists and turns and more warnings from the mouse, they found the door that led outside.

"That was sort of lame," she said as they walked toward his car.

"From what I've heard, this is a really popular attraction among the teenagers in town. And as Kevin said, Jason and Hannah and their friends enjoy it."

"Probably because the girls scream and clutch on to the nearest testosterone-filled boy," she replied drily.

He smiled. "You want to get some dinner before I take you back to your room?"

Knots of tension twisted in her stomach and the taste of panic still filled the back of her throat. "I'm really not that hungry right now. Maybe you could just stop someplace and I'll grab a sandwich to take back to the room for later. I can put it in the mini-fridge until I'm ready to eat."

"There's a sub place not far from here—we can stop there."

They got into the car and Jordon was more than grateful to leave Mouse's Maze of Mirrors behind. She hated her own weakness. She hated that she still felt a bit shaky and dark memories clutched at her heart and invaded her brain.

The last thing she wanted was for Gabriel to sense any weakness in her. "So, what's on the agenda for tomorrow? A roller-coaster ride through a cave? A tour through Ripley's Believe It or Not?" She forced a flippant tone in her voice, determined not to let the memories pull her down.

"Nothing quite so grand. We need to chase down all the men Kevin said he was with Sunday night and confirm his alibi."

"Even if his alibi is confirmed until around midnight, that doesn't clear him for the murder, which took place much later than that," she replied.

"True, but in order to make a solid record, we need to corroborate everything." He pulled into the parking lot of a small place called Subs and Such.

"I'll just run in and grab something," she said. "You want anything?"

"Nah, I'm good. I've got some leftover meat loaf waiting for me at home."

It took her only minutes to get a submarine sandwich, several bags of chips and peanuts and then return to the car. All she wanted now was a long soak in the tub and time to put the mirrors and her memories behind her.

She might not have been woman enough to make her marriage work and she might not have been the daughter her parents wanted her to be, but she was one hell of an FBI agent. That was all she needed to be.

"Do you want me to drive into the station tomorrow morning or are you planning on picking me up?" she asked once they were back in the Diamond Cove parking lot.

"Why don't I come here around seven in the morning to get you? That way I can start the day with one of Joan's breakfasts."

"Sounds good to me." She gathered her purse and the white bag holding her sandwich and snacks. "Then I'll see you in the dining room at seven in the morning."

She gladly escaped the car and stepped into the cold night. She just needed a little time to get herself centered again. The little foray through the maze of mirrors had definitely shaken her up more than she'd expected.

She carried both her purse and her bag of food in her left hand, leaving her right hand to rest on the butt of her gun as she made her way down the path toward her cabin.

The night was once again silent around her and smelled of the clean evergreen that reminded her of Gabriel's attractive woodsy cologne.

She breathed a sigh of relief as she reached her door. She stepped into the warmth of the room and noticed a folded white piece of paper that had apparently been slid beneath the door at some point while she'd been gone.

It was probably something from Joan and Ted, perhaps concerning breakfast the next morning.

She dropped her purse and the sandwich bag on the coffee table and then picked up the paper. She unfolded it and a sizzle of adrenaline whipped through her as she read the message written in red block letters.

U R Next.

Chapter Four

For the first time in months Gabriel's thoughts weren't filled with mayhem and murder. Instead they were filled with a woman who smelled like spring and had almost had a panic attack in a tourist attraction meant to be fun.

She'd played it off well, but he'd picked up on the signs of her distress while they'd gone through the maze. Although she'd made a few jokes, her voice had been slightly higher in pitch and with a hint of breathlessness. When she'd grabbed his hand hers had been icy cold and had trembled. What had caused her such distress?

She was a curious contradiction—tough enough to insist that she stay in a room that might put her at risk as a target for a vicious serial killer, yet shaken up by a silly maze of mirrors. Definitely intriguing.

He turned onto the road that would eventually lead to his house, thoughts of Jordon still taking up all the space in his mind. She was not only beautiful, but also intelligent and with a sense of humor that reminded Gabriel he had a tendency at times to take life and himself a little too seriously.

He'd been sorry that she hadn't been up for dinner

with him. Her company was far more appealing than leftover meat loaf and complete solitude.

His cell phone rang. He punched the button on his steering wheel to answer. "Chief Walters," he said.

"Gabriel, can you come back here?" Jordon's voice held a touch of simmering excitement.

"Of course. Is there a problem?"

"Unless I'm the victim of some sort of a sick prank, I think our killer just made contact with me."

Every nerve in his body electrified. "Are you safe?"

"Yes, I'm safe. We'll talk when you get here." She disconnected before he could ask any other questions.

He turned around in the closest driveway and headed back the way he'd come. Adrenaline rushed through him, along with a mix of uneasiness and cautious excitement.

The killer had made contact. What did that mean? His investigation into the other murders hadn't indicated any kind of contact between victim and killer.

He drove as fast as possible and within five minutes was back at the Diamond Cove and out of his car. He hurried toward unit seven, his heartbeat racing.

A rivulet of relief flooded through him when Jordon opened the door to his knock. She'd taken off her coat and boots and appeared to be just fine.

"Thanks for coming back," she said as she closed the door behind him. She pointed to a white piece of paper on the bed. "That was slid beneath my door at some point or another while I was gone today."

He walked over to the bed and stared down at the note. Jordon moved to stand next to him, her fresh scent filling his head as the blatant threat of the words on the paper tightened his gut.

"Do you think it's really from the killer?" she asked. "I didn't see anything in the case files about notes to the victims."

"This is something new and we have to treat it as a serious threat."

"Not that many people know I'm here," she replied.

"This is a small town with a healthy gossip mill. By now probably dozens of people know you're in town and staying here." He turned to look at her. "You need to get out of here. Pack your things and I'll check you into a nearby motel."

She took a step back from him and put her hands on her hips. "I'm not going anywhere." Her eyes flashed and her chin thrust upward. "If that note is from the killer, then it's the first real piece of evidence we have. Hopefully, you can lift a fingerprint off it."

"And it shows that you now have a bull's-eye on your head. I can't allow you in good conscience to remain here." The idea of anything happening to her absolutely horrified him.

She laughed, a low husky sound. "Guess what, Chief Walters—you don't get to allow or not allow me to do anything. You aren't my boss."

He stared back at the note and then looked back at her. "Jordon, be reasonable. You're setting yourself up as bait for somebody who has already killed three people." A new frustration burned in his chest. She was right. He couldn't force her to do anything, but he definitely wanted to change her mind.

"I am being reasonable." She stepped closer to him and placed a hand on his chest. "Gabriel, please don't fight me on this. This is what I'm trained for. This is what I do."

The warmth of her hand seemed to burn right through his coat, through his shirt and into his bare skin. He fought a sudden impulse to grab her in his arms and pull her tight against him.

Crazy. These cases were definitely making him crazy. She dropped her hand back to her side and grinned up at him. "This little gun just might be your best opportunity to catch a killer."

"I would prefer for the little gun to stay safely in a holster," he replied.

"Hey, you made a joke," she said.

He frowned, not comforted by her light tone. This was serious business. "I can't change your mind?" he finally asked.

"No way. I'm a chatty, cheerful morning person and I'm stubborn as hell. Just ask my ex-husband."

He released a deep sigh. "I've got an evidence bag and gloves in my car trunk. I'll just go get them and I'll be right back."

A wealth of worry rode his shoulders as he headed back outside to his car. There was no question he wanted the killer caught, but not at the expense of Jordon's safety.

She's trained, he told himself. *She's an FBI agent. She knows the risk and obviously embraces it.* But that thought certainly didn't comfort him in any real way.

He grabbed an evidence bag and a pair of gloves from his trunk and then hurried back to the room with a heavy concern still burning inside him.

As he placed the paper in the bag, she sat on the edge of the bed, her eyes glittering brightly. "This is the break you've needed," she said. "I feel it in my bones and my bones rarely lie."

He sealed the bag and then sank down in the chair next to the fireplace, reluctant to leave her alone. "You know I'd feel better if you'd leave here and stay someplace else."

She shook her head. "This is where I need to be. First thing in the morning I'll talk to Ted and Joan and ask them if they saw anyone unusual on the premises today."

He frowned thoughtfully. "Kevin Rollings didn't have time to get here and leave a note after we left the maze."

"That note could have been slipped under my door at any time during the day after we left here. He's not coming off my suspect list so easily and neither are his brothers."

"As far as I'm concerned, all of the Rollings brothers are up there on the list. Before I head home I'll stop at the Overtons' and see if they saw anyone on the property today who shouldn't have been here." He released a deep sigh. "I should put a couple of men on duty here so that you aren't so vulnerable."

"Don't you dare," she replied fervently. "This place is relatively isolated and any men you put here would be visible. Their presence would drive the killer underground. If he doesn't come after me, then he might be patient enough to come after another guest when Joan and Ted open the doors again."

She leaned forward. "You have to trust me, Gabriel. You have to believe that I know the risk and I accept it. He's not going to get the jump on me."

A helpless inevitability swept through him. She was right. The last thing he wanted was for the killer to fall off the radar only to target another guest, and sooner or later, the Overtons would need to open their doors and have paying guests staying here again.

The only thing he could hope was that the note might yield a clue, a fingerprint, an unusual watermark…anything that might lead to the guilty.

"Now, unless you want to watch me slosh around naked in a tub of bubbles and hot water, you'd better get out of here," she said.

His mind was suddenly seized with erotic visions that heated his blood. He consciously willed them away and stood. "I hope whatever you do you'll keep your gun right next to you." He picked up the bagged note from the coffee table.

"Don't look so grim," she said as she got up from the bed. "You need to remember that the other three victims weren't armed and were unaware of the danger that was present here."

There was some comfort. Still, even as she walked him to the door, he realized he'd never been so reluctant to leave a woman. "Stay alert," he said.

"Always. I'll see you in the morning." She opened the door and he walked out into the cold, a cold that couldn't begin to rival the chill in his heart as he thought of Jordon being the next potential victim.

JORDON BOLTED UPRIGHT and grabbed for her gun. She gasped for air as she struggled to leave her nightmares behind. The room was cast in shadows, partially lit by the bathroom light she'd left on all night.

As her breathing returned to normal, she placed her gun back on the nightstand. There was no danger here except for in the dreams she'd left behind.

A glance at the clock on the nightstand let her know

it was just after five. It would be another hour before her alarm would ring, but she knew there was no way she'd go back to sleep.

She flopped back on the mattress and stared up at the dark ceiling. It had been months since she'd had any nightmares, but last night her sleep had been filled with them.

Ralph Hicks and his mirrors had invaded her dreams, yanking her back to that cellar and the terror of those long hours. She'd also dreamed of a faceless figure she knew was the killer who had now marked her for death if she was to believe the note left for her.

And there was no reason for her not to believe. Like the other victims, she was the only guest here, and from past actions, that was what the killer liked.

She'd be stupid not to feel a healthy dose of fear, but she knew that specific fear would help her stay alive. She hadn't been afraid on that day a year ago when she'd knocked on Ralph Hicks's door to ask him some questions about the murders going on in the neighborhood.

The forty-six-year-old man hadn't been on anyone's radar as a suspect, but he had lived next door to the latest victim and so was on the list to be interrogated. She hadn't known she was in danger until he smashed her over the head and rendered her unconscious.

The experience had taught her a valuable lesson, that everyone was a potential suspect and danger could leap out of nowhere. With a sigh she slid out of the bed, grabbed her gun once again and padded into the bathroom to get ready for the day.

As she dressed she thought of the people they'd interviewed the day before. Certainly Kevin Rollings hadn't hidden his resentment of this place, but did that make him their killer? Or was he simply a bitter man who verbally railed against all the perceived injustices of his world? Billy Bond had been sketchy, but that didn't make him a killer, either.

They just didn't have enough information yet. Today they would be pounding the pavement and asking more questions, and hopefully something they stumbled on would help break the case wide open.

She was huddled by the dining room door, freezing her butt off, when Joan unlocked and opened the door at quarter till seven.

"I positively hate winter," she exclaimed as she shrugged off her coat and then headed for the coffee.

"I really don't mind it too much." A frown dug into Joan's forehead and her eyes were dark. "Gabriel told us about the note you got. We didn't see anyone around your door yesterday and we didn't notice any strangers on the property. I wish we would have seen somebody. I can't tell you how much I wish we would have seen the person responsible and you and Chief Walters could make an arrest and end all this."

Jordon poured herself a cup of coffee and then sat at the table and gestured for Joan to join her. "Is running a bed-and-breakfast something you always dreamed about doing?" she asked in an attempt to change the subject and erase Joan's worry at least for a few minutes.

"Always, although it took me some time to get Ted completely on board with the idea. I think he worried that it would be too much work for me, but I absolutely love it. I love that the entire family is involved, and

I was ready to get the kids out of the city and into a more family-oriented environment."

"Were you having problems with the children?" Jordon asked curiously.

"No real problems, although Jason had started hanging out with some kids I didn't really approve of and his grades were dropping and Hannah had started getting attitude."

Jordon smiled. "What fifteen-year-old girl doesn't have a little attitude with her mother?"

Joan laughed, but the laughter was short-lived and once again her eyes darkened. "We took such a gamble by making the move here. We put our entire life savings into buying this place. If it doesn't work out for us I don't know what we'll do."

"We're going to get this person, Joan. We're going to get him, and all of your rooms will fill up once again and you all will be just fine."

Joan gave her a grateful smile. "Chief Walters has been wonderful through all of this. He's been working so hard and I know these murders are eating him alive. I'm glad you're here to help him."

"We're definitely doing everything we can," Jordon replied.

Joan leaned back in her chair. "I'm just sorry you aren't going to get a chance to see some of the sights and have some fun while you're here."

"Actually, I did manage to go through Mouse's Maze of Mirrors."

"Hannah and Jason love that place," Joan replied.

"I wasn't a big fan," Jordon admitted.

"Really? Why not?"

"I don't like mirrors, but that's another story altogether."

Both women turned toward the door as Gabriel came inside. "Good morning," he said.

"Back at you," Jordon replied.

Joan got up from the table. "I'll just go see to breakfast." As Joan left the room, Gabriel took off his coat and sat across from Jordon.

His gaze was dark and intense. "You doing okay?"

"I'm fine as a fiddle."

"No problems overnight?" he asked.

"None at all. Do you know it takes more muscles to frown than it does to smile?"

He sat back in the chair and a smile curved his lips. "Is that better?"

It wasn't just better—it was freaking amazing. He had a smile that could light up the darkest corner of the earth. There was no question that she was intensely attracted to him and she thought he might be more than a little bit drawn to her.

But she also had a feeling Gabriel wasn't interested in a hot sexual fling, and that was all it would be. That was all she would ever be to any man. That was her choice.

For the next fifteen minutes they drank coffee and talked about the plans for the day. Joan brought in plates of biscuits and gravy with sausage patties on the side and a fresh fruit salad. Ted came in and joined them for small talk while they ate.

It was just after eight thirty before they were in Gabriel's car and headed to their first stop for the day to check Kevin's alibi for the night Sandy Peters had been murdered.

"Dave Hampton and I have a bit of a history," Gabriel said. "I've had to arrest him several times for drunk and disorderly. The man loves his booze, and when he drinks too much, he gets stupid and nasty."

"Are you expecting trouble with him? Because if you are, I've got your back, partner."

He cast her a quick glance. "Are you always so sure of yourself?" he asked wryly.

"Only when I'm on the job," she replied. "I know what I'm good at."

"And what are you good at besides being a kick-ass FBI agent?"

Not much. She shoved the two hurtful words away. "I'm great at zapping food in a microwave. I can do five cartwheels in a row without getting dizzy, and when I sing I can make every dog in a five-mile area howl."

He cast her a charming grin. "I'm impressed."

"What about you? Besides being a kick-ass chief of police, what else are you good at?"

He frowned thoughtfully and then the frown lifted, and when he shot her a quick glance, his eyes were a lighter, more inviting blue that she hadn't seen before.

"I can twist an aluminum can into a work of art. I can get almost any dog to eat out of my hand if I'm holding a good piece of steak, and I know all the lyrics to Manfred Mann's 'Blinded by the Light.'"

"Whew, now I'm the one impressed." What impressed her more than anything was that he had responded with the same silly lightness as her. She didn't think he had it in him. There was nothing sexier than a man who didn't always take himself and the world too seriously.

However, the light mood disappeared as he pulled into Charlie's Brake and Muffler Repair. "Dave works here as a mechanic," he said.

"Let's go talk to Dave the drunk and see if he can corroborate Kevin's alibi."

Gray clouds hung low in the sky as they walked toward the large building with four bays. Men's voices rang out along with the sound of noisy tools being used.

They entered into a small office where a man stood behind a counter. "Charlie," Gabriel greeted the man. "How's business?"

"A little slow, but not too bad." His gaze swept the length of Jordon. "I'm hoping you're here because you or the little lady needs a brake job."

"This *little lady* doesn't need brakes," Jordon said drily.

"Actually, we're here to speak to Dave," Gabriel said.

Charlie frowned. "Good grief. What has he done now?"

"Nothing. We just need to ask him a couple of questions," Gabriel replied.

Charlie pointed to a nearby door. "You can use the break room. I'll go get Dave and send him in."

The break room held a card table that cast slightly to one side and was littered with what appeared to be petrified crumbs from meals past, a couple of chairs and a soda machine. The air smelled of grease and oil. Neither of them sat.

Dave Hampton was a big man with a shock of thick dark hair and a scowl that appeared to have been etched permanently into his face. "I haven't done anything wrong. What's this all about?" He glared first at Gabriel and then at Jordon as he wiped his hands on a filthy rag.

"We just need to ask you a couple of questions and then we'll let you get back to work," Gabriel said.

"Questions about what?" He stuffed the rag into his coverall's pocket.

"About last Sunday night," Gabriel said.

Dave narrowed his eyes. "What about it? I didn't do anything stupid. If somebody said I did then they're a damned liar."

"It's nothing like that," Gabriel assured him. "We just need to know where you were and who you were with."

"A bunch of us went to Hillbilly Harry's to shoot some pool and have a few beers." Dave visibly relaxed.

"Who was with you?"

"Wesley Mayfield, Neil Davies, Tom Richmond and Kevin and Glen Rollings. Is this about that woman's murder?"

"What time did you all leave the bar?" Gabriel asked, ignoring Dave's question.

"I guess it was around midnight or so."

"And none of you left early?"

Dave rocked back on his heels and smiled slyly. "It's Kevin, isn't it? You're wondering if he killed that woman." Dave shook his head and released a small laugh. "Those Rollings boys are thick as thieves, and Kevin hates anything and anyone that has to do with Diamond Cove."

"I got the impression that Kevin didn't get along well with his brothers." Jordon spoke up for the first time.

"That's definitely not true. Kevin raised Glen and

Ed after their mother died," Dave said. "According to what Kevin told me, their father was a no-account drunk and Kevin had to step up to be both mother and father to his younger brothers. Like I said before, those three are thick as thieves."

"Was Kevin drunk when you all left the bar?" Jordon asked.

Dave frowned. "We were all a little toasted, but he was no drunker than the rest of us. Is that all? I really need to get back to the shop."

"That's it for now," Gabriel replied.

She and Gabriel didn't speak again until they were back in his car. "There's definitely no honor among thieves," he said as he started the car. "Dave threw Kevin under the bus pretty quickly."

"Kevin told us he got completely trashed, but Dave didn't indicate that Kevin was all that drunk," Jordon replied.

"He was sober enough to drive himself home," Gabriel said. "And Ed has always given me the impression that Kevin isn't close to him or Glen."

Jordon pulled her collar up more tightly around her neck as a cold wind of uneasiness blew through her. "What worries me now is the possibility that we aren't looking for just one killer, but maybe we have a brotherhood of murderers, and that's definitely only going to complicate things."

Chapter Five

"Where to now, boss?" Jordon asked as they pulled back on the main road.

"How do you feel about a little shopping?"

"Like any reasonable woman, I'm always up for some retail therapy," she replied.

"In the store we're going to you can buy a Branson T-shirt or a corncob pipe, a refrigerator magnet or any one of a thousand other items."

"And I'm guessing that Glen Rollings might be my personal shopper?"

He flashed her a quick smile. "Glen is definitely the charmer of the Rollings boys, but I doubt that you need a personal shopper. You strike me as the kind of woman who usually knows exactly what she wants and you don't stop until you get it."

"You've got that right." She turned her head to look out of the passenger window. At the moment she'd like Gabriel Walters's very kissable mouth to be on hers.

The errant thought could only be because she was cold and she knew being in his arms and kissing him would warm her. She'd been cold since she'd arrived in Branson, if not because of the wintry weather, then from the chill of hunting down a cold-blooded serial killer.

Were they up against a single murderer or was it a tag-team effort? Were Glen and Ed helping the brother who raised them get his revenge on Diamond Cove? It was crazy to think somebody would go to such lengths to destroy a business, but revenge killings had happened for far less.

She turned back to look at Gabriel once again. "What I don't understand is if Kevin really wants to destroy Diamond Cove then why not just set fire to the place? Why not build a bomb and blow it all up?"

He turned into the parking lot of the Ozark Shed of Souvenirs and released a deep sigh. "I don't know. I haven't been able to get a handle on this from the very beginning. This is far more evil than a fire or a bomb. It takes a special kind of killer to stab somebody. This person apparently likes to kill up close and personal."

With his words ringing in her ears, they exited the car and headed for the huge shop.

Evil. The word echoed in her brain. Yes, whatever was going on here was definitely evil.

She knew all about evil. She'd been locked in a cellar with evil personified for hours, just praying for death to take her quickly.

She shoved the thought away when they entered the store. She gazed around in amazement. Never had she seen so much stuff in one place. Tote bags and camping lanterns, wooden signs and toilet-paper holders in the shape of outhouses fought shelf space with traveler-size toothpaste and T-shirts and blinged-out wallets and purses.

She followed Gabriel to a sales counter where a

gray-haired woman greeted them. "Gabriel," she said with a big smile that lifted all of her wrinkles upward. "I hope that's a girlfriend with you and you've come in to buy one of our real, stunning Ozark gold rings."

Gabriel laughed, a low, deep and appealing sound. "Special Agent James, meet Wanda Tompkins, the orneriest woman in the entire town."

"Nice to meet you, ma'am," Jordon said.

"You, too," Wanda replied and looked back at Gabriel. "So, if this pretty woman isn't your girlfriend and you aren't here to buy anything, then what can I help you with?"

"We need to speak with Glen," Gabriel said.

"He's upstairs in the back room." Wanda gave Jordon a sly smile. "A shame you aren't his girlfriend. He's a good man who needs a good woman."

"Be careful or I'll arrest you for attempted matchmaking," he replied in a mock-stern voice. "And do I need to remind you that this isn't your first offense."

Wanda laughed and waved a hand at him. "Go on with your bad self." She turned her attention to a group of tourists who had entered the store.

"So Wanda has tried to hook you up?" Jordon asked as they climbed a narrow set of wooden stairs to the second floor.

"When I first arrived in town this store was robbed and that's when I first met Wanda. There was about six months after that when she made finding me a wife her life's mission. She still calls me occasionally to tell me about some nice woman I should meet."

"And did you ever meet any of them?" she asked.

"A few."

"They weren't wife material?"

"They were for somebody, but just not for me."

They reached the top of the stairs and she followed behind him as they wound through several aisles of merchandise. The man was drop-dead gorgeous, wore a respected uniform and seemed to be a genuinely nice guy.

There must be plenty of women in this town who would love to get hitched to a man like him. Cautious, that was what he'd told her he was, but she wondered if maybe he wasn't just super picky.

Jordon had believed she'd married a man like Gabriel, a man who was well respected, principled and moral. She'd been head over heels in love with Jack and after that debacle she never wanted to give any man her heart. Although something about Gabriel made her think some time in a bed with him would be totally awesome.

As they reached the doorway to a storage room, she mentally kicked herself for her errant thoughts. She wasn't here to have a quick, hot hookup. They had a killer to catch.

Like his brothers, Glen Rollings had pleasant features, blond hair and light blue eyes. He was tall and thin, and when Gabriel made the introductions, Glen's gaze swept the length of her.

"You're an FBI agent? Wow. That's hot." He gave her a wink that she assumed he thought was sexy. It was totally lame.

"We want to ask you a few questions," Gabriel said.

Glen gazed at Jordon once again. "Maybe the superhot FBI agent wants to tie me up to interrogate me." He winked at her again.

"Knock it off, Romeo. We're here on serious business," she said with narrowed eyes.

The smile on his face slowly faded. "I know why you're here. Everyone knows a woman was murdered at Diamond Cove." He shook his head. "I wish my brother had never bought that damned place and I also wish he'd keep his mouth shut about how much he hates it."

"So where were you last Sunday night?" Gabriel asked.

As Glen told the same story that Dave had told them earlier, Jordon listened carefully for any inconsistencies.

"And what did you do after you left the bar?" she asked when he was finished.

"Went home…unfortunately alone," he replied.

"Did any neighbors see you? Anyone call you?" she pressed.

"My closest neighbors are a retired couple who go to bed at the crack of dusk, and no, I didn't get any calls." Glen frowned and gazed at Gabriel. "I told you the last time you talked to me that you're barking up the wrong tree. I'm a lover, not a killer."

"Do you text?" Jordon asked.

Glen's frown deepened. "Occasionally. Why?"

"Just curious. Can I see your phone?" Jordon asked.

Glen cast her a sly look. "I may be a dumb country hick, but I've watched enough cop shows to know you need a warrant for that."

Jordon wasn't surprised that he didn't hand it over. Cell phones were as intimate as underwear. You could tell a lot about a person just by looking at their text messages.

Their questioning ended and they headed back downstairs. "I can't leave here without buying a Branson T-shirt," she said. "I love sleeping in oversize T-shirts."

It took her only minutes to find a hot-pink shirt with *Branson* written in bold black letters across the chest. She paid Wanda and then they returned to the car.

They managed to hunt down two more of the men who had been at Hillbilly Harry's with Kevin and Glen on the night of the murder, and then at six thirty they stopped in a pizza place for dinner.

"So, we know Kevin and Glen have a solid alibi until midnight on the night Sandy was murdered," Jordon said as she pulled a piece of the pie onto the smaller plate in front of her.

"But none of the Rollingses can prove that they were home all night after midnight except Ed, who was supposedly home with his wife." He frowned. "We need to touch base with her."

"Could you prove where you were on a specific night between midnight and five or six in the morning?" She didn't wait for his reply. "Unless you have somebody in bed with you, it's hard to have an alibi for that time."

"It's a good thing I don't need to provide an alibi for the middle of the night." He took a bite of the pizza and stared off into the distance.

A lonely man. He wore his loneliness in quiet moments. She recognized it. She understood it because she had a same core of emptiness inside her. She'd had it before her marriage and even more so since the day she'd walked out on her husband. It was a part of her that she tried not to acknowledge.

"I love pepperoni," she said to break the silence that had stretched too long between them. She picked a piece of it off her pizza slice and popped it into her mouth. "Thick crust and pepperoni—there's nothing better."

For the next ten minutes they talked about the merits of different kinds of pizza. It was a welcome respite after the murder talk that had been the subject of most of their conversations during the day.

It was almost eight when he pulled up in the Diamond Cove parking area. The sun had gone down and dusk had given way to night.

"See you for breakfast?" She grabbed her purse and her shopping bag with the T-shirt.

"I'll be here. Stay safe through the night."

"Stop worrying about me. I'll be just fine," she replied. She got out of the car and opened her coat so she had easy access to her gun.

As she walked to her room, the loneliness she'd sensed in Gabriel resonated deep inside her. There were moments when she wished she had somebody meaningful in her life, somebody to share the ups and downs of the days and hold her in big strong arms through the night.

At one time she'd wanted that, she'd believed she deserved that, but she no longer believed.

"Been there, done that," she muttered as she unlocked her door and went inside. And it had been a heartbreaking experience that she never wanted to repeat.

She tossed her purse on the bed and pulled the

T-shirt out of the shopping bag and carried it and her gun with her into the bathroom.

After a quick shower she pulled on the soft cotton shirt and then climbed into the comfortable big bed with her laptop. As she had before, she typed notes into a growing file she'd named Means and Motive.

It was often those two elements that ultimately solved a case. Who had the means to execute the crime and who had the motive?

She'd been typing in notes for about half an hour when a bump sounded against the building near her door. Every nerve inside her electrified. Her heartbeat raced as she grabbed her gun from the nightstand.

U R Next.

The words screamed inside her head as she slid out of bed and approached the door. If she opened it, would she be met by somebody wielding a deadly sharp knife, ready to follow through on the threat? Was this potentially an attack like the one that had taken Sandy Peters's life?

She gripped her gun more firmly. She wasn't Sandy Peters and nobody was going to take her by surprise. Drawing a deep breath to steady herself, she reached out, turned the lock and then jerked open the door.

She was greeted only by a cold gust of wind that momentarily stole her breath away. No knife-wielding maniac, no quick attack.

Nobody.

She took a step outside onto the porch and looked around. Nothing. She wouldn't see anyone in the area. The darkness of night would cover anyone's presence.

It was only when she turned to go back into the

room that she noticed one of the rocking chairs in front of her window had been moved.

It looked as if somebody had been trying to peer into her window and had accidentally bumped into the chair. Whoever it was, there was definitely no sign of the person now.

She stepped back into the room and closed and locked her door. Her heart still raced as she climbed back into the bed and pointed her gun toward the door.

"Come and get me, you creep," she whispered.

THE NEXT FOUR days passed far too quickly. Jordon had told Gabriel about the Peeping Tom incident and again he'd tried to get her to move to another motel, but she was adamant that she was right where she wanted... where she needed to be.

She'd been right. She was definitely stubborn and he'd tried a dozen ways to change her mind, but she wasn't budging. The fact that she'd been warned that she was the next victim and she continued staying at Diamond Cove had given him several nightmares over the last couple of nights.

They had interviewed all the men who had been at Hillbilly Harry's on the night of Sandy's murder, they'd pored over the files in an effort to find something they might have missed, and by late Sunday afternoon, Gabriel had all kinds of anxiety burning in the pit of his stomach. He figured by the time these cases were solved he'd have ulcers as big as the Ozark foothills.

The Rollings brothers remained high on the suspect list, along with Billy Bond, who as groundskeeper had easy access to all the victims and might have known their routines, but no new evidence had been revealed to make an arrest.

Unfortunately, the note that had been left for Jordon had yielded nothing…no fingerprints and no distinctive features. The paper was ordinary copy paper that could be bought almost anywhere in town and beyond.

Because it had been written like somebody would write a text, they had questioned everyone again about texting, including Jason and Hannah Overton, who might have thought leaving such a note would be funny.

The two teenagers had proclaimed their innocence passionately and Gabriel had been surprised to learn that almost everyone these days texted in abbreviated language. It had made him feel like an ancient old man.

He now closed the file that held the crime-scene photos and looked across the conference table where Jordon had been reading through the interviews they'd conducted over the last several days.

"Why don't we knock off early, and instead of grabbing a burger out somewhere, I'll take you to my place and fix us a home-cooked meal," he said.

"That sounds absolutely marvelous," she replied. Her eyes were a warm green as she rose from the table and reached for her coat. "A little break will be nice. I've been thinking about murder for the past week."

"Then let's make a pact that for the next couple of hours we won't talk about work at all."

"That's a deal," she instantly agreed.

Within fifteen minutes they were in Gabriel's car and headed to his house. Although he'd certainly had his head immersed in these cases for the last seven days, he'd also had far too many inappropriate thoughts about his "partner."

Her scent invaded his senses when he was sleeping; the visions of her clad only in bubbles in the oversize tub haunted his dreams. He could easily imagine her in bed and clad only in the hot-pink oversize T-shirt she'd bought.

He had no idea if taking her to his house for a meal was a good idea or not, but he did know they both needed a break from the mind-numbing routine of the investigation and the endless fast food they'd eaten over the past week.

"It doesn't look like you're going to make that beach in Florida unless we get a break pretty fast," he said.

"I already canceled my reservations. I also heard on the weather last night that we're supposed to get a big snowstorm here starting tomorrow night." She leaned forward and adjusted the heater vents as if just thinking about the upcoming snow made her cold.

"I'm sorry about your vacation plans."

She leaned back in the seat again. "The beach will still be there after we catch this creep. What's for dinner?"

"How does spaghetti with meat sauce sound?"

"Fantastic. Do you like to cook?"

"I do. I find it a good stress reliever." He shot her a quick glance. "What do you do to relieve stress?"

"I've always thought primal screaming sounded like a great idea but it's hard to find an empty forest when you need one," she said jokingly. "Actually, stress rolls off my back pretty easily."

"I've noticed that about you." He'd definitely no-

ticed that she used humor to ease tension and allevi-
ate any stress that might be in the air. He wondered
what might lurk beneath her humor. What depths of
emotions, if any, did she mask with laughter?

And then he wondered why he cared. She was here
only temporarily. Despite his visceral attraction to her,
there was no way he intended to pursue anything re-
motely romantic with her.

"Nice place," she said as he pulled up in front of
the three-bedroom house he called home. It was a neat
place painted a dark brown and flanked by two tall,
beautiful evergreen trees.

Still, the Christmas tree lights remained hung and
an inflatable Santa had lost his wave as the air had
seeped out. He'd had more important things on his
mind than taking down Christmas decorations.

"Santa looks pretty sad," she said as they walked
up to the front door.

"Yeah, it was a pretty grim Christmas," he replied.

"Have you been here long?" she asked.

"It's a rental but I've been here for the last three
years, ever since I moved here from Chicago." He unlocked the front door and ushered her inside.

They entered into the large living room with the
open kitchen to the right. "Make yourself at home,"
he said as he hung his coat in the closet and then did
the same with hers.

She walked around the room, her eyes narrowed
as they had been when she'd looked at the crime
scenes. He looked around the space in an effort to
see it through her eyes.

The overstuffed gray sofa was comfortable for sitting and watching the flat-screen television on the op-

posite wall. The black coffee table held only a small fake flower arrangement that a woman he'd briefly dated had given him. Lamps were on each of the end tables.

She looked at him and smiled. "Your living space is exactly what I expected it to be."

He raised an eyebrow. "What does that mean?"

"It's neat and uncomplicated. A place for everything and everything in its place." She released a short laugh. "You'd go stark raving mad if we lived together."

"You're messy?"

"I like to call it controlled chaos," she replied.

"Interesting," he said. "How about you bring your controlled chaos into the kitchen so I can start working on the meal."

"Sounds like a plan."

Fifteen minutes later he had a pot of seasoned tomato sauce simmering on one burner and stirred a skillet of frying hamburger, garlic and onions on another.

Jordon sat at the table with a beer and filled what was normally the silent hours he'd grown accustomed to with cheerful chatter that he welcomed.

She was so bright and witty and he was vaguely surprised to realize how much he enjoyed her company. Within thirty minutes he learned that she loved old rock and roll, Chinese food and her neighbor's Yorkie named Taz. She loved to dance in her underwear in her living room and preferred white cheddar to yellow.

As they ate the salad, garlic bread and spaghetti, they argued politics and discovered they watched the same television shows and had read many of the same books.

She asked him about his time working in Chicago and he related many of the cases he'd worked on there. She helped clean up the dishes and they settled side by side on the sofa for coffee.

"I needed this," she said as she eased back against the gray cushion.

"The coffee?"

"No, silly man. I needed this break away from thinking about serial killers and the potential demise of Diamond Cove."

He smiled at her. "Nobody has ever had the nerve to call me a silly man before."

She gave him a brash grin. "I call 'em like I see them, cupcake."

He laughed. "I needed this, too. Maybe after this little break we'll approach everything with fresh eyes tomorrow."

"What we need is fresh evidence, and until this creep makes another move, we're in a holding pattern." A frown danced across her forehead as she lifted her coffee cup to her lips.

"And we're doing exactly what we said we wouldn't do by talking about the case."

She took another sip of the coffee and nodded her head. "You're right. So, tell me, Gabriel Walters, what is your deepest fear?"

She constantly surprised him. A long look at her features let him know the question was serious. He feared being alone for the rest of his life. He feared that he would never have the family he desperately wanted, but those were things he didn't share with anyone.

"I'd say my biggest fear right now is that we won't catch this guy and somebody else will wind up dead." He couldn't tell her that he worried that particular somebody would be her. "What about you? What's your deepest fear?"

"Big hairy spiders, especially the jumping kind," she replied flippantly.

He gazed at her for a long moment. "Are you ever serious?"

"I'm serious about getting bad guys off the streets," she replied with a slight upward thrust of her chin.

God, she looked so beautiful with that spark of defiance in her eyes. She intrigued him like no other woman had ever done before.

Despite their long hours of working together over the last week, in spite of all the conversations they'd shared, he felt like he'd just scratched the surface of her. He shouldn't want to go any deeper. A superficial relationship was all he needed for them to work well together.

However, right at this moment with her scent wafting in the air and her eyes the soft green of a beautiful spring day, he wanted more. "Tell me why you're afraid of mirrors," he said.

Her eyes instantly darkened and her chin shot up once again. "What makes you think I'm afraid of mirrors?"

He held her gaze intently. A faint color danced into her cheeks. She set her coffee cup on the table in front of them and wrapped her arms around herself.

She shifted her gaze to someplace in the distance just behind him and released a shuddery sigh.

"His name was Ralph Hicks." Her voice was soft and her eyes remained shadowed. "He had already tortured and killed five women before I knocked on his door to interview him. I was officially off duty for the day, but I decided to go ahead and get the interview done on my way home from work." She shook her head and her face paled. "I should have gone straight home and danced in my underwear."

He fought the impulse to move closer to her. She looked small and achingly vulnerable as she pressed herself farther into the corner of the sofa.

She drew in a deep breath and continued. "He was so pleasant and unassuming-looking. He invited me inside and nothing rang a bell of alarm in my head. I stepped in and he bashed me over the head with a small bat. I never saw it coming."

She unwound her arms and leaned forward to grab her coffee cup, but before she did, he reached out and took her hand in his. Icy cold and so achingly small. She wound her fingers with his and he slid closer to her. Her face had paled to an unnatural white and her lower lip trembled for just a moment.

"I'm sorry I asked," he said regretfully.

"It's okay." She gave him a small smile that did nothing to light up her eyes. "Thankfully, after he hit me, the last thing I did before I passed out was slide my cell phone under his sofa. When I regained consciousness I was in my underwear and strung up with chains and there were three floor-length mirrors in front of me. Ralph liked his victims to watch themselves as he tortured them."

Gabriel tightened his hand around hers, his stomach churning with sickness as he could only imagine the horrors she had endured. He wanted to rescue her from her past, from that horror, something that he knew wasn't possible.

"I was lucky. By the time he had me trussed up, he decided it was his bedtime. I didn't see him again until midmorning the next day. By the time he came down the stairs to have his fun with me, my fellow agents already knew I was in trouble because I hadn't shown up for work and I never, ever missed work."

"They traced your phone," he said.

She nodded. "They came in hard and fast, but not before Ralph had played on my hip with a lit cigarette." She released his hand and leaned back once again. "The good news is Ralph got a bullet in his chest and I walked out of there with just a heart-shaped scar."

"And an aversion to mirrors," he added.

"Only if there's more than one," she replied as her face regained most of its color. "And now I think it's time you get me back to Diamond Cove."

He wanted to protest. He wanted more time with her, but her eyes remained hollow and he realized that sharing her story had taken an emotional toll on her.

Twenty minutes later they were back at the bed-and-breakfast and Gabriel got out of the car as she did. "What are you doing?" she asked.

"I just thought I'd walk you to your door," he replied. She'd been quiet on the way back and he'd cursed himself for digging deep enough to dredge up what must have been horrendous memories for her. If he had any questions about whether there was something behind her humor and laughter, he now had the answer.

"That isn't necessary," she protested.

"I know, but it's something I feel like doing. Besides, if the weather forecast is right, by Tuesday morning I might not be able to make it here at all." He walked behind her on the small path.

"Ugh, don't remind me. More snow, more winter— it makes me want to throw up," she replied.

They reached her door and she turned to face him. Her features were softly lit by the nearby solar lamps. "Thank you for the meal and the conversation."

"I'm sorry some of the conversation was difficult for you."

She smiled up at him. "It's something that happened to me, but it's in the past and I survived." Her gaze softened. "When I first arrived here I was sure you were going to be an inflexible, boneheaded pain in my butt, but I was wrong about you. Thank you for putting up with me, Gabriel."

He watched her lips moving, and before he realized his intent, he covered her mouth with his. The evening air was cold, but her lips were wonderfully hot and inviting.

She opened her mouth to him, welcoming him as his tongue deepened the kiss. White-hot desire seared through him. All rational thought momentarily left him, and it wasn't until she raised a hand to gently touch his cheek that rational thought slammed back into his head.

He broke the kiss and stepped back from her, appalled by what he'd just done. It had been a total lack of control. "I'm sorry. That was completely unprofessional and wrong."

"It sure didn't feel wrong," she replied, her cheeks flushed with a becoming pink.

He took another step backward. "Still, it won't happen again."

"Don't bet on it." She dug her key out of her purse and then smiled at him. "Good night, Gabriel. I'll see you in the morning." She opened her door and disappeared inside.

He stared at her closed door for a long moment as he waited for the desire inside him to ebb. Finally, with the frigid night air seeping into his bones, he turned and hurried to his car.

Jordon James was like no other woman he had ever dated. *She's a partner, not a date*, he reminded himself firmly as he started his engine and pulled out of the Diamond Cove parking lot.

They needed to get this case solved sooner rather than later. They needed to find the murderer so Jordon could get back to Kansas City before he really did something boneheaded.

Chapter Six

The snow began to fall at six o'clock the next evening. Jordon sat at the conference room table and stared out the window at the fat, fluffy flakes drifting down from the heavy gray skies.

She was alone in the room. Gabriel had left almost twenty minutes ago to deal with an armed robbery that had taken place at one of the convenience stores.

She'd been distracted all day…distracted by a single kiss. It surprised her how much she'd liked that darned kiss, how much she wanted to repeat it…and more.

Neither of them had mentioned it throughout the day and she had a feeling Gabriel definitely wished it had never happened. But it had and she'd thought about it far too often as the long hours had gone by.

Releasing a deep sigh, she focused back on the files in front of her. Although neither of them had said it out loud, they were at a dead end.

They had checked and rechecked the Rollings brothers and Billy Bond, and while they remained on the suspect list, she and Gabriel had no real evidence to point a finger at anyone. They had also dug a little deeper into the Overtons' background, but nothing in their past had raised a red flag or indicated any reason why somebody would want to hurt either one of them.

Now there was a blizzard forecast for overnight and it would probably stymie any further investigation at least through the next day or so. Jeez, she hated winter and she hated this killer.

She stared out the window once again, her thoughts flittering back to the evening before. She hadn't meant to tell Gabriel about Ralph Hicks and what had happened in that cellar. She'd thought she'd covered her anxiety well, but Gabriel had obviously picked up on her panic attack in the mirror maze.

He'd offered her just the right amount of support... a warm and strong hand holding hers and not so much sympathy that she felt guilty about sharing the events of that dark moment in her past.

He'd seen her more vulnerable, more fragile than she liked anyone to see her, but for some reason Gabriel felt safe. She knew instinctively that he was a man who would keep all of her secrets. Funny. She was a woman who didn't trust easily and yet within seven days she trusted Gabriel implicitly.

Not that any of that mattered. Once they caught the killer she'd go back to Kansas City, and within a month or two Gabriel probably wouldn't even remember her name. She wasn't sure why that thought depressed her a bit.

"Sorry about that," he said as he breezed back into the room.

"Not a problem. I know as head of this department you have lots of other things to attend to besides this case."

"Thank God I've got good men and women working with me and for the most part the department practically runs itself." He sank down in the chair across from hers and raked a hand through his thick, shiny hair. "I assigned a couple of men to investigate the armed robbery, but before I could get out of my office, I got a butt-chewing phone call from the mayor."

She raised an eyebrow. "Does he think we're not doing whatever we can to solve this?"

"He was all puffed up like a peacock and talking about his responsibility to the town. He reminded me that a serial killer running amok hurts the tourist trade Branson depends on, as if I'm too dense to know that."

"You might be a silly man, but I would never call you dense," Jordon said in an effort to lighten the dark frustration in his eyes.

It worked. His eyes lightened a bit and he leaned back in his chair. "What I'd like to be right now is a magician. I'd like to wave a magic wand and have all the answers to solve this case in my hand once and for all."

"Unfortunately, we're both short on magic wands at the moment," she replied. "Face it, partner. We've conducted a solid, thorough investigation but we're kind of at a dead end at the moment. We've hit a brick wall."

He leaned forward and released a deep sigh. "I know and it's frustrating as hell."

"Look on the bright side. The perp could attack me at any moment and then I'll nab him," she said lightly.

His gaze darkened once again. "Jordon, don't even joke about that." He scooted his chair out and stood, walked to the window and peered outside. "We probably need to head out of here. The snow is coming down pretty hard. We should also stop someplace on the way and pick you up some supplies in case I can't get to you first thing in the morning."

"Don't worry about supplies—I'll be fine. Before you arrived for breakfast this morning, Joan told me no matter how bad the weather gets, breakfast will be served as usual and she'd make sure additional meals would be available if we all get snowed in."

"Should we pick you up a sub sandwich or something else for later tonight?" His gaze once again went out the window.

"Not necessary. I'm still full from the burgers we ate earlier. I've also got some chips and peanuts left in the room if I get the munchies. I'll be fine for the rest of the night." She got up and pulled on her coat.

As they left the building to get into Gabriel's car, she was surprised to see how quickly the snow was piling up on the road. Already a couple of inches of new snow had fallen on everything.

"Just drop me off and get yourself home safe and sound. The roads look like they're already getting treacherous," she said.

Minutes later her words proved true as Gabriel slowly maneuvered the snow-covered streets with blowing snow that made visibility difficult.

She grasped the edges of her seat as the back wheels slid out and he quickly corrected. A muscle throbbed in his jawline as he frowned in concentration. They didn't speak until he reached the Diamond Cove parking lot.

"Don't wait another minute. Get someplace safe for the night," she said as she unbuckled her seat belt.

"I'll call you in the morning," he replied.

She nodded and got out of the car. The wind stole her breath and the snow stung her face and any bare skin as she hurried up the path that would take her to her room. When she reached her door she looked behind her, grateful to see the faint red glow of Gabriel's taillights as he drove away.

She hated winter more than she hated fried liver, more than she despised her ex-husband. She hoped Gabriel got home safe and sound. This was definitely not a good night to be out on the roads.

Her fingers trembled from the frigid air as she put her key into the doorknob and opened the door.

A person exploded out of the room toward her. She had only a second to register a black ski mask, a black or navy coat and the glint of the long, sharp knife as it slashed at her.

She stumbled backward, dropped her purse and fumbled for her gun as she raised her other arm defensively in front of her. She gasped as the blade sliced through the arm of her coat.

Before she could clear her gun from her holster, the figure shoved past her and ran toward the woods. Jordon nearly fell backward, but quickly regained her balance and followed. There was no way she was going to let the perp get away.

"Halt, or I'll shoot," she cried just before the person darted behind a tree.

Jordon raced ahead, the wind howling in her ears and her face and fingers freezing. She had no time to process the attack that had just occurred, a surprise attack that might have killed her. All of her training kicked in and she had only one goal in mind.

This was the perfect opportunity to bring him

down. She refused to let the cold and the near-blinding conditions stop her. She absolutely refused to give in to any fear that tried to take hold of her. She didn't have time for fear.

There was no question in her mind that this was the serial killer they sought. He'd obviously hoped to stab her in the chest, to incapacitate her and then finish her off, just like he'd done to Sandy Peters.

If he'd been successful just moments before in his attack, then Gabriel or somebody else would have found her body on the porch sometime the next morning.

The only sound in the woods was the sharp pants of her own breaths as she raced forward and tried to see the dark, deadly figure who shared the area with her.

She paused and swiped at the snow on her face. Where had he gone? Was he hiding behind a tree just waiting to strike out at her again?

Was he behind her? She whirled around, every nerve tense and her heartbeat racing frantically. Her head filled with images of Samantha Kent, who had entered these woods to take pictures but instead had wound up stabbed in the back.

Swirling wind-driven snow made it impossible for her to see more than five feet in front of her. Her lungs ached with the freezing air.

Each tree she passed was a potential hiding place. Every tree in front of her could hide the knife-wielding killer. She walked slowly now, pausing often to listen to see if she could hear anything, but there was nothing but the thundering boom of her heartbeat in her head.

Bitter disappointment filled her as she realized she

had no idea where he'd gone. It was possible he wasn't even in the woods anymore.

The wind cut through her, and her face and fingers had gone numb. The snow was coming down so hard now she could barely see her hand in front of her face. It was a whiteout condition.

She had to give it up. It was foolish to hunt a person in these circumstances, especially not knowing the area or if her prey was even still nearby.

She turned to head back to her room and froze in her tracks. She was in a snow globe and completely disoriented. She hadn't paid attention to the direction she'd run.

Was her cabin in front of her or to the left? Was it behind her or to the right? How far away was she from her room? How long had she been running?

Squinting, she tried to see something that would orient her, but there was nothing but snow and wind. She was in trouble. She hadn't been truly scared before, but now she was terrified. She was lost in a blizzard and had no idea where to go.

It was going to be a long night. Jordon had assumed Gabriel was going to go home to ride out the storm in the comfort of his own home, but that wasn't happening.

As chief of police, he needed to be out on the road, seeing to stranded motorists or any accidents that were certain to occur with this kind of weather.

He'd left her and driven straight back to the station, where the garage mechanic had put snow chains on his tires. He should have had them put on earlier in the day before the storm was upon them, but he'd been busy.

Thankfully, it took only a few minutes and then he headed for the main drag, grateful to see that it appeared everyone had taken the storm warnings seriously.

Branson appeared like a ghost town. All the stores and restaurants had closed up. Shows had been canceled and there was virtually nobody on the streets.

With the near-whiteout conditions, he intended to park in one of the lots in the middle of the strip and ride out the worst of the storm. Hopefully, from here he could respond quickly to anyone who needed help. His police radio crackled as his men on duty gave updates from where they were located.

He'd just parked when his cell phone rang. A jangle of nerves coursed through him as he recognized the number as Jordon's.

"Jordon?"

"I'm sorry… I'm lost, Gabriel. I'm lost and so cold."

He sat up straighter, his heart racing. "Jordon, where are you?"

"In the woods. I'm someplace in the woods. He came after me and I chased him, but now I don't know where I am. There's so much snow. Everything is white, so white." Panic screamed from her voice and a sickness surged inside him.

"Jordon, stay where you are. I'm coming to find you."

"Okay, and, Gabriel, please hurry."

He was already racing down the street as fast as the conditions would allow him, which wasn't half-fast enough for his panicked alarm. Damn the snow that now fell in sheets.

He kept her on the phone as he radioed for more men to meet him at Diamond Cove. Once he'd called for help, she told him in a halting voice about the person waiting for her in her room and attacking her with a knife.

His heartbeat thundered inside his chest. She'd nearly been stabbed but he couldn't fully process that now. The biggest threat to her at the moment was the weather, and if she'd run from her room as soon as Gabriel had left the bed-and-breakfast, then she'd been out in the elements far too long.

By the time he reached Diamond Cove, her chattering teeth were audible over the phone as she kept up a stream of conversation.

He was grateful to see two of his men already there and waiting for him. "Agent James is someplace in the woods. We'll stick together and cover the area," he said to them. "It's also possible that our killer is someplace out here, so stay alert.

"Jordon, we're here and we have flashlights," he said into his cell phone. "Let me know when you see or hear us."

"I'm officially now a snow cone. A cherry snow cone because that's my favorite flavor. If I was from Italy I'd be an Italian ice," she said and released a small burst of laughter that bordered on hysteria.

He wasn't surprised that she'd defaulted to humor. He'd known her long enough to realize it was her way to deal with stress or fear. "We're on our way, Jordon."

"Maybe it's better to be a snow angel than a snow cone," she said and rambled on about making snow angels when she'd been younger and had lived in Denver with her parents.

Gabriel led the men to her suite, where the door was still open; her key remained in the doorknob and her purse was on the ground. He threw her purse inside the room, pulled the key out, shoved it into his pocket and then closed the door.

It was impossible to follow any footprints. The wind and the falling snow had already covered whatever prints there might have been. As they stepped off the porch and entered the woods, all three of them began to yell her name as their flashlights scanned the snowy landscape.

Gabriel could only pray they were going in the right direction. After only a few steps, the cold ached inside him and his face stung. He couldn't imagine how frozen she must be.

It was slow going as visibility was nearly down to nothing, and the men walked side by side so that none of them would get lost, as well.

As Jim and Bill yelled her name, Gabriel kept the phone pressed tightly against his ear. "Maybe I'm a snow woman," Jordon said. "If somebody is making me into a snow woman then I definitely want bigger boobs."

Gabriel was grateful he didn't have her on speaker. He knew without a doubt she wouldn't want anyone else hearing this conversation but him.

How much longer could she stay out here in the cold? She already sounded half-delirious. He was also aware that she could be vulnerable to another attack by whoever had gone after her in the first place.

His brain flashed with visions of what Samantha Kent must have looked like when Billy Bond had found her. According to the groundskeeper, she'd been facedown on the ground and bleeding out from the vicious stab wounds she'd suffered.

They had to find Jordon. They had to find her right now. The wind seemed to swallow the men's cries and Gabriel realized Jordon had stopped babbling.

"Jordon?" he asked urgently.

"I'm here… I think I heard somebody shouting my name."

"Scream…scream as loud as you can," he replied. He took the phone away from his ear.

A raw, ear-piercing scream shattered the silence. It not only sounded from the cell phone in his hand, but also from someplace to the left of them.

"This way," Jim said urgently and headed in that direction.

Suddenly she was in front of them. Snow covered her dark hair and her shoulders, and her eyes glowed wild in the light. "Jordon!" Gabriel shut off the cell phone and stuffed it into his pocket as he ran toward her.

"Gabriel!" She met him and slammed her body into his, her arms wrapping tightly around his waist. "Thank God you found me," she said with a half sob.

He held her tight for only a couple of seconds. "Let's get you out of here." With his arm around her shoulders, the four of them headed back to the cabin.

First he wanted her safe and warm, and then he wanted to know every single detail that had led up to her being out in the woods in a blizzard.

Once they reached her suite, he thanked Bill and

Jim and they left to get back on the road to help anyone else who might be in trouble.

Gabriel's first order of business was Jordon. As she stood shivering, he shrugged out of his coat and then pulled hers off. "Sit," he said and pointed to the chair next to the fireplace. He turned on the flames and then hurried to the bathroom for a towel.

His blood ran cold as he saw that the window in the small room was open and the screen was nowhere to be seen. He grabbed a hand towel and used it to slam it shut. He tried to lock it, but the lock didn't work. This answered how the perp had gotten inside.

He took a couple of bath towels from the stack on the back of the commode and hurried back to her. She'd taken off her boots and socks and rubbed her bare feet together. At least she didn't appear to be drowsy or suffering from hypothermia.

"I'm sorry. I didn't mean to be any trouble." Her voice broke with a hiccuping sob.

"Here, dry off your hair," he replied softly. She did as he instructed, and he went to the small closet and pulled down a blanket that was folded on the top shelf.

He wrapped the blanket around her. "Let me see your fingers."

He took one of her hands in his, grateful to see her fingertips were red but didn't show any indication of frostbite. "Now your feet."

She hesitated a moment but then raised her legs so he could grab her ankles. Her toenails were painted a pearly pink and he was grateful again that her toes were cold, but didn't appear to suffer frostbite.

"Okay," he said and she lowered her feet back to the floor. For the first time since he'd answered her call on his phone, his stomach slowly began to un-clench. He leaned over her, pulled the blanket more tightly around her and then sat opposite her chair on the edge of the bed.

The beige blanket emphasized the bright green of her eyes and her dark, damp tousled hair. She looked so fragile and he wanted nothing more than to pull her into his arms and comfort her…warm her. But he had business to attend to.

"Feeling better?"

"A little," she replied.

"Now, tell me exactly what happened after I dropped you off here," he said.

She grimaced and sat up straighter in the chair. "He was waiting for me in here. I opened the door and was met by a knife. He tried to stab me but thankfully only sliced through the arm of my coat. Before I could grab my gun, he pushed past me and ran into the woods. I didn't want him to get away."

Her eyes blazed bright. "I didn't think about the weather. I didn't think of anything except catching him. But it didn't take long for the storm to make it impossible for me to find him."

"Did you get a good look at him?" He asked the question even knowing that if she'd been able to iden-tify him she would have already done so.

"Black ski mask, black or navy coat." She frowned. "It all happened so fast."

"Height…weight?" he asked.

"I…I'm not sure. Maybe taller than me? And with his coat it was difficult to tell body weight." She shrugged the blanket off her shoulders and ex-pelled a deep breath of obvious frustration. "I'm an

FBI agent and I can't even tell you exactly what my attacker looked like. I can't even tell you what material his coat was made of."

"Jordon, cut yourself some slack. You were caught by surprise in the middle of a snowstorm. Whoever it was, entry was made through the bathroom window. It looks like the lock doesn't connect right."

She frowned and pulled the blanket back around her shoulders. "I wonder who around here knew the lock wasn't working properly?"

"Our handyman, Ed Rollings, might know," he said grimly.

She stared at him for a long moment. "Don't tell me again you want me to move to another motel. You're right—I was caught by surprise tonight, but that won't happen again and I'm not going anywhere."

Gabriel grimaced. It was as if she'd read his mind and he wanted to shake her for her stubbornness. He walked over to the window and moved the curtain aside to peer outside.

There appeared to be about five inches of snow already on the ground and it was still coming down fast and furiously. Even if there hadn't been any weather conditions to contend with, his decision would be the same.

He turned back to look at her. "I'm not leaving you alone here until that window is fixed, and that won't happen before tomorrow."

"So, I get a snuggle buddy for the night. I like it." Her lips curved into a smile and her eyes held an inviting light that twisted Gabriel's gut with a new kind of tension.

Chapter Seven

She couldn't get warm.

She felt as if she'd never be truly warm again. Even with the blanket clutched tightly around her shoulders and the knowledge that Gabriel was going to be with her through the night, Jordon still possessed a stubborn inner chill that wouldn't go away.

It wasn't the fear of the close call with the killer that kept her frozen, but rather the moments when she'd been surrounded by the harshness of winter. At least that was what she told herself.

Gabriel wandered the room, obviously looking for something...anything the killer might have left behind before his attack. His shoulders were rigid with tension and his frown was as deep, as dark as she'd ever seen it.

How she wished things had played out differently tonight. If not for the damned winter weather she was certain she would have managed to capture the killer and the case would have been solved.

It would be nice if they found the killer's body in the woods sometime tomorrow, frozen to death and no longer a threat to anyone. But she knew fate wouldn't be so kind.

They wouldn't find anything in the woods. The snowstorm would have effectively erased or covered any evidence the killer might have left behind.

Gabriel disappeared into the bathroom, and she closed her eyes and tried to access any minute detail about the attacker that she might not have thought of before. Hidden face, dark bulky coat and big, wicked knife—that was all she'd seen and it wasn't enough.

She'd been anticipating a potential attack, had been so careful, so cautious whenever she'd come and gone from her room. In her wildest nightmares she'd never dreamed the danger would explode out at her from inside her suite.

The whole room felt slightly tainted now. Her privacy, her safe place had been violated by the mere presence of the killer. Still, she was more determined than ever to remain here.

"I should go get a print kit from my car and see if I can lift anything," Gabriel said as he came back out of the bathroom.

"It wouldn't do any good. He had on gloves." She'd seen the knife and she now realized she'd also seen the hand that held it. "Big, black gloves. You won't find anything in here. You didn't find anything in Sandy Peters's room or at the other two crime scenes. This creep is careful and he still hasn't made a mistake."

Once again he sat on the edge of the bed facing her. She pulled the blanket closer around her throat. "I don't think it was Ed."

He sat up straighter. "Why do you say that?"

She frowned and once again went over every detail of the surprise assault. "Ed is a bit heavyset and I think our killer is leaner."

"Even if it wasn't Ed that still leaves Glen, Kevin and Billy Bond as potential suspects. None of them are particularly big men."

"Billy Bond would know the woods intimately. As groundskeeper, he probably knows the trails better than anyone else," she replied. "The person I was chasing didn't seem to be running willy-nilly. He seemed to know exactly where he was going."

"You shouldn't have gone out there all alone. You could have been killed, Jordon." His gaze remained dark and troubled as he looked at her.

"Then I would have died doing what I love. Besides, it worked out okay. The only way things would have been better is if I'd managed to get him and you hadn't had to ride to my rescue. Did you search all of the woods after Samantha Kent was killed?"

"Every inch of them," he replied.

"Is there anything on the property besides trees and brush?"

"A couple of old outbuildings," he said. "One of them is nothing more than a lean-to shed where lawn equipment is stored. The other one is just a little bit more substantial."

"Substantial enough to harbor somebody overnight in a snowstorm?"

He ran a hand down his jaw where a five o'clock shadow had begun to appear. "Doubtful. There are no windows or doors in it and it lists badly to one side."

She couldn't control a shiver that overtook her as she remembered the horror of the frigid temperature and the snow that had been everywhere.

"You're still cold. I saw a little coffeepot on the

vanity in the bathroom. Do you want me to make some?"

"Not unless you want a cup." She knew what would warm her up. He could. If he'd just wrap her in his arms and kiss her, the inner chill would finally ease. If he took her to bed and made love to her, she'd be wonderfully warm.

With the deep frown cutting across his forehead and the set of his shoulders, the last thing he appeared to have on his mind was any kind of intimacy with her. He probably thought he was going to spend the night on one of the chairs rather than sharing the bed with her.

But he had kissed her and his lips had held the heat of desire and the taste of deep yearning. In the past week she'd felt his attraction toward her. Furtive heated glances, a casual touch that lingered a little too long. Whether he knew it or not, he'd definitely been sending signals she'd received.

"There's only one way for me to get warm," she said. She shrugged off the blanket and stood. "I need a nice hot bubble bath."

His eyes widened. "Now?"

"Right this very minute." She walked over to the oversize tub and started the water. He turned on the bed to continue to stare at her.

She ignored him and adjusted the water temperature and then added some of the lilac-scented bubble bath to the tub. When she looked at him again, his eyes were still widened with an expression she couldn't quite read.

He cleared his throat. "If you're going to take a

bath then I'll just go sit in the bathroom until you're finished," he said.

"Don't be silly. If it makes you that uncomfortable then you can just sit there and stare at the fire." She began to unbutton her blouse.

He whipped his head around to face the opposite direction but not before she saw the searing desire, the raw, stark hunger that lit his eyes momentarily.

"You like baths," he said, his voice sounding slightly strained.

"I love a nice soak. Now that I think about it, I guess it's one of my major stress relievers," she replied.

By the time she'd stripped off the rest of her clothes, the tub was full of steamy, scented water. She eased down into the warm depths and pushed the button to get the jets working.

Leaning back in the tub built for two, she knew it wouldn't be enough. She wanted a bath, but at the moment what she needed, what she wished for more than anything was the man who sat on the bed.

She wouldn't be happy, she wouldn't find the warmth she craved until Gabriel held her in his arms.

Torture.

The sounds of sloshing water, the whir of the jets, and the faint sensual moans she emitted were sheer torture to Gabriel.

He stared intently into the fireplace, but instead of seeing the dancing flames there, his head filled with visions of a very bare Jordon in the tub.

Her skin would be warm and soft and sweetly scented by the fragrance of lilacs. He was jealous of the jetted water that swirled around her naked body. He was on fire with the desire for her that had simmered inside him for the last week.

The memory of the kiss they had shared burned in his head. Her lips had been so soft, so hot, and just thinking about it heated his blood.

"I think this is a perfect night to open this bottle of complimentary wine," she said. "Would you like a glass?" There was a sweet invitation in her voice.

She was seducing him.

It was evident in her tone of voice, in the fact that she'd gotten into the tub with him sitting right here. She was seducing him and he was helplessly faltering in his desire to not respond.

Don't turn around, a little voice whispered in his head. He somehow knew that if he turned around, if he saw her in that tub, he'd be lost.

Still, even knowing that he was making a mistake, in spite of all the internal alarms that rang in his head, he stood and turned around.

Her beauty squeezed the air out of his lungs and shot a burst of fiery adrenaline through his veins. Her hair looked even more charmingly curly than it had before, and her creamy shoulders and a hint of her breasts were visible above the bubbles.

He had no conscious memory of crossing the room, but suddenly he stood by the edge of the tub. She smiled up at him and held out a glass of wine. "Why don't you join me. The water's just fine."

She was a wicked temptation, and any good sense he had fled beneath the sensual assault she presented to him. He was cold, and the only way he could get warm was to join her in the tub.

Her eyes beckoned him like a silent siren song. As if in a trance, he took off his belt and dropped it to the floor and then unbuttoned his shirt and shrugged it off. He was making a mistake and someplace in the back of his mind he knew it, but nothing short of the apocalypse could keep him out of that tub.

He took out his gun and set it on the tiled area next to the bathtub and then kicked off his shoes, bent down and peeled off his socks. As he unfastened his slacks and stepped out of them, that inner voice whispered that this was his last chance to stop the madness, but he didn't listen.

He'd never been a shy man. He knew he was physically fit, but as he took off his boxers and then eased down into the tub, the smile Jordon gave him made him feel like Adonis himself.

She was curled up on one side of the tub and he was on the other. His legs stretched out to the left. She did the same so they didn't touch each other. She leaned forward and handed him the glass of wine and then grabbed hers.

"Here's to warm baths and snuggle buddies," she toasted and then clinked her glass with his.

He didn't draw a full, deep breath until she leaned back again. If he didn't touch her then there would be no harm, no foul.

If this was the only intimacy they shared, then they could face each other in the morning without any regrets. He took a big swallow of the wine.

"I'll admit, this does have its merits," he said as the warm water swirled around him.

She smiled. "And you're going to smell like a beautiful spring flower when you get out." She downed her wine and then poured herself some more. She held the bottle out to splash more in his glass but he shook his head.

"I'm good." The last thing he needed was to add too much alcohol to the fire. Besides, he was already half intoxicated by her.

She took another sip from her glass and then set it on the side of the tub, closed her eyes and released a sigh of obvious pleasure.

How could she look so relaxed? Only hours before, she had been attacked by a killer and faced freezing to death in the middle of a snowstorm.

He'd wanted to be angry with her for chasing the perp without calling for backup, without giving any thought to the consequences. However, it was difficult to be angry with her when he knew he would have reacted the same way.

It was equally difficult to sit across from her and gaze at her without wanting her. The bubbles were slowly dissipating and in desperation he looked up at the ceiling. The last thing he needed was to do something stupid that might complicate their partnership.

The water sloshed and he knew she was changing positions, but he kept his gaze upward. "Gabriel? Would you mind washing my back?"

Every muscle in his body tensed as he looked at her once again. She held out a wet washcloth and a small beige soap bar, and there was not only a warm invitation in her eyes but also that damned soft seduction. "Please?"

He was helpless to deny her. Hell, he was helpless to deny himself. He took the washcloth and soap from her and moved his legs so that he was sitting cross-legged, and she sat the same way directly in front of him with her back turned toward him.

He wasn't touching her—the washcloth was, he told himself as he caressed the soapy cloth over her slender back. But he knew he was only fooling himself. He wanted her and it was obvious she wanted him, too.

Good sense be damned, he knew with a sweet inevitability there was no way they would exit this room in the morning without having made love if that was what she wanted.

As soon as the thought filled his head, she turned to face him. The washcloth and soap slid from his hand the second she leaned into him.

Her bare breasts pressed against his chest at the same time their lips met. As the kiss deepened, he stretched out his legs and pulled her fully on top of him.

Warm soft skin, hot lips and the heady scent of lilacs cast all other thoughts out of his head. There was just him and Jordon and this single night.

"I want you, Gabriel," she said softly as their kiss ended. Her eyes shone with a brilliance he could drown in.

"I want you, too, Jordon." The words issued forth from the very depths of him.

She placed a finger over his lips. "I love the way my name sounds on your lips. I love the way your body feels against mine. Now I think it's time we move this to the bed." She moved away from him and hit the knob that would empty the water.

He stepped out of the tub and onto the bath mat and then grabbed one of the fluffy oversize towels and quickly dried himself off. He took a second towel and beckoned her out of the tub.

He'd officially lost his mind and he knew it, but they were both in too deep to stop now. She stood with her back to him and he began drying her shoulders. As he did so he leaned forward to kiss just behind one of her earlobes.

She leaned her head back and released a small moan that shot fire through his blood. He moved the towel down the length of her slender back, over her perfectly rounded butt and then down her shapely legs.

The tight control he'd maintained since the moment she'd started the water in the tub snapped. He dropped the towel, scooped her up in his arms and carried her to the bed.

There was no time to fold down blankets or turn out the lights. They were on each other like two hungry animals. He took her mouth in another kiss and reveled in the full-body contact with her.

This time when he broke the kiss, he moved his mouth slowly down the length of her neck, across her delicate collarbone and then to the raised nipple of one of her breasts. He teased it with his tongue, loving the taste of her and the way her fingers splayed in his hair as if she couldn't get enough of him.

He definitely couldn't get enough of her. He raised his head and gazed at her. "You are so beautiful, so perfect."

"I almost believe it when you say it," she replied in a husky voice.

With his desire a barely controlled beast inside him, he continued to explore her body. It was only when his fingers touched the raised scars on her left hip that desire was tempered by empathy and an anger that she had ever been in a cellar where a madman had played on her body with a lit cigarette.

He ran his fingers over the raised area and then followed the caress with his lips. He'd like to be able to kiss away not only the physical scar, but also the memory of that time, of that horrible pain she had to have endured. He wished he could kiss away the fear that she must have experienced knowing she was in the hands of a brutal serial killer.

He moved his hand to her inner thigh and then to the soft folds of her center. She moaned and whispered his name as he moved his fingers faster against her.

She arched her hips upward to meet him, and within minutes she gasped and stiffened as she climaxed. She shuddered and reached up to grab his shoulders.

Her eyes glowed a deep green. "Take me now, Gabriel. I want you inside of me."

He didn't hesitate. He moved between her thighs and slowly entered her. Her warm, moist heat surrounded him as her fingernails dug into his back.

He fought to maintain control, to last for as long as he possibly could. But as he began to stroke inside her, intense pleasure washed over him and he feared he'd lose it far too quickly.

His lips took hers once again in a fiery kiss that stole all thought from his mind. She met him thrust for thrust as fevered pants escaped them both.

She cried out his name as she stiffened against him and then moaned as she found her release once again. Gabriel's climax came hard and fast. He groaned and half collapsed on top of her.

He remained there only a moment and then rolled to the side of her and waited for his heartbeat to resume a more normal pace.

She rose up on one elbow and gazed at him with a soft smile. "I don't know about you, but I think that was pretty amazing."

He reached up and caressed her cheek. "'Amazing' doesn't even begin to describe it."

She leaned over and kissed him, a soft sweet kiss that stirred him on a completely different level altogether. "And now I'm wonderfully exhausted. All I need to do is get you out of this bed so that we can get under the covers."

She got off the bed and he did the same. As she stood, he saw the heart-shaped scar on her hip and once again his heart squeezed tight for the fear, the pain she must have gone through.

"Get your gun," he said. "I'll be right back." He took his gun from the edge of the bathtub and then went into the bathroom and closed the door behind him.

This night had been all kinds of wrong. He checked the window to make sure it was properly locked and then stepped up to the mirror and stared at his reflection.

From the moment the attacker had leaped out at Jordon, mistakes had been made, first by her and then by him. Making love to her had definitely been a huge mistake. Hell, they hadn't even used protection.

She touched him like no other woman had ever done before in his life. She made him laugh and she made him think. He wanted to know all of her thoughts, every one of her innermost emotions and dreams.

She was exactly the kind of woman he wanted in his life and she couldn't be more wrong for him. She'd told him she wasn't interested in marriage. Footloose and fancy-free—that was the way she wanted to live her life. They just wanted different things in their lives.

Starting tomorrow, he had to distance himself from her. They had to get back on the course of being strictly partners trying to hunt down a killer and nothing more.

But first, he was going to return to the bedroom and climb into bed with her. She would snuggle against him and he would want her all over again.

He leaned closer to his reflection. "Bonehead," he whispered to the man in the mirror.

Chapter Eight

Jordon awoke before dawn. Gabriel was spooned around her back with his arm thrown across her waist and his deep, even breathing warmed the back of her neck.

She closed her eyes again and embraced the moment of feeling loved even though she knew it was a false sentiment. Gabriel Walters could never love a woman like her. Nobody could really love her. Still, it was nice to pretend for a little while.

Certainly making love with him had rocked her world. He'd been so passionate and so wonderfully intense. He'd made her feel incredibly beautiful and desired.

They'd come together again sometime in the middle of the night, and then their lovemaking had been sleepy and slow and all kinds of wonderful.

However, she knew when dawn broke and a new day began, it would be business as usual between them. She didn't expect the soft glow in her heart to remain. She wasn't here for romance. She didn't *do* romance. She was here to catch a killer.

She remained in bed, wrapped in Gabriel's warmth and listening to her heartbeat mirror the slow steady beat of his until the sound of a snowblower shattered the silence. Gabriel stirred and slowly unwound himself from her.

"Good morning," he said as he sat up and raked a hand through his hair.

"Back at you," she replied.

He leaned over and grabbed his cell phone from the nightstand. "Jeez, it's just after seven. I haven't slept this late since before the first murder."

She slid out of bed. "I get the bathroom first." She grabbed a fresh pair of slacks, a blouse and her underwear and then went into the bathroom.

She hoped he didn't want to talk about last night. She didn't want to hear the regrets he was probably feeling in the light of day.

While she suffered not a single regret about what they had shared, she also wasn't eager to delve too deeply into exactly what her own feelings were.

Dressing as quickly as possible, she tried to get her head back into the game of murder and away from the night of passion. The killer was escalating in his quest. He'd almost gotten to her last night. She'd been lucky that the first knife strike hadn't hit her chest and incapacitated her.

When she left the bathroom Gabriel had already dressed and made the bed. He stood at the window with the curtain pulled back allowing a faint stream of sunshine to seep into the room.

"If you don't like the weather in Missouri just wait a minute and it changes," she said.

He turned away from the window with a nod. "It's hard to believe we were in blizzard conditions last night. It looks like the sun is going to shine today."

She walked over to stand next to him and peered outside. The morning sun sparkled on the five or six inches of additional snow that had fallen overnight. In the distance she saw Billy Bond working a snow-blower around the dining room porch and Ted Overton was shoveling off the paths in front of the cabins.

"It looks like everyone is working hard except us," she said.

"Why don't we head in for coffee and breakfast and then we'll get to work."

Within minutes they were both in their coats and snow boots and heading toward the dining room. Billy and his snowblower had disappeared, but Ted greeted them on the path with a quick, cheerful "good morning" as he continued to shovel.

WHEN THEY ENTERED the dining room, not only was Joan there, but also Jason and Hannah were seated at the table eating breakfast. Billy had apparently come in to get warm and stood by the fireplace sipping a cup of coffee.

"Good morning, everyone," Gabriel said.

They all returned his greeting except Billy, who gave a curt nod and then turned to face the fire. All of Jordon's muscles tensed. Was it guilt that had him facing away from them or just the desire to warm up?

They each got a cup of coffee and then sat at the table with the two teenagers while Joan scurried into the kitchen to see to their breakfast.

"Billy, why don't you join us?" Gabriel said. His tone of voice indicated it was a command, not a simple request. Billy got the message, for he moved away from the fire and sat in the chair opposite Jordon.

She stared at him but he refused to meet her gaze. He looked at a place just over her shoulder and then into his cup as if the contents were of great interest.

Was he the person who had been in her room last night? Was he the cold-blooded killer they sought? He'd probably know about the window lock and could have even set it so that it appeared to be secure when it wasn't.

"Heck of a night," Gabriel said. He took a sip of his coffee then turned to look at the groundskeeper. "How are the roads out there?"

"Side streets are a mess, but it looked like the road crews had already hit the main streets when I came in," he replied.

"Where did you ride out the storm, Billy?"

The man shot Gabriel a quick glance. "At home, where any sane person would be in that kind of weather," he replied.

"Anyone with you?" Jordon asked.

For the first time since they'd entered the room, his gaze met hers. Cold and flat, his eyes stared into hers and she fought against an inner chill. "It wasn't exactly a good night for socializing."

"What about for a walk in the woods?" Gabriel asked. Jason and Hannah had stopped any pretense at eating as they listened intently to the conversation.

"I don't know what you're talking about." Billy took a sip from his cup and then leaned back in the chair. "Why would I go for a walk in the woods in the middle of a snowstorm?"

"That's what we're trying to figure out. Jordon thought she saw somebody in the woods last night," Gabriel said. It was apparent by the way he framed his words that he intended to play the attack close to his chest.

"Well, it wasn't me," Billy said. "Getting out in weather like that for a walk would be just plain stupid. I might be many things, but I'm not that dumb."

At that moment Ted came in from outside. "Billy, you warmed up enough to get back to work?"

"I am." Billy got up from the table, put on his coat and then headed out the door.

"Do you think Billy is the killer?" Hannah asked half-breathlessly.

"We're still investigating," Jordon replied as the snowblower outside once again started up.

"He's always been kind of weird," Jason said and then popped a piece of bacon into his mouth.

Ted wore a deep frown. "Is Billy a suspect?"

"Like Agent James said, we're still investigating," Gabriel replied.

Joan entered the room carrying their plates and then sat at the table next to her husband. "I see you two got through last night okay. According to the weatherman, we're supposed to get above-freezing temperatures tomorrow and it's supposed to be in the midforties for the rest of the week."

"Ah, sweet music to my ears," Jordon said. She took a sip of her coffee and then looked at Ted. "I was wondering about the outbuildings in the woods. Gabriel said there is a lean-to shed out there and also a building that's a little more substantial."

"That's right," Ted replied. "They're really nothing but eyesores. One of my goals for this spring is to tear them both down and put up a nice, new shed."

"Is there electricity out there?" Jordon asked.

"Not in the lean-to shed but in the other building there is, although we don't use that building at all," Ted replied.

"Mom, can we be excused?" Jason asked Joan.

"Go ahead, but get your morning chores done. Just because you have a snow day at school doesn't mean you don't keep your usual routine."

"We know, we know," Hannah replied, earning her a stern look from Joan. The two kids quickly got up, grabbed their coats and left.

"What's with all the questions about the outbuildings?" Ted asked.

"Jordon was attacked last night and whoever did it ran into the woods," Gabriel replied.

"Attacked?" Joan raised a hand to her lips in horror. "What happened?"

"He was waiting for me in the room. He got in through the bathroom window. He tried to stab me and then ran off into the woods," Jordon explained.

"Oh, sweet Lord," Joan exclaimed. "I'm so glad you're okay."

"I'm fine," Jordon assured her. "The arm of my coat was the only casualty."

"Thank goodness," Joan replied, her voice still filled with a touch of shock.

"That lock on the window in Jordon's room needs to be replaced or fixed," Gabriel said. "And hopefully it can be done today."

"Ed should be in within the next couple of hours. I'll get him right on it," Ted replied and then looked at Jordon. "Did you see who it was?" He grimaced. "I guess you didn't since you're sitting here instead of making an arrest."

Jordon shook her head. "He had on a ski mask and it was impossible for me to make an identification."

"We're hoping maybe there might be something in the woods or in one of those outbuildings that might yield a clue," Gabriel said.

"I certainly hope so. I want this nightmare to be over," Joan replied fervently.

Jordon ate quickly as did Gabriel. If they were going to head into the woods to see what they could find, then she wanted to do it sooner rather than later.

The very idea of traipsing through the snow made her want to shiver, but if they found something that would help them catch the murderer then it would be worth every agonizing cold moment.

It was almost eight thirty by the time they left the dining room. There was no sign of Billy and the sound of the snowblower had stopped.

"You might want to put your gun in your coat pocket so you can zip up your coat," Gabriel said and his breaths hung on frosty puffs.

"I definitely want my coat zipped," she replied. "That hot beach in Florida would be nice right about now."

"A beach anywhere sounds good to me," Gabriel agreed.

They took off walking toward the woods. Both of them had their guns in hand.

"I've got to confess, I'm not feeling optimistic about us finding anything out here," she said.

Gabriel smiled at her, that beautiful smile that sparked warmth through her entire body. "I thought you were the optimist in this partnership." His smile faded and he stopped in his tracks, his eyes slightly darker in hue. "Do we need to talk about last night?"

"As far as I'm concerned, there's nothing to talk about. We were just two cold souls who warmed each other up on a cold wintry night." She forced a lightness into her voice. As crazy as it sounded, it had been more than just a hot hookup for her.

He held her gaze for a long moment, his features radiating with an emotion she couldn't discern. "Okay, then let's get this done." He trudged ahead and she quickly followed.

As they got deeper into the woods, Jordon tried not to remember the panic that had nearly crippled her the night before when she'd been lost in a snow globe.

She also had to swallow down the fear that had gripped her, knowing that at any moment a knife could stab her and she would become the fourth victim to die at Diamond Cove.

There were places where the snow had drifted and others that appeared barely touched by the new snowfall. The tree branches sparkled in the sunlight. It would have been a beautiful winter wonderland if they weren't hunting for clues that would lead them to a savage killer.

They walked slowly, scanning the area silently and with focused concentration. If only they could find a scrap of material from a torn coat, something dropped out of a pocket, anything that would identify who had been in her room and had tried to stab her.

When they approached the lean-to shack that Gabriel had described, he motioned for her to go to the left and he went to the right.

She tightened her grip on her gun, even though she

didn't really expect trouble. Whoever had been in the woods last night would have beat feet to get out of the area long before now.

The shed held a riding lawn mower, rakes and shovels, and other yard equipment, but nothing that didn't belong there. They checked the entire structure but didn't find anything that would indicate that anyone had been there the night before.

The sun grew warmer on her shoulders as they left the shed and continued on. Once again she scanned the pristine landscape for anything that was out of place, something that didn't belong.

In the distance was the other outbuilding Gabriel had mentioned. It was bigger than the other shed and had a doorway without a door and two windows with no glass.

It appeared completely abandoned and like a stiff wind would bring it down. She couldn't imagine anyone huddling inside for the duration of the snowstorm. A sigh escaped her. This whole search had been nothing but more dead ends.

How she wished she would have been able to catch the person the night before. She'd been so taken by surprise. Somehow, she should have managed to take down the perp before he ever shoved past her and jumped off her porch.

The crack of gunfire split the air and a bullet dug into the snow at Jordon's feet. She scarcely had time to register it when Gabriel slammed his body into hers and took her down to the ground.

GABRIEL'S HEART THUNDERED as he returned fire into the building. Jordon wiggled out from beneath him.

"See if you can get around to the back," she said. "I'll cover you and get behind a tree trunk."

Although his first instinct was to protect her, he reminded himself she was a trained professional and as it was they were both sitting ducks with their dark coats against the white snow. They needed cover.

He gave a curt nod. She fired into the building and he raced to the right, praying that she would manage to get behind something before a bullet found her.

As he darted to the back of a tree, he looked back and sighed in relief when he saw that she had rolled sideways and now crouched behind the trunk of a large oak.

Several more shots came from the shed, one of the bullets pinging off the tree behind which he hid. Who was in the shed? There had been nothing to indicate in the past that the killer they sought had a gun.

Jordon returned fire and Gabriel darted to another tree, moving him closer to the back of the shed. There was no way he intended to allow whoever was inside to escape.

If it was the killer, Gabriel had no idea why he would be here now. But certainly with the attack and the flight last night, he had to believe that the person they had sought was the same person shooting at them.

Adrenaline pumped through him as he moved again. Jordon was no longer in his sight, and as gunfire sounded from the shed once again, he could only hope that no bullet found her.

At least he didn't hear a scream of agony or any cry for help. But would she shout for aid if she'd been shot, or would she lie in the snow and die silently? She was so tough and obviously a lone wolf.

He made it to the rear of the shed just in time to see a figure dart out of the back door opening. He recognized the cut of the dark coat and the baggy jeans beneath. He'd seen them earlier in the dining room.

Billy Bond.

"Jordon, in the back," he yelled and took off running after Billy.

Billy ran fast, but Gabriel ran faster, fueled by anger and determination. "Billy, halt! Don't make me shoot you in the back."

Instead of shooting at him, Gabriel got close enough to lunge at his back. Billy hit the ground hard with Gabriel on top of him.

Jordon appeared and leaned down to place the barrel of her gun against the side of Billy's head. "If you twitch, I'll shoot," she said firmly.

"Please, don't shoot me!" Billy exclaimed.

"Billy, what in the hell are you doing?" Gabriel said as he got to his feet and yanked the man up by the back of his coat. As Gabriel handcuffed Billy, Jordon searched his pockets and pulled out his gun, then did a more thorough pat-down.

"It's a meth lab," Jordon said. "I ran through the shed and there's enough material in there to keep the whole state high for a very long time."

"I don't know what you're talking about," Billy replied, a surly snarl curving his lips.

"Then why were you shooting at us?" Gabriel asked as he led the man back the way they had come.

"I wasn't shooting at you. It must have been somebody else. I was just out here trimming some tree branches."

"And I'm the freaking queen of Scotland," Jordon retorted with a laugh.

Gabriel led Billy into the shed, where he looked around in stunned surprise. A hot plate was plugged into an electrical socket that hung from the lightbulb in the ceiling. Mason jars gleamed red and purple, and jugs of drain cleaner, paint thinner and a variety of other items used to make the deadly drug littered what was left of the workbench.

Anger once again ripped through Gabriel. Fighting the making and use of meth was a full-time job. It was a scourge that not only ripped apart families, but killed. And this had been going on right under his nose.

Was Billy just a dope manufacturer and dealer or was he a killer, as well?

"Let's go," he said and roughly yanked Billy out of the door.

Within minutes they were in his car and headed to the police station. They rode in silence. Gabriel drove slowly although he was eager to get Billy into an interrogation room and have a long talk. He needed to find out if they now had the killer under arrest.

Thankfully, the main roads had been cleared, but the side streets remained a grim testimony to the storm that had roared through overnight.

He felt the tension that wafted from Jordon and knew that she had the same questions that he had about Billy Bond and his potential relationship to the murders that had taken place.

Had he been the person who had attacked Jordon?

Had he climbed through the window with the intention of killing her? Gabriel gripped the steering wheel tightly and tried to quell his anger.

Once at the station, he put Billy into the small interview room and then instructed his right-hand man, Lieutenant Mark Johnson, to gather up the team trained for cleaning up drug labs in the area and get out to Diamond Cove.

Jordon stood just outside the interrogation room door, peering in through the small window to where Billy sat at the table with his head in his hands.

"We now know why we thought he was a creep," she said. "He definitely had something to hide."

"A damn meth lab." Gabriel shook his head.

"And potentially our killer?" Jordon looked at him with darkened eyes.

"Let's get in there and see just how much he has to hide," Gabriel replied, hoping that this would be the end of the search for their murderer.

Billy looked up as the two of them entered the room. His smirk was gone, replaced by eyes that held nothing but despair and hopelessness.

Gabriel sat across from him and Jordon remained standing just behind Gabriel's chair. He read Billy his rights and thankfully the groundskeeper waived his right for a lawyer.

"I'm in big trouble, aren't I?" he asked.

"You're looking at fifteen years just for the drug charges. If I add in attempted murder then you're probably looking at life," Gabriel replied.

Billy's eyes widened slightly. "I wasn't trying to kill you. I just wanted to scare you off. Dumb, huh."

"Duh, we're the law. We run toward bullets, not away from them," Jordon said drily.

"Methamphetamines? What on earth were you thinking, Billy? Just how long has this been going on?"

Billy grimaced and shook his head. "My sister was diagnosed with breast cancer three months ago. She needs money for treatment and I was desperate."

"Desperate enough to murder three innocent people?" Jordon asked.

Billy's gaze shot to her and then back to Gabriel, his eyes widened once again. "Don't try to pin that on me. I don't know anything about those murders—you've got to believe me." He leaned forward, his eyes filled with fire as he held Gabriel's gaze. "I'll admit I'm guilty of the meth lab, but I did not kill those people."

A weight dropped inside Gabriel's chest and lay heavy in the pit of his stomach. He believed Billy. And if Billy wasn't their killer, then who was?

Chapter Nine

They interviewed Billy for almost two hours, and it was only when Gabriel wanted the names of anyone else involved in the meth operation that Billy finally demanded a lawyer.

He was taken to a jail cell to await a meeting with legal counsel, and Jordon and Gabriel got in his car to head back to Diamond Cove.

"I hate to admit it, but I believe him," Jordon said as she adjusted the car heater vents for maximum warmth on her face. "I believe that he wasn't in the woods last night and I believe him when he said he wasn't the person who attacked me. I just don't think Billy is our man."

"I agree and that's good news and bad news," Gabriel replied. "The good news is we can take him off our suspect list. The bad news is that means our murderer is still out here somewhere."

Jordon stared out the passenger window, her mind working over the few suspects they had left. The Rollings brothers, they were it. Was one of them the killer or was the person they sought completely off the grid, flying under their radar? That was definitely a depressing thought.

She gazed back at Gabriel. "I'm assuming we'll be checking some alibis for last night at some point today?"

"Definitely, although the first order of business is seeing to it that the window in your room is fixed."

He pulled into the Diamond Cove entrance, where two police cars and an evidence van were already parked. Several officers stood around, and it appeared that the van had been packed with all the items that had been in the shed.

"Chief," Mark greeted them as they got out of the car. "We're loaded up and ready to leave. Thank God it looked like he hadn't cooked for a couple of days and the fumes weren't too bad at all. It definitely helped that there were no closed windows or doors and the storm blew through the building."

"Good," Gabriel replied.

"Did you find any actual meth?" Jordon asked.

Mark grinned. "Enough to keep Billy cooking up slop in prison for a very long time."

"One more bad apple off the streets," Jordon replied.

"We'll just let you finish up." Gabriel touched her arm. "Let's go check in with Ted and Joan."

She followed behind Gabriel as they headed inside. She couldn't help but think about how nice it had been to have his arms around her through the night, how comfortable she felt with him. Their conversations were so easy, as if they'd known each other for months instead of days. She didn't feel the need to censor herself with him. She trusted that she could just be herself and that was okay with him.

She'd misjudged him at first impression. He wasn't

inflexible; he was determined. He wasn't uptight—he was focused, and he was so much more than those things. He was intelligent and could be funny. More important, he seemed to *get* her.

Maybe she was just feeling particularly soft about him because he'd thrown her to the ground and covered her body with his own when the bullets had flown. His first instinct hadn't been to get to cover himself, but rather to protect her.

Not that any of that mattered. She tamped down a strange wistfulness that tried to take hold of her as they entered the main dining room.

Ted sat on one of the chairs by the fireplace and Joan sat at one of the tables. There was an underlying thrum of tension in the air. Joan stood as they entered and worried her hands together.

"We didn't know," she said. Her blue eyes were darker than Jordon had ever seen them. "You have to believe me—we had no idea what Billy was doing out there in the shed."

"A meth lab…murder," Ted said in disgust and gazed at his wife. "All of it happening right here where we live with our children. This would have never happened if we'd stayed in Oklahoma City, where we belonged."

It was obvious the crimes were fracturing what Jordon had presumed was a good and loving relationship.

"Sit down, Joan," Gabriel said calmly. "Nobody believes that you and Ted had anything to do with Billy's meth business."

Jordon walked over to the coffeepot to get a cup of the hot brew while Gabriel took a seat next to Joan.

"How long has this been going on? How long has

Billy been cooking drugs on this property?" Ted asked, his voice almost a growl.

Jordon sat at the table next to Gabriel and faced the fireplace and Ted. A rich anger radiated from the man, an anger that appeared to be pointed not only at the circumstances, but also specifically at his wife.

"I checked that shed when Samantha Kent was killed in the woods and there was nothing there. According to what Billy told us, he started just after Christmas when he found out his sister had cancer and needed money," Gabriel said.

"Did he kill those people?" Ted asked. "Is he the killer who is trying to destroy us?"

"We don't believe so," Jordon said.

Ted frowned. "So, we still have a killer running loose around here." He shook his head and gazed at Joan once again. "Happy wife, happy life—yeah, right." He got up from his chair and slammed his coffee cup down on the table. "I've got work to do in the office."

"I'm sorry," Joan said as soon as he'd left the room. "He's upset. We're both upset. This has all been so difficult." She looked utterly miserable as the glint of tears shone in her eyes.

"Don't worry—we understand," Jordon said softly.

"Has Ed come in yet?" Gabriel asked.

"He arrived just a few minutes before you did." She glanced at Jordon. "I sent him right to your room to take care of the window issue."

Gabriel stood. "We'll go check out the progress."

Jordon took a big gulp of her coffee and then got up, as well. "Joan, stay strong. We're going to get this all taken care of."

"I hope so. I was the one who insisted we make this move. Ted really only did it to make me happy." Her hand trembled as she reached up and tucked a strand of hair behind her ear. "I just want this to all go away so we can live the dreams we had."

"We'll do everything we can to make that happen, Joan," Gabriel replied.

"Tensions are definitely rising," Jordon said once they were on the path to her room. "I hate to see what's happening between Joan and Ted."

"Collateral damage," Gabriel replied. "There are always more victims than the dead ones when something like this happens."

"The ripple effect," she replied. Her stomach clenched. "I want to get this guy so badly I can taste it."

"Speaking of tasting it, we'll stop and get lunch after we leave here and before we start interviewing anyone."

Jordon glanced at her cell phone, shocked to see that it was already almost three. It was amazing how a chase in the woods and an interview with a drug dealer could eat up the hours of the day.

The door to her room was unlocked and they walked in to find Ed in the bathroom installing a new window lock. "I put up a new screen and this should take just a minute," he said after their initial greetings. "I told Ted a month ago that this lock had an issue, but with everything else going on around here, I guess we both forgot about it."

He finished using his screwdriver and then opened the window and tried the new latch several times. "That should do it," he said.

"Just a minute, Ed," Gabriel said before the handyman could leave the suite. "We have a few questions to ask you."

"Questions about what?"

"Where were you last night?"

Ed looked at them in surprise. "I was at home. In fact, Kevin and Glen came over and wound up spending the night. We played cards and drank some beer, and this morning Millie made us all sausage and French toast with my favorite strawberry syrup."

Jordon stared at the man with a rising frustration. She still couldn't be certain if he was off the hook for being the man who had attacked her, but how convenient that he'd just provided an alibi not only for himself but also for his brothers.

"Is there anything else?" Ed asked with his usual pleasantness. "I've got some other work to attend to around here."

"That should do it," Gabriel replied. Once Ed was out the door, Gabriel turned and looked at Jordon. "We'll grab some lunch and then I think it's time we talked to Millie."

"Do you really think she'll say anything different than what Ed told us?"

"Doubtful, but maybe we'll see something in the house that will tell us something different."

"If you don't mind, I'd rather talk to her first and grab lunch afterward," Jordon said. She wanted to tie up any loose ends that they could from the attack the night before as soon as possible.

He shrugged. "Fine by me."

"Will she even let us in the front door?" Jordon asked as they left her room.

He flashed her a quick smile. "It would be down-right rude to keep people standing on the front porch on a cold winter's day."

"And Branson is known for its down-home friend-liness," she replied.

Why couldn't she get Gabriel's *friendliness* out of her brain? Throughout the interview with Billy, she'd flashed back to the night before and the intimate moments with Gabriel. When they'd entered the room to find Ed, her gaze had shot to the bed where they'd made love the night before.

He'd somehow managed to get under her skin in a way no man had done since Jack. She'd hoped never again to feel the wild electricity, the slight flutter in her heart, for any man. As crazy as it sounded, when she left here the chief of police would have more than just a little bit of her guarded heart.

She mentally shook herself and realized there was an unsettled piece of her brain, as if she'd forgotten something important. But, try as she might, she couldn't figure out what it was, like having a snatch of a lyric to a song going around and around in her head and she couldn't quite remember the title.

Gabriel pulled down a narrow road that thankfully had been plowed earlier in the day. The houses were small and set far apart.

"Unfortunately, Ed's house is fairly isolated and the last place before a dead end. It's doubtful that anyone in the neighborhood would know whether Kevin's and Glen's cars were parked there overnight or not."

Jordon released a deep sigh. "A dead end is where we're at. Nothing is coming easy with this case. I can't go back to Kansas City without this being solved. It would totally ruin my reputation."

"And what reputation is that?" he asked.

"My kick-ass-and-get-it-done reputation," she replied.

He cast her another one of his charming grins. "I certainly wouldn't want to mess with that reputation, so that means we need to kick ass and really get it done."

"Amen," she replied.

He parked in front of a little house painted a dreary brown with a bright red front door. Unfortunately, the driveway was completely shoveled, making it impossible to see whether one car or three cars had been parked there overnight.

She definitely hoped an answer was inside. She not only wanted to catch this guy sooner rather than later, but she also needed to get back to Kansas City before Gabriel dug any deeper into her heart.

MILLIE ROLLINGS WAS a painfully thin woman with mousy brown hair and faded blue eyes that gazed at them warily as she ushered them into a small neat living room that smelled of lemon furniture wax and old coffee.

Gabriel had never had much to do with Ed's wife, whom he saw only occasionally at the grocery store. He'd always gotten the impression of a nervous little bird, and as he introduced her to Jordon, his impression of Millie didn't change.

"Ed told me there was a pretty FBI lady staying at Diamond Cove," she said and self-consciously reached up to touch a strand of her limp hair.

"Do you mind if we have a seat and ask you a few questions?" he asked.

"Of course, please, although I can't imagine what you would want to ask me." She gestured toward the sofa and sat in a chair opposite them.

"We spoke with Ed earlier and he mentioned you had houseguests last night," Jordon said. "Is that correct?"

"Yes. Ed's brothers came by to play cards and got snowed in until this morning. I made them a big breakfast of sausage and French toast and the strawberry syrup that's Ed's favorite." She reached a hand up once again to pat her hair and her gaze shifted slightly above Jordon's head.

Interesting that she'd used almost the precise same words that Ed had used when he'd described the morning meal. Gabriel would love to get a look at her phone to see how quickly Ed might have called his wife after they'd spoken to him.

"You do realize we're searching for the person who has killed three people in cold blood. If you know anything about these crimes or if you're lying about Kevin and Glen being here last night, you could go to prison for a long time," Gabriel said.

Millie shot back in her chair as if he'd physically struck her. Her lower lip trembled slightly, and this time when she reached up to her hair, she grabbed a strand of it and twirled furiously.

"I'm not a liar. I'm not," she replied. "I'd never risk going to prison for anyone, especially the likes of those two. Me and Ed, we're good people."

"Sometimes good people make mistakes when it comes to protecting their family," Jordon said softly.

"I wouldn't do that and now I think it's time you both leave." She stood and looked at them expectantly...and defiantly.

The mouse had roared, Gabriel thought. He didn't know whether to be amused or ticked off. He and Jordon rose from the sofa.

"Mrs. Rollings, if you know anything about these murders, anything at all, now is the time to speak up," Jordon said.

"I can't help you and if you have any more questions you talk to Ed." She opened the front door. "Now, please go."

"What do you think?" Jordon asked when they were back in the car.

"I honestly don't know what to think." He started the engine and then pulled away from the house. "She might be telling the truth and she might be lying."

"Have you heard any rumors about her being an abused wife? Is it possible that she's scared of her husband and so would say anything to us that he told her to say?"

"I haven't heard any whispers of abuse," he replied. "But you never know what goes on behind closed doors."

"True. Maybe we should check with the neighbors. Maybe somebody saw or didn't see the cars here that would either prove Millie truthful or a liar."

It took them almost an hour to check with the other people who lived on the same street as Ed Rollings. Unfortunately, it had been a night where most people had hunkered down and weren't paying attention to what their neighbors were doing.

"Now I need to eat," Jordon said as they drove back

toward the main strip. "Breakfast seems like it was served a lifetime ago."

"What sounds good?" he asked. Another night in her bed sounded good. Another night of holding her sweet, soft body against his sounded great. "How about a juicy steak?" He hoped his voice didn't betray his physical frustration.

"Hmm, perfect," she replied.

It was almost six when they pulled into a popular steak house where Gabriel often ate. There were only two cars parked in front of the building despite the dinner hour.

As they got out of the car, Gabriel was struck by a bone-weariness. Between the trauma of the night before, the shoot-out with Billy and all the other events that had occurred within the past twenty-four hours, it was no wonder he was tired.

This case was eating him alive, and when he wasn't thinking about murder, he was thinking far too much about Jordon. Before he'd gone to sleep the night before, he'd been determined to put a little distance between himself and his partner. However, they'd shared another bout of lovemaking in the middle of the night, and so far the distance he'd thought he'd be able to maintain wasn't happening. Hell, he wanted her again right this minute.

The owner of the restaurant, Bob Carson, greeted them at the door. "Slow night with the weather, Chief. You've pretty much got your pick of tables or booths." He held out two menus.

"Thanks, Bob." Gabriel took the menus and then led Jordon to a booth toward the back of the restaurant. There was only one other couple seated at a table in the same general area.

They had just gotten situated and peered at the menus when Bob appeared at the booth with an order pad. "My waitresses didn't show up tonight due to the snow."

"Does this mean you'll also be cooking our meals?" Gabriel asked with a touch of humor.

Bob laughed. "No. You're in luck—the chef actually made it in along with one busboy. Now, what can I get for you two this evening?"

Jordon ordered a strip steak and a loaded baked potato and Gabriel got the rib eye with creamy mashed potatoes. They both ordered soft drinks and then Jordon leaned against the high, red leather booth back.

She looked achingly beautiful but her eyes appeared tired and slightly hollow.

"You look exhausted," he said softly.

"I am," she admitted.

"I think we've done enough today. After we eat I'll take you back to your room, unless you're finally ready to agree to get a room at another motel," he said, desperately wishing she would agree to go someplace safe.

She laughed, the slightly husky sound that stirred him on all levels, and shook her head. "You're nothing if not consistent, Chief Walters."

"Jordon, I care about your safety," he replied.

"I care about my safety, too, but that doesn't mean I'm going to run and hide. Ed fixed the window lock, and if it makes you feel better then you can walk me to my door each night and check the room before I settle in."

"Do you have some sort of a death wish?"

"Of course not," she replied quickly. "I'll admit I take some risks, but they're always calculated ones."

Their conversation was interrupted by the arrival of their meals. Unlike most of the meals they had shared, Jordon was unusually silent and appeared distracted.

Gabriel didn't know if it was because she was tired or if he might have made her angry with his death-wish question. Although he would have liked to prod her into telling him more about herself, about her current mood, instead he gave her space and remained quiet.

They were halfway through the meal when she placed her fork down and stared at him thoughtfully. "Something has been bothering me all afternoon and I finally figured out what it was."

"What's that?" he asked curiously.

"Ted."

Gabriel looked at her in surprise. "What about him?"

"I'm just wondering how hard Joan really had to twist his arm to move here." Her eyes darkened slightly. "I'm wondering what lengths he might go to in order to get back to life in Oklahoma City."

Gabriel sucked in a deep breath. Was it even possible? Would Ted sabotage the family business by killing three people in cold blood to ruin his wife's dream and get her and their children back where he thought they belonged?

"That's sick and it's crazy," he finally said.

"I know, right?" she replied. "But we knew we might be chasing crazy. Ted lives right across the street. He'd have access and intimate knowledge of the area."

"But he had a solid alibi for Samantha Kent's murder. He was having breakfast in the dining room with other people when she was killed," Gabriel protested.

"The medical examiner only has to be wrong about the time of the attack by twenty minutes or so. That would have given Ted time to stab her, clean himself up and appear for breakfast."

She leaned forward, her eyes blazing with the spark of life that had been missing before. "Ed mentioned that he'd told Ted about the window lock not working a month ago and yet he put me in that very room. Why not one of the other empty rooms? I know we checked into their backgrounds, but we were looking at it from the viewpoint that they were victims. I'm just saying maybe we need to approach an investigation into Ted from a new angle."

She picked up her fork once again and Gabriel set his down, his appetite gone as he realized they had managed to take one suspect off their list but had just added another one.

Chapter Ten

Another week passed far too slowly. The cases had all gone cold, and although the investigation continued, they were grasping at straws. One of the only good things that had happened was the weather had warmed up and the snow had finally melted away.

Jordon now sat in the conference room alone. Gabriel was attending to other duties in his office and she'd been reading through the interviews and the background material they'd gathered throughout the past week.

They'd spoken to Glen's, Ed's and Kevin's neighbors and friends in an effort to get a handle on the three brothers who topped their list of suspects.

They'd also spent hours on the phone speaking to anyone they could find who had been in Ted's and Joan's lives in Oklahoma City before they'd bought the Diamond Cove. This time the investigation wasn't seeking to find somebody who was an enemy of the couple.

Much of their efforts had been focused on digging into Ted's past to see if there was any indication that he harbored a dark and twisted soul. He had no criminal record other than a speeding ticket he'd received four years ago.

They'd spoken with former coworkers, and Jordon had spent hours digging into social media where he was fairly active. She'd studied his posts and stared at his photos for so long he invaded her dreams, but she'd found nothing out of the ordinary.

She'd not only delved into Ted's social media, but had also looked at Joan's. She'd even been desperate enough to study Jason's and Hannah's online presences, figuring sometimes children might share something about family tension.

Joan had posted fairly regularly when she'd been a teacher but had apparently put her blogging efforts into the official Diamond Cove website when they'd moved here. Her cheerful, inviting blogs had fallen off after the first murder.

Jason posted irregularly, mostly sharing things that teenage guys would find interesting. He had been unhappy about the move and talked about leaving his friends, but later posts indicated that he'd adjusted okay and had made new friends. Hannah had little social media, which was rather surprising for a fifteen-year-old girl.

Jordon sighed and cast her gaze out the nearby window where dusk was just beginning to paint the world in deep purple shadows. Another night nearly gone and they weren't any closer to solving the case.

However, she had definitely grown closer to her partner. He invaded her dreams, as well. They were not just sizzling erotic dreams, but also sweet and filled with all kinds of wonderful that she knew she'd never have in her real life.

She'd grown to care about him deeply and she had a feeling he was feeling the same way about her. That only made her need to solve this case more pressing than ever.

Even though they'd known each other for only a little over two weeks, they had probably spent more time together than most couples who had been married for six months or so.

They'd learned each other's little quirks. She knew he liked his burgers without ketchup and with extra mayo and that he refused to drink cold coffee. His energy level fell somewhat in the late afternoons, but he got a second wind after eating dinner.

Those were just the superficial things she'd discovered about him. She'd also learned he had a kind heart, that he had a secret passion for supporting animal rights and that his eyes softened and lightened in hue whenever he gazed at her.

The very last thing she wanted to do was break his heart. He was such a good man and he deserved a good woman. As much as she'd like to think otherwise, that woman would never, ever be her.

A wave of loneliness, of quiet sorrow struck her, piercing through her heart and bringing an unexpected sting of tears to her eyes.

She'd once had such dreams of sharing her life with a special man. She'd once believed she'd have a husband who would be her soft place to fall, a man who would be by her side until death. But those dreams had been stolen and she refused to believe in anything like that ever again.

This case was definitely not only getting to her on a professional level, but also on a personal one. Angrily she swiped at her eyes and sat up straighter in the chair. She was good alone. That was the way it was supposed to be and there was no sense getting all teary-eyed about it.

The conference room door opened and Gabriel swept in, filling the room with his solid presence, with his male vitality. "Now, where were we?" he asked.

She shoved the files away. "At the same dead end we were at a week ago," she replied with an uncharacteristic pessimism darkening her tone. "It would be nice if we could just identify somebody with the means and a clear motive, but I'm beginning to wonder if any of our suspects are really good for these murders." She released a heavy sigh.

He frowned. "That doesn't sound like the kick-butt partner I've come to know and love."

"I guess I'm just not feeling it right now," she replied.

"Has all work and no play made Agent James a grumpy woman?"

"Possibly," she admitted.

"My recommendation is we grab our coats, get out of here and go someplace where we can kick back and have a couple of drinks," he replied.

She immediately stood and pulled her coat from the back of her chair. "Just lead me to the nearest bar."

He grinned at her. "Now, that's the go-get-'em spirit."

Fifteen minutes later he pulled up in front of a small tavern off the main drag. A wooden sign across the doorway proclaimed the place to be Joe's.

"I know, it's a bit of a dive, but it's my favorite place to come and unwind," he said as he turned off the car. "The music is low, the drinks are good and strong, and here nobody expects anything from me except that I pay the tab before I leave."

"Sounds like the perfect place to end a fairly depressing day," she replied.

They got out of the car and he ushered her inside with his hand in the middle of her back. It was just one of many of the casual touches they'd shared since the night they'd made love, but tonight she felt particularly vulnerable and it affected her more deeply than ever before.

Joe's held a long polished bar with a dozen stools. Two men sat on opposite sides of the bar and an older man with a graying beard stood behind it and nodded in greeting to them as they entered.

Gabriel led her to one of the handful of booths where a small bowl of peanuts was the centerpiece. A country song about lost love and a broken heart played on speakers overhead. Jordon took off her coat and then slid into the black leather booth.

"What can I get for you?" Gabriel asked her.

She frowned thoughtfully. "A gin and tonic with a twist of lime," she finally replied. She didn't want a civilized glass of wine. She wanted…needed something stronger to take the edge off her uncharacteristic blue mood.

She watched Gabriel as he walked to the bar. It wasn't her growing feelings for him that had her so discouraged. It wasn't, she told herself firmly.

The real problem was that she was afraid she'd be called back to Kansas City before they caught the bad guy. The job was the only successful part of her life, and she was afraid she'd leave here as a failure, and she'd already been a failure in so many other areas of her life.

He returned to the booth with their drinks and sat across from her. "What is your poison tonight?" she asked.

"Scotch and soda. My father introduced me to the pleasure of fine scotch when I got old enough to have an occasional drink with him."

"You're close to your parents?"

"Very," he replied. "They moved from Chicago to Florida several years ago, but they come up to visit me at least once a year and we stay in touch by phone."

"They must be very proud of you," she replied.

He smiled. "They are, but I think they'd be proud of me no matter what I chose to do for a living."

The front door opened and she glanced over to see Glen Rollings come in. The relaxation that had been about to take over her came to a screeching halt as every muscle in her body tensed.

Gabriel followed her gaze and muttered a small curse under his breath. "What in the hell is he doing here?"

Glen ambled over to their booth with a wide smile. "What a small world. Chief Walters, I didn't know we shared the same drinking hole. I was just driving by here and saw your car and thought I'd stop in to say hello." He winked at Jordon. "Figured I'd take the chance at seeing the hottest woman in town one more time."

"Hello and goodbye," Jordon replied, not attempting to mask her irritation.

"Move it along, Glen. We're busy here," Gabriel

said, his eyes narrowed as he glared at the blond-haired man.

"Jeez, you guys don't have to be so unfriendly," Glen replied.

"We're both not feeling too friendly right now," Jordon said.

"Wow. Okay, then. I guess I'll just see you later." Glen turned around and headed for the bar, where he sat on one of the stools.

"In all the times I've been here, I've never seen any of the Rollings brothers," Gabriel said. "I don't like this sudden appearance."

Jordon cast Glen another glance. He had a beer in front of him and was half-turned on the stool so that he could see them. She looked back at Gabriel. "Do you think he followed us here?"

"I don't know. Maybe he is a regular here and I've just never seen him." He took a drink and then grabbed a handful of peanuts. "Just ignore him."

For a few minutes they sat silently. Jordon felt Glen's steady gaze on her, making it impossible for her to just ignore him as Gabriel had advised.

Was he their man? Was it possible he had seen the car outside and wondered if maybe she was inside here by herself? Alone and vulnerable?

All the other murders had taken place on Diamond Cove property, but that didn't mean the next one would. The killer could always change up his game. Maybe for him it was enough that she was a "guest" at the resort.

Thankfully, Glen finished his beer fairly quickly and then left. It was only then that her muscles began to slowly unknot. "That was weird," she said.

"Maybe it wasn't as weird as it felt. It's possible he really did see the car and maybe thought he could charm you. I think he has a crush on you."

Jordon was somehow grateful that Gabriel's thoughts about the situation hadn't gone as dark as hers had. She sat up straighter in the seat and picked up some peanuts.

"Tell me about your parents," he said. "You've heard all about mine, but you never mention yours."

"That's because we aren't real close. My mother and father own a successful law firm back in Denver. They're both defense lawyers who specialize in high-profile cases. They wanted me to follow in their footsteps and work at the firm, but that wasn't the side of the law I wanted to work."

"They were unhappy with your decision to become an FBI agent?"

An old pain attempted to grab hold of her, but she shoved it away. She'd long ago made peace with the fact that she hadn't been the daughter her parents had wanted.

"They weren't happy about my career choice and they weren't happy that I never had an interest to rub shoulders with their society friends." She smiled at him wryly. "I think they were probably disappointed that I had curly dark hair instead of beautiful gleaming blond tresses, too."

"I love your hair," he replied. "And I love that you're an FBI agent and here with me right now." His eyes gleamed in the low lighting.

"Thanks." She grabbed some of the peanuts, aware that his gaze was a little too soft and filled with a lot of inviting heat.

"So, what are some other places where you hang out in your downtime?" she asked, determined to steer the conversation onto a lighter topic.

"I occasionally go to the local animal shelter and play with the dogs."

"Why don't you have one?" she asked curiously. "You know, man's best friend and all that."

"My lifestyle wouldn't be good for a dog. I work long hours and it wouldn't be fair."

"Working long hours makes any kind of a relationship difficult," she replied.

He nodded. "People who aren't in the life don't understand the drive, the passion we feel for this work." He cocked his head to the side and gazed at her curiously. "Was that an issue in your marriage?"

"Not really. Jack loved the fact that I sometimes worked long hours. It gave him an opportunity to cheat with women who were better than me." She looked down into her empty glass, shocked that she'd spilled this particular piece of her past.

"Better than you? What in the hell does that mean?"

She looked up to see his intense gaze boring into her. "Can I get another drink?"

He held her gaze for another long moment and then got up from the booth and headed for the bar. Jeez, what had made her dredge up the failures of her marriage? With the arrival of Glen and now the conversation, this downtime definitely wasn't as refreshing as she'd expected when they'd left the station.

As she stared at Gabriel's back, she knew the answer as to why she'd brought up her marriage. She had to remind herself that she wasn't fit to be a wife, that she wasn't good for any real relationship. Something about the way Gabriel watched her made her want to believe differently about herself, but she knew the truth and she had to cling to it.

He returned to the booth with her drink. "Now, tell me all about this creep that you married."

She took a big swallow of her gin. "He wasn't a creep," she said as she set her glass down. "I met Jack at a charity function. He owned an insurance company and was a well-respected figure in the community. He was handsome and smart and charming, and I fell hard for him. We dated for eight months and then got married."

She'd been so happy, so certain that she'd found her soul mate. Even her parents, who had never been particularly pleased with anything she did, had approved of Jack.

"We had a blissful couple of months before the cracks started to appear," she said. "He thought I was messy, so I tried really hard to keep things neat and tidy. He didn't like my jokes and so I tried to be more serious. The first year was definitely an adjustment for us. And then I heard from a mutual friend that he was seeing another woman."

It was an old hurt that had scabbed over long ago, but as she remembered that time, she was surprised to realize it still hurt just a little bit.

"Did you confront him?" Gabriel asked softly.

She nodded. "I did, and he confessed that he'd met her a few times for drinks and that was all there was to it. He swore he wouldn't see her again, that he wanted our marriage to work, and I believed him."

"And so the marriage continued."

"I didn't want another failure. Marrying Jack was

the one thing I'd done that my parents approved of, so I was desperate to make it work. Then I found some sexy text messages on his phone that made it clear he was having an affair, and yes, I was snooping."

She took another big gulp of her drink and realized she was more than a little bit buzzed. She'd always been a lightweight when it came to hard liquor.

She offered Gabriel a rueful smile. "The problem wasn't Jack—it was me. I didn't know how to make him happy. I didn't know how to be a partner. I'm just not good wife material."

"That's not true." His eyes filled with a warmth that washed over her. "You just weren't Jack's wife material and I still think he's a creep."

She laughed. "Partners are supposed to be loyal to each other. I promise I'll hate anyone who breaks your heart, and now I think it's time for me to get back to my room for the night."

They got up and pulled their coats on, and Jordon stood by the door while Gabriel paid the tab. When he ushered her outside, a deep scowl possessed his features.

"What's wrong?" she asked him once they were in the car.

He buckled his seat belt and then turned to look at her, his eyes so dark she fought against an inner shiver. "Joe just told me that he'd never seen Glen in the bar before tonight."

All the black thoughts she'd momentarily entertained when Glen had sat on the bar stool staring at her rushed back into her head.

"He implied to us that he was a regular customer," she said.

Gabriel pulled out on the road to take her back to the bed-and-breakfast. "I don't know if he's a real threat or if he just really drove by and saw the patrol car like he said. We know for sure now that he's a liar."

Jordon leaned her head back and closed her eyes. The travel back to her broken marriage, coupled with the new concern of a stalking Glen, swept away any pleasant buzz the alcohol might have given her.

She turned in her seat and glanced behind them, but no cars shared the secondary road with them.

"Don't worry. I'm watching, too," Gabriel said.

"I just don't understand these men. It's like Kevin and Glen are intentionally doing things to make them look like suspects. Are they just stupid or are they that calculating and they're trying to muddy things up for us?"

"Neither of them are rocket-scientist material, but they are cunning. I'll call Mark and have him assign somebody to keep an eye on Glen. I want to know what he's doing and when he's doing it."

"Sounds like a plan," she replied.

"I'm sorry the night ended up like this. I was hoping we'd both relax and kick back a bit."

"It's not your fault Glen showed up and ruined the mood."

It took only minutes to arrive back at Diamond Cove. They both got out of the car and walked up the path to her room, guided through the dark night by the solar lights.

Gabriel pulled his gun as she unlocked her door. This had become their routine since the night she'd been attacked.

She opened the door and they both went inside fast.

Immediately he went to the bathroom, where she knew he'd check to make sure nobody was hiding and that the window remained securely locked.

She checked in the closet and under the bed, and when the room was cleared, he sat in the chair next to the fireplace and she sat on the edge of the bed facing him.

"Looks like I'm good for another night," she said.

He nodded, his eyes holding a gleam of hunger. "Jordon, about your marriage… The only mistake you made was not marrying a man who loved your sense of humor, a man who didn't care about housekeeping or cooking and such nonsense. You just need to be with a man who understands you and loves you just the way you are."

She jumped up from the bed, afraid that he was going to say something stupid, afraid that she would fall for his sweet words and ultimately he'd only wind up being another person she disappointed.

"I'm tired, Gabriel. I don't want to talk anymore about my past or Glen Rollings or murder or anything else." She stood by the door. "I just need to get some sleep."

He got up from the chair and joined her at the door. "Then I guess I'll just say good-night." There was a wistfulness in his tone that held the promise of the warmth of his arms, the heat of his body against hers.

She could have him if she wanted him for the night. All she had to do was ask him to stay and she knew he would. The idea was definitely tempting, but she steeled her heart.

"Good night, Gabriel," she said and opened the door.

He stepped outside and then turned to look at her.

"You know I'm more than just a little bit crazy over you."

Her heart squeezed tight. "Get over it," she replied forcefully. "I've never lived up to anyone's expectations, Gabriel, and I certainly wouldn't live up to yours."

She closed the door before he could respond and leaned her head against the wood. She wished he'd never told her what he felt about her. She wished he was the antagonistic bonehead she'd initially thought he was going to be.

Instead he was a man she could love, a man who could fill the empty spaces of her life. But she refused to love him. She cared about him too much to fall into a rosy glow with him that would only end in flames of regret.

Chapter Eleven

He'd wanted her tonight. He'd wanted to hold her in his arms and make love to her. He'd needed to somehow erase whatever insecurities her ex-husband had scarred into her soul. Although she hadn't gone into great detail, she'd said enough to let Gabriel know that the marriage had wounded her in a way to make her believe she was unworthy.

Instead of going home, Gabriel returned to the station, thoughts of the conversation they'd shared in the bar still haunting him. She had so much to offer a man who captured her heart, but she didn't believe she had anything to give.

There was no question that she'd rebuffed him tonight. She'd shoved him out of the door as if he was the devil himself. He didn't know what to do with the feelings he had for her, but it was obvious she had no interest in them.

He parked in front of the station and went inside, unsurprised to find Mark working at his desk. "You know we don't pay overtime," he said and sank in the chair across from Mark.

Mark smiled. "Sheila flew out this morning to spend a couple of weeks with her parents. The house was so quiet without her I decided to come in and catch up on some paperwork. What are you doing here so late? I thought you and Agent James had knocked off for the day."

"We had," Gabriel replied and then told Mark about Glen showing up at the bar. "I want a tail put on him. I don't know what his game is, but I don't like it. Him showing up at Joe's just didn't feel right."

"I'll take care of it," Mark replied. "I'll talk to Ben before I leave here. You know how good he and his team are at undercover surveillance."

Gabriel nodded and released a deep sigh. Ben Hammond ran a private investigation agency in town and was often tapped to help out the small police department.

"This is a tough one," Mark said.

Gabriel didn't have to ask him what he was talking about. Mark had been part of the team of officers working alongside Gabriel and Jordon on the cases.

"I thought when I left Chicago behind I was also leaving behind these kind of tough cases," Gabriel said.

"You probably also thought you'd be working for a mayor who was a normal, rational human being," Mark said wryly. "He's thrown us all under the bus in his last couple of news conferences."

Gabriel leaned back. "We're all busting our butts to solve this case and he's whining about our lack of progress." He shook his head ruefully.

"How's Agent James holding up?"

"Like all the rest of us she's frustrated and weary." And she'd never lived up to anyone's expectations. Gabriel frowned as her parting words played in his head. Something about the funny, brash Agent Jordon James broke his heart just a little bit.

"She's a tough one," Mark said.

"She is," Gabriel agreed.

"I heard from the grapevine that Ted Overton has been spending a lot of time alone in some local watering holes lately," Mark said.

Gabriel frowned thoughtfully. "Wish I knew if he's trying to drown his guilt or just drinking his misery away."

"I don't know, but from all my sources he's definitely trying to drown something."

Gabriel stood abruptly and released a weary sigh. "Go home, Mark. Get a good night's sleep."

"And you do the same," Mark replied, although he made no move to get out of his chair.

A few minutes later Gabriel was back in his car, but he wasn't heading home. He wouldn't rest easy unless he knew exactly where Glen Rollings was right now. He needed to make sure the man wasn't parked down the street from Diamond Cove and potentially planning some sort of an attack on Jordon.

Glen lived not too far from Ed, but unlike Ed's small neat house, Glen's place was a tiny cabin that appeared not to have enjoyed any outside maintenance for the last twenty years or so.

The window shutters had either fallen off or hung by a single nail, and it was impossible to tell what color the cabin might have once been painted, for it had weathered to a dull gray.

Gabriel breathed a sigh of relief as he saw Glen's car parked outside and lights beaming out from the windows. He pulled to a stop just past the house and called Mark.

"I just wanted to let you know that Glen Rollings's current location is his home. I thought you might want to tell Ben that when you speak to him."

"I already talked to him. I gave him Glen's address and he's going to have somebody in place within the next half hour."

"Thanks, Mark. I appreciate it."

The two men hung up and Gabriel left, this time heading for home. If he couldn't put a man on Jordon, then this was the next best thing. He would have liked to put a tail on all their suspects, but it simply wasn't financially feasible. Glen's appearance in the bar had been odd and unsettling enough that he could justify the expense of a tail. Although he was certain that Mayor Donald Stoddard would bitch and moan about the use of the private agency.

I've never lived up to anyone's expectations.

Jordon's words haunted him as he entered his house and as he undressed and got into bed. She'd far exceeded his expectations of her professionally, and she'd also exceeded his expectations of her as a desirable, exciting woman.

He fell into a troubled sleep filled with images of a shadowy person with a wicked-looking knife chasing Jordon through the woods. He ran after them, desperate to help her, but the trees all came to life, their limbs grabbing at him to hold him back.

It was just after seven the next morning when he walked into the Diamond Cove dining room, where Jordon and Joan were already seated at a table.

Joan looked haggard and as if she hadn't slept in

days. The pleasant sparkle that normally lit her eyes was gone, replaced by the dark pall this case had cast over everyone involved.

Joan and Jordon greeted him before Joan jumped up from the table and hurried into the kitchen. "Everything all right?" he asked after he'd poured a cup of coffee and sunk down in the chair opposite Jordon.

After the conversation they'd had the night before, he wasn't sure what kind of mood to expect from her this morning. "According to Joan, Ted is drinking too much, the kids are starting to act out and she feels like her entire world is falling apart." Her eyes sparked with anger. "This case is really ticking me off."

"We can only chase what leads we get, and right now there aren't any to chase," Gabriel replied. "We've now got a tail on Glen, so if he's our man and he makes a move, we'll be on him before anyone else gets hurt."

"And if he isn't our man?" She raised one of her eyebrows.

Gabriel frowned. "Then we'll find the person who is our man. I don't know what else to say." He still couldn't quite gauge her mood.

"I know you don't. I'm just frustrated." She released a deep sigh. "Maybe I just need to make myself a bigger target. I need to appear as more vulnerable bait. I could spend the nights sitting in a rocking chair outside of my room…or maybe…"

"Stop." Gabriel interrupted her in horror and leaned forward in his chair. "You aren't going to do anything like that."

"You're right—I'm not. I just wish this creep would make another move." She took a sip of her coffee and then set the cup back down on the table. "You know I can't stay here forever." Her gaze held his intently and then she stared down into her coffee cup.

"Do you know how much longer we've got with you here?" His heart suddenly felt too big for his chest and he had to talk around a lump that rose up in his throat.

He'd known she was here only temporarily, but in the past week or so he'd somehow buried that fact deep in his mind. It had been easier to not think about the time she'd have to go.

"I spoke to my director last night and he's giving me another two weeks and then it's time for me to go back home," she replied.

"Here we are," Joan said as she entered the dining room carrying two plates of scrambled eggs, toasted English muffins and strips of crispy bacon.

Two weeks. It wasn't a lot of time. Gabriel picked up his fork even though his appetite had fled. They had fourteen days to catch the killer.

And he had two weeks to try to stop falling deeper in love with her.

JORDON SAT IN the center of her bed and stared at her laptop monitor. It was just after nine and the frustration of another fruitless day burned hot in her belly.

That wasn't all that burned inside her. She was in love with Gabriel and she wished he was beside her right now, in her bed…in her life forever.

The night that they'd slept together she'd thought he would just be a fling, a warm memory for her to embrace on lonely nights. Gabriel in her bed had been exciting and wonderful, but Gabriel out of her bed was everything she had ever wanted, everything she had ever dreamed of in a man.

But she knew he wouldn't settle for anything less than marriage and she wasn't willing to go through that again. He was terrific husband material and she was nothing more than mistress material. And to believe anything otherwise would be a disservice to them both.

With a deep frown, she got up from the bed, refusing to think about all the things she wouldn't allow in her life. She knew who and what she was, and whether Gabriel knew it or not, he deserved much better.

She'd almost been grateful when Director Langford had told her he was pulling her off the case after another two weeks. All she had to do was hang on to her heart and remember she was a lone wolf for the next fourteen days.

What she needed now was a cup of coffee from the guest shed and then a good night's sleep. She wrapped on her gun belt, pulled on her coat and stepped out of her room.

The temperature had dropped again but not before the last couple of warm days had melted the snow left by the night of the blizzard.

As always when she left her room at night, she kept her hand on the butt of her gun and her senses on high alert. The night was silent around her, but she scanned the area with narrowed eyes.

There was no way she was going to let somebody get a jump on her. She was ready for anything that might come out of the darkness. She would never be taken by surprise again.

She reached the guest shed and opened the door.

Instantly every nerve in her body electrified and her muscles tensed. There had been no welcoming tinkle of the bell. In fact, the small silver bell that had hung over the door was gone.

Her breaths became shallow as she yanked her gun from her holster and fell into a crouch. Was he inside here with her, or was he just outside and had hoped she wouldn't notice that the bell was missing.

Was he just waiting for her to turn toward the coffee machine and watch a drink fill a cup and then he'd come at her and stab her in the back like he had Rick Sanders?

She twirled toward the door and then pivoted to face both the laundry room door and then the storage room door. Her heart ticked like a time bomb in her chest. Despite the cold of the night, her fingers grew slick with sweat on the gun handle.

Where was he? She turned sideways so both the laundry room door and the entry into the shed were in her vision. She pulled the laundry room door open and released a frantic gasp of air.

Nobody there.

She refused to give in to the shudders of fear that attempted to possess her. She still had to clear the small storage room and watch her back for anyone coming in from outside.

Heart still racing, she grabbed the storage room door handle, turned it and then kicked the door open. Despite the relative darkness of the room, it was easy to see that nobody was inside.

She whirled to face the door that led back outside. Any desire she might have had for a flavored coffee was gone, vanished by the sick knot of nerves that twisted inside her.

The bell over the door had been there two nights ago when she'd come inside to get coffee. It hadn't just dropped off to the floor and there was absolutely no reason Ted and Joan would have had it removed.

She stepped back outside, her gaze frantically shooting in all directions. She got back safely to her room and sank down on the edge of her bed, and only then did her heartbeat begin to slow.

It was him. The killer had taken down the bell. He was toying with her. Had he been someplace nearby? Watching her search the room? Laughing at her fear?

Her stomach clenched, this time not in fear, but rather in anger. He was so close…so damn close. He had to have known about the bell over the door. He had to know that about every other evening she made the trek to the shed for a late-night cup of coffee.

Had he hoped she wouldn't notice the missing bell? Had he hoped that she'd be unaware enough to go into the shed, stand in front of the coffeemaker and be attacked from behind?

If that was the case then he must think she was stupid. She frowned. And why wouldn't he believe that? They hadn't caught him yet even though apparently he was moving around right under their noses.

She carried her simmering anger with her the next morning into the dining room, where Gabriel was already seated at a table, chatting with Joan.

"Good morning," she said curtly. "The bell over the door in the guest shed is gone," she added before either of them could reply.

"What do you mean gone?" Joan asked in surprise.

"The bracket is still there but it looks like the bell was torn off." Jordon stalked over to the coffeemaker.

"Who would have done such a thing?" Joan asked. Jordon turned to look at her.

Joan raised a hand to her mouth. "The killer. He didn't want anyone warned of him coming in behind them."

"Give the little lady a stuffed bear," Jordon replied as she poured herself a cup of coffee. Once she was finished, she walked back to the table and sat across from Gabriel.

He gazed at her with a deep frown. "When exactly did you discover this?"

"Last night it was just after nine when I decided to get myself a cup of coffee from the shed. The minute I stepped through the door I realized the bell hadn't tinkled."

"How often at night are you leaving your room to get coffee?" he asked, his voice holding a wealth of disapproval as his gaze bored into hers.

"I'll just go see to breakfast," Joan said and quickly left the room.

"Every other night or so," Jordon said in response to Gabriel's question.

"Tell me, Agent James—on those nights do you really want a cup of coffee or are you taunting the killer to make a move on you?"

He was definitely angry. As if calling her Agent James wasn't enough to let her know, the deepening frown across his forehead and the taut slash of his lips was a sure sign of his ire.

She smiled at him. "I told you when we first met

that if you hung around me long enough you'd get irritated with me."

"This isn't funny, Jordon," he replied. "I have nightmares about something happening to you."

She looked at him in surprise. "You dream about me?"

He shook his head. "Don't change the subject. Answer my question."

"I forgot what the question was."

He leaned back in his chair and released a deep sigh of obvious frustration. "Have you been intentionally taunting the killer to come after you?"

She thoughtfully stared down into her coffee cup and then looked back at him once again. "I don't know," she finally answered truthfully. "I mean, I'm definitely a coffee freak and I like to drink a cup in the evenings, but maybe subconsciously I was hoping the killer would come after me."

"You aren't alone in this. We're a team, Jordon. It's bad enough that you're staying here. The last thing I want is for you to take any additional chances that put you in greater danger." His gaze softened and his mouth relaxed a bit.

"I won't get coffee at night anymore," she said quickly, afraid by the look on his face that he was going to say something stupid…something that might twist her heart.

"That only makes me feel a little better," he replied.

Joan came in with their breakfast plates, thankfully ending that particular conversation. "I'll have Ed hang another bell in the shed as soon as he comes in this morning."

Jordon exchanged a pointed gaze with Gabriel and

she knew he was thinking the same thing. It was very possible that the man who would be replacing the bell was the same one who had yanked it off.

Was she mistaken in her belief that her attacker on the night of the snowstorm hadn't been Ed? In retrospect she really couldn't be sure. It had all happened so very fast.

Or had he taken down the bell to clear the way for one of his brothers to make a move on her? The idea of three of them working in concert was so disturbing.

The day had barely begun and already a dull throb pressed tight across the back of her skull. She had a deadly man to find and a wonderful man to forget.

Chapter Twelve

Ten days.

And tomorrow it would be nine more days and Jordon would be gone. Gabriel turned around at his desk and stared out the nearby window where another day had ended and night had fallen.

When the bell had gone missing in the guest shed, he'd added a tail to both Kevin Rollings and Ted Overton, but over the past couple of days neither one of the men had gone anywhere or done anything suspicious.

Gabriel knew he couldn't justify the tails remaining in place for too long, especially not having any concrete evidence to tie them to the crimes other than Kevin's vocal hatred of Diamond Cove.

A knock on his door turned him around in the chair. Mark entered the office and sank down in the chair in front of his desk. "Another frustrating day, huh," he said. "Maybe the killer is done. Maybe he figures the three murders have already ruined business for Diamond Cove and he's finished."

Gabriel smiled. "Thanks for trying to inject a little optimism into my heart, but we both know he isn't finished." His smile fell. "And right now it appears that we're stuck just waiting for his next move."

"He's marked Agent James as his next victim, but so far he's been unsuccessful in getting to her. Let's just hope he doesn't change his mind and decide to go after somebody else, like a member of the Overton family."

"There's been no indication that the family is at risk, which makes Ted even better as a potential suspect," Gabriel replied. "However, I have warned them all to not be on the property alone, especially at night."

"I know Agent James is leaving town soon. What happens when his target goes away?"

Gabriel's gut tightened, and he didn't know if it was because Jordon would be gone or knowing that the killer would probably find another target.

"I don't know," he finally replied. "I can't stop Ted and Joan from reopening their business and that means any of their guests could be potential victims."

"If they have any guests."

"Oh, they'll have guests. If nothing else they'd get stupid people who want to stay in a place where murder has taken place." Gabriel swallowed against a bit of disgust.

"So, I guess the only thing we can hope for is that our man comes after Agent James within the next week or so," Mark said.

That was the last thing Gabriel hoped would happen. He wanted the killer caught but he didn't want Jordon involved. He was torn between being a chief of police who trusted that an FBI agent could take care of herself, and being a man who wanted nothing more than to protect the woman who held a big chunk of his heart.

"I guess I'm out of here," Mark said and got up from the chair. "I'll see you in the morning."

"Good night, Mark." Gabriel shut down his computer and then stood. It was time to get Jordon back to her suite. He put on his coat, left his office and then walked down to the conference room where she had been working alone for the last hour while Gabriel caught up on all the other crimes in the area.

He opened the conference room door and her fresh, floral scent instantly assaulted his nose. She looked up from whatever she'd been reading and her smile warmed him to his very soul.

"Another day is done," she said. She slid the paper into one of the manila folders on the table and then stood.

"Another day of more dead ends," he replied.

She pulled on her coat. "Don't beat yourself up, Gabriel. We both know we're at a point in the investigation where the ball is in the killer's court."

"Don't remind me," he said drily. "Are you hungry? Want to grab something before I take you back to Diamond Cove?" They had eaten a late lunch, but he'd much prefer the final meal of the day spent with her than alone in his kitchen.

"I'm really not very hungry. I'm good just going to my room," she replied.

He nodded despite his disappointment. She'd been rather distant with him all day. During lunch she'd been quiet, far more introspective than he'd ever seen her. It was as if mentally she was already moving on and putting him and these crimes behind her.

She was quiet as they left the building, got into his car and left the station. "The weather report says more snow coming in sometime tonight," he said to break the silence.

"Hopefully it isn't going to be another blizzard," she replied.

"Nah, right now they're just calling for an inch or two."

"That's good." She stared out the passenger window and the silence resumed.

He tried to think of something inane, any light topic that would draw her out, but the things he really wanted to talk about with her weren't light or inane.

Tonight the depth of his feelings for her begged to be spoken out loud. They filled his heart with a fullness that was difficult to hold in. As crazy as it was, he knew in his very soul that she was the woman he wanted not just for the next ten days, but rather for the rest of his life. And until this moment he'd believed that she was falling in love with him.

They reached Diamond Cove and they both got out of the car. As always, he drew his gun as she unlocked her suite door. Once the room was cleared, they took off their coats and he sat on the chair next to the fireplace.

"How about a cup of coffee before I take off?" he asked.

"Okay, I'll make a pot, although this isn't as good as the flavored ones in the guest shed." She walked over to the vanity where the little coffeepot sat next to a small basket that held coffee packages, creamers and sugar packets.

He watched her covetously as she poured the water into the back of the machine, set the coffee packet inside and then turned it on to brew.

She was so beautiful and seemingly so unaware of her own attractiveness. It wasn't just her physical charm that drew him to her, but also the spirit and beauty that shone from within.

As she turned around to face him, he got up and flipped the switch that made flames jump to life in the fireplace. He sat back down in the chair and knew this night wouldn't end without him speaking exactly what was in his heart.

"Long day," she finally said when the coffee was finished and she'd poured them each a cup. She set hers on the nightstand and moved aside what appeared to be a red nightgown that was on her bed, along with a can of hair product and a tube of mascara, and then sat down.

"They're all long lately," he replied. When he'd worked as a cop in Chicago, he'd once faced down a man high on PCP and armed with a machete. He and his partner had gotten into a firestorm of flying bullets with a handful of dangerous gangbangers.

However, nothing he'd ever experienced before in his life had made him as nervous as he now was as he faced a woman with soft curls and green eyes and a spirit that made him smile.

"You've been terribly quiet all day," he observed.

She nodded. "I guess I've just been trying to figure out where we go from here."

"I know where I'd like us to go from here." He set his coffee cup on the table and ignored the sudden dryness of his throat as he held her gaze intently.

"Where is that?" she asked. She picked up her coffee cup and took a sip.

"Jordon, I'm not talking about these cases. I'm talking about us…you and me."

Her eyes became guarded as she set her cup back on the nightstand. "Gabriel, there is no you and me."

"Jordon, I'm in love with you and I think you feel the same way about me." His heart thundered in his chest as he spoke the words that had been burning inside him.

She averted her gaze from his. "You just feel that way because we slept together."

"Jordon, I loved making love with you, but my feelings for you certainly aren't just based on a physical level. I love the way your eyes light up just before you say something funny. I adore how they narrow when you're deep in thought."

He leaned forward, the words now falling out of his mouth as if released from a pressure cooker. "Jordon, at the end of this, no matter how the investigation goes, I don't want to tell you goodbye. I want you in my life forever. I want…" He paused as she held up her hand.

"Stop, Gabriel. Please stop." She got up from the edge of the bed and walked several steps back from where he sat.

He drew in a deep breath and then continued. "I know the distance thing might be a bit of an issue at first, but it's less than a four-hour drive from here to Kansas City. There's no reason why we couldn't continue to see each other on days off and eventually I'd be willing to relocate."

There was no joy on her beautiful features. Instead she gazed at him in what looked like stunned horror. She closed her eyes for a brief moment, and when she opened them again, a reckless smile curved her lips. "Sorry, sailor. You've obviously got me mixed up with somebody else."

"Stop it, Jordon." He stood, all of his muscles tense. "Don't make jokes when I'm pouring out my heart to you."

A slight flush filled her cheeks and she averted her gaze from him. "Then stop pouring out your heart," she replied in a soft voice.

"Okay, I'll shut up after you tell me you don't love me." He took several steps closer to her. "Tell me that I mean nothing to you and I'll leave here and won't speak of this again."

He saw it in her eyes, a soft yearning, a sweet wistfulness, but it was there only a moment and then her chin shot up and her gaze was once again shuttered.

"I told you I wasn't marriage material, that I'd never lived up to anyone's expectations," she replied.

"Oh, Jordon, you've not only lived up to mine, but you've far exceeded them," he said softly.

Her lower lip began to tremble and she turned away from him. "Please go, Gabriel. Before you say anything more that you'll regret."

He stared at her stiff back and he didn't see an impenetrable wall. Rather, he saw a woman who was afraid to believe she was worthy of being loved by anyone.

He didn't know how to make her not be afraid. He didn't know what else to say and so he simply stood still and loved her.

JORDON WAITED FOR the sound of the door opening and then closing, indicating to her that Gabriel had left. But several long minutes passed and it didn't happen.

Her heart hurt as it had never ached before in her life.

Falling in love with Gabriel had been so incredibly easy, but this…this rejection of him was so achingly difficult. She desperately wanted what he was offering her, yet of all the men in the entire world she knew, she couldn't be more wrong for a man like him.

She stiffened as his hands fell on her shoulders. "Jordon," he whispered, his breath a warm delight on her ear. She closed her eyes and fought against the sting of tears. "Jordon, don't throw away what we have."

She drew in a deep breath and whirled back around to face him, dislodging his hands from her. "You obviously took things too seriously. We don't have anything, Gabriel. We slept together. It was no big deal. We've had a few laughs and some good times, but that certainly doesn't equate love."

He stared at her and the intensity of his gaze made her feel as if he was peering into her mind, into the very depths of her soul. "What are you so afraid of?"

"I'm not afraid of anything," she replied with a rise of anger filling her. Why was he making this so difficult? Why couldn't he just accept the words she said and go away?

"You know what I think? I believe your parents and your ex-husband did a real number on your head. They have made you feel like you're unworthy of loving…of being loved, and nothing could be further from the truth."

"Thank you, Dr. Gabriel, for the quick psychoanalysis," she retorted.

He had the audacity to smile at her. "You have no idea how adorable, how utterly wonderful I find you.

I've been waiting years to find you. You're the woman I want to build a life with. I want you to have my children and I want to grow old with you."

His words painted a picture of a beautiful future, one that she'd once dreamed of and one that still resonated with desire in a small piece of her heart.

There was a part of her that wanted to reach out and grasp on to what he offered, but there was a bigger voice inside her head that told her she'd be all kinds of fool to believe that kind of future with him could be hers.

"You're just trying to grasp on to something good because your investigation has stalled out and you're frustrated," she replied.

A flash of anger lit the depths of his eyes. "You really believe my feelings for you are simply born out of my frustration with the investigation?" He released a dry laugh and shook his head. "Don't try to tell me how I feel and why. I'm not afraid to take a leap of faith with you."

"Then you're a fool," she exclaimed. "And stop implying that I'm afraid. I'm a realist, Gabriel, not a coward."

"I think you're a coward," he replied. "I think you love me, Jordon, and you're just too scared to give us a chance. You'll invite a serial killer into your life, but you won't allow in a man who loves you. You're more afraid of giving your heart than you are in giving your life."

"Get out." A deep rich anger filled her. "Get out now." She stalked to the door. She didn't want to hear anything else he felt the need to say to her.

He stood perfectly still, the only movement his

gaze as it searched her features. He finally walked over to the chair, grabbed his coat and put it on.

She opened the door, allowing in the cold of the night, a cold that couldn't begin to compete with the chill that encased her heart.

He walked over to her and reached up as if to stroke her cheek, but she jerked away from him, not allowing him the touch. A muscle ticked in his jaw and his eyes darkened.

"You aren't just a coward, Jordon. You're also a beautiful fool," he said and then walked out.

She slammed the door after him. She locked it and then leaned with her back against it as tears blurred her vision. A beautiful fool…a coward. How dare he say such things to her.

Who did he think he was? He didn't really know her and he certainly couldn't be in love with her. He was just kidding himself and she refused to be pulled into his fantasy.

Still, her heart squeezed tight, so tight in her chest she could scarcely draw a breath. He was the fool to think that she could be the woman he wanted in his life.

She moved away from the door and sank down on the bed, tears still stinging her eyes and an imminent threat of sobs only making her even angrier with him.

He was just a silly man who had confused a wonderful bout of lovemaking and a few laughs with love. She'd told him right up front how she felt about marriage and relationships. He should have just kept his feelings to himself.

But what if he does really love you, a little voice whispered in her head. *What if fate brought you to-*

gether to finally know happiness? To finally have what you've always dreamed of in the deepest recesses of your heart?

"No," she said aloud, effectively silencing the voice in her head. She wasn't a coward, but she just wasn't willing to put her heart on the line again.

She'd be gone from here before long and eventually Gabriel would find the woman who was really right for him. She'd be a woman who had a place for everything and everything in its place. She'd be able to cook hearty meals for him and whatever children they might have. She'd be everything Jordon wasn't and couldn't be.

Damn him for his bedroom eyes and gentle ways. Damn him for making her love him when she didn't want to love anyone. Tears began to chase themselves down her cheeks, and instead of attempting to stanch them, she gave in to them.

She curled up on the bed and wept. She grieved for the woman she had once been, a young woman who had believed in dreams of marriage and happily-ever-after.

She mourned the fact that she no longer believed in those dreams, that they had been shattered by a man who had taken her love and then betrayed it over and over again.

It felt as if she cried for hours, and finally, her tears wound down to little gasping sobs. She rolled over on her back and stared up at the ceiling. How was she going to continue working with Gabriel when she was so angry with him?

And why are you so angry?

The reason wasn't clear, but she embraced the emotion and held tight to it. She was a lone wolf and he should respect that. The idea that he thought she could be anything else just ticked her off.

She got up from the bed and went into the bathroom, where she sluiced water over her face and then stared at her reflection in the mirror.

Finish this assignment and then get the heck out of Dodge, she mentally said to her reflection. *Do your time and then get back to the safe, alone life you've built for yourself.*

Eventually she'd forget that she'd ever loved a good man like Gabriel. She had to forget him because there was no place in her life for him.

She left the bathroom and started to unbuckle her holster, but stopped as she spied a piece of paper peeking out from under her door. Her heartbeat clanged a discordant beat as she pulled her gun. She raced to the door, unlocked it and yanked it open. The porch was empty and she narrowed her eyes to attempt to see through the darkness.

She remained standing on alert for several long moments, the night feeling ominous and fraught with new danger. Slowly she bent down, picked up the paper and then closed and locked her door.

The white paper burned in her hand as she carried it with her and perched on the edge of the bed. When had it been shoved under her door?

It had to have been left after Gabriel had gone, otherwise he would have seen it. While she'd been crying about broken dreams and Gabriel's love, the killer had left her a new calling card.

Her hands trembled as she opened the paper and read the bold letters.

Play a game of cat and mouse
In Mouse's Maze of Mirrors
Come alone or I won't play
At midnight face your fears.

She read the note a second time and then looked at the clock on the nightstand. It was twenty till midnight.

She jumped up off the bed and pulled her cell phone from her pocket. *Come alone or I won't play.* The words reverberated in her head.

This was a final showdown. She knew it in her gut. With her hand still trembling and a healthy fear squeezing her lungs, she repocketed her cell phone.

She threw on her coat and then grabbed the keys to the patrol car that she hadn't used since she'd been here. She left the room and headed for the parking lot.

She was a lone wolf, and she was going to meet the killer in a place where her nightmares began.

Chapter Thirteen

Who was she going to face in the mirrors? Jordon clenched the steering wheel tight as she drove through the dark night toward the tourist attraction.

Would it be Kevin Rollings, who worked the admission gate and probably knew every inch of the maze? Was he the one they sought?

Or would it be one of his brothers? Was Ed not the pleasant handyman he pretended to be? Had Glen managed to lose his tail? Had he parked his car at his home and then sneaked out of a door or window to come here for a final confrontation with her?

A simmering panic rose up the back of her throat and she swallowed hard against it. Would she get into the maze and get lost in her past? Captured and helpless by visions of Ralph Hicks and that cellar where she'd thought she would die?

She couldn't let that happen, otherwise whoever was in the maze would manage to accomplish what Ralph hadn't managed. If she gave in to her panic, then she knew without a doubt she would wind up dead.

It was three minutes until midnight when she pulled into the Mouse's Maze of Mirrors parking lot.

There were no other cars in the lot and the place was dark and formidable.

She got out of the car with her gun in her hand, every muscle tensed and her heart racing a familiar rhythm of fear. Would he be here? Or was this just another little game of taunting like the missing bell in the guest shed?

She wouldn't know until she went inside. She licked her dry lips and drew on every ounce of training she'd had. She had to remain cool and calm and completely in control.

The front door was unlocked, an invitation to enter and face the killer. She eased the door open and went inside in a crouched position. Security lights gave the small lobby a ghostly illumination.

She checked behind the counter where Kevin had sat when she and Gabriel had been there before. Her lungs expelled a deep breath as she saw that nobody was there.

She stared at the turnstile, knowing that once she went through it she would be in the maze of mirrors. *You can do this*, she told herself. *You're a kick-butt FBI agent and it's time to put an end to the killer's madness.*

Her stomach twisted in knots so tight she was half-nauseous. Her lungs constricted, making deep breaths impossible. *Just do it*, a voice screamed in her head.

She pushed through the turnstile and stepped into the maze. Lights turned on and five reflections of herself stared back at her. She appeared wild-eyed and terrified…just like she'd appeared in Ralph's mirrors.

She drew in several deep breaths to center herself. She refused to be that frightened woman in the reflection. She didn't move until she'd calmed herself and was prepared for whatever might happen.

"Hello?" she called out.

Silence.

Was she here all alone or did she share the space with the person who had brutally killed three people? Somebody had to have turned on the lights. She couldn't be alone. After taking several steps to her right, she found herself facing another set of mirrors.

Which way had Gabriel led her out of here? She couldn't remember how to find the exit, and in any case, she expected to meet somebody before she ever reached the end of the maze. "Is anybody here?"

"Beware. If you aren't fast enough, I'll pull you into my mouse hole and nobody will ever find you again."

The words boomed overhead and ended on the mouse's cackle. Jordon whirled around and five Jordons moved in the reflections. Her taut nerves ached as she waited for somebody to show themselves.

Was she supposed to wait for someone to appear or walk the maze to meet her tormentor at another junction? The uncertainty of the situation had her silently screaming inside her head.

She took several steps forward only to realize it was a mirror and not a passageway. She walked to the left and found another corridor.

A flash of movement behind her spun her around, but then she realized it had been a reflection and she had no idea where the person was and how close he was to her.

The vision had been so brief there was no way she could make an identification. She didn't even know if it had been a man or a woman. It only confirmed to her that the killer was here and toying with her.

She walked slowly, the panic still attempting to close off her airway as she faced her own reflection again and again. The odor of cigarette smoke seemed to linger in the air, along with the acrid scent of burning flesh.

The scars on her hip burned and itched, a reminder of her nightmares, of Ralph and his torture. *Be in the moment*, she commanded herself. She couldn't be pulled back to that cellar where she'd thought she was going to die a slow and painful death.

"Bring it on, you little creep," she yelled.

A girlish giggle filled the air. "You're gonna die in here tonight, Agent James."

Jordon froze, her mind working to make sense of the familiar voice. It couldn't be… Hannah? Was this some sort of a teenager's sick joke? Was she here with some of her friends? Spooking the FBI agent? Was this their idea of a little fun?

"Hannah? Stop playing. This isn't funny. Stop this nonsense and come out and talk to me right now," she said.

"I don't want to talk. You're the next victim, Jordon. You're staying at Diamond Cove and that means you have to die."

Jordon's skin crawled. Was it possible? Surely the murders couldn't have been committed by a fifteen-year-old girl. But even as she tried to deny the possibility, she knew the facts, and the fact was even teenagers could be deadly killers.

Something flashed in her peripheral vision on her left and pain sliced into her upper arm. She whirled around, but Hannah was gone, once again hidden within the maze. Her breath caught in her throat as the warmth of blood leaking down her arm attested to the depth of the wound.

This was definitely no joke. This wasn't a silly game, not when blood had been drawn. Her brain whirled. None of the murdered guests would have felt threatened by Hannah. Hannah knew the woods and she would have known the guests' routines. She had the means to commit the murders, but more than anything Jordon needed to understand the motive.

"Why, Hannah? Why are you doing this? Why did you kill those people?"

"Because I want to go home!" Hannah's voice was filled with a bitter rage. "I didn't want to move to this stupid place in the first place. I don't belong here. Now nobody will want to stay at Diamond Cove and my mom and dad will take us back to Oklahoma City, where I have my own friends."

Jordon was stunned, first by the vitriol in Hannah's voice and second by the unbelievable cunning that had hatched this whole deadly plot.

She tightened her grip on her gun and a vision of Joan's face flashed in her mind. Joan, with her sweet blue eyes and her love for her family—there wasn't going to be a happy ending for her.

But could Jordon shoot Joan's daughter? Could she really take the life of a fifteen-year-old girl? Hopefully, it wouldn't come to that, but if it came to which one of them was going to walk out of here alive, Jordon would pull her trigger without regret.

She screamed as a knife sliced out at her from the left, catching her in the middle of her thigh. She pivoted and ran to the left and caught a glimpse of Hannah ahead of her.

"Stop! Hannah, don't make me shoot you!"

Hannah laughed and instantly disappeared from Jordon's view. Jordon stopped her forward run and instead crept forward slowly…cautiously, unsure from where the next attack might come.

Her biggest fear was that the attack would come from behind. That she wouldn't see Hannah coming, she wouldn't hear her approach until a knife plunged into the center of her back.

There was no question the surroundings were disorienting for Jordon, and it was equally obvious Hannah was perfectly at home in the maze. Like the mouse that ruled this environment, Hannah was the rodent that knew all the secrets of the mirrors.

The sticky wetness on her arm and the blood that now had soaked through her slacks concerned her, but she couldn't focus on that now. She had to figure out a way to somehow disarm and contain Hannah without either of them getting killed.

GABRIEL DROVE AIMLESSLY in his car, the argument with Jordon playing and replaying in his head and sickening his heart. He'd been a damned fool to tell her how he felt about her.

He should have at least waited until the day before she was leaving. Maybe with another week of spending more time together she would have been more open to the possibility of a continuing relationship.

She obviously hadn't been ready to hear what he had to say. Maybe his timing sucked, but he didn't believe she didn't care about him. He'd seen love or something very much like it shining in her eyes when she gazed at him in quiet moments of their days. He'd felt it wafting from her when they touched and when they laughed.

What he hated was that they'd parted with harsh words. While he believed what he'd said to her about being afraid to reach out for love, he'd probably been too harsh with her. He'd let his emotions get ahead of him.

He hated that her cold, demanding parents and a cheating ex-husband had made her believe that she was unlovable. He hated that she didn't believe she deserved to be loved.

He found himself parked back in the Diamond Cove parking lot and realized he was here to apologize to her. He'd pushed her too hard and he didn't want to go to bed until he told her he was sorry.

A glance at the clock told him it was a few minutes before midnight. It was possible she was already sleeping. He could always apologize to her in the morning. Still, he didn't turn around and leave.

Just as he'd needed to tell her how he felt about her earlier, he knew he needed to apologize to her this very moment. The cold air gripped him as he got out of his car. The same cold had encased his heart since he'd left her room earlier.

He certainly didn't intend to apologize for loving her, but he wanted her to know he hadn't meant to get upset with her and that he just wanted her to be happy. At least that way hopefully there would be no unresolved tension between them in the morning.

The last week with her shouldn't be uncomfortable

for them both. That wasn't the impression he wanted her to take away from here.

As he approached her door, he was relieved to see light casting out from her window. Good—apparently she was still awake.

He rapped lightly on the door and waited for a reply. When none came he knocked a little harder. "Jordon, it's me. I'd like to talk to you. Please open the door."

Several seconds passed and a rivulet of uneasiness swept through him. There was no way he believed her to be the kind of woman to just ignore him. He knew her well enough to know that if she was still angry with him she'd open her door and meet him with both barrels loaded.

He froze. Had the patrol car he'd left for her to use while here been in the parking lot? He'd been so buried in his own head, so deep in his own thoughts, he hadn't paid any attention.

He turned and raced back to the parking lot. The uneasiness turned to panic as he saw the car was missing. Where could she have gone? Why would she leave her room at this time of night?

Would she have been angry enough to get in the car and go for a drive? That just didn't feel right. For several long seconds his brain refused to fire.

Had something happened after he'd left her earlier? What could have possibly led her to leave her room at this time of night?

Had the killer made contact with her again?

He stared across the street where the Overton house was dark. He needed to get into Jordon's room. He had to see if there was any clue inside as to her whereabouts. Maybe she just needed to get out and clear her head, he thought again as he raced across the street. Maybe she got hungry and decided to grab something to eat.

However, in winter in Branson on a weeknight, most places shut down early. Besides, he just didn't believe one of those rational explanations was right.

Although he hated to bother the Overton family, an alarm bell was ringing loudly in his head, an alarm that told him Jordon might just be in trouble.

He pushed the doorbell and heard the ding-dong echo someplace inside the house. He waited only a minute and then rang it again. Lights went on inside and Ted came to the door clad in a T-shirt and plaid sleep pants and holding a gun.

"Chief Walters," he said in surprise.

"I need you to open Jordon's door for me," Gabriel said without preamble.

"Give me a minute." He opened the door to allow Gabriel to step into a small entry and then Ted disappeared down a hallway. He returned a few moments later wearing his coat and jeans and they both left the house.

"Is there a problem?" Ted asked.

"I'm not sure." Gabriel's gut twisted into knots of tension. He'd half hoped that by the time they got back to her suite she'd have pulled in, sheepish that she'd worried anyone and carrying a bag of goodies from the nearest all-night convenience store.

"I hope I didn't wake everyone in your house," he said.

"Just me and Joan. It would take a bomb going off

to wake up Jason or Hannah at this time of the night," Ted replied.

When they reached her room, Ted pulled from his pocket a ring full of keys. He fumbled with them for a moment and then got to the one that would unlock her door.

Gabriel stepped into the room and gazed around, his heart beating wildly. Almost immediately he saw the white folded piece of paper on her bed.

His chest tightened. It looked just like the previous note she'd received from the killer. He picked it up and opened it. His blood chilled as he read the sick poem.

"I've got to go," he said to Ted. "Don't touch anything in here. Just lock up after me."

He didn't wait for Ted to reply. He ran out of the room and down the path to his car, his heartbeat thundering loudly in his head. He had to find her. Dear God, he had to get to her as soon as possible.

When he got into his car, he looked at the time. Twenty after midnight. She'd met the killer twenty minutes ago in a place where she'd frozen in a panic attack when they'd been there before.

She would not only be vulnerable to a bloodthirsty, knife-wielding killer, but also to the horrible demons of her past. Why hadn't she called him the minute she'd received the note?

Even as the question formed in his mind, he knew the answer. She'd been so angry with him and the note had said for her to come alone. Dammit!

He tore out of the parking lot and tried to call her, but the call went directly to her voice mail. What was happening? He glanced at the clock. What had already happened? It had been almost half an hour since the rendezvous was supposed to occur. So many horrible things could transpire in that amount of time.

He tried to call her again and got the same result. He then called Ben Hammond. The private investigator answered on the second ring.

"You have men on Glen and Kevin Rollings?"

"Yeah. When my guys last checked in they were both at their homes."

"Have them knock on the doors and get a visual confirmation that those two are where they're supposed to be and then get back to me as soon as possible," Gabriel said urgently.

Ben called back just as Gabriel turned into the Mouse's Maze of Mirrors parking lot, where Jordon's car was the only other vehicle in the lot.

"Both men are confirmed at their homes," Ben said. "My men spoke to each of them."

"Thanks, Ben."

Gabriel pulled his car to a stop, his brain whirling with not just fear, but complete confusion. If Ted was at home, and Kevin and Glen Rollings were also in their houses, then who the hell was inside with Jordon?

"HANNAH, COME OUT and talk to me," Jordon shouted. For the last few minutes the girl had been ominously silent. Jordon had no idea where she was in the maze now or how to find her to end the madness.

She'd wandered down corridors, wound up in dead ends, and all the while her nerves had screamed with tension as she anticipated another attack.

She thought the bleeding of her wounds had finally stopped, but the anxiety of the situation was definitely wearing on her. She had no idea how much time had passed since she'd first entered the maze but it felt like an eternity.

The recorded cackle of the mouse split the air and Jordon dropped into a crouch, prepared for an attack that might come from any direction.

Her own reflections haunted her. Her mind attempted to drag her back into the torment of her past. There were times she saw only herself and other times she saw the ghost of Ralph Hicks just behind her. She wanted to scream with the anxiety that bubbled inside her.

"Hannah, this needs to stop now."

"You're right."

The girl's voice came from all around her and a sharp pain in the back stole Jordon's breath away. She jerked around to see Hannah's reflection in four mirrors. The girl smiled and held up her bloody knife.

Jordon's knees tried to buckle as she took a step forward and the warmth of blood worked down her spine. Her gun hand shook as she stared at the four Hannahs.

Which one was real?

Time seemed to stand still and then everything happened in the space of a single heartbeat. Jordon fired at one Hannah. Glass shattered to the floor. Damn, she'd shot a mirror.

She gasped in agonizing pain and tears blurred her vision. If she had to shoot out every mirror in the place, she'd do it. She scarcely took time to breathe before she fired again, and this time her bullet found its mark.

Hannah screamed and dropped her knife as she

bent over to grab just above her left knee. She took a step forward and then fell out of the reflections and to the floor.

It was over.

Case solved.

Jordon tucked her gun into her holster, the simple action taking up nearly all of her energy as her chest squeezed tight and her back screamed in pain.

She walked over close enough to kick the knife out of Hannah's reach and then took several steps backward. She was so tired…so very tired as the adrenaline that had pumped through her for so long seeped away.

She'd just sit for a minute to catch her breath and then she'd call Gabriel. She sank down and leaned back. She was light-headed and cold chills raced through her.

Hannah continued to yell and curse and cry, but the sound seemed to come from very far away. Jordon saw herself in three reflections and she was vaguely surprised that no visions from her past haunted her, no images of Ralph Hicks and that cellar tried to intrude. She saw only herself, alone as she had always been.

The pain in her back intensified, making it difficult to breathe. She wondered if she might be dying. The thought made her so sad.

She should have called Gabriel. Her heart squeezed tight at thoughts of him. He'd have to clean up this mess she'd made. At least Hannah would no longer be able to hurt anyone again.

White dots like snowflakes danced in her vision.

Cold. She was so very cold. She was back in a snow globe, immersed in a brutal, bitter winter.

She closed her eyes.

She should have gone home and danced in her underwear.

Chapter Fourteen

Gabriel approached the front door of the maze with his heart beating out of his chest. He had no idea what to expect or who besides Jordon he might encounter inside.

Billy Bond was in jail and all their other suspects were accounted for, so whoever had written that note hadn't even been on their radar. Who could it be?

He went into the front door fast and with his gun ready. The small lobby was empty. He shoved through the turnstile and entered the maze. Instantly he heard female cries for help coming from someplace within the mirrors.

His nerves electrified. Was it Jordon? No...he didn't think so. Whoever it was, she was not only cursing but she was also crying for her mother.

Definitely not Jordon.

His mouth dried. So, where was Jordon? The unknowns of the situation balled a huge knot of anxiety in his stomach. He should call for backup, but until he knew what he faced, he was afraid that the extra manpower might only complicate things.

He stood in a corridor where he saw nothing but

visions of himself. He walked forward and took the first turn to the right. Another empty passageway.

The cries for help had stopped and a frightening silence ensued. A horrible dread seeped into his bones as he continued walking slowly, aware that somebody could jump out and attack him with every step he took.

Had the cries for help been a ploy? A ruse to get him to rush to the rescue only to be stabbed by the killer? Was that what had happened to Jordon?

Oh, God—please, no. She might not want to have a meaningful relationship with him, but he certainly wanted her alive and well and with a future that would hopefully bring her to the point where she could love some special man. He didn't want her hurt. He prayed she wasn't hurt.

Walking the maze was agonizingly slow as he constantly turned first one way and then the other to clear any corridors he came to.

He finally stopped with his back to a dead end. "Jordon!" Her name released from the very depths of him with more than a hint of despair. "Jordon, where are you?"

"I'm here. Please help me. I'm hurt." The female voice came from his left and he suddenly recognized it.

"Hannah?" he called out incredulously. What on earth was she doing in here?

"She shot me. I just came here to help her and she accidentally shot me," Hannah cried.

"Where's Jordon?" Gabriel tried to move in the direction of the voice.

"She's here. She's…she's dead. He stabbed her and then he ran away."

Gabriel stumbled into one of the mirrors as all the breath in his body whooshed out of him. *No!* The single word screamed in his brain. It couldn't be. An all-encompassing grief pierced through him as he shoved off the mirror and continued walking.

He couldn't think about Jordon right now. He had to shove the grief away. He needed to focus. He pulled his radio from his belt and called in the troops.

From what little he knew, this was definitely a crime scene and the killer was still on the loose. With the call made, he reattached the radio to his belt.

"Hannah, keep talking so I can find you." He pulled on every ounce of professionalism he had. Jordon was gone. Jordon was dead. Despite the utter tearing of his heart, he had a job to do.

Hannah continued to yell to him, and with two more turns, he was there. His brain worked to take in the scene before him. Hannah lay on the floor, bleeding from what appeared to be a gunshot wound in her leg. A bloody knife was also on the floor not too far away.

It was the sight of Jordon that once again stole his breath away and squeezed his lungs so hard he could scarcely breathe. She was seated and leaning against one of the mirrors, eyes closed and utterly lifeless.

He rushed to her side and crouched down, his fingers going to her neck to check for a pulse. *Please be there*, he prayed. *Please don't be dead.*

Yes! Yes, there was a pulse.

He grabbed his radio once again. "I need an ambulance at Mouse's Maze of Mirrors. Officer down. I repeat, officer down!" He touched her face. Her skin was cold and pale.

"Jordon? Jordon, can you open your eyes? Can you talk to me?" There was no response.

Her slacks were ripped and bloody across her thigh, but it appeared that the wound had stopped bleeding. He had no idea what other injuries she might have sustained.

He was afraid to move her to even check. Hannah had said she'd been stabbed by the killer. More injuries had to be in her back or someplace where he couldn't see them beneath her coat.

"What about me? I'm hurt. She shot me," Hannah cried plaintively.

Reluctantly, he left Jordon's side and moved to Hannah. The bullet had caught her just above her knee, and while she was bleeding, it was apparent that nothing vital had been hit because there wasn't too much blood.

"Just hang on," he said to the girl. "Help is on its way."

"Is Agent James going to be all right?" Hannah asked and there was a glint of fear in her dark eyes.

Gabriel took a step back and surveyed the scene once again. Hannah shot and Jordon apparently stabbed and the knife was on scene.

There was no way the killer would have left his weapon behind. It didn't make sense and the murderer they'd been chasing didn't make those kinds of mistakes. There was no way he could believe things had happened as Hannah had said.

A new quiet horror swept through him as he looked back at her. Was it possible that the tall, slender girl was responsible for all the deaths and destruction?

"It's over, Hannah," he said in calculation. "Agent

James is going to be just fine and she'll be able to tell me everything that happened here tonight." He wanted to believe it. He needed to believe that Jordon would be okay.

Hannah's features twisted with rage. "I just wanted to go home! If nobody stayed at Diamond Cove because of the murders then Mom and Dad would move back to Oklahoma City and I'd be where I belong."

"Chief Walters," a deep voice cried out. "We're here."

Gabriel recognized the voice as belonging to Ty Kincaid, an EMT. "We need two boards," Gabriel replied.

It seemed to take forever for the medical team to find them in the maze and then get both Hannah and Jordon loaded into the ambulance.

Jordon didn't regain consciousness as they took off her coat to reveal the bloody wound on her back. Gabriel officially placed Hannah under arrest before the ambulance pulled away.

He followed the ambulance to the hospital, where both patients were whisked back into the emergency room and he was left alone in the lobby.

Gabriel paced the room, his thoughts a riotous mess in his head. Hannah was their killer. How deep were Jordon's wounds? A fifteen-year-old kid had kept them all hopping around like maniacs all because she didn't want to live here. Had he gotten there in time or had Jordon been stabbed deep enough in her back to cause her death?

Only now did he fully process the sheer anguish that ripped through him, bringing the sting of tears to his eyes and squeezing his heart with an agony he'd never known before.

He was ragged with emotions by the time Mark walked in to join him in his vigil. "How is she?" he asked.

"Nobody has told me anything yet." He sank down on a chair and Mark sat next to him.

"She's a fighter," Mark replied.

"She is that," Gabriel agreed, but that didn't stop the frantic claw of despair inside him.

"The men were all working at the crime scene when I left them. I contacted Kent Myers to let him know he'd have to keep the attraction closed until we're finished with it."

"At least it's over now except the evidence gathering and the cleanup," Gabriel replied as he stared at the emergency room door and willed a doctor to come out with good news.

"Who would have thought our perp would turn out to be a teenage girl? You think the prosecutor will push to try her as an adult?"

Gabriel turned to look at Mark. "I'm certainly going to encourage him to. These murders weren't the result of a school yard fight or something else spontaneous. She carefully plotted this out. She showed enormous cunning in both the planning and the execution. She needs to be locked up for a very long time."

He turned to stare at the door once again. What was taking so long? Why didn't somebody come out to talk to him?

"Want some coffee?" Mark asked.

"No, thanks. I'm good." As sick as his stomach

was at the moment, there was no way he wanted to attempt drinking anything.

Dr. Gordon Oakley came through the emergency room door. Gabriel and Mark both sprang to their feet. "Chief... Mark," he greeted them.

Gabriel searched the ER doctor's features. "How is she?"

"Agent James is resting easy now. She needed seven stitches in her leg and twenty-one in her back. Thankfully, both were slashing wounds and not stabbing injuries. She was also cut on her arm, but that didn't require any stitches."

Gabriel released a deep sigh of relief and then frowned. "So, why was she unconscious?"

"I'd say she might have suffered a touch of shock and utter exhaustion. She's hooked up to an IV. We've cleaned her up and administered pain meds. We'll keep her under observation until sometime tomorrow."

"Can I see her?"

"I'd prefer that she not be disturbed for the rest of the night. From what I understand, she's been through quite a trauma and what she needs now is complete rest," Gordon replied. "You can see her in the morning."

Although disappointed, Gabriel nodded. He wanted whatever was best for her. For the next ten minutes the doctor filled them in on Hannah's wound. At the moment she was in surgery. Her parents had been contacted and were in a private waiting room.

"I'll go talk to the Overtons," Mark said when the doctor had left them again.

"And I want a full-time guard on Hannah while

she recuperates here," Gabriel replied. "I need to get back to the crime scene."

"I'll take care of everything here," Mark assured him.

The two men parted, as Mark headed to talk to the Overtons and Gabriel left the building. It wasn't until he was in his car that the emotions of the night nearly overwhelmed him.

As his car warmed up, he leaned his head back and closed his eyes. She was going to be just fine. Tears of relief burned at his eyes.

He'd been so scared for her. He'd been so afraid that this night would end differently. It was already tragic enough that a girl's life, for all intents and purposes, had come to an end.

It was utterly inconceivable that three innocent people had been brutally murdered because a kid didn't like where she was living. But if Jordon had lost her life tonight, the depth of the tragedy would have been beyond anything he could even imagine.

She was fine. The case was solved, and within the next twenty-four to forty-eight hours, she would be gone from here, gone forever from his life.

He tightened his hands on the steering wheel, opened his eyes and realized it had begun to snow.

JORDON AWOKE SLOWLY. Before she opened her eyes the scent of fresh coffee and bacon drifted to her nose along with a faint antiseptic smell. Shoes squeaked on the floor from someplace in the distance and a blood-pressure cuff began to pump up on her arm.

She opened her eyes to find herself alone in a hospital room. The cuff around her arm released and the blood-pressure monitor displayed numbers that assured her she'd made it through the long night despite the aches and pains that attempted to tell her otherwise.

She glanced out the nearby window and frowned. It was snowing again. She couldn't wait to get to that beach in Florida, where it would be wonderfully warm and sunny.

"Ah, good—you're awake." A blonde woman in purple scrubs entered her room. "My name is Marjorie and I'll be your nurse for the day." She walked over to Jordon and held out a thermometer. "Open."

Jordon did as she was told.

"You're normal," Marjorie replied as she removed the thermometer.

"I know some people who would argue with you about that," Jordon replied and then frowned as Marjorie didn't react. Great—a nurse without a sense of humor.

"On a scale from one to ten, how do you rate your pain level?"

Jordon changed positions and winced. "About a seven, but I don't need any more pain meds." She almost welcomed the pain that was a reminder that she'd survived. "What I would like is a big cup of coffee."

"I'll contact the kitchen and let them know you're ready for a breakfast tray."

"Perfect," Jordon replied.

She stared back out the window as Marjorie left the room. Gabriel. A vision of him jumped into her head. So handsome and with those piercing blue eyes that warmed her from the inside out.

She channeled her thoughts into another direction.

She didn't want to think of him with his gentle touches and strength of character.

Instead she closed her eyes and thought about Hannah and the confrontation from the night before. She'd been a fool to go in there alone, especially not knowing whom she might face.

It had been a reckless move not to call for backup. She wasn't a cat with nine lives. She'd already had two near-death experiences because of her lone-wolf attitude. It was past time to be a team player.

Thankfully, these troubling thoughts were interrupted by the arrival of breakfast. As she ate she was haunted by every breakfast she had shared with the Overtons, by each conversation she'd had with Joan.

Hannah's crimes would haunt them. Their lives would never be the same again. How did a parent ever find any kind of peace knowing that one of their children had committed three horrible murders? That she would be in lockup for years to come?

She cleaned off her plate and then fell back asleep. She had no nightmares haunted by Ralph Hicks or Hannah. Rather it was Gabriel who filled her dreams. They were sweet dreams of laughter and love, and she awakened with both deep longing and agonizing regret.

By that time lunch was served and then the doctor arrived. "When can I get out of here?" she asked him.

"How are you feeling? We did a lot of stitching on you last night."

"I'm sore," she admitted. "But I'm hoping to get a ride out of here as soon as possible and get back home to Kansas City. I can see my doctor there for any follow-up."

"Why don't you enjoy dinner on us this evening and then we'll see about releasing you," he replied.

She nodded her agreement, but there was no way she was spending another night here. She needed to get home. She had to get her feet back on the ground in her own space and put this place and a certain man far behind her.

After the doctor left the room, she called Director Tom Langford to fill him in on everything that had happened. He arranged for a helicopter to pick her up the next afternoon.

She'd just hung up when Gabriel came in. She stared at him in stunned surprise. In one arm he carried a huge, inflatable palm tree and in the other he had a pink fruity drink with a little umbrella stirrer.

"If Jordon can't get to Florida, then a piece of Florida will come to her," he said. He set the palm tree next to her bed. "Unfortunately, there's no alcohol in here." He held out the drink.

She took it from him and fought against the huge lump in her throat that made speech impossible for a moment. He looked so wonderfully handsome in his uniform and without the stress of the cases weighing him down.

He sat in the chair next to her bed and smiled at her. "Go on—take a sip. I wasn't sure exactly what you liked, so it's a strawberry smoothie with chunks of pineapple, berries and mango."

She took a drink and she didn't know if it tasted so good because she loved smoothies or if it was the fact that he'd gone to all this trouble just for her. The silly man was breaking her heart.

"Delicious," she said and then pointed to the palm tree. "Where did you manage to get that?"

"A couple of years ago the police department threw themselves a luau. There are five more of those in storage." His smile faded. "How are you doing?"

"I'm okay. I guess I'll be sporting a new scar across my back."

"She could have killed you." His voice was husky and his beautiful eyes were dark and filled with an emotion she didn't want to acknowledge.

"Is this the part where you yell at me for being a reckless fool?"

He leaned back in the chair. "It's enough for me that you recognize that you were reckless."

"I should have called you the minute I got that note. I'm done being a cowboy. I got lucky when Ralph Hicks had me in that cellar. I got lucky again last night, but I can't depend on luck anymore."

"If you've realized that then I guess your time here wasn't for nothing." His gaze on her was so intense she had to look away.

"How is Hannah?"

She needed a conversation about something…anything that would ease some of the tension in the room.

She stared out the window and listened absently as he caught her up on everything that was going on with the teenage killer. Hannah had come through surgery fine and was recuperating with a guard at her door.

"We found Joan's car parked a block away from the maze. She sneaked out of the house and took the car. Ted and Joan heard nothing. Hannah intended to kill you and then get home and back into bed before morning," he said.

"How are Ted and Joan?"

"Broken and in complete shock."

"They'll eventually get through this," Jordon replied. "They're strong people." She cast her gaze out the window. "And now, on another note, I should be released sometime this evening and I've made arrangements to leave tomorrow. I was wondering if you could pick me up later and take me to a motel for the night," she said.

She looked at him once again and saw in his eyes words he wanted to speak, emotions he wanted to share. But she didn't want to hear him. They had said everything necessary the night before.

"You know I'll be here whenever you need me," he finally replied.

Once again the lump was back in her throat and the pain that had been in her back moved around to pierce her in the heart.

"I'll call you later," she said and set the drink on her tray. "I think what I need right now is a nap."

He got up from the chair. "Then I'll just wait for your call." With those words he was gone.

She squeezed her eyes closed against a sudden burn of unexpected tears. The whole visit had been stilted and uncomfortable, nothing like the relationship they'd shared in the time she'd been here.

He'd brought her a palm tree and a fruity drink. His eyes had spoken of a love that invited her into something she'd never believed she could have.

She was doing what was best for both of them.

She had to tell him goodbye.

GABRIEL PARKED IN front of the motel room door and dreaded the goodbye that was to come. The sun was bright and the snow that had fallen the day before had been negligible. It was a beautiful day for a helicopter ride.

He'd brought Jordon to the motel room the night before and their ride from the hospital had been quiet, their only conversation dealing with the aftermath of the cases.

He now opened his car door and started to get out, but Jordon flew out of the door with her two bags in hand. "Don't get out," she said. "I've got this."

She opened the back door and threw her bags into the seat and then got into the car. She cast him a cheerful smile that only managed to break his heart just a little bit more.

"Thanks for taking me to the airport," she said.

"No problem," he replied and pulled out of the motel parking lot. "How are you feeling today?"

"Not too bad. I'm going to be sore for a while, but it's nothing I can't handle."

Her scent filled the car, evoking desire and love even as he drove her to the place where she'd leave him forever. Throughout the long night a weary resignation had set in. He loved…and he'd lost.

He couldn't make her love him if she didn't. He couldn't force her to understand that they belonged together if she didn't believe that in her very soul.

He could only let her go to find her own kind of happiness. She was the bravest woman he knew and yet he still believed it was fear that held her back.

"Nice day to fly," he said. "And now you can take that vacation you've been waiting for. You've definitely earned it."

"What about you? When was the last time you had a vacation?" she asked.

"I haven't taken one since I took this job," he admitted. He wasn't going to tell her that the idea of going off somewhere alone simply wasn't appealing to him.

"I'd definitely say you've earned one, too."

Why were they talking about vacations when his heart ached so badly? He didn't want inane conversation and yet he knew that was all that was left between them.

They reached the small airport, and as he parked, he had a perfect view of the helicopter that waited to take her home. "Looks like your ride is here."

"You don't have to get out." She unbuckled her seat belt.

"I'll walk you to the door," he replied. Just like he had every night since she'd been attacked by Hannah and had gotten lost in the snowstorm.

He got out of the car and grabbed the larger bag from her. Silently they entered the airport and then exited to the tarmac, where the helicopter pilot stood waiting.

When he saw them approaching, he climbed into the plane and the blades began their whooping swirl as they prepared for takeoff. Jordon took her bag, and when she looked back up at Gabriel, her green eyes simmered with emotion.

"Gabriel, I can't thank you enough for everything you've done for me while I've been here," she said.

"Jordon, I…"

She held up a hand. "Please don't say anything. This is hard enough already. Goodbye, Gabriel."

She didn't wait for his reply. She hurried to the helicopter door and climbed inside. He backed away, grief ripping another hole in his heart.

The helicopter blades spun faster and the engine began to whine. An empty, hollow wind blew through him as he turned to go back to the parking lot. It had taken him so long to finally find the woman he wanted forever in his life and now she was gone.

"Gabriel!"

His name carried on the breeze and he turned around to see her running toward him. Had she forgotten something? When she reached him, she threw her arms around his neck and smiled up at him.

"I want it," she said. Her eyes sparkled with a light that half stole his breath away. "I want life with you. I thought I could just walk away from you, but I can't. I love you, Gabriel, and I'm willing to take a chance on us."

He couldn't speak. Instead he took her lips with his in a kiss that held all his hope, all his dreams and every ounce of his love for her.

"I'd wrap you up in my arms right now if you didn't have stitches in your back," he said when the kiss ended.

She laughed, that husky sound that delighted him. "I don't know how this is going to work, but I do know my vacation is going to be right here with you."

"What about the beach?"

"To heck with the beach. I want to spend my time wherever you are."

"I want that, Jordon," he replied fervently. "We're going to make this work. We'll figure it all out as long as we love each other."

"You know I'm messy and I don't cook."

"And I love that about you," he assured her.

She cast a quick glance back at the helicopter. "I've got to go."

"I know." He kissed her again and this time he tasted her love for him and the promise of a future together. "I'll call you."

"I'll be waiting." She backed away from him and then turned and ran back and disappeared into the helicopter.

Gabriel remained in place and watched as the bird lifted off to carry her away. He missed her already, but his heart was filled with a wealth of happiness.

The sun glinted on the helicopter as it circled the airport once, and the shine was warm in Gabriel's heart. He loved and she loved him back, and he'd never been more certain of his future.

She might not know it yet, but Jordon was the woman he was going to marry. She was the woman who would have his children.

This wasn't a goodbye; it was only the beginning. He had no doubt in his mind that life with Jordon would be a wonderful adventure and he was more than up for the challenge.

Epilogue

The sun was hot in Florida in late August. Jordon sat on the chaise lounge and sighed with happiness. "This is positively wonderful," she said as she closed her eyes and raised her face.

"You just think it's wonderful because you have a handsome devil to rub sunscreen on your back," Gabriel said as his hands sensually worked the coconut-scented cream across her skin.

"You're right—the beach is definitely better with you," she replied.

He kissed the back of her neck and shivers of pleasure worked up her spine. "If you keep doing that we won't have much time in the sun. We'll wind up back in the room like we have done every afternoon since we arrived here."

He laughed and moved back to his chair next to hers. "Vacations are definitely better with a snuggle buddy."

She looked at him and grinned. "You're a great snuggle buddy." She leaned back in her chair and closed her eyes once again.

There were still moments when she needed to pinch

herself to make sure this was real and not a dream. The last six months had been magical.

She and Gabriel had taken every opportunity to see each other despite the distance. She'd spent weekends at his house and he'd come to Kansas City every chance he got and had stayed with her.

Each and every day their love had only grown deeper, her confidence in what they had together grew stronger. He had made her believe in herself in a way nobody had ever done before. He made her a better woman and she liked to believe she made him a better man.

She hadn't been surprised when he'd told her Joan and Ted Overton had decided to remain in Branson and continue to run Diamond Cove. The couple had decided that despite their heartbreak over Hannah's crimes, they couldn't allow her plot to succeed.

She'd been happy when Gabriel had told her that the couple appeared to be closer than ever, and while they planned to support their daughter, they also believed she belonged behind bars.

"Whew, it's really hot out here," Gabriel said, pulling her from her thoughts with a seductive lilt to his voice. "I'll bet our room is nice and cool. We could probably crank up a little music and dance in our underwear in the air-conditioning."

Jordon laughed, but didn't open her eyes. "You definitely look hot dancing in your underwear," she replied. She was so in love with this man.

"If we go inside we could probably even request room service to bring us a bottle of champagne to celebrate."

She turned her head to look at him. "And what would we be celebrating?"

He swung his legs over the side of his chair to face her and pulled their beach tote bag closer to him. His ocean-blue eyes gazed at her softly. "Jordon, these last six months have been the happiest I've ever been in my life."

Her heart squeezed. "You know I feel the same way. I thought I knew what love was, but it took you to really show me what it's all about."

"You know I'm all in with you, Jordon."

"Since you put in your resignation and are going to be part of the men in blue in Kansas City and move in with me next month, you'd better be all in," she said with a laugh.

"The real question is, are you sure you're really all in?" He slipped a hand into the tote bag and pulled out a small velvet box.

Her breath caught in her throat and she sat up to face him as he got down on one knee in the sand. His eyes suddenly held a touch of uncertainty. He opened the ring box to display a sparkling princess-cut diamond ring. "Will you make me the happiest man in the world and marry me, Jordon?"

Her heart trembled inside her, not with fear, but rather with a kind of wild joy she'd never known before. "You silly man, take that worried look out of your eyes. Yes, yes, a thousand times yes, I'll marry you."

He slipped the ring on her finger and then pulled her up off the chaise and into his arms. The kiss they shared was filled with unbridled passion and enduring love.

"Hey, get a room," a male voice called from nearby.

She broke the kiss and turned her head to see a skinny old man eyeing them. She grinned at him. "We have a room and we're going there right now." She placed a hand over Gabriel's heart. "This is the man I'm going to have babies with."

The old man's lips turned up in a smile. "Then get off the beach before you start that kind of business."

"Come on, fiancé. You heard what he said," she said to Gabriel.

He grasped her hand and together they ran across the sand toward the hotel, toward their future filled with love and laughter and family.

* * * * *

"They left a note."

She handed him a piece of paper, the message on it typed in block letters: YOUR BOY WILL BE SAFE AS LONG AS YOU COOPERATE. YOU AND YOUR BOYFRIEND BRING TEN THOUSAND DOLLARS TO THE ADDRESS WE'LL GIVE YOU TOMORROW AND WE WILL TALK THEN. DO NOT GO TO THE POLICE OR TELL ANYONE ELSE. WE HAVE PEOPLE WATCHING YOU AND WE WILL KNOW. MAKE ONE WRONG MOVE AND YOUR BOY WILL DIE A HORRIBLE DEATH.

Andrea sank into a chair, her hand over her mouth, stifling a sob.

Jack read the note again. "Who is this boyfriend they're talking about?" he asked.

"I don't know. I'm not dating anyone. I haven't, since before my marriage. I think they mean you."

CHRISTMAS KIDNAPPING

BY
CINDI MYERS

First Published in Great Britain 2016
By Mills & Boon, an imprint of HarperCollins*Publishers*
1 London Bridge Street, London, SE1 9GF

© 2016 Cynthia Myers

978-0-263-91923-3

46-1116

Our policy is to use papers that are natural, renewable and recyclable products and made from wood grown in sustainable forests. The logging and manufacturing processes conform to the legal environmental regulations of the country of origin.

Printed and bound in Spain
by CPI, Barcelona

Cindi Myers is the author of more than fifty novels. When she's not crafting new romance plots, she enjoys skiing, gardening, cooking, crafting and daydreaming. A lover of small-town life, she lives with her husband and two spoiled dogs in the Colorado mountains.

For Jim and Jim

Chapter One

Experience had taught Andrea McNeil to trust her first impressions of a man. She had learned to read temperament and tendencies in the set of his shoulders and the shadows in his eyes. Whether they were heroes or the perpetrators of heinous crimes, they all revealed themselves to her as much by their silences as by what they said.

The man who stood before her now radiated both strength and anxiety in the stubborn set of his broad shoulders and the tight line of his square jaw. He wore his blond hair short and neat, his face clean shaven, his posture military straight, though he was dressed in jeans, hiking boots and a button-down shirt and not a uniform. He moved with the raw sensuality of a hunter, muscular shoulders sliding beneath the soft cotton of his shirt, and when his hazel eyes met hers, she saw pride and courage and deep grief.

"All I want you to do is help me remember the face of the man who killed my friend," he said, before she had even invited him to sit on the sofa across from her chair in her small office just off the main street of Durango, Colorado.

She didn't allow her face to betray alarm at his state-ment. This certainly wasn't the worst thing she had heard from the people who came to her for help. "Please sit down, Agent Prescott, and I'll tell you a little more about how I work."

FBI special agent Jack Prescott lowered himself gingerly onto the sofa. He grimaced as he shifted his weight. "Is something wrong?" she asked.

"I'm fine."

She kept her gaze steady on him, letting him know she wasn't buying this statement.

He shifted again. "I took a couple of bullets in a firefight a couple of months back," he said. "The cold bothers me a little."

The window behind him showed a gentle snowfall, the remnants from the latest winter storm. A man who had been shot—twice—and was still on medical leave probably ought to be home recuperating, but she might as well have told a man like Jack Prescott that he needed to take up knitting and mah-jongg. She didn't have to read the information sheet he had filled out to know that much about him. Even sitting still across from her, he looked poised to leap into action. She would have bet next month's rent that he was armed at the moment and that he had called into his office at least once a day every day of his enforced time off.

Her husband, Preston, had been the same way. All his devotion to duty and reckless courage had gotten him in the end was killed.

She focused on Agent Prescott's paperwork to force the memories back into the locked box where they be-longed. Jack Prescott was single, thirty-four years old and a graduate of Columbia with a major in electrical engineering and robotics. Twelve years with the FBI. A letter of commendation. He was in Durango on special assignment and currently on medical leave. He took no medications beyond the antibiotics prescribed for his gunshot wounds, and he had no known allergies. "Tell me about this firefight," she said. "The one in which you were injured."

He sat on the edge of the sofa cushion, gripping his knees. "What happened to me doesn't matter," he said. "But my friend Gus Mathers was killed in that fight. I saw it happen. I saw who killed him."

"That would be traumatic for anyone," she said.

"You don't understand. I saw the man who killed Gus, but I can't remember his face."

"What you're talking about is upsetting, but it's not unusual," she said. "The mind often blocks out the memory of traumatic events as a means of protection."

He leaned forward, his gaze boring into her, his expression fierce. "You don't understand. I don't forget faces. It's what I do, the way some people remember numbers or have perfect pitch."

She set aside the clipboard with the paperwork and leaned toward him, letting him know she was focused completely on him. "I'm not sure I understand," she said.

"I'm what they call a super-recognizer. If I look at someone for even a few seconds, I remember them. I remember supermarket clerks and bus drivers and people I pass on the street. Yet I can't remember the man who murdered my best friend."

"Your talent for remembering faces doesn't exempt you from the usual responses to trauma," she said.

"Your memory of the events may come back with time, or it may never return."

He set his jaw, the look of a man who was used to forcing the outcome he desired. "The cop who referred me to you said you could hypnotize me—that that might be a way to get the memory to return."

"I do sometimes use hypnosis in my therapy, but in your case, I don't believe it would work."

"Why not?"

Because there are some things even a will as strong as yours can't make happen, she thought. "Hypnosis requires the subject to relax and surrender to the process," she said. "In order for me to hypnotize you, you would have to trust me and be willing to surrender control of the situation. You aren't a man who is used to surrendering, and you haven't known me long enough to trust me."

"You're saying I'm a control freak."

She smiled at his choice of words. "Your job—your survival and the survival of those who work with you—requires you to control as many variables as possible," she said. "In this case, your need to control is an asset." *Most of the time.*

"I want you to hypnotize me," he said.

"Consciously wanting to be hypnotized and your conscious mind being willing to relax enough to allow that to happen are two different things," she said. "I'm certainly willing to attempt hypnotic therapy at some point, but not on a first visit. It's too soon. Once we have explored the issues that may be causing you to suppress this memory, we may have more success in retrieving it, through hypnosis or by some other means."

He stood and began to pace, a caged tiger—one with a limp that, even agitated, he tried to disguise. "I don't need to talk about my feelings," he said, delivering the words with a sneer. "I don't need therapy. I know the memory of the man who shot Gus is in my head. I just have to find a way to access that information again."

"Agent Prescott, please sit down."

"No. If you can't help me, I won't waste any more of your time."

He turned toward the door. "Please, don't go," she called. His agitation and real grief touched her. "I'm willing to try things your way. But I don't want you to be disappointed if it doesn't work."

He sat again, tension still radiating from him, but some of the darkness had gone out of his eyes. "What do I do?"

"You don't do anything," she said. "The whole point is to relax and not try to control the situation. Why don't you start by taking off your shoes and lying back on the couch? Get comfortable."

He hesitated, then removed his hiking boots and lined them up neatly at the end of the sofa. He lay back, hands at his sides. His feet hung over one end and his shoulders stretched the width of the cushion. There probably wasn't an ounce of fat on the man, but he had plenty of hard muscle. He wasn't the type you'd want to meet alone in a dark alley, though maybe a dark bedroom…

The thought surprised her, and she felt a rush of heat to her face, glad Jack had his back to her so he couldn't wonder what was making her blush. He folded his arms across his chest, a posture of confrontation and protection. "Put your hands down by your sides," she suggested. "And close your eyes."

"Aren't you going to swing a pendulum or a watch or something in front of my eyes?" he asked.

"That's not the approach I use. I prefer something called progressive relaxation."

"Is that the same as hypnosis?"

"It's a way of readying your body for hypnotic suggestion. Now, close your eyes and focus on your toes."

"My toes?"

"Agent Prescott, if you're going to question every instruction I give, this isn't going to work."

"Sorry. I'll focus on my toes."

"Relax your toes. Now focus on your ankles." She made her voice as low and soothing as possible. "Imagine a warm wave of relaxation moving up your legs, from your toes and feet to your ankles and then your calves and knees. Your body feels very comfortable and heavy, the muscles completely relaxed. The sensation moves up your thighs to your torso. Every bit of tension is leaving your body. Each vertebra of your spine relaxes, one by one. You're feeling very heavy and languid."

She continued the journey up his body, instructing him to relax his shoulders and arms and hands. "How are you feeling?" she asked.

"Fine." His voice was clear and alert, his posture still as stiff as if he were standing for inspection.

"Think of someplace pleasant and relaxing," she said. "A mountain meadow with a waterfall or a beautiful beach with ocean waves rolling in. Choose whatever place you like to go to relax."

"Okay."

"What are you thinking of?" she asked.

"The gym."

She blinked. "The gym?"

"Working out relaxes me."

That explained those impressive shoulders and biceps. "That kind of relaxation is a little too active. What about vacations? Do you like to go to the beach? Or to a lake in the mountains."

"The last vacation I took, Gus and I and some other guys went hiking. We climbed a mountain."

She could imagine—all macho competitiveness: heavy packs, miles logged, not bathing or shaving for days, eating food out of cans. She shuddered. "I don't think this is going to work," she said.

He sat up. "Let's try again. Do the thing with the pendulum. I think I would do better if I had something to focus on."

She hesitated, but if he left here, she would feel she had failed him. She reached up and unclasped the necklace she wore—a gold chain with a gold heart-shaped locket. An anniversary gift from Preston a few months before he died. "Sit back and relax as much as you can," she said.

Jack settled back against the sofa, his gaze fixed on the necklace. "Focus on the heart," she said, and began to gently swing the locket from side to side. "As you focus, count back slowly, from ninety-nine."

"Ninety-nine," he said. "Ninety-eight. Ninety-seven."

She shifted her own gaze from the locket to Jack and found herself staring directly into his gold-green eyes. The naked pain and vulnerability revealed in his gaze startled her so much she almost dropped the necklace. He took her hand. "Please. You have to help me."

His grip was strong and warm but not painful. Far from it. His touch sent warmth coursing through her, as if someone had injected heated platelets into her bloodstream. The heat settled in her lower abdomen, reminding her in a way she hadn't been reminded in many months that she was a woman with a very attractive, virile man touching her. She carefully extricated her hand, which still tingled from the contact. "I want to help you, Agent Prescott," she said. "But the mind is the most complicated machine imaginable. There isn't a formula or solution to solve every problem."

The clock on her desk chimed and she glanced at it. "I'm afraid our session today is over, but I hope you will make an appointment to see me again."

He looked away, frustration clear in the tension along his jaw and the defensive set of his shoulders. "Do you really think it would help me remember Gus's killer?"

"I can't promise you will ever remember what you saw the day your friend was killed," she said. "But I can help you come to terms with what happened."

"Maybe I'll come back," he said.

"I really do think it would help you to talk to someone," she said. "Not only about Gus, but about your own injuries. Being forced into medical leave must be difficult for you."

He looked startled, his eyes locked to hers once more. "The other team members kidded me, said I should enjoy the paid vacation. But it's driving me crazy knowing Gus's killer is out there and I'm not doing anything to help stop him."

"That's something we can talk about the next time you're in." She stood, and he rose also and followed her to the door.

"Do you have another client now?" he asked.

"No, it's time for my lunch break."

He checked his watch, a heavy stainless model she recognized as designed for mountaineers and other outdoorsmen. "Let me take you to lunch. I want to make up for wasting your time this morning."

Her heart sped up at the prospect of being alone with him in a nonclinical setting. "Agent Prescott, I don't think—"

"Call me Jack. And I just want to talk. Not therapy talk, just, you know, conversation. I'm bored out of my skull not working, and I don't know many people in Durango. Not outside of work, anyway. You seem like you'd be good company, that's all."

She should say no. Professional ethics aside—and really, there was nothing unethical about having lunch with a client—spending more time with Jack was dangerous to her equilibrium. He was exactly the type of man who attracted her most—powerful, dedicated, intelligent and virile. And all those traits made him the worst sort of man for her to be with.

But the temptation to sit across from him and learn more of his story, to have his attention fixed on her for a little while longer, won out over common sense. "All right," she said. "I can have lunch with you."

SITTING ACROSS FROM Dr. Andrea McNeil in a café down the street from her office, Jack felt better than he had since the shoot-out. Maybe it was being with a pretty woman. He hadn't dated in a while and she was definitely a looker—her businesslike blue suit did nothing to hide her shapely figure, and her high-heeled boots showed her gorgeous legs to advantage. Her sleek brown hair was piled up on top of her head, drawing attention to the smooth white column of her throat, and she had lively brown eyes above a shapely nose and slightly pouty lips.

But though he could appreciate her beauty, he attributed most of his good mood to the way she focused on him. As if anything he had to say were the most interesting thing she had heard today. That was probably just her therapist's training, but it was doing him a lot of good, so he wasn't going to complain.

"How did you hear about me?" she asked when they had ordered—a salad for her, a chicken sandwich for him.

"I have a friend—Carson Allen, with the Bureau's resident agency here in Durango. He and I have done some hiking and stuff. Anyway, he said you're the counselor for the police department and the sheriff's office. How did you end up with that job?"

"My husband was a police officer." She focused on buttering a roll from the basket the waitress had brought.

"Was?"

"He was killed three years ago, by a drug dealer who was fleeing the scene of a burglary."

The news that she was a widow—a cop's widow—hit him like a punch in the gut. "I'm sorry," he said. "That must have been tough."

She met his gaze, serene, not a hint of tears. "It was.

But I lived through it. I have a son, Ian." She smiled, a look that transformed her face from pretty to breathtaking. "He's five. I had to be strong for him."

"Sounds like he's a pretty lucky little boy." And her husband had been a lucky man. Jack envied his coworkers who had found women who could put up with the demands of a law enforcement job. He had never been that fortunate.

"Tell me more about this talent of yours for remembering faces," she said. "What did you call it?"

He recognized the shift away from any more personal conversation about her, and he accepted it. "I'm a super-recognizer. I think it's one of those made-up government descriptors the bureaucrats love so much."

"I'll admit I'm unfamiliar with the concept. It must be pretty rare."

He shrugged. "It's not something that comes up in casual conversation. Scientists are just beginning to study facial-recognition abilities. More people may be super-recognizers than we realize. They just don't admit it."

"Why not admit it?" she asked.

"It makes for awkward social situations. You learn pretty quickly not to admit you recognize people you haven't been introduced to. I mean, if I tell someone I remember seeing them at a football game last fall or on the bus last week, they think I'm a spy or a stalker or something."

"I guess that would be strange." She speared a tomato wedge with her fork. "How old were you when you realized you had this talent?"

"Pretty young." For a long time, he had thought that

was the way everyone saw the world, as populated by hundreds of individual, distinct people who stayed in his head. "In school it was kind of a neat parlor trick to play on people—go into a store to buy a soda and come out three minutes later and be able to describe everyone who was in there. But as I got older, I stopped telling people about it or showing off."

"Because of the social awkwardness."

"Because it made me different, and if there's anything teenagers don't want to be, it's different."

She laughed, and they waited while the waitress refilled their glasses. "Did your ability get you the job with the Bureau?" she asked. "Or did that come later?"

He shrugged and crunched a chip. "You know the government—they test you for everything. I was doing a different job—one that used my electrical and robotics background—when someone in the Bureau decided to put together a whole unit of people like me and I got tapped for it. Gus was a recognizer, too." A familiar pain gripped his chest at the mention of Gus. Jack didn't have any brothers, but he had felt as close to Gus as he would have any brother. They had been through so much together.

"Is that what brought you two together?" she asked.

"Not at first. We were in the same class at Quantico and we hit it off there. We had probably known each other a year or so before I found out he had the same knack I had for remembering faces. We used to joke about it some, but we never thought anything of it. Not until both of us were recruited for this special project."

"That's really fascinating." She took a bite of her salad and he dug into the chicken sandwich. The si-

lence between them as they ate was comfortable, as if
they had known each other a long time, instead of only
a few hours.

But after a few more minutes he began to feel uneasy.
Not because of anything she was doing. He glanced
around them, noting the group of women who sat at
a table to their left, shopping bags piled around them.
A trio of businessmen occupied a booth near the front
window, deep in conversation. A family of tourists, an
older couple and two clerks he recognized from the
hotel where he had stayed his first two nights in town
months ago filled the other tables. Nothing suspicious
about any of them. He swiveled his head to take in the
bar and gooseflesh rose along his arms when his gaze
rested on a guy occupying a stool front and center, directly beneath the flat-screen television that was broad-
casting a bowling tournament. Average height, short
brown hair, flannel shirt and jeans. Nothing at all re-
markable about him, yet Jack was positive he had seen
the guy before. Probably only once—repeat exposure
strengthened the association. But he had definitely been
around this guy at least once before.

"What is it?" Andrea spoke softly. "You've gone all
tense. Is something wrong?"

He turned to face her once more. "That guy back
there at the bar—the one in the green plaid shirt—he's
watching us."

She looked over his shoulder at the guy and frowned.
"He has his back to us."

"He's watching us in the bar mirror. It's an old surveillance trick."

"Do you know him?" she asked.

"I've seen him before. Maybe only once. I think he's in our files."

"Why would he be watching you?"

Jack shoved back his chair. "That's what I'm going to ask him."

He pretended to be headed for the men's room, but at the last second, he veered toward the guy at the bar. The guy saw him coming and leaped up. He overturned a table and people started screaming. Jack took off after him, alarmed to see the guy was headed right toward Andrea, who stared, openmouthed. Jack shoved aside a chair and dodged past a waitress with a tray of plates, but his bum leg made speed difficult and the guy was almost to Andrea now.

But the perp didn't lay a hand on her. He raced past, headed toward the door, Jack still in pursuit. Andrea cried out as Jack ran by her. "My purse," she said. "He stole my purse!"

Chapter Two

Andrea stared at the water glass on its side, ice cubes scattered across the cloth. Jack had taken off after the purse snatcher so suddenly she hadn't had time to process everything that had happened. One moment he was saying something about the guy at the bar watching them, and the next her purse had disappeared, and so had Jack.

"Would the gentleman like the rest of his meal boxed to go?"

Andrea blinked up at the waitress, whose face betrayed no emotion beyond boredom, as if purse snatchings and overturned tables were everyday occurrences.

"No thank you," Andrea said. "Just bring the check." She glanced toward the door, hoping to see Jack. Had he caught the thief? Had he been hurt in the attempt? She needed to get out of here and make sure he was okay.

The waitress returned with the check and Andrea realized that, without her purse, she had no way to pay the bill.

"I'll get that." Jack's hand rested atop hers on the tab. He dropped into the chair beside her, his face flushed and breathing hard. "He got away," he said. "I'm sorry about your purse." He shifted his hip to retrieve his wallet and winced.

"You're hurt," she said, alarmed.

He shook his head. "I'm fine." He removed his credit card and glanced around. Two busboys were righting the overturned table and most of the other diners had returned to their meals. "Where's our waitress?" Jack asked. "I'm ready to get out of here."

He helped her with her coat and kept his hand at her back as they left the café. "What was in your purse?" he asked. "I'm assuming a wallet and credit cards. Driver's license?"

She nodded. "And my car keys, house keys and cell phone." She took a deep breath. "I can call and cancel the cards, get a new license, and I have spare keys at home. I'll have to get a new phone."

"Let me take you by your place to get the keys," he said.

"You don't have to do that. I can call someone." Maybe Chelsea, who was babysitting for her, would come—though that would mean bringing along Ian and Chelsea's baby, Charlotte.

"I have the whole afternoon free, so you might as well let me take you."

"All right. Thank you."

Jack drove a pickup truck, a black-and-silver late-model Ford that was the Western equivalent of a hot sports car. She gave him directions to her home and settled back against the soft leather seats, inhaling the masculine aromas of leather, coffee and Jack Prescott. If some genius were to bottle the combination, it would be a sure bestseller, the epitome of sex appeal.

"Nice place," he said when he pulled into the driveway of the blue-and-white Victorian in one of Durango's quiet older neighborhoods. Snow frosted the low evergreens around the base of the porch and dusted the large pine-and-cedar Christmas wreath she had hung on the front door. Jack had to move Ian's tricycle in order to get to the walkway to the steps.

"Sorry about that," Andrea said. "I keep telling him not to leave it in the way like that, but he forgets."

"He'll be ready for a bicycle before long," Jack said. "If he's five."

"He's been asking for one for Christmas but I don't know…" The thought of her baby riding along the narrow and hilly roads of her neighborhood filled her with visions of collisions with cars or tumbles in loose gravel.

Chelsea opened the door before they were up the steps, Charlotte in her arms. "Oh, hi, Andrea." She sent a curious glance toward Jack. "I didn't know who was here in that truck."

"My purse got stolen at lunch," Andrea said. "I came home to get my spare keys. This is Jack. Jack, this is Chelsea. She's my best friend and she looks after Ian while I work. I don't know what I'd do without her."

"Hello, Jack." Chelsea pushed a corkscrew of black curls behind one ear and smoothed the front of her pink polo shirt.

"I'll just get my keys and get out of your hair." Andrea started to step past her, but at that moment, Ian barreled out of the house.

"Hey, Mom!" He grinned up at her, the dimple on the left side of his mouth and the thick fall of dark hair across his forehead foreshadowing the lady-killer he would no doubt be one day. Just like his father. "You came home early," Ian said.

"Not to stay, I'm afraid." She hugged him and smoothed the hair out of his eyes. But his attention had already shifted to Jack. Ian ducked his head behind her leg and peeked out.

Jack squatted in front of the boy—it had to be an awkward movement, considering his injuries, but a slight wince was the only sign of difficulty he gave. "Hello, Ian," he said. "My name is Jack."

"Mr. Prescott," Andrea corrected. She nudged her son. "Say hello, Ian."

"Hello." The words came out muffled against her leg, but Ian's eyes remained fixed on Jack, bright with interest.

"What's your favorite food, Ian?" Jack asked.

Ian looked up at his mom. "You can answer him," she said.

"Grilled cheese sandwiches," Ian said.

Chelsea laughed. "He would eat grilled cheese every meal if his mother and I would let him."

"I like grilled cheese, too," Jack said.

"I'll just get my keys." Andrea slipped inside and went to the drawer in her bedroom where she kept her spare set. She paused to study the photo on her dresser, of her and Preston and eighteen-month-old Ian on her lap. Ian liked to hold the picture and ask questions about his father, but one day pictures and her memories weren't going to be enough. A boy needed a father to help him learn to be a man.

She returned to the porch to find Jack and Ian in the

driveway, studying something on the tricycle. "What's going on?" she asked Chelsea.

"Guy talk." Chelsea dismissed the two males with a wave of her hand. "What's this about your purse being stolen?" she asked.

"A purse snatcher. Jack chased him, but the guy was too fast." She jingled her keys. "I'll have to call when I get to my office and cancel my credit cards and see about getting a new driver's license."

Chelsea sidled closer and lowered her voice. "Jack is definitely a hottie," she said. "How long have you two been an item?"

Andrea flushed. "Oh, no, it's not like that. I mean, we just met."

"You don't act like two people who just met." Chelsea grinned.

"I don't know what you're talking about."

"You can't take your eyes off him. And he feels the same way."

Andrea glanced at Jack, something she realized now she had been doing every few seconds since she had returned to the porch. He was kneeling beside the trike, listening while Ian gave some long explanation about something. Just then Jack looked up and his eyes met hers, and she felt a jolt of pleasure course through her.

Jack stood and patted Ian's shoulder. Then the two rejoined the women on the porch. "Ian was telling me about the pedals sticking on his ride," he said. "I'll bring some oil over sometime and fix the problem for him."

"Oh, you don't have to do that," she protested. Jack was a client. They were supposed to have one casual lunch and some conversation. Now he was getting involved in her personal life.

"I'm going to help Jack fix my bike," Ian said.

"Mr. Prescott." Her voice sounded faint, even to her, as she made the automatic correction.

"It's no trouble," Jack said.

Arguing about it, especially in front of Ian and Chelsea, seemed a waste of breath. "All right." She knelt and hugged her son. "I have to give a speech tonight for a police-officer spouse group, so I won't be home until late," she said. "But Chelsea has a special treat for you."

"Pizza and a movie." Chelsea put a hand on the boy's head.

"And root beer?" Ian asked.

Chelsea looked to Andrea. "All right. You may have one glass of root beer with your pizza," Andrea said.

"A big glass," Ian said.

Jack laughed. "You're quite the negotiator, pal," he said.

Ian beamed at the praise. Butterflies battered at Andrea's chest. This wasn't good. She didn't want Ian so focused on a man she hardly knew. Especially a man like Jack, with a dangerous job and a reckless attitude. "We'd better go," she said. "I have clients to see this afternoon."

"I like your truck," Ian said to Jack.

"Maybe I'll give you a ride sometime," Jack said.

Andrea waited until they were in the vehicle and driving away before she spoke, choosing her words carefully. "You shouldn't have said that, about giving him a ride in your truck," she said.

"I would want you to come along, too," he said.

"Saying you'll take him for a ride promises some kind of ongoing relationship."

His knuckles whitened on the steering wheel, the only sign of any emotion. "Would that be so bad?"

She turned toward him, her hands fisted in her lap. "You're my client. I hardly know you."

"I had a good time today," he said. "I'd like to see you again. You and Ian."

"I don't think that would be a good idea."

"Why not?"

"It just…wouldn't."

"Because of the client thing? What if I decided not to see you in a professional capacity anymore?"

"It wouldn't matter." She looked out the window, at the passing lines of shops crowded along the highway in Durango's downtown area. Evergreen garlands, wreaths and hundreds of tiny white lights decorated the Victorian buildings, making the scene look right out of a Christmas card. People filled the sidewalks, hands full of shopping bags, or carrying skis or snowboards, fresh from a day at Durango Mountain Resort.

"Is there someone else?" he asked. "Do you have a boyfriend? I didn't get that vibe from you."

What kind of vibe would that be? But she wasn't going to go there. "I'm busy with my job and raising my son," she said. "I don't have time to date."

"You don't have time to date a cop."

His perceptiveness momentarily silenced her. She stared at him.

"I'm not a trained therapist, but if your husband was killed in the line of duty, it doesn't take a degree to figure out you might not want to repeat the experience." He glanced at her, then back at traffic. "But even civilians can get hit by buses or fall off of mountains or have a heart attack while mowing the lawn."

She shook her head. "I don't want to date you, Jack."

"Fine. But I will have to see you again."

"Why is that?"

"I'm going to try to find out more about the guy who snatched your purse. I'm going to try to find him."

"Don't worry about it. Everything in there can be replaced."

"Maybe. But I don't think he was in that café this afternoon for the sole purpose of stealing a random stranger's purse. He was watching us—watching me—for a while before he made his move. I want to find out why."

"I doubt you'll get my purse back," she said.

"Maybe not. But I have to see you again anyway."

"Why?"

"I promised Ian I'd fix the stiff pedal on his tricycle. And I always keep my promises."

Yes, Jack Prescott would keep his promises. He would do his duty and live by his pledge, whether that pledge was to a friend or a woman or a little boy like Ian. But he would also keep his promise to give all he had for his country. Even if that meant his life. That last promise was one she wasn't sure she could live with.

AFTER JACK DROPPED Andrea at her office, he called Special Agent Cameron Hsung, one of his fellow Search Team Seven members. "Hey, Jack, how are you doing?" Cameron's cheerful voice greeted him. The half-Asian twentysomething was one of the younger members of the team, an IT specialist who had been recruited, like the other members of Search Team Seven, because of his super-recognizer skills.

"I'm doing great." Jack rubbed his thigh, which burned with pain as a result of his pursuit of the thief and squatting to put himself at eye level with Ian McNeil. "There's no reason I couldn't come back to work right now."

"I'm guessing your doctor has a different idea," Cameron said.

"He says at least two more weeks of leave. But what does he know. How's the case going?" The case—the sole focus of the team at the moment—involved a terrorist cell headquartered here in western Colorado. The suspected leader of the cell, a man named Duane Braeswood, had jumped from the Durango and Silverton tourist railroad two months ago, but a subsequent search hadn't turned up his body.

"We got a lead that a man matching Braeswood's description had shown up at a hospital in Grand Junction," Cameron said. "But by the time local law enforcement made it there, he had disappeared."

"So he was injured?"

"Pretty badly, I guess," Cameron said. "After a bit of a hassle, we got a copy of the medical report. He had a broken leg, some busted ribs, and a bruised liver and kidneys."

Jack winced. "So he probably didn't get to the hospital—or out of it—on his own."

"That's what we're thinking. We got some security video but it's pretty blurred. Typical cheap system that hasn't been maintained. Nobody thinks about these things until they actually need the equipment to do its job. Then it's too late."

"The man doesn't seem to have any shortage of helpers," Jack said.

"Yeah, well, money buys a lot of things—even friends."

"Right. And speaking of friends, I need a favor."

Cameron groaned. "Something tells me I should say no before I even hear this."

"It's nothing complicated. A friend of mine had her purse stolen while we were at lunch today."

"You have a woman friend?"

"Don't act so surprised."

"At least you're using your leave productively. Who is she? How did you meet?"

"Her name is Andrea McNeil. She's a therapist."

"You mean the police therapist you were going to see? Man, what did you do, put the moves on her from the couch?"

"We were having lunch. That's all." Though he definitely wanted more. A guy didn't meet a woman like Andrea every day, and he wasn't buying her argument that she didn't want to date him. He understood her reluctance, given her history, but she must have felt the connection between them. And he thought he was savvy enough to have picked up that she hadn't agreed to have lunch with him because she fell for his "I'm so lonely" line. She was really interested. All he had to do was take it slow and prove that exploring the chemistry between them was worth the risk. "I thought I recognized the purse snatcher. I think he's in our database."

"Uh-huh. And what is this favor you want from me?"

"I want a copy of the database so I can look for this lowlife and find him."

"That database is classified," Cameron said. "It's not supposed to leave this office."

"It's not like you're releasing it to a civilian. I'm a member of your team."

"Technically, you're not on the team right now. You're on medical leave. You're not even allowed to come to the office."

"Because some bureaucratic pencil pusher is afraid of getting sued if I slip and fall on a wet floor or something before my doctor has cleared me to return to work. That's why I need a copy of the database on my personal computer."

"Jack, it'll cost me my job if anyone finds out."

"No one will find out. It's not like I'm going to go around showing the thing off. I just want to track down this guy."

He thought he heard Cameron's teeth grinding together. "All right. But don't go all Lone Ranger on me. If you find anything, you bring it to us."

"I will. I promise."

"Okay. Meet me when I get off at six, at that tavern around the corner."

"The Rusty Moose."

"Yeah. Dumb name, good beer. You can buy me one and I'll get you what you need. And hey, if your therapist friend has a friend, maybe you could introduce us."

"You have to find your own dates, Cam. That's where I draw the line."

"Hey, I figured it was worth a try."

Jack hung up the phone and started the truck. He

couldn't shake the feeling the purse snatcher had been up to more than looking to steal a handbag. There had to be a connection to his case. Even if he was supposed to be on medical leave, that didn't mean he couldn't do a little investigating on his own. He was out of the hospital and doing pretty good. He had never been the type to sit around and do nothing, and he wasn't about to start now.

BY THE TIME Andrea made it home from her meeting, she was drained. As much as she enjoyed sharing her expertise with groups, she identified a little too closely with the challenges faced by members of the Law Enforcement Spouses organization. She remembered what it was like to be in their shoes and deal with the constant worry about her loved one. Though she was happy to listen to their concerns and offer strategies for coping, she knew her words weren't really enough.

She was surprised to find the house dark when she arrived. Chelsea usually left the porch light on for her. She fumbled her way up the steps and opened the door. Silence greeted her—another oddity. Even though it was past Ian's bedtime, Chelsea liked to stay up and watch movies or her favorite reality TV shows. "Chelsea? Is everything okay?" she called as she reached for the light switch.

A half-eaten pizza sat on the coffee table, an almost-empty glass of root beer tipped on its side next to the pizza box, the brown liquid pooling on the table and dripping on the floor. One of the couch pillows was on the floor, too. Heart in her throat, Andrea took a step forward. Then she saw the blood.

Or at least, she thought it was blood. The pool of brownish-red liquid on the rug beside the coffee table definitely wasn't root beer. It could have been spilled syrup, except that no one would be eating syrup with pizza, would they?

She reached for her phone to call 911, but of course, the thief had stolen it, along with her purse. "Chelsea!" she shouted, headed toward the kitchen and the phone there. "Ian!"

She stumbled over something in the hallway—Chelsea lay on her back, her hands and feet tied, a gag in her mouth. She stared up at Andrea, eyes wide. Shaking, Andrea dropped to her knees and pulled the gag from the babysitter's mouth. "What happened?" she demanded. "Where is Ian?"

"Ian's gone." Tears spilled out of Chelsea's frightened eyes. "Two men took him. He's gone."

Chapter Three

Jack spent most of his evening stretched out in the recliner in his apartment, his laptop propped on his stomach, scanning the database Cameron had loaded onto a flash drive. A football game on the TV played in the background, and he was debating getting out of the chair and hunting in the refrigerator for a beer when his cell phone rang. He didn't recognize the number on the screen, though it was a local exchange, and he almost let the call go to voice mail but decided to take a chance. "Hello?"

"Jack, they've taken Ian. You've got to help me. Please. They've taken my baby."

He didn't recognize the voice of the hysterical woman on the other end of the line, but the name Ian meant it had to be Andrea. "Andrea? Is that you?"

"Yes. Oh, God—Jack. Ian will be terrified. You have to help me find him."

"I'll be there in five minutes." He was already moving toward the door. "Can you sit tight until then?"

"Yes. But hurry, please."

He broke several traffic laws on the way to Andrea's house, but traffic was light off the highway this time of evening, and in less than five minutes he roared into her driveway. Every light in the house was illuminated. He raced onto the porch and knocked. "Andrea! It's me, Jack."

"Come in. We're in the kitchen."

He found her at the back of the house, applying a cold washcloth to a nasty-looking bruise near the babysitter's temple. Chelsea held her baby close, tears pouring from her eyes as she rocked and cooed at the infant. Andrea had been crying, too, her eyes red and swollen, cheeks streaked with tears. "What's going on?" Jack asked.

"Ian and I were watching a movie and eating pizza and these two men dressed in black and carrying big guns burst in and grabbed him," Chelsea said. "I tried to stop them, but one of them hit me in the head with the butt of the gun. When I woke up, I was tied up and gagged in a back bedroom and Ian was gone." She gulped and swallowed hard. "I was so afraid they'd taken Charlotte, too, but they left her sleeping in her crib."

"Have you called the police?" Jack asked.

"They said not to," Andrea said. "They said they would kill Ian if I contacted any law enforcement." Her voice wobbled at the word *kill* and she looked ready to collapse.

Jack put his hand on her shoulder to steady her. "Who told you not to?" he asked.

"I don't know who. They left a note."

She handed him a piece of paper, the message on it typed in block letters.

YOUR BOY WILL BE SAFE AS LONG AS YOU COOPERATE. YOU AND YOUR BOYFRIEND BRING TEN THOUSAND DOL-LARS TO THE ADDRESS WE'LL GIVE YOU TOMORROW

AND WE WILL TALK THEN. DO NOT GO TO THE POLICE
OR TELL ANYONE ELSE. WE HAVE PEOPLE WATCHING
YOU AND WE WILL KNOW. MAKE ONE WRONG MOVE
AND YOUR BOY WILL DIE A HORRIBLE DEATH.

Andrea sank into a chair, her hand over her mouth, stifling a sob. Chelsea leaned over and squeezed her hand.

Jack read the note again. "Who is this boyfriend they're talking about?" he asked.

"I don't know. I'm not dating anyone. I haven't since before my marriage."

"I think they mean you," Chelsea said.

"Me?"

"Jack isn't my boyfriend," Andrea protested.

"If the kidnappers saw the two of you together this afternoon, they might think so," Chelsea said. "I mean, I did."

Andrea moaned and covered her mouth again.

Jack sat across from her. His leg throbbed, but he ignored it. "The only person watching us this afternoon was that guy in the restaurant," he said.

"Did you find out who he is?" Andrea asked.

He shook his head. "I'm still looking into it." He glanced around the room. "He probably got your address from your license in your purse. And he has your keys, too." Why hadn't he thought of that before? He should have made Andrea change her locks. Or he should have insisted on staying here at her house tonight. He turned to Chelsea. She looked as wrecked as Andrea, clutching the child in her arms so tightly it was a wonder the infant didn't wail. "What did these two look like?" he asked.

She shook her head. "They were wearing masks, dressed all in black. They carried big guns. Everything happened so fast..."

"How tall were they? How much did they weigh? Did they have accents? Could you see their hands, get an idea of race?" He knew he sounded like a bully, firing questions at the upset woman, but he couldn't help himself. In situations like this, gathering as much evidence as possible as quickly as possible could make the difference between life and death.

Fresh tears spilled from Chelsea's eyes and she shook her head again. "I'm sorry. I don't know. I was so focused on Ian and the guns. And then they hit me." She began to sob, and Andrea pulled her close.

"Why would someone do something like this?" Andrea asked. "How did they know I had a child? Have they been following me for a while now?"

Jack considered the questions. "This doesn't make sense as a kidnapping." He tapped the note. "For one thing, the ransom is too low. Kidnappers ask for millions of dollars, not a few thousand."

"They must have known I don't have millions," Andrea said.

"Maybe this doesn't have anything to do with you," Chelsea said. "Maybe they got their houses mixed up. You see that on TV sometimes. What do they call them—home invasions."

"Maybe." Jack reread the note. "But I don't think so. How long would you say they were in the house?"

Chelsea frowned, concentrating. "I don't know. They burst in and knocked me out right away. They were here long enough to tie me up and put me in the bathroom.

After I woke up, I spent a half hour or more crawling down the hall, trying to get to the phone."

"It sounds to me as if this was planned," Jack said. "They came in fast and hard, took out Chelsea, grabbed the boy and left. They didn't kill Chelsea, though they easily could have, and they left her baby alone. They wanted Ian." His eyes met Andrea's. "And they wanted you to cooperate. They knew taking your son would make you do whatever they wanted."

"But why me?" she asked. "I've never hurt anyone in my life."

"Your husband was a cop," Jack said. "Maybe he made enemies. It could be someone he put in prison. They're out now and seeking revenge."

"Preston has been dead three years. Anything they do to me or Ian now doesn't touch him. These people would be taking a lot of risk for nothing."

He nodded. While he'd learned not to discount some people's drive for revenge or the irrational ways evil people could act, this didn't feel like that kind of situation. The note hadn't mentioned Andrea's husband at all.

But it had mentioned her "boyfriend." "Maybe whoever did this was trying to get to me," he said.

"To you?" Confusion clouded her eyes. "But, Jack, I hardly know you. We just met."

"I can't prove it yet, but I think the man I saw in the restaurant this afternoon is connected to a case I've been working on. He may have seen the two of us together and assumed a relationship. He stole your purse in order to learn where you live. He may even have meant to kidnap you and send the ransom note to me, but when they found Ian instead, they decided to use him."

"That's crazy," Chelsea said.

"It is. But this group has done this kind of thing before." Months before, Duane Braeswood and his men had kidnapped the sister of a woman who worked for the head of the Senate Committee on Homeland Security. They had threatened to kill the sister if the woman, Leah Carlisle, didn't cooperate with them. Once Leah was in their power, they had killed her sister and held Leah hostage for six months. Search Team Seven had rescued her in the same raid in which Gus had been killed. "They know that most people will do almost anything to save their loved ones, more than they would do, even, to save themselves."

"But I'm not your loved one," Andrea said. "I'm just an acquaintance you had lunch with."

"No. But I'm not going to turn my back on you when you need my help." And he cared about her. And Ian, too. In the short time he had known them, they had worked their way into a corner of his heart.

She looked away. "I don't have anyone else I can call," she said. "Not anyone who would be safe. If you can pretend to be my boyfriend until we get through this…" She let her voice trail away, as if she thought she were asking too much.

"I'm not going to leave your side until we're through this." He gripped her shoulder again. "You've got to be strong now. For Ian."

She sat up straighter and took a ragged breath. "What do we do now?" she asked.

"Can you get ten thousand dollars together?"

"I can take it out of my savings as soon as the bank opens in the morning."

"Let's wait until the kidnappers call with instructions. Right now, you can't stay here tonight."

"No." She hugged her arms across her chest and shivered.

He turned to Chelsea. "What about you?"

"I want to go home to my husband. I haven't told him about any of this yet. I'd rather do it face-to-face."

"He'll want to call the police." Andrea clutched Chelsea's hand. "You have to convince him to keep quiet."

"I will," Chelsea said. "He won't like it, but he won't want anything to happen to Ian, either."

Jack stood and walked to the phone on the wall. "What are you doing?' Andrea asked. "Who are you calling?"

"I'm forwarding this number to my cell phone. That way you can come with me and we won't miss a call from the kidnappers."

"The note says they have someone watching me," Andrea said. "Maybe we shouldn't leave the house."

"They think I'm your boyfriend. They won't be alarmed if you come with me." At least, he hoped that was the case.

Andrea packed an overnight bag and Chelsea retrieved the baby's car seat from her vehicle. "My husband can bring me by to get my car later," she said. "I'm too scared to drive home alone right now."

"I don't mind taking you home. And I'll talk to your husband, too. I'll persuade him to keep quiet."

Chelsea's husband turned out to be a burly mechanic who worked for the local Ford dealer. He listened to the story Chelsea told with growing signs of alarm. When she got to the part about needing to keep quiet, he started shaking his head.

Jack stepped forward. "Mr. Green, I'm with the FBI," he said. He opened his ID folder to show his badge and credentials. "I'm going to be doing everything I can to get Ian back to his mother safely, and for that, I need your cooperation."

"FBI!" Chelsea gasped. "Andrea, you didn't tell me he was a fed."

Andrea said nothing, her face pale and drawn. She looked as if the slightest breeze might make her collapse. Jack resisted the urge to gather her close and hold her tightly. "Will you promise not to contact police and not to say anything to anyone—coworkers, friends, relatives, anyone—until this is resolved?" he asked.

Mr. Green nodded. "Sure. I'll keep quiet. I didn't know the FBI was involved."

Not officially, Jack thought. *Not yet.*

They drove in silence to his apartment. Andrea made no protest when he took her arm and guided her up the stairs to the furnished unit he had rented when the team relocated to Durango the month before. The television still broadcast the ball game, the sound turned down low, and the harsh overhead light illuminated the wrappings from the sub sandwich and chips that had been his dinner.

"The bedroom is back this way," he said, steering her toward the short hallway that led to the unit's single bedroom and adjoining bathroom. "You can sleep here. I'll take the couch."

Covers spilled onto the floor, silent testimony to

a restless night. The pillow still bore the imprint of his head. He rushed forward to jerk the comforter into place. "I'll get some clean sheets," he said, moving past her.

"You don't have to go to all this trouble," she said, her hand on his arm. "I can take the sofa."

"No, it's okay."

He found the sheets, and together they made the bed, an ordinary, intimate activity that broke some of the tension between them. "Do you have a washer and dryer?" she asked, gathering up the old linens. "I can wash these."

"I'll get them later." He took the mound of sheets from her and stuffed them into the closet behind him. "Can I get you anything else? Tea? Bourbon?"

A smile flickered across her lips. "The latter is tempting, but I want to keep a clear head."

"Try to get some sleep." He hesitated, then reached out and squeezed her shoulder. She leaned her cheek against his hand, her skin silky and warm, and no man with feelings would have been able to resist pulling her to him.

She welcomed the gesture and snuggled against him, her head buried in the hollow of his shoulder. "I'm so afraid," she whispered. "If they hurt Ian…"

"Shh." He cradled the back of her head, his fingers threaded through her hair, which was coming loose from the pins that held it atop her head. He removed the pins one by one and combed out her locks with his fingers. She sighed and settled against him more firmly, so that he was aware of the soft weight of her breasts against his chest and the vanilla-and-honey perfume of her hair. He wanted to bury his face in those silky tresses—and bury the rest of himself in her, as well.

She raised her head and tilted her face up to his, her expression questioning. "Why do I feel so safe and comfortable with you?" she asked.

"Because you are safe with me." He stroked her cheek, silken and warm. "I'm not going to do anything to hurt you."

"Kiss me." She whispered the words, but they had the force of a command. One he was all too ready to obey.

Her lips were as soft and supple as he had imagined, and she responded to the gentle pressure of his mouth by rising up on her toes and angling her head to deepen the contact. This was no meek surrender to his will, but the urgent encouragement of a partner who wasn't afraid to take the lead. She traced her tongue along his bottom lip and he opened to her and shifted to snug her body between his thighs, letting her feel how much he wanted her.

She was the first to break contact, looking up at him with heavy-lidded eyes. "That was as amazing as I thought it might be," she said. "Thank you."

"I'm the one who should be thanking you."

She gently moved out of his embrace. "That was very selfish of me," she said. "I was feeling so helpless and lost… I thought if I kissed you then, just for a moment, I could forget how terrible everything is."

He rubbed his hand up and down her upper arm, as much to avoid breaking contact with her as to comfort her. "Did it help?"

Her eyes met his, the desire he'd seen there only a moment before edged out by sadness. "It did. But it doesn't change our situation." She stepped back, putting space between them. "I'm not trying to lead you on. I think I'm so stressed and upset, and I've been on my own so long…" She shook her head. "It's like my emotions have gone all haywire."

"You don't have to apologize for anything." He understood her more than she would probably believe. The combination of stress and many months of living alone had no doubt intensified his desire for her, but that didn't explain the tenderness beneath the lust, and the fierce desire to make things right for her. He wanted to return her son safely to her, and he wanted to see her smiling and happy again.

"We're going to find Ian," he said. "Hold on to that thought." He turned away. "Try to get some sleep." All he wanted was to crawl into that bed with her and hold her all night long, but she'd probably misinterpret his actions, think he was taking advantage of her vulnerability. If he was going to help her, she had to trust him, and that meant letting her dictate the pace of their relationship. So, while he wanted to stay, he made himself leave the room and shut the door quietly behind him.

ANDREA DIDN'T KNOW how long she stood where Jack left her, clinging to the memory of his warmth and strength. How long had it been since a man had touched her with such tenderness? She had savored the feeling, even as shame lurked in the background, mocking her for enjoying even a minute while her son was in danger. But she'd needed those few moments in Jack's arms to pull herself together and to gather her own strength to keep from breaking down. Though the urge to collapse onto the bed and give in to the sobs that pressed at the back of her throat almost overwhelmed her, doing so wouldn't bring Ian back to her.

She went into the bathroom and washed her face and brushed her teeth, then returned to the bedroom and contemplated the freshly made bed. No way would she sleep tonight, not with thoughts of her boy, frightened and with strangers, haunting her.

She went into the living room and found Jack seated on the sofa, a laptop opened on the table in front of him. He had turned off the TV and a cup of coffee steamed at his right hand. He looked up when she moved into the light. "I couldn't sleep," she said, and sat beside him.

"I figure we're both in for a long night," he said. "Would you like some coffee? I just made it."

"Maybe in a minute." She nodded to the laptop. "Are you looking for the purse snatcher?"

"Yes." He shrank the screen and picked up the coffee cup. "No luck so far, but I'm just getting started."

"I don't mean to keep you from your work." She sat back and grabbed a small throw pillow to hug across her stomach. "I promise not to look."

"I'll take a break for a few minutes." He sipped the coffee and neither of them said anything for a long moment. The refrigerator hummed in the small kitchen behind her, and somewhere below, a car door slammed.

"Why did you call me tonight?" he asked.

A reasonable question, but one she wasn't sure she could answer. "I don't know. I wasn't even thinking. I guess…you're an FBI agent. And you knew Ian. Or at least, you met him and talked to him." She looked at him, the truth of her next words making her a little shaky. "I believed you could save him." But why would she believe such a thing about a man she scarcely knew? Still, she couldn't shake the conviction that if anyone could help her, it was Jack. The stubbornness and commitment and need for control that had struck her as negative traits in her office now stood out as exactly the characteristics needed to fight the evil responsible for her son's disappearance.

"I'll do everything I can to get him back to you," he said.

She forced herself to stand on shaky legs. "I think I'll have some of that coffee now."

When she returned from the kitchen, he was focused on the computer once more. She moved around the room, then studied the few books on a shelf by the door—an acclaimed biography of Theodore Roosevelt, a guide to Colorado's Weminuche Wilderness, a few thriller novels and a thick treatise on the history of terrorism. A single photograph graced the shelf by the books: two men, dressed in hiking gear and standing side by side atop a mountain, beaming at the camera. If she had to guess, she would say the man next to Jack in the photo was his friend Gus, the one whose death tormented him.

"I think I've got something," Jack said.

She hurried to the sofa, scooting close to him to study the picture on the computer screen. A man looked back at her from a grainy black-and-white photo. "It's from a surveillance camera," Jack said. "Not the best quality, but good enough I can recognize him. This is the guy in the restaurant—the one who stole your purse."

She leaned forward and squinted at the image. It was of a white man, fairly young, with light brown hair and a sharp nose. But nothing about him looked familiar. She shook her head. "I don't recognize him. But I wasn't really paying attention in the restaurant and his back was to me."

"That's all right," Jack said. "I got a good look at him and this is the guy." He clicked to the next screen and she read the name there. Anderson.

"Is that a first or a last name?" she asked.

"We don't know." Jack scanned the few lines of information under the name. "We don't know a lot, but we suspect he's connected to a terrorist cell we've been tracking here in Colorado."

"Terrorists? You think Ian has been kidnapped by terrorists?" The knowledge refused to sink in. What would terrorists want with her little boy? Tears stung her eyes. Where was Ian now? What were they doing to him? If they hurt him…

Jack gripped her hand, pulling her back from the nightmare of horror she was capable of imagining. "We're going to find them, and we're going to get Ian back," he said.

She nodded, struggling for control. "Yes." That belief was the only life preserver she had. "We're going to get him back."

Jack turned to stare at the picture on the computer screen once more, and when he spoke, his voice was colder and harder than she had imagined it could be. "Tomorrow Anderson and his friends will be sorry they ever messed with me."

Chapter Four

The call came at 6:13 a.m., forwarded from Andrea's home phone to Jack's cell. He sat up on the sofa, where he'd fallen into an exhausted doze sometime after three, and snatched up the phone as the last notes of "What It's Like" sounded. "Hello?"

"Agent Prescott. Are you alone?"

The voice wasn't familiar, and the echoing quality of it made Jack suspect it was being filtered electronically to disguise it. "Andrea is here with me, but no one else."

"Good. Let me talk to Dr. McNeil."

Andrea was already standing in the doorway to the bedroom, staring at him with equal parts hope and dread. Jack held the phone out to her. "It's him. Or somebody with him."

She pressed the phone to her ear, clutching it with both hands. "Hello? Is Ian all right? Please let me speak to Ian."

"Your son is safe. For now. Do you have the money we asked for?"

"I'm going to the bank to get it as soon as they open. I don't keep that kind of cash in the house."

"That's fine. You haven't told anyone about what happened?"

"Only Jack. And my babysitter and her husband know, but only because she was there when he was taken. She doesn't remember much and we made them both swear not to tell." The words came in a rush, all her anxiety translated to speech. She wanted these men to know she was cooperating with them. She would do anything to see her son safe.

"Good. I'm going to give you an address. Write this down."

"Hold on. I need paper and a pen." She motioned and Jack thrust a notepad and pen into her hand. She copied down the address the man dictated and read it back to him. "Where is this?" she asked. "It doesn't sound like Durango."

"It isn't. But I'm sure you can find it. Bring the money to this address by noon today. Agent Prescott can come with you, but no one else. If we even suspect police or FBI or anyone else is around, we'll slit Ian's throat and let him bleed to death right in front of you." He ended the call.

Andrea sank to the floor, her legs no longer able to support her. Jack lowered himself beside her and pulled her close. "I heard," he said. "He's trying to intimidate and frighten you."

"It's working." She covered her mouth with her hand in a vain attempt to stifle her sobs. "My poor baby."

Jack let her cry for a minute or so. Then he held her away from him and shook her gently. "Come on. We've got work to do. We're going to get Ian back today. Focus on that."

She nodded and sucked in a shaky breath. "Okay. What do we need to do?"

"Take a shower and get dressed. I'll make more coffee. Then we'll plan our strategy."

When Andrea emerged from the bedroom fifteen minutes later, showered and wearing fresh clothes, Jack handed her a cup of black coffee. "I've decided I should go by myself to meet these people," he said. "This smells of a trap and there's no need to put you in danger when I'm the one they really want."

"My son is in danger. There's no way I'm not going with you to get him." Her eyes blazed and her face had taken on some color for the first time in hours.

He hadn't really thought he could convince her to stay behind, but he felt he had to try. He nodded and picked up a gun from the kitchen table and handed it to her. "Then you'll need this." She stared at the compact weapon, matte black and deadly looking.

"It's a Beretta Storm," he said, pulling the slide back to reveal an empty chamber. "Nine millimeter, double- or single-action trigger, ambidextrous safety." He placed the gun in her hand. "Do you know how to shoot?"

She nodded. "Preston took me to the range and made sure I was competent."

"Good." He nodded toward the box of ammo on the table. "Load it, and be ready to use it if you have to, though I hope you don't have to."

He pulled out his Glock and checked the load. The last time he had fired the weapon was the day Gus died.

"Preston had a Glock like that," she said. "I still have it in the gun safe at home."

He holstered the weapon again. "We could be walking into a trap," he said. "We're going to have to be on our guard."

She nodded. "We have to find the address first."

He picked up the notepad with the scrawled address and walked to the laptop on the coffee table. A few minutes of searching online and he came up with a location. "It's about twenty-five miles out of town, near the community of Bayfield. Do you know it?"

She sat next to him and laid the now-loaded weapon beside the computer, the barrel facing away from them. "I've driven through it a few times. From what I remember, there isn't much there—a few houses, maybe a gas station. I guess the kidnappers chose it because it's remote and probably not very busy this time of year."

"Let's see if we can get a look at it." He pulled up Google Earth and keyed in the address. By zooming in and maneuvering the mouse, he was able to get a bird's-eye view of a cluster of buildings alongside a river. "Pine River," he read. "This address looks like a fishing camp."

He switched to Street View and studied the image of what appeared to be boarded up buildings. The image had been captured in the summer and showed a dirt road leading into the property, and the surrounding woods. "It's a pretty good setup," he said. "The river protects them on one side and there are dense stands of trees on the other sides. It's well hidden from the road, and from the looks of the place, no one has lived there for years."

"If we drive in there, we'll be trapped," she said.

"We're not going to drive," he said. "At least, not right away. We're going to park some distance away and hike in cross-country. And we're going to do it long before noon. I want a look at this place and whoever is there before they expect us."

"I just realized the man on the phone referred to you as Agent Prescott. How did he know your name?"

"Because I'm the one they're really after." He looked at her. "If things go bad out there, I want you to take Ian and run, as far and as fast as you can. Don't worry about me."

Her eyes shone with tears and her face was the color of paper. She nodded. "I don't want to leave you," she said. "But I have to save Ian."

"We'll need to dress warm, with good boots and warm coats, hats and gloves," he said. "We can swing by your house on the way to the bank and get what you need. The weather forecast is calling for a major storm cell to move into the area by afternoon."

"The bank opens at nine," she said. "If we leave here at eight thirty, we can go to my house, then the bank, and leave from there. I can change shoes in the truck on the way down."

Now that the pressure was on, she had pulled herself together and was all business. "You would have made a good cop," he said.

Her expressive face revealed anger and pain. "I know you probably mean that as a compliment," she said. "But I don't see it that way." She picked up the gun again and stood. "I'll be ready to go when you are."

THE FIRST FLAKES of snow began to fall as they moved away from Jack's truck. They had parked the vehicle off the road, hidden by a thick stand of juniper, to the west of the fishing camp. It had taken almost an hour to reach the camp from Durango, the last thirty minutes on a winding snow-packed road that crossed and recrossed the Pine River. "We've got to hike about two miles," Jack said. "We'll have to find a place where we can watch the camp without being seen."

Andrea pulled down the knit cap on her head and checked that the gun was secure at the small of her back beneath her winter coat. She hoped she wouldn't have to fire it, but she would if it meant saving Ian. "I'm ready," she said.

Jack led the way into the snowy woodland. He moved swiftly but silently, sinking to his shins in snow with each step. Andrea tried to follow in his tracks but was soon out of breath and sweating beneath her layers of clothing. As the snow began to fall harder, she told herself this was a good thing. The storm would keep everyone at the camp inside and the snow would help muffle the sound of their approach.

After they'd walked for half an hour or so, Jack stopped. Andrea moved up beside him and looked down on the river some ten feet below. Ice rimmed the frothing brown water. "If we walk along the riverbank from here, we should come to the camp," he said.

She shivered, as much from fear of what lay ahead as from the cold soaking through her clothing. Jack pressed something into her hand—the key to his truck. "Do you think you can make it with Ian back to my truck by yourself?" he asked.

She stared up at him. "You're coming with us, aren't you?"

"I plan to. But just in case something happens—can you find your way by yourself?"

She folded her hand over the key, then slid it into her coat pocket. "I can do it. I follow the river, then turn left. That will eventually take me to the road. Your truck is parked just past the telephone pole with the sign tacked to it about a farm auction next month."

Jack clapped her shoulder. "Good job, remembering that sign."

"How's your leg?" she asked. All this hard hiking couldn't be good for his wounds.

"I'm fine. Don't worry about me." He turned away and started walking again before she could say anything else.

When he stopped again, she could make out the corner of a building maybe fifty yards ahead, the wood siding painted dark green, icicles hanging from the metal roof. Jack dropped to his knees and motioned for her to do likewise.

Snow soaked into her jeans and wet the cuffs of her coat as she crawled along behind Jack. She couldn't see anything from this height other than snow and Jack himself ahead of her. Then the undergrowth receded and they were in the clearing, behind a building. At the corner of the structure, Jack stood, his weapon drawn. She rose also, her back to the building, heart thudding painfully.

Jack peered around the side of the building. "What do you see?" she whispered.

"Nothing," he said. "But there are a lot of buildings here. We're going to have to get closer if we're going to find Ian."

The camp looked deserted, the windows in the cabins boarded up, the sign that read Office on one building hanging crooked from a single nail. But the tire tracks in the packed snow of the drive looked fresh, and the smell of wood smoke mingled with the scents of pine trees.

There were nine cabins overall, eight arranged in a half circle, with the office, a larger structure that looked as if it had once contained a residence as well as a store, sitting to one side, nearest the narrow drive that led from the main road. A rusting metal arch marked the entrance to the camp, the sign hanging from the top unreadable from Jack's position.

He waited, ears straining to hear any sound beyond the whistle of wind through the trees. The cabin they were standing behind was probably empty. In the five minutes or so they had been standing here, he hadn't heard any sounds from inside. If someone had so much as walked around in there, he and Andrea would have known about it.

Behind him, Andrea shifted her weight from foot to foot, feet crunching on the snow. He checked his watch. A few minutes past ten thirty. If Anderson or whoever he worked for was planning an ambush, they were probably already in place. They'd done a good job concealing themselves, though it would be easy enough to take up positions in the cabins and wait for Jack and Andrea to drive into the yard. Then the kidnappers could converge and take them prisoner or simply open fire and kill them before they had a chance to act.

Well, that wasn't going to happen. He was going to find Anderson and whoever else was here before they found him. But first he needed to know where they were keeping Ian.

He turned and leaned toward Andrea, his mouth against her ear. The vanilla-and-honey scent of her seemed out of place in the midst of danger, but it made him more determined than ever to save her son and get her out of harm's way as quickly as possible. "We're going to have to search the cabins," he whispered. "We'll approach from the back and listen for sounds of movement inside. If we don't hear anything from any of them, we'll have to try to get a look inside somehow, by prying the boards off the back window or something."

She nodded.

"I'll go first," he said. "When I give the signal, you run to me."

He checked the area again. Still no sign of life. He took a deep breath, blew it out, then made a dash for the next cabin in line.

Cursing his throbbing leg, he leaned against the side of the building, waiting for his heart to slow and his breath to grow more even. No signs of movement in the yard. He looked toward Andrea and nodded. She didn't hesitate but raced toward him.

The back of the cabin contained a single boarded-up window. Jack pressed his ear to the plywood and Andrea did the same. She closed her eyes as she listened, so he took advantage of the moment to study her. Blueish half-moons beneath her eyes testified to her sleepless night, and tension traced fine lines around her mouth. Snow dusted the top of her head and the shoulders of her coat, and as he watched, a shiver ran through her. But she hadn't uttered a word of complaint.

She opened her eyes, and the sadness of her expression pulled at him. "I don't hear anything," she whispered.

He shook his head and indicated that they should move on to the next cabin.

Once again, they pressed their ears to the boarded-up back window and listened. Andrea's eyes widened as the low rumble of male voice reached them. Jack nodded and strained to make out the words. "Better...kid... boss..." Frowning, he drew back. Whoever was speaking was in the cabin's front room, too far away to be heard clearly. He pulled Andrea away from the building.

"I'm going around to the side," he said. "There's another window there. If I can hear their conversation, that might help us find Ian and figure out the best way to get to him."

"I'll go with you," she said.

"No. It's too dangerous. Anyone walking by the front of the cabin could see us."

"Two sets of ears are better than one," she said. "Besides, I think we'll both be safer if we stick together."

He didn't have time to waste arguing with her, and maybe she had a point. "All right. Let's go before they leave the cabin."

Two windows looked out from the side of the cabin. Jack led the way to the front window and crouched low beside it. Andrea moved in close behind him, bracing herself with one hand on his back. Her touch reminded him that there was more at stake with this mission than perhaps any other he had undertaken. He pressed his ear to the bottom of the plywood that covered the window.

"Where are they? Shouldn't they be here by now?"

The speaker's voice was high and thin, with a flat Midwestern accent.

"It's not even eleven. They'll be here." The second speaker had a deeper, rougher voice, with no identifiable accent.

"This snow might slow them down. The radio said there's a winter storm warning."

"It's just a little snow. If they want to see their kid, they'll be here."

"We can't screw this up. Not after what happened last time." Footsteps followed these words, as if the first man had begun to pace.

"You and I don't have to worry about that. We'll blame the kid getting away on Leo."

Andrea lurched against him. Jack reached out a hand to steady her and squeezed her arm.

"That's not going to happen with this one," the first speaker said. "I told Leo not to let this one out of his sight."

"He's only what, five?" the second man said. "The other one was practically a grown man. We should have been more careful."

"It doesn't matter. His old man wasn't cooperating anyway. I say we tell the boss he was causing trouble and we finished him off. It's not like he's going to make us show him a body."

"I wouldn't put it past him. He doesn't overlook details like that."

"So we do a good job with the fed and he doesn't worry about anything else," the first man said.

"When they get here, I get first shot at the fed," the

gravel-voiced man said. "In the gut, so that he dies slowly."

"Don't make a mess," the first man said. "We have to haul the body out of here. I don't want blood all over the car."

"I'm not worried about your car. If you had been thinking at all, you would have got a van. We wouldn't have to worry about anyone seeing inside one of those."

"There's no one out here to see into anything," the first man said. "What about the woman and the kid? What are we going to do with them?"

"What do you think?" Gravel Voice said.

"I ain't killing no little kid."

Andrea's fingers dug into Jack's back.

"I'll do it, then. Or Leo will do it. He already has orders to silence the kid if Prescott and the woman bring anybody else with them."

"As long as I don't have to do it," the first man said.

"We don't have a choice. He knows what we look like. We can't afford to leave him behind."

"The woman is pretty," the first man said. "We ought to keep her around for a little while."

"It's just like you to think that way. We haven't got time. The boss wants all of those feds out of the way."

"You mean Roland wants them out of the way," the first man said. "I'm not so sure the boss even knows what's going on. I think Roland is calling all the shots these days."

"You had better not let anyone else hear you say that—especially Roland."

"How much longer do we have to stay out here in the middle of nowhere? I'm ready to get back to the city."

"When the big job goes down, we'll be a part of that."

"Yeah, well, I've been hearing that for a while now and I ain't seen any sign that anything is going to happen. I think Roland and the rest of that bunch are just stringing us along."

"You're wrong," Gravel Voice said. "It would have happened before now if it wasn't for those feds. That's why what we're doing is so important. We get rid of them and the rest of the plan can be executed."

"Listen to you and your five-dollar words." The pacing stopped. "All right, let's go. I don't want Prescott and that woman sneaking into camp when we're not looking."

"They won't get past the traps we set," Gravel Voice said. "We'll know if they try to get in." Footsteps moved toward the door.

Jack grabbed Andrea's arm and they raced to the cover of the woods behind the cabin. The front door slammed and he caught a glimpse of two men moving away.

Neither of them said anything for a long moment as they caught their breath. Finally, Andrea leaned toward him. "What traps?" she asked.

Jack shook his head. "I don't know. Either he was bluffing, or we got lucky and didn't set off anything. I think the other man, the one with the higher voice, was Anderson, the man we saw in the restaurant."

"He mentioned seeing me before." A shudder ran through her. Jack pushed down his own revulsion at the man and his proposal to keep Andrea alive for a while longer than the others. He couldn't deny that emotion added urgency to his desire to stop these men, but he couldn't let feelings guide him. He had to think coldly and logically and rely on his training.

"They were holding a child here before Ian," Andrea said. "And he got away."

"Not a little boy like Ian," Jack said. "They said this one was 'almost a grown man.' So a teenager." He frowned. "No one has reported a missing child in the area. Our office would have heard."

"Maybe the child wasn't from here," Andrea said.

"The names of missing children are in a national database. Still, we don't know when this happened."

"They talked as if they had been here awhile," she said. "Who is Roland?"

"Roland is part of the suspected terrorist cell we've been tracking." Roland had been Duane Braeswood's right-hand man, but it sounded as if, with Braeswood's injuries, he might be taking a more prominent role. Jack filed the information away to share with the team. "I can call in my team," he said. "They could be here in less than an hour and they've got the manpower and equipment to surround this place."

"No! You heard what they said—if anyone else shows up, they'll kill Ian."

"We'd have a plan to prevent that. I could move in right away to protect him."

"I won't take that kind of chance with my son." She gripped his arm, her fingers digging in. "I'm really afraid of these people," she said. "Not just for Ian's sake, but for yours. They hate you."

"Most of the people we hunt down hate us. That doesn't stop us."

"I knew the people Preston was trying to stop were

terrible, and I thought I understood that they were dangerous. But I never met them or saw them, so the danger was always more abstract." She hugged herself. "This is so much more real and frightening."

"They're just people," he said. "They're not smarter or stronger or luckier than us. Don't underestimate them, but don't make them bigger than they are."

She took a deep breath and nodded. "You're right. That makes sense. What do we do now?"

"We need to figure out where they're hiding Ian, and we need to determine if anyone else is in the camp."

"They mentioned someone named Leo," she said. "It sounds as if he's with Ian."

"There may just be the three of them. If so, the odds aren't so bad. But we can't assume anything. We need to be sure."

The two men who had been speaking had moved in the direction of the office, so he and Andrea continued down the row of cabins, pausing to listen at each one. But all were silent and seemingly empty. After another twenty minutes or so, they reached the last cabin in line. Smaller than the others, it was also farthest from the entrance. The kidnappers might have chosen it as the best place to keep Ian for these reasons.

Jack paused by the back window and sniffed the damp air. "Do you smell that?" he asked.

"What?" Andrea tilted her head back and sniffed also.

"Wood smoke. It's stronger here. As if someone had a fire in the woodstove recently." He stepped back and looked up at the black stovepipe that jutted from the roof. No smoke curled from it, but the odor in the chill air told him it might have, and recently.

They pressed their ears to the plywood over the back window, tensed. Jack listened to the roaring of his own pulse. After a long moment Andrea's shoulders slumped and she shook her head. "I don't hear—"

Thump!

They both jumped and Andrea covered her mouth to stifle a cry. She stared at the window, then pressed her ear to the plywood once more. The sound came again. *Thump! Thump! Thump!*

"Hey! Knock it off, kid. Be still in there!" The man's voice was broad and nasal, definitely not either of the two men they had overheard earlier. It was a good bet they had found Leo.

Andrea practically vibrated with tension. She hugged Jack to her, then released him. *What do we do now?* she mouthed.

They could burst into the cabin and try to overpower whoever was in there with the boy—if Ian really was the one making those noises—but they risked being trapped if Anderson and Gravel Voice came running. And they still weren't certain there weren't other men in the camp. He pulled Andrea away from the cabin, back into the woods, where they could talk with less chance of being overheard.

"We need to find out for certain how many people we're up against," he said.

Her gaze darted back to the cabin. Her focus now was on her son. "How do we do that?"

He needed a way to draw them out without endangering Ian or Andrea. The scent of wood smoke tickled his nose, giving him an idea. "If we set one of the empty cabins on fire, that will draw them out," he said. "While they're distracted, we'll run in and grab Ian."

She frowned. "How are we going to set anything on fire when it's snowing?"

"We need an accelerant. Gasoline or kerosene or something like that."

"Where are we going to get that?"

"There might be some up by the office. It looks like it used to be a store. We'll need matches or a lighter, too."

"Why can't we just go in, grab Ian and get out of here? We both have guns, and if we're fast, we'll be gone before whoever is in there guarding him can call for help."

"We still have to make it back to my truck without them catching us," he said. "We can't exactly move quickly in this rough country, in the snow, carrying a child. They might cut us off or corner us."

"What if they do that now, before we can get to Ian?"

"If we can't find what we need to start a fire, then we may very well have to grab him and make a run for it. But let's try it my way first."

She sighed. "All right."

"You stay here," he said. "I'll check the office. If I find what I need, I'll start the fire. As soon as Ian's guard leaves, you go in and get Ian. But be ready to shoot if you run into a second guard."

"What do I do if I see someone heading your way?" she asked.

If this were an FBI operation, they would have radio communication, but Andrea hadn't even had time to replace the cell phone Anderson had stolen. "Stay out of sight," he said. "Look after yourself and Ian. I'll watch out for myself."

He retraced his route behind the row of cabins. The snow was falling harder now, a white curtain over the landscape. The compound remained empty and silent save for the soft crunch of their footsteps. He would be able to hear a car approaching in the storm, if reinforcements showed up in anticipation of Jack and Andrea's scheduled arrival with the ransom money.

Like the other buildings in the camp, the office was a simple rectangular board-and-batten structure with a small front porch, a metal roof and boarded-up windows. But this building was twice as large as the others and boasted a back entrance in addition to the front door. Jack hoped this back door led to a storeroom where he could find the materials he needed for starting a fire.

The steps leading to the back door had long since rotted away, but someone had positioned a plastic milk crate on the ground below the threshold, which enabled Jack to reach the doorknob. The door was locked, but the mechanism was cheap and flimsy. He took out his pocketknife and had the lock open in less than a minute.

As soon as the door was open, Jack slipped inside and closed it again. The interior of the building was black and smelled of mouse and mold. He waited, his back to the door, and allowed his eyes to adjust to the dimness. After a few minutes he could make out the bulky shapes of stacked boxes and old furniture. A second, closed door must lead into the main part of the building. He pressed his ear to it and listened. Nothing.

Confident that he was alone, Jack risked switching

on the flashlight on his phone. He played the beam across the piled junk in the storeroom: a sagging upholstered armchair, a leaning stack of yellowing newspapers, a table with a broken leg, some old flowerpots, a case of bottled water and another of chicken noodle soup, several unlabeled cardboard boxes, and a shelving unit filled with canned goods—some of them so old the labels were barely legible.

No gas cans. No cans of kerosene. Treading carefully, Jack moved over to the canned-goods shelf. He scanned the items there—mostly beans and canned peaches or tomatoes. But on the bottom shelf he found a gallon container of cooking oil. If he let the oil soak into the dry wood of one of the cabins, he might be able to get a good blaze going in spite of the damp.

He picked up the oil and flinched when a mouse raced out from behind it. Heart pounding, he searched the shelves for matches or a lighter. Behind a box of assorted fishing flies he found a butane lighter, the long-handled kind used to light campfires or candles. Perfect.

He pocketed the lighter, switched off the flashlight and stowed the phone, then picked up the cooking oil. He stopped beside the pile of newspapers and stuffed a few under his jacket to use as kindling. Andrea was probably wondering what had happened to him. He hoped she was staying put and not attempting anything rash. She struck him as a controlled, reasonable woman, but a mother whose child was in danger had plenty of reasons to set aside caution.

Outside once more, the cold wind hit him with a force that made him grit his teeth and hunch against the onslaught. His leg throbbed from the dampness and his recent exertions. A hot blaze was going to feel good, though he wouldn't have time to enjoy it.

He stopped at the corner of the office and thus the most distant point from the building where Ian was being held. Or at least, they had assumed the thumping noise came from Ian. Assumptions were dangerous in his business, but what other "kid" would Anderson and his men be keeping prisoner out here?

What about the boy or teenager or whoever he was they had alluded to earlier? The two men they overheard said he had escaped, but where had he gone? And why hadn't the FBI heard anything about this?

He dropped the container of cooking oil at the back corner of the building and wadded the papers against the foundation, sheltering them from the snowfall as best he could with his body. When he was satisfied with the arrangement, he uncapped the bottle of oil and splashed it onto the side of the building. The siding, even damp from the storm, sucked up the oil, which smelled rancid, as if it had sat in that storeroom for many years. Careful not to get any oil on himself, Jack emptied the bottle, tossed it aside, then pulled out the lighter.

"Don't make another move, Agent Prescott, or I'll blow a hole through your guts."

Chapter Five

Andrea's stomach churned with nerves as she waited for something to happen. Would Jack really be able to set a fire in all this snow? Would he even find anything to start a blaze with? And if he did, would she be able to get inside the cabin and rescue Ian before someone spotted her?

She drew the gun from the back of her jeans and eased off the safety. Then she pressed her ear to the plywood covering the window and listened. Someone was moving around in there—someone a lot bigger than Ian, from the sound of it. What had they done to her poor baby? Was he tied up? Gagged?

She took a deep breath. No time to panic here. She could be furious about all this later. Right now she had to be calm. Cold as ice. She was a woman on a mission to save her son and she couldn't afford to think about anything else.

What was taking Jack so long? She had expected flames by now. Shouting. Slamming doors. People running to put out the fire. At the very least, she expected Jack to come back and tell her they were going to have to go to plan B, whatever that was.

Still holding the gun with both hands, stiff-armed

and pointed at the ground the way she'd seen on TV, she crept to the other end of the building. She had to move out a few steps in order to see the first cabin in line. Something shifted in the curtain of snow. Then Jack stepped out of the shadows beside the building.

And another man, dressed in the kind of camouflage coveralls hunters sometimes wore, a stocking cap pulled low over his forehead, stepped out behind Jack. Andrea gasped and started toward them, then thought better of it. The last thing she wanted was for Jack's captor to spot her. She shrank back against the building. *Think!* she ordered her brain, which had frozen in fear, like a streamed movie stuck buffering.

There was still someone moving around in the cabin with Ian. So the man with Jack was probably one of the two men they had overheard earlier—or maybe he was a fourth man. There might be any number of people hidden in the other cabins or in the woods nearby. Her stomach churned at the idea and she forced it from her mind. Right now she needed to get closer to Jack and his captor and try to figure things out. At least that way she could find out where they were taking Jack.

Keeping close to the cabins and moving as quickly and quietly as possible, she crept toward the office building. She stopped at the corner of the last cabin before the office and her stomach plummeted as Jack's captor prodded him up onto the office's front porch and in through the door. Raised voices sounded from the office—at least two men in addition to Jack, who, as far as she could determine, wasn't talking.

Two men in the office, plus one person in the cabin with Ian—three people besides her and Jack in the camp. Were there more in the other cabins? They hadn't bothered to show themselves. Maybe while the two in the office were dealing with Jack, she should bust into the end cabin, shoot the guy with Ian and rescue her son.

And leave Jack to die? Nausea rose in her throat at the thought. She flipped the safety back on the gun, stuffed it in the waistband of her jeans and pushed a wet lock of hair out of her eyes. At least all this cold was shocking her out of the stupor she'd slipped into the moment she had discovered her son was missing. Why hadn't she called the police or let Jack call his colleagues with the Bureau?

That was easy enough to answer—she hadn't wanted to do anything to jeopardize Ian's safety. The kidnappers had counted on that. It was the same psychology that made people fall for scammers who posed as stranded grandchildren who needed money to get out of jail. The grandparents who fell prey to such traps were so worried about the safety of their loved ones that they didn't think logically. She would have judged herself too savvy and educated to fall for such a ruse, but at least when it came to children, apparently, emotion trumped common sense every time.

Though there were no windows on this side of the office building, she still worried someone might spot her, so she moved along the side of the cabin to the back. She stopped and studied the structure again. It was built like all the others, except that this one was larger and also included a back door. How could she help Jack? Alone, she wasn't sure she had the nerve to burst in there, waving the pistol around as if she knew what she was doing. That would probably distract his captors for a few seconds—until they shot her or over-powered her.

Her gaze shifted to the back door. Maybe she could creep in that way and get the jump on them. There weren't any steps leading up to the door, but someone— Jack?—had positioned a milk crate underneath it. She frowned at the other items near the crate—an over-turned plastic jug and what looked like a bunch of paper.

She glanced toward the front of the building—no movement. Then she raced toward the back door. The empty gallon jug lay on its side in the mud, a camp-ing lighter beside it. The label on the jug read Cooking Oil. The paper—yellowing newsprint—was crumpled around the corner of the cabin. The outer layer of paper was soaked, but when she pulled this away, she found a drier layer. Maybe dry enough to light.

Muffled voices rumbled from the office at the front of the building, but she couldn't make out any words. If she set the fire as Jack had planned, she could force Jack's captors out of there. But would Jack be in even more danger, trapped in flames?

It would take a while for the building to burn down, so she didn't think Jack was in much danger. And get-ting his captors away from him and occupied with put-ting out the blaze would give them all more time to escape. "Here goes nothing," she muttered, and flicked the lighter. The paper flared instantly, and seconds later, flames licked at the old wood of the cabin. Andrea re-treated to the edge of the woods and waited.

ANDERSON SHOVED THE rifle barrel into the small of Jack's back and Jack took another step forward into the front room of the office. He studied the man who lounged on a faded green sofa, keeping his expression impassive. This man was older than Anderson, maybe midfifties, with a hawk nose and deeply recessed eyes. Nothing about him was familiar. He wasn't in the database Jack had combed through last night and he wasn't on the hours of surveillance videos from terrorist targets the team had reviewed.

"We were beginning to think you had stood us up, Agent Prescott," the man said, his voice gravelly and low—the other man Jack and Andrea had overheard earlier. "Of course, I expected you to do something underhanded, which is why my friend here was watching for you."

Jack remained silent, giving nothing away.

"Did you bring the money we asked for?" the man asked.

"Does your boss know you only asked for ten thousand?" Jack asked. "That seems pretty small-time for a guy like him. That kind of money won't pay his expenses for a day."

The man's eyes shifted, uncertain. "I'm the only boss around here," he said, though to Jack's ears the words carried more bluster than conviction.

"So Braeswood and Roland don't have anything to do with this," Jack said. "You just happened to know my name and what I do and who I'm connected to. And you came up with the idea to kidnap that little boy to get to me all by yourself."

"Are you saying you don't think I'm smart enough to come up with an idea like that?" He stood.

"If you were smarter, you wouldn't be stuck out here

in the middle of nowhere, babysitting a kid," Jack said. "Braeswood would have given you something more important to do."

A vein pulsed at the corner of Gravel Voice's right eye. "This isn't about the kid," he said. "It's about you and the rest of the jackbooted thugs who pass yourselves off as law enforcement in this country."

"Jackbooted thugs. I haven't heard that one in a while. Classic conspiracy-theorist rhetoric. Did they teach you that in the indoctrination camps?" If he made the man mad enough, would he blurt out something Jack could use later to tie him to Braeswood's group? Gravel Voice hadn't denied the connection, a sign that Jack's assumption of a connection was on the money.

Anderson, who had remained still and silent all this time, suddenly spoke. "Do you smell something funny?"

Gravel Voice glared at him. "What do you mean?" He sniffed. "All I smell is wood smoke."

The tang of wood smoke hung in the air, stronger than it had been earlier, Jack thought.

"Didn't you tell Leo to put out that fire?" Gravel Voice asked.

"He put it out. I watched him do it," Anderson said.

"He must have lit it again," Gravel Voice said. "I smell smoke."

Anderson made a face. "He was whining about being cold. He don't like being stuck down there with the kid."

"It's not like he's got the tough job, guarding a toddler. He's just a whiner. Go tell him to put the fire out. Somebody is going to smell it and come nosing around."

Anderson glanced at Jack. "What about him?"

Gravel Voice pulled out a pistol—a long-barreled
.44. The kind of gun that would blow a hole the size of
a dinner plate in Jack at this close range. "He'll be fine
here with me."

"Okay." Anderson slouched out the door, leaving
Jack and his boss alone.

"Where's the woman?" Gravel Voice asked. Then,
as if there might be more than one woman involved, he
clarified, "The boy's mom."

"I came alone," Jack said.

"Liar." The gunshot echoed off the walls, leaving
Jack's ears ringing. The bullet bit into the doorframe behind Jack's head. "Where is she?" Gravel Voice shouted.

"I don't know," Jack said. True enough. He hoped
Andrea had stayed behind the last cabin, but he had no
way of knowing.

The front door burst open, hitting against the wall.
"Fire!" Anderson yelled.

The smell of smoke was much stronger now. "What
the—?" Gravel Voice leaped to his feet.

"This building is on fire!" Anderson shouted. "You
need to get out now, Jerry." Not waiting for an answer,
he ran outside again.

Gravel Voice looked toward the door, then at Jack.
"I don't have time to waste with you," he said, and
raised the pistol.

The gunshot exploded through the room. Gravel
Voice staggered forward, a stunned expression on his
face, then sank to his knees, blood staining the front
of his shirt, his own weapon unfired. Jack lunged and
twisted the gun from his hand, then looked past him as

Andrea stepped through the door from the storeroom, the Beretta in her hand.

"Let's go," Jack said. Still holding the .44, he grabbed her free hand and pulled her toward the back door.

"Is he dead?" she asked, looking over her shoulder toward the man's slumped figure.

"I don't know." Probably. He doubted anyone could survive a direct hit like that.

"He was going to kill you," she said,

"Yes. You saved my life." He pulled her along after him. They could talk through her guilt or confusion or whatever she was feeling later. Right now they had to take advantage of the opportunity they had. "Come on," he said. "We have to hurry."

"Where are we going?" she asked as they ran out the front door, across the porch and around the side of the building, which was completely engulfed in flames now. In spite of the damp, the old, dry wood had caught quickly.

Jack put up a hand to shield his face from the intense heat and guided her around the back of the row of cabins. "We're going to get Ian!" he shouted over the crackle of the flames.

As they raced past the opening between the first and second cabins, he caught a glimpse of the commotion in the front of the buildings. Anderson raced past, shouting, but not at Jack and Andrea. Right now all his attention was on the burning building, but before too long, someone would remember the outsiders and come looking for them. They had to act quickly.

Jack and Andrea reached the last cabin in time to

see a compact, balding man emerge from the building. He stared toward the flames, then took off running.

Jack didn't hesitate, but raced into the cabin. Inside, Andrea pushed past him. "Ian!" she called. "Ian, Mommy's here!"

Frantic thumping led them to a back room, where Ian lay on a mattress on the floor. Though his hands and feet were tied and a bandanna served as a gag, he kicked his feet against the floor. "Oh, Ian!" Andrea knelt and pulled her son close.

Jack joined her and worked the knot on the bandanna loose and removed the gag. "We'll untie you later, buddy," he said, scooping the boy out of Andrea's arms and standing, biting down hard to keep from crying out as pain shot through his injured leg. "Right now we have to get out of here."

After checking to make sure no one was looking their way, he ran out of the cabin and around the side, into the woods behind the camp. They made no attempt at stealth this time as they slogged through the heavy snow, followed the riverbank back toward where he had parked his truck. Behind him, he heard Andrea stumbling through drifts and shoving aside the branches of scrub oak and piñon.

Ian lay still in Jack's arms, staring up at him with huge, frightened eyes. "It's okay, buddy," Jack said. "You're safe now."

"Jack!" Andrea's scream froze him. He whirled to find her tangled in camouflage netting. She clawed at the wet jute that covered her head and shoulders.

"Hang on—let me help." He carefully laid Ian on the

ground. "Hang on just a minute, buddy," he told the boy. "I'm going to get your mom."

He approached her slowly, wary of any other traps. The netting had dropped from a tree overhead and Andrea was thoroughly tangled, her legs and arms partially protruding from the mesh, her body tilted upside down. "Hold still and I'll cut you loose," he said. He pulled out his pocketknife and began sawing at the thick jute.

"Hurry," she pleaded. "They could be right behind us."

"Just a few more cuts… There!" He sliced at a last cord and pulled the netting from around her. "This must be one of the traps they set for us," he said. "We were lucky we didn't run into one on our way to the camp."

"Let's hope our luck holds out." She looked over her shoulder. "Do you think they realize we're gone yet?"

The noise from the camp faded, and it had begun to snow harder. The fire might already be out. Anderson and Leo had probably checked the cabin by now and discovered that Ian had disappeared. "We'd better hurry," he said, and picked up Ian again.

Another five minutes of stumbling through the woods and he spotted the truck up ahead. "Do you have the keys?" he called over his shoulder.

Andrea moved alongside him and hit the button to unlock the vehicle. She ran ahead and opened the passenger door. He deposited Ian inside, then took his knife from his pocket and handed it to her. "You can cut him loose while I drive," he said, taking the key from her and moving around to the driver's side.

"Oh, honey, I'm so glad to see you," she said as she slid into the passenger seat and pulled Ian onto her lap.

Jack was sure those were tears running down her cheeks and not melted snow, though the storm had returned in earnest, a blanket of white falling from the sky.

"Anderson and Leo are probably looking for us by now," he said as the truck's engine roared to life.

"Do you think there were others?" she asked, her arms tight around Ian.

"I didn't see any sign of anyone else. I think it was just the three of them." Two now, he thought. "They'll have a hard time catching up to us now." At least, he hoped that was the case. He had no idea what kind of arsenal those three had at their disposal. Previous experience with Braeswood's group had suggested they had almost limitless resources. Braeswood had a fortune of his own and had managed to recruit more than a few wealthy donors to his cause. Plus, the Bureau suspected foreign groups contributed to his efforts. The feds, on the other hand, had to deal with numerous budget constraints.

"Those are bad men," Ian said.

"They are," Andrea agreed. "But you were very brave." She sawed at the ropes that bound his hands. Once they were severed, she turned her attention to the ties around his ankles.

"I peed my pants." Ian sounded as if he was about to cry as he made this confession. "I couldn't help it. The man wouldn't untie me so I could go to the bathroom."

"It's okay, honey," Andrea said. "That doesn't matter. And the snow has washed you all off now anyway."

"There are some blankets behind the seat you can wrap up in," Jack said. He hit the controls to turn up the heat. Now that they were out of the storm, a chill was setting in. He had to gun the engine to guide the truck through the fast-accumulating snow. He braked at the edge of the woods and prepared to turn out onto the road. As soon as they were well away from the camp, he would call his team and let them know to be on the lookout for Anderson and the rest.

He nosed the truck up onto the shoulder of the road, then stopped to wait for a car to pass. "Do you think the people in that car could see the fire at the camp from the road?" Andrea asked.

"They saw the fire, all right," Jack said, his fingers tightening around the steering wheel. "That was Anderson driving, and Ian's guard, Leo, was beside him."

"Where are they going?" Ian asked, his face creased with worry.

"They're running away, honey." Andrea pulled Ian against her, as if to hide him from his kidnappers.

Or they were looking for their escaped prisoner. Or rushing Gravel Voice to the hospital. But Jack didn't want to say anything to upset Ian more. Better the boy see them as having the upper hand. Which, in this case, maybe they did have. He shifted into gear and roared out onto the highway, the back end of the truck fishtailing as he fought for purchase on the slick pavement. He glanced toward Andrea and Ian. "Buckle up," he said. "We're going after them."

ANDREA WRAPPED BOTH arms around Ian and braced her feet against the floorboards as the truck rocketed down the snow-covered pavement in pursuit of Ian's captors. She couldn't believe that after all they had risked to get away from these guys, Jack was going after them.

"Leave them," she pleaded. "Let the police take care of this. I just need to get Ian home."

"If we let them go, they're liable to come after you again." Jack hunched over the steering wheel, his expression grim.

The thought sent an icy cold through her that the truck's roaring heater couldn't touch.

"Mom, you're squeezing me too tight." Ian squirmed and shoved against her.

"Sorry, honey." She loosened her hold and he shifted around to sit in her lap, facing forward. She tried not to think what would happen if they crashed. But she hadn't thought to bring Ian's booster seat with her, and now didn't seem the right time to try to belt him into the backseat. "Don't be scared," she said. "Everything is going to be all right."

"I'm not scared," he said. Eyes bright, he focused on the taillights of the car ahead of him. "This is just like in the movies."

What kind of movies has he been watching? she wondered as the truck skidded around a curve. They were close enough to read the Colorado license plate on the car ahead, but the kidnappers hadn't slowed down. "I just hope they don't start shooting at us," she said.

"Get down!" Jack shouted as the muzzle of a gun appeared in the passenger window.

She dived to the floorboards, on top of Ian. "Mom!" he yelped.

"Just stay still, honey." She closed her eyes, waiting for the shots she was sure were coming.

Instead, she heard the whine of the tires change cadence. "We're crossing the first bridge," Jack said. "The road's getting icy, but I think we can make it."

Think? But the tires found purchase and she breathed a sigh of relief. She raised her head, trying to see what was going on.

"Stay down," Jack said. "They might try to fire at us again."

"What are they doing?" she asked.

"They've sped up." He pressed down on the accelerator and the truck fishtailed, sliding back and forth as he fought to bring it under control. Jack shook his head. "The road's too slick. They're having a hard time, too."

"They'll have to slow down at the second bridge, won't they?" she asked. She remembered a rickety-looking wooden structure, scarcely two lanes wide.

"They ought to, but with the snow coming down, they may be worried about getting to the highway before it becomes impossible to travel."

"What happens if we can't reach the highway?" she asked.

"We'll be stuck on this side until the weather clears."

And the bad guys might be stuck with them. Her stomach clenched at the idea and she hugged Ian more tightly.

"Why are we down here on the floor?" he whined. "I want to sit up where I can see."

"That isn't safe, honey. We can't get up until Jack tells us to."

"This is a dumb game," Ian said.

Andrea only wished it were a game. "Just stay down there until I tell you the coast is clear," Jack said. "Do that, and you'll win a special prize."

"What prize?" Ian asked.

"Do you like race cars?" Jack asked.

"Yes!"

"I have a friend who owns a real race car. I'll get him to take us for a ride in it."

"Wow!" Ian pressed himself even closer to the floor-board of the truck. Clearly, nothing Andrea could have offered would have appealed to him more than the prospect of a daredevil ride in a real race car. Never mind that they were already racing much too fast down a snow-slicked road. Apparently, in their brief acquaintance Jack had already figured out something about her son that she hadn't known—that Ian had a love for speed. She was both touched that he had paid so much attention to the boy and disturbed that there was something about her son she hadn't known. Was this only the first of many secrets that would be hidden from her because she was female?

"We're almost to the second bridge," Jack said. The truck slowed, then stopped altogether.

"What is it?" Andrea asked. "What's wrong?"

"The road is blocked. It looks like an avalanche from the cliffs above."

"What is Anderson doing?"

"He's stopped, too... Now he's backing up."

Andrea sat up. "Is he trying to ram us?"

Jack put the truck into Reverse. "I don't know." He began backing up as well, putting more distance between them and the sedan.

But Anderson didn't ram them. Instead, he stopped again, about a hundred yards back from the bridge.

Then his brake lights went out and tires screeched as he shot forward. "What is he doing?" Andrea asked.

"I think he's going to try to bust through the snow," Jack said.

"Can they do that?" she asked.

"So far, they've proved they won't let anything keep them from getting what they want," he said, his expression grim. "But I won't let them succeed this time."

Chapter Six

Wanting to close her eyes but unable to look away, Andrea sat up and stared in horror as the sedan hit the wall of ice and snow. A spray of white exploded up on either side as the car hit the obstacle, then skewed sideways. The driver fought for control, but the car slid off the pavement and into a deep drift. "They're not going to make it," she said.

Smoke poured from beneath the battered hood. "They're not going anywhere now," Jack said. He started the truck and rolled forward.

"What are you doing?" she asked.

"I want to be close enough to nab them when they bail and make a run for it."

The sedan's driver shoved open his door, but he managed to force it only a couple of inches before the snow blocked it. A few seconds later, Anderson climbed from the driver's side window. Leo exited from the other side. Jack stepped out of the truck and drew his gun.

"This way, gentlemen," he shouted. "Keep your hands where I can see them and no one gets hurt."

Anderson glared at Jack. He shouted a curse, then climbed onto the bridge railing and dived into the rushing water. On the other side of the bridge, Leo jumped, as well.

Cursing under his breath, Jack began peeling off his jacket. "What are you doing?" Andrea asked..

"I'm going to pull them out before they drown." He bent to untie his boots. "And then I'm going to arrest them."

"Jack, that water is freezing. And the current is really fast. They're not worth it."

But he kept peeling off his coat. Snow plastered his shirt to his back, his muscles rippling as they moved. When he turned to face her, she stared at a single melted snowflake making its way down his throat.

"Andrea."

She swallowed hard and told herself to breathe again. Now was definitely not the time to be lusting after a man. He'd just…surprised her. She'd been so focused all day on saving Ian that she had forgotten how strong and good-looking Jack was. He pressed the .44 he had taken from one of the kidnappers into her hands. "Keep this for me." Then he handed her his shoulder holster with the Glock. "And this."

"You can't go after them unarmed."

"The guns are no use to me soaked in the river, either." He touched her cheek and gave her a half smile. "Don't worry. I'm a strong swimmer."

He was also recovering from a gunshot wound. No matter how much he pretended otherwise, she knew the wound still bothered him. As he made his way toward the bridge, clad in only jeans and a flannel shirt, she detected the slight hesitation every time he put weight on his injured leg.

"Where is Jack going?" Ian asked. While she and Jack had argued, the boy had climbed onto the seat beside her.

She sighed. "He's going to do his job," she said. A job he clearly took very seriously. Just like Preston. The night her husband had died had been like this. She had begged him not to go on that raid. He was officially off duty and the SWAT team was prepared to handle things.

"It's my case," he had said as he'd slipped on his Kevlar vest, then buttoned up his shirt. "I need to be there."

She'd stood at the front door, baby Ian in her arms, and watched him walk away from her, toward danger. *He is always going to choose duty over his family*, she had thought to herself. It was the way things were supposed to be, but that didn't make it any easier for her to live with.

She slid out of the truck. "You stay inside," she told Ian. "You can watch out the window."

With the shoulder holster draped around her and the .44 in her left hand, she took a few steps toward the bridge until she had a clear view of Jack making his way down the snowy embankment and of Anderson in the icy water. She couldn't see the other man, on the other side of the bridge, but Anderson was making slow but steady progress toward the opposite shore. Waves swamped him, and he had been carried a ways downstream, but before Jack reached the water's edge, Anderson crawled out onto the bank.

The kidnapper looked at Jack, then turned to look downstream. The other man stumbled toward him. Jack stood with his hands on his hips, staring after him. Leo made a rude gesture in his direction, and then both men began walking up the road, soon disappearing from view in the curtain of snow.

Andrea walked out to meet Jack. "I'm sorry they got away," she said. "But I'm not sorry you didn't have to go in after them."

"I couldn't be any colder than I am already." He followed her back toward the truck. "How's Ian?"

"He's okay. He's a lot calmer about all of this than I am."

"Kids are a lot tougher than we think sometimes. And he's with you now, so that makes everything all right."

"Everything doesn't feel all right. What are we going to do?"

He walked her around to the passenger side of the truck and held the door for her, then reached into the backseat and pulled out a gym bag. He grabbed a towel from it and rubbed at his hair as he walked around to the driver's side. "Hi, Jack," Ian said when Jack climbed into the truck. "You're wet."

"You're right, buddy. And I didn't even get to go swimming."

"It's snowing so hard you could almost go swimming on land," Ian said.

Jack laughed, and the boy joined in. The deep, masculine chuckles mingling with little-boy giggles made Andrea's breath catch. How was it possible to feel such joy and such fear at the same time? "You must be freezing," she said.

"I'll be okay." He shrugged back into his coat. "I've got a spare change of clothes here in the truck." He tossed the damp towel into the backseat, started the truck again and put it in gear. "We're going back to the camp," he said. "We can stay out of the weather in one of the cabins, get warm and decide what to do next."

JACK PARKED THE truck on the road and walked into the camp alone. This time, Andrea hadn't argued with him. She had slumped in the seat, her arms locked around her son, looking too exhausted for words. Ian, however, had cheerfully offered to come with him. "You'd better stay here, buddy," Jack had said, smiling in spite of his own weariness and the stabbing pain in his leg. "You'll get too cold out there."

"I like to play in the snow," he said.

Jack laughed. "Maybe we'll do that some other time. Right now I need you to stay with your mom and keep her company. She'd be pretty lonely if we both left her."

"Will you be back soon?" Ian asked.

"Soon. I promise."

He crept through the woods alongside the track leading into the camp and approached the compound obliquely, keeping an eye on both the entrance and the row of cabins. The office had been reduced to charred ruins, the acrid smell of smoke hovering in the air around it. The other buildings stood silent and still, their boarded-up fronts adding to their look of desolation.

He had reclaimed his Glock from Andrea and as he entered the camp, he drew it. Alert for any sign of life, he checked each cabin and found them all empty. The middle one, where they had overheard Anderson talking with Gravel Voice, contained a pair of faded green plaid recliners, a kitchen table and chairs, and a single mattress on an iron frame. The stale odors of cigarettes and coffee hung in the air. Jack was careful not to touch anything. An evidence team might be able to lift fingerprints or DNA from the furniture and kitchen utensils.

The end building, where Ian had been held, contained a sofa and a small table and a woodstove, as well as the mattress. The other cabins looked as if they hadn't been occupied by anything but mice and squirrels for years.

Jack left the camp and returned to the truck, grateful for the respite from the icy wind. "They're all gone," he said. "We'll be safe there. As soon as we're inside, I'll call my boss and fill him in."

"Do you think we'll have to stay here very long?" Andrea asked.

"I don't know. I'll get a weather report, too, and find out what the status is for the roads."

He parked the truck in front of the end cabin. Later he'd move the vehicle out of sight back in the trees, just in case anyone showed up again. "This one is in the best shape," he said. "And it has the woodstove, so we can keep warm."

"Warm sounds good." She picked up Ian and followed Jack up the steps. Ian made a noise of protest. "I don't like it here," he said.

"It's okay." Andrea rubbed his back and kissed the top of his head. "The bad men are gone and Jack and I are staying right here with you."

"I'm going to start a fire to warm us up." Jack knelt in front of the woodstove, relieved to see a supply of firewood against the back wall and a basket of kindling near the hearth. "We'll get dry. Then I'll see what I can find for dinner."

The boy didn't say anything, but he seemed content to sit in Andrea's lap on the sofa and watch Jack build the fire. Soon he had a good blaze going. He closed the glass-fronted door to the little stove. "That should warm us up quickly," he said. He stood. "I'm going to get my things out of the truck. You might look around here and see what kind of supplies we have."

He retrieved his gym bag from behind the seat and brought it inside, along with the damp towel. When he returned, he found Ian wrapped in a blanket and Andrea draping the boy's wet clothing on chairs in front of the fire. She looked up when he entered. "There's a lot of canned food and some dishes in the kitchen cabinets," she said. "And I found sheets and blankets for the bed."

"You should get out of those damp clothes," he said. "You'll feel a lot better when you're dry."

"Maybe." She looked doubtful.

"You can wrap up in a blanket," he said. "I promise not to look." But he wouldn't promise not to let his imagination fill in the details about her figure. The damp had made her clothing formfitting, making it pretty obvious that she was a very shapely woman. Even exhausted from their ordeal, her hair a wet tangle about her shoulders and any makeup she might have once worn long since washed away, she made him want to do things that might have made her blush if they had been alone and he had revealed his desires.

He turned away. They weren't alone, and they weren't out of danger yet. He picked up his bag. "I'll change in the other room," he said.

After he had finished dressing in the sweats and

a sleeveless T-shirt he usually wore to the gym, Jack called his boss. "Sir, this is Jack Prescott."

"Agent Prescott." Special Agent in Charge Ted Blessing had a deep, sonorous voice and the demeanor of a drill sergeant, which Jack suspected he had once been.

"Sir, I'm involved in a situation I believe relates to our case."

"Agent Prescott, you are on a medical leave. You are supposed to go to doctor's appointments and go home. How did you become involved in a 'situation'?"

"I was at a medical appointment, sir. Or at least, I went to see a therapist I hoped could help me remember who killed Gus Mathers." He had to force out the words. Admitting he had sought help from a counselor felt like confessing to a weakness.

"And what happened?" Blessing asked.

Jack explained about spotting Anderson in the restaurant, the theft of Andrea's purse and the subsequent kidnapping of her son.

"Why didn't you call me and alert the local police as soon as Dr. McNeil contacted you?" Blessing's words held an edge sharp enough to cut.

"She insisted I keep quiet," Jack said. "The note left at her house said if she contacted anyone other than me, the kidnappers would kill her son."

"The note specifically mentioned you."

"It said she could call her boyfriend, but she doesn't have a boyfriend. Anderson saw us together in the restaurant. I think he assumed a relationship." From the first he had felt drawn to Andrea, but he couldn't possibly have given that away over a casual lunch, could he?

"We're going to set aside the question of why you

were having lunch with your therapist—for now," Blessing said. "What happened next?"

"The next morning a man called and instructed us to bring the ransom money to an address, which turned out to be an abandoned fishing camp on the Pine River, near the small town of Bayfield. We arrived early and hiked in to assess the situation. We located the boy and determined there were three men in the camp—Anderson and two others I had never seen before."

"And you still didn't call the police?"

"We were concerned if authorities arrived, the kidnappers would carry out their threat to murder the boy. Then the kidnappers discovered our presence. After an exchange of gunfire, one of them was killed. The other two fled."

Blessing made a sound like grinding his teeth. "I'll expect a full report detailing why you discharged your weapon—in triplicate."

"Yes, sir." Jack would fill in the details later to clarify that it was Andrea who had fired, killing a man in order to save Jack's life. "I pursued the remaining two kidnappers as far as the river. An avalanche had blocked the road and they ran their car into a ditch. They fled on foot and jumped into the river and swam the rest of the way across and escaped. If you can get some men out here, you might be able to pick them up."

"Where are you and Dr. McNeil now?" Blessing asked.

"We're back at the fishing camp with her son. We're stuck here until the weather clears."

"Are you all right?"

"Yes, sir. No one is hurt and we have food and shelter."

"The weather report is calling for blizzard conditions to continue into the night, so plan to stay put," Blessing said. "Give me some directions and a description of the two men we're looking for and I'll get some agents out there. I'll also alert local authorities."

Jack gave directions and descriptions. "What makes you think this is connected to our case?" Blessing asked. "Is it because of Anderson?"

"Yes, sir. He's in our database of suspected associates of the terrorist cell we've been tracking. Also, Dr. McNeil and I overheard Anderson talking with the man who was shot, and they mentioned Roland. There was also another man, their boss, whom they didn't mention by name, but I think they were talking about Braeswood. They implied that this bigger boss wasn't in a position to keep tabs on the operation right now, and Roland had taken over. That fits the scenario of Braeswood recovering from wounds sustained when he jumped off that railroad bridge."

"Having another man named Roland involved would be a big coincidence," Blessing said. "But we both know coincidences do happen in our line of work. The information you've given me is very interesting, but we'll have to dig deeper to find proof of a connection. It's possible, even more reasonable, to believe the kidnappers targeted Dr. McNeil for a specific reason. Has she suggested anything in her past or her other relationships that might lead her to be targeted?"

"Her late husband was a police officer who died in the line of duty three years ago," Jack said. "But she's sure this doesn't have anything to do with him. And this whole scenario echoes methods the group has used before. I think Anderson kidnapped Ian McNeil in order to get to me."

"It sounds as if it almost worked. I'll look into it. In the meantime, sit tight until the weather clears."

Jack ended the call and returned to the front room. Andrea still stood in front of the fire, shivering in her wet clothes in spite of the blaze. He pressed a sweatshirt and socks into her hands. "Put these on," he said. "You'll feel better."

"All right." She glanced toward Ian, but the boy was curled on his side on the sofa, sound asleep.

While Andrea changed, Jack hung his jeans and shirt to dry, then went into the kitchen, where he found coffee and a coffeepot. He got the coffee started on the little three-burner gas stove, then opened two cans of chili, dumped them into a saucepan and started that heating. A few minutes later, Andrea, wearing his sweatshirt, which came to midthigh, and a pair of his gym socks, shuffled into the kitchen. He let his gaze linger briefly on her long, shapely legs before he forced himself to turn away.

"What smells so good?" she asked. "I'm starved."

"Canned chili. We'll have it with crackers. Do you think Ian will wake up and eat some?"

"I hate to wake him, but if the men holding him wouldn't even let him go to the bathroom, I doubt they fed him anything to eat." Her face crumpled and he thought she might cry.

He pulled her close and held her tightly against him.

"It's okay," he murmured. "He's safe now, and they didn't hurt him."

"Thanks to you." She lifted her head to look into his eyes. "I don't know what I would have done without you," she said. "I never could have rescued him on my own. I owe you everything."

"You don't owe me anything," he said. "You saved my life, remember?"

He was sorry as soon as he said the words. She stiffened and bowed her head and he silently cursed his thoughtlessness. He should never have reminded her of the man she had shot, who had probably died and whose burned body he suspected lay somewhere in the wreckage of the office. "Andrea, look at me," he said.

She raised her eyes to meet his. "You did the right thing," he said. "If you hadn't fired when you did, he would have killed me. And then he would have killed you, and probably Ian, too."

She took a deep breath and her shoulders straightened. "You're right, of course. I just… I never expected to have to do something like that."

"I know. Yesterday morning you were an ordinary workingwoman. You and your son were safe. I'm sorry I brought these people into your life."

She searched his face. "I was so terrified they would kill you," she whispered.

"I'm not going anywhere." He traced the curve of her jaw with his thumb. Her skin was so incredibly soft, yet she was as tough as any man he knew. She had been terrified for her son's safety, yet had found the courage to do whatever it took to save him. Her combination of vulnerability and strength stirred him.

She closed her eyes and leaned into his palm. The tenderness and sensuality of the gesture fired his senses. He bent, his lips hovering over hers. "If you don't want me to kiss you, you'd better say so now," he murmured.

In answer, she slid her arms around his neck. "Kiss me," she said, and drew him to her.

The attraction he had felt for her flared into the full heat of desire when her lips touched his. Her mouth claimed him, erasing all other thought or sensation. He angled his head to explore her lips more fully, tracing his tongue across the seam, tasting her and feeling her breath hot and silken against his cheek. He caressed the satin of her neck with one hand and slid the other down to the curve of her hip.

Her lips parted and she made a breathy sound of welcome as he deepened the kiss. All the tension and fear of the last hours melted away in the fire of that embrace. He felt lighter and freer than he had in weeks, and when at last she gently pulled away, he found he was smiling.

She returned the smile, shy and maybe a little dazed. "You'd better see to the food," she said. "I'll go wake Ian."

He moved to the stove to turn off the pot of chili, but the memory of her lingered on his skin like warm silk. He hated that he had brought danger into her life, but he couldn't be sorry he had met her. Yes, she had saved his life when she fired on Gravel Voice, but she had rescued him even before that moment. With Andrea, he could feel himself healing, becoming whole again in a way he had begun to think was out of reach.

Chapter Seven

Andrea stood beside the sofa, staring down at her sleeping child, her lips still tingling from Jack's kiss, her skin pebbled with goose bumps from the loss of his warmth. She had never intended to kiss him. She wasn't a woman who behaved impulsively or who had casual relationships with men. Or any relationships, really. She was a working mother with a son to raise. She didn't have time for all the drama and risk of dating.

But kissing Jack had felt so right. She had grown so close to him in the last two days as they worked together to save her son. When she looked into his eyes, she found no pity or false promises, only a steady faith in her that had melted some of the chill she had carried inside her ever since the night Preston was killed.

Still, she needed to be careful, she reminded herself. She had just met Jack and knew very little about him. With scarcely a second thought, she had trusted her life and that of her son to him, and so far he had proved worthy of that trust. But could she take the next step and trust him with her heart, as well? Every instinct for self-preservation told her to back away and protect herself. But in Jack's arms she wanted nothing more than to surrender to feelings she hadn't allowed herself to experience in years.

"Mommy?" Ian's voice, soft and sleepy, pulled her from her reverie. She hurried to sit beside him.

"I'm right here, baby," she said, rubbing his leg. "Are you hungry? Jack made some chili for us."

"Chili sounds good." He sat up and rubbed his face. "I'm thirsty, too."

"I'm sure we can find something to drink."

"Do we have any root beer?"

She laughed. "I'm afraid not." She stood and leaned down to pick him up, but he slid off the sofa.

"I can walk." Trailing his blanket, he hurried into the kitchen, his feet making soft slapping sounds on the bare floor.

Smiling, she followed. She had to keep reminding herself that he wasn't really a baby anymore. Every day he asserted his own personality more, an odd mixture of hers and Preston's quirks—and new traits that were clearly all his own.

What would Preston think of his son if he could see him now? she wondered. He'd been a good husband during the pregnancy and birth and was proud to be a father, but he wasn't the kind of man who was very involved in child care. He came from a tradition where men provided for and protected their families but women did most of the hands-on parenting.

Jack looked up from ladling chili into bowls when Andrea followed Ian into the kitchen. "Grab a seat and have some chili, buddy," he said.

Ian climbed onto one of the rickety folding chairs. "I like it when you call me buddy," he said.

"That's because you are my buddy." Jack looked up and caught Andrea's eye, and she swallowed the sudden knot in her throat. He was so good with Ian. So natural. She never would have expected that the big tough FBI agent would have such an easy way with kids.

"Do you have brothers and sisters?" she asked as she pulled out the chair across from Ian. "Nieces and nephews?"

"I have a younger sister, but she's still single. Why?"

"You're so good with kids. I just wondered."

"I like kids. Well, maybe not all kids, but I like Ian."

"I like you, too." Ian looked up from crumbling crackers on top of his chili. "How long are we going to stay here?"

"We have to wait until the snow stops and the road is clear," he said. "It could be a while."

"One of the men we overheard said something about a radio," Andrea said. "If we found it, we could listen to the weather report."

"I'll look for it later," Jack said. "I'm going to take the plywood off these windows, too, and let in some light."

"Good idea." She suppressed a shudder and focused on the hot chili. Maybe the cabin wouldn't seem so gloomy without the boarded-up windows.

"How long do we have to stay?" Ian asked, with a child's insistence on specifics.

"The weather report on my phone calls for snow most of the night," Jack said. "Think of it like a sleepover."

Warmth curled through Andrea as she contemplated spending the night in this small cabin with Jack. Of course, they had a five-year-old chaperone to keep anything from happening, but after the kisses they had shared, being near him felt so much more intimate. Now that he'd reminded her that she was a woman with sensual needs, she couldn't seem to think of anything else.

"Just as long as we don't miss Christmas," Ian said.

"Oh, honey." Andrea smoothed the back of his head. "Christmas is over a week away. We won't be here nearly that long." At least, she hoped not.

After their late lunch, Andrea washed dishes while Jack used a pry bar from his truck to remove the plywood from the cabin's side and back windows. "I'm leaving the front boarded up," he said. "So that it doesn't look different to anyone driving in. If anyone returns, I don't want to make it too obvious we're here. I'm going to move my truck behind the cabin, too."

"Having the windows uncovered makes it feel less claustrophobic," she said. "Thank you."

He toweled off his hair, leaving it uncombed and sexy looking. Melted snow beaded on his forearms and a stray droplet rolled down his neck. She had to fight the urge to lick it off.

"Is something wrong?" he asked. He put a hand to his neck. "Did I get mud on me or something?"

She turned away, her face burning. "Can I borrow your phone?" she asked. "I need to call my office and let my assistant know what's going on."

Though she had left a message early this morning that she wouldn't be in today, she told Stacy to cancel tomorrow's appointments as well, once she got in touch with her. "Is everything okay?" the assistant asked. "Is there anything I can do?"

"Everything is going to be fine. I just had a family emergency that I need to take care of. There's nothing you can do. I should be back tomorrow afternoon or the next day." Surely the snow would have stopped by then.

"Be careful traveling," the assistant said. "The weather is awful and a lot of roads are closed, including most of the mountain passes."

She ended the call, then phoned Chelsea. "Are you all right?" her friend asked after she had answered on the first ring. "Is Ian okay?"

"Ian is fine. We're both fine. Ian, do you want to say hello to Chelsea?"

"Hello, Chelsea." Ian sat on a quilt in front of the woodstove with Jack, who was showing him how to make a "telephone" with the two washed-out chili cans and a piece of string he'd unearthed in a kitchen drawer.

"What happened?" Chelsea asked. "If I didn't hear from you soon, I was going to call the police."

"It's okay," Andrea said. "Jack and I found Ian at the address the kidnappers gave us and they ended up running away." She saw no need to mention the dead man or the frightening race to the river.

"That's it? They just ran away?"

"Well…it was a little more complicated than that, but the main thing is, we're all right and they're gone. How are you doing?"

"I have a headache and I'm still a little shook up, but I'll be fine. Will you be home soon?"

"That's one of the reasons I called. All this snow means the roads into this fishing camp are impassable. We won't be able to leave until the snow stops and the county plows clear the way."

"Where did you say you are?" Chelsea asked.

"It's a fishing camp—a bunch of cabins on the banks

of the Pine River, outside Bayfield. We've moved into one of them. It's dry and there's a woodstove and we have food. Not gourmet, but we'll be fine."

"So you're spending the night there?" Chelsea asked. "With Jack?"

"And Ian."

"Uh-huh. Well, the kid has to sleep sometime. And a cabin in the woods with the snow outside and a nice fire inside sounds pretty romantic to me."

"Chelsea!" Andrea would have protested that she scarcely knew Jack and she didn't think of him that way. But Jack was sitting only a few feet away. And the humming in her body whenever he was near told her that she did indeed think of Jack "that way."

Chelsea laughed. "Hey, he's gorgeous and he seems really into you. I say go for it. A guy who will go out of his way like that for you and your son is a keeper."

Her heart fluttered at the words and she looked across the room at Jack, who was patiently showing Ian how to knot the string so that it wouldn't slip out of the can. "It's too soon to tell," she said.

"Coward," Chelsea said. "Trust me, you don't forget how to have sex just because you haven't had it in a while."

"Uh-huh. I have to go now, Chelsea."

"I want a full report when you get home." Laughing, Chelsea ended the call.

"Here's your phone." She crossed the room and returned it to Jack.

"We made a phone, Mom. Look." Ian giggled and put the empty chili can to his ear. "Hello. Mr. Jack, can you hear me?"

Jack peered from around the kitchen door and spoke into his chili can. "Hey, Mr. Ian. How are things at your end of the room?"

"My mom wants to talk to you." Ian thrust the can into Andrea's hand. "Say hello, Mama."

"Hello, Jack."

"Mom! You have to talk into the phone."

Andrea nodded and moved the can to her mouth. "Hello?"

Jack said something she couldn't make out. Ian erupted in giggles. "Mom! Now you have to put the phone to your ear."

Sheepish, she moved the can to her ear. "You're the sexiest playmate I ever had." The words, issued in a low, masculine whisper, sent heat to more than just her face.

"I want to talk now," Ian said, and reclaimed the can.

Andrea curled up on the sofa and watched her son and Jack play. The telephone call morphed into a mock wrestling match, which ended with Jack giving Ian a ride on his shoulders all through the cabin while they both sang loudly, and off-key, a song with made-up lyrics about slaying monsters.

Jack had slain Ian's monsters, turning this cabin from a place of fear into a place of fun. He had beaten back some of Andrea's fear, too, though she needed to hold on to some of it for a little longer. Some of her fears—of letting go or giving in, of trusting someone else with her happiness—had kept her going in the years since Preston's death. She couldn't afford to give that up just yet.

The warm fire and her son's happy laughter lulled her into a doze there on the sofa. When she woke, someone—probably Jack—had covered her with a blanket.

He sat in the cabin's one armchair across from her, Ian on his lap, both of them studying something on his phone. "How long have I been sleeping?" she asked, sitting up and raking a hand through her hair.

"A long time," Ian said.

"A couple of hours." Jack's smile was like a caress, sending a rush of pleasure through her.

"Jack and me have been playing games on his phone," Ian said.

"Jack and I," she automatically corrected, worry raising its familiar head as she came more fully awake. As much as she loved seeing Ian so happy, she knew he would be crushed when Jack left. And Jack would leave. His job would take him away from them, both physically and mentally. One of the great disappointments of her marriage had been discovering that even when Preston was with her, part of him was focused on criminals and clues and the work that consumed him.

"I'm hungry," Ian announced.

"I'm hungry, too." Jack stood, lifting the boy with him. "Let's go see what we can rustle up for dinner, bud."

Andrea retreated to the bathroom, where she frowned at the sleep marks on her face and the tangles in her hair. She wasn't exactly a sexy playmate now. And it was just as well. As flattering as it was for Jack to see her that way, it wasn't a good idea if she intended to keep her distance. No sense starting something with him that would only end badly.

Dinner was canned beef stew and biscuits from a mix Jack found in the cupboard. "Jack is a good cook," Ian announced, beaming at his new best friend.

"I'm sure your mom does a much better job," Jack said.

"But she always makes vegetables and fish and stuff." Ian made a face. "Healthy food."

Jack laughed and winked at Andrea. She looked away.

After supper she helped Jack clear the table. "You cooked, so I can do the dishes," she said.

"We'll do them together." He took out his phone and handed it to Ian. "Hey, buddy. Why don't you go play in the other room while your mom and I clean up in here."

Ian took the phone. "I wanna play with you," he said. "Mom can do the dishes by herself."

"Ian McNeil," Andrea said. "You've monopolized Jack all afternoon. You can play by yourself for a little bit."

"Okay." With all the reluctance and drama of a stubborn five-year-old, he shuffled out of the room.

Andrea began gathering up the plates, scraping them into the garbage can under the sink. Jack filled the basin with hot, soapy water. "He's a great kid," he said.

"Yes, he is."

"I think he's going to bounce back pretty well from this." He took the plates from her and slid them into the water.

"I have a colleague who specializes in children's issues. I'll probably have her talk to him, just to be sure he's okay." She picked up a dish towel and stepped to one side to make more room for him at the sink.

"That sounds like a good idea." He handed her the first clean plate.

"I'm sorry you're stuck here with us," she said. "I

mean, I'm not sorry you're with us, but I regret that we've intruded on your life this way."

"I thought I'd made it clear that I don't see you as an intrusion." He scrubbed at dried food in a pan. "Besides, I'm on medical leave. My days were full of bad TV and too much brooding about whatever was going on with the case without me."

"That must be frustrating," she said. "Being involved in an investigation for months, then suddenly finding yourself left out."

"It is." He paused, both hands immersed in the soapy water. "Being here makes me feel less useless, at least. And though I haven't found a solid connection yet, I'm sure the people who took Ian are connected to the men I'm hunting."

"Maybe the Bureau's investigators will find the connection when they search the camp."

"Maybe." He began rinsing the next dish. "But they'll just shut me out again. If I found the connection myself—the proof that what happened to you and Ian is linked to Braeswood and his activities—they would have a tougher time excluding me, medical leave or not."

He sounded so wistful, frustration clear in the set of his jaw and the tension in his shoulders. She put a comforting hand on his arm. "I hope you find what you need," she said. "I'd help you if I knew what to look for."

"Thanks." His gaze met hers, and she felt a renewed rush of pleasure—and uneasiness. She was still so unsure of where the two of them were headed. She looked away and pretended to focus on drying a plate.

"What's wrong?" he asked. "Are you worried about what's going to happen tomorrow?"

She hadn't even let herself think about tomorrow yet. "What is going to happen?" she asked.

"As soon it's safe to travel, we can leave. The Bureau is sending a team out to take this place apart. At some point, they'll want to interview you about what happened."

She fumbled the plate she was drying. He put a steadying hand on her wrist. "Don't worry. You're not in any kind of trouble. They just want to gather as much information as they can in order to find these guys."

She slid her hand from his grasp and focused on drying the plate. "Do you think those men will try to go after Ian again?" The possibility made her feel sick.

"I doubt it. But in case they do, I'm not leaving your side until this is settled."

She looked up, alarmed. "You don't have to do that."

"I'm officially on medical leave, so I don't have any other pressing duties. And it's my fault this happened in the first place. I'm going to make sure they don't have a chance to hurt you again."

She believed he could protect her and her son, and knowing he was watching over them would probably make her feel much safer. But spending more days or even weeks in close proximity to him could cause all kinds of other problems. Ian would grow even more attached to him and she…she would grow more attached to him, too. She rubbed the dish in her hand so hard it squeaked. "I'm sure we'll be fine on our own. I can always call the police if I see anything suspicious."

He let the dishrag slide into the water. "What's

wrong?" he asked. The dampness from his hands soaked into her shirt as he gripped her shoulders.

She shrugged away from him. Everything was wrong. She and Ian shouldn't even be here. They should be home, on a normal night after work, eating a meal she had cooked and getting ready for his bedtime story. "Nothing's wrong," she lied.

He released her but didn't return to washing dishes. "Something has upset you," he said. "Something to do with me. What is it?"

She tossed the dish towel onto the counter and faced him. Maybe he was right. Maybe they did need to talk about this. "I'm worried about what's going to happen to Ian when you leave," she said. "He's clearly crazy about you."

"What about you?" His gaze searched her face. "How do you feel about me?"

"How I feel doesn't matter. I have to think of my son."

"We've already established that Ian likes me. I want to know how *you* feel about me." He took a step closer, crowding her against the counter but not quite touching her. "When we were kissing earlier, I got the impression you thought I was okay." His voice was low, rough with emotion, sending a shiver across her skin.

She folded her arms across her chest. "That kiss was a mistake. Yes, I'm attracted to you, but…"

"But what?" He cupped her chin in his hand, and she leaned into his touch, in spite of her determination not to. "Do you think because you're a mother, you don't get to act on your feelings?" he asked.

"If I let you get closer to me, it's only going to hurt

Ian when you leave." *And it's going to hurt me, too. I don't want to deal with any more pain.*

He slid his hand down her neck and moved nearer, the front of his shirt brushing her breasts, his eyes dark with desire, mesmerizing her. "Who says I'm leaving?" He kissed her cheek, a feather brush against her sensitive nerves.

"You have a job to go back to." She forced herself to focus on the issue at hand, to ignore her racing heart and the tension building inside her.

"So do you," he said, and kissed her other cheek.

She put her hands up to push him away but only rested her palms against the hard plane of his chest. She fixed her gaze on him, stern and determined. "Your job is different," she said. "Police work is— It's consuming. It's not something you can leave behind at the end of the day."

He leaned back, his mouth set in a hard line. "You mean it's not something your husband could leave behind. I'm not him."

"I counsel plenty of law enforcement officers," she said. "One of the traits of the good ones is that they're very focused."

"In your work, I'm guessing one of the things you work on with people is balance," he said. "You help your clients find that equilibrium between work and the rest of their life."

She nodded. "It's a common problem for law enforcement."

"It's a common problem for everyone. But no life is ever perfectly balanced. Sometimes the scales tip more toward work. When I'm on an important case, I have to put in long hours and devote a lot of my attention to the job. What I'm doing is important to the safety of the country. To the safety of people like you and Ian."

"I realize that. But I also know that you came to me because you couldn't let go of your guilt over your colleague's death. Something that happened on the job was affecting every aspect of your life."

"One reason that happened, I think, is because the job, and the friendships I've made there, were all I had in my life. At the end of the day I came home to an empty apartment. I didn't have anyone else who mattered to me. Now I do."

Her therapist's training had taught her to read between the lines of what her clients told her, and to pick up on subtle cues of body language to divine their feelings. But she didn't trust her instincts when it came to Jack. "What are you saying?" she asked.

"I'm saying that you and Ian have become important to me. I had this void in my life and you two have moved in to fill it up." He cradled the back of her head, fingers threaded into her hair. "I know we haven't known each other long, but from the moment I met you, I felt a connection. It was as if I had been looking for you and I hadn't even realized it until I found you."

"I felt the connection, too." She curled her fingers against him, no longer pushing him away but reluctant to pull him to her. "It caught me off guard. I don't know what to think. I…I don't want to lose you."

"Life is all about risk." He moved his hands to her shoulders again, reassuring and gentle. "Relationships are never easy. But I think the two of us are smart enough to figure this out. I want to try."

Instinct told her to shy away from complications she didn't need, but a small voice in her head—or maybe from her heart—told her she would be a fool to pass up a chance with a man with whom she had felt such an immediate connection. "Maybe we could try," she said.

"You're right about one thing," he said. "I am focused. When I'm at work, I'm focused on work. And when I'm with you, I'm very focused on you." He tipped her head up, his gaze fixed on her mouth, which tingled as if he had touched her.

She wet her lips and tried and failed to draw a steady breath. He was like a tide, pulling her under, and when he bent to her, she closed her eyes and surrendered.

Chapter Eight

Andrea had expected a repeat of their earlier kiss, forceful and almost overwhelming in its passion. Instead, Jack teased her with the slightest brush of his lips against hers. Then he trailed a line of similarly gentle caresses along her jaw until his mouth rested against the pulse at the base of her throat. Her body hummed with awareness, every nerve attuned to the heat and strength and *maleness* of him.

She gripped his biceps and arched to him, the sensitive tips of her breasts pressed into his muscular chest. "What are you doing to me?" she whispered.

"I want you." He nipped at her neck, just beneath her ear, his words as much as his touch sending a tremor through her. "But I don't want to rush you. We've got all night. Or longer, if you need it."

All she needed right now was him. All her fears and worries seemed petty in the face of that fundamental longing. Tomorrow or the next day or next week or next month he might leave her, but tonight they were together, and she knew if she pushed him away now, she would regret it for the rest of her life. She rose on tiptoe and pressed her lips to his. "Let me check on Ian," she said.

He followed her into the cabin's front room, where they found Ian asleep on the sofa, curled on his side, Jack's phone still in his hand. Jack retrieved the phone, then added wood to the fire while Andrea covered her son with a blanket. Then Jack took her hand and led her into the bedroom. "We'll hear him if he wakes," he said.

"He probably won't even stir," she said. "He's always been a hard sleeper. Nothing to trouble his dreams, I guess." Unlike her. Many of her nights were restless.

"Does he miss his father?" Jack asked.

His genuine concern for the boy touched her. "I don't think he really remembers Preston. I keep his picture in Ian's room and Ian asks about him sometimes, but the way he might ask me about an actor on TV or a character in his favorite storybook. Now that he's in school and he hears other children talk about their dads, I think he's more curious about the idea of a father." Some of those conversations were so painful, trying to explain to Ian why other boys had fathers and he didn't.

Jack massaged the back of her neck, kneading at the knotted muscles. "Do you miss Preston?"

"Sometimes." She let out a deep breath, trying to release the tension inside her, too. "I miss what we had when we first married. That sense of being the most important person in the world to someone else. Later on, after he made detective and joined the drug task force, we lost some of that closeness. I felt as if Ian and I only got whatever energy Preston had left over from the job."

"The job has a way of sucking some people in," he said. "The excitement and the feeling that you're making a difference can be a real rush. Home life can seem dull in comparison."

"I'm not blaming him," she said. "I expected too much of him sometimes and didn't try hard enough to see things from his perspective. Counseling other spouses of law enforcement officers has taught me so much. It's the regrets that trouble me now more than the grief."

He put his arms around her and pulled her close. She welcomed the embrace and laid her head on his chest, the steady beat of his heart a calming rhythm. "I think whenever a relationship ends unexpectedly, we try to understand and cope by playing that what-if game," he said. "What if I had said this or done that or not done or said those other things?" His lips brushed the top of her head. "But that's a game you can't win. You can't change the past."

"So I'm fond of telling my clients." She pulled away enough to look up at him. "I also tell them they can't control the future, so it's important to focus on the now."

"That word again. *Focus.*" He slid his hands down to rest at the small of her back, pulling her tight against him. The hard ridge of his erection nudged at her belly, leaving no doubt of his feelings for her. "I can think of a few things I'd like to focus on right now."

"Oh?"

"I'd like to focus here." He slid one hand up to stroke the side of her breast, sending ripples of pleasure through her. "Or here." He arched against her, letting her feel the evidence of his desire. "And here." He slid his thigh between her legs, pressing against the center of her arousal.

"Those…those all sound like good ideas," she gasped. She pulled his head down and found his lips, blotting out her nervousness with a long, drugging kiss. Then he was pulling her down onto the mattress, laying her back and half covering her with his body. The bed was made now, with fresh sheets and blankets. Jack must have done this, perhaps while she was napping on the sofa. Was it because he'd planned to bring her here later, or merely because he had wanted a comfortable bed for the night?

And then the answer didn't matter as he slid his hand beneath the sweatshirt, reclaiming her full attention. He skimmed his hand up her thigh and over her stomach to caress her breast. She tugged at his shirt until he lifted enough for her to push it up so that she could run her hands over the smooth muscles of his abdomen and chest. A fine dusting of hair tickled her palms as she traced the outline of his pecs, and his nipples pebbled at her touch.

He sat up and removed his shirt, then helped her out of hers, as well. His gaze lingered on her so long she began to feel self-conscious, and she tried to cross her arms over her breasts, but he pulled her hands away. "You're beautiful," he said. "So beautiful," he murmured again as he bent and drew one taut peak into his mouth.

Desire lanced through her, sharp and urgent. She bit her knuckle to stifle her cry and bowed her body against him. He slid his hand under her back, pulling her closer, and transferred his attention to her other breast. To be held this way, so intimately and tenderly, after too many years alone made her eyes burn with threatening tears. Then he raked his teeth across her sensitive nipple and any lingering sadness fled. Skimming her hand down his torso, she fumbled for the drawstring of his sweat pants, aware of the hard length of him straining at the fabric.

He shoved her hand out of the way and slid back from her long enough to strip off his pants, then removed her panties, as well. She gasped at the rush of cool air across her naked flesh and then he was beside her once more, cupping between her legs, one finger parting her folds, his touch warming and exciting her until she was panting with need.

She reached for him, wrapping her fingers around his erection and smiling when his breath caught. "Don't make me wait any longer," she said.

In answer, he pushed onto his knees and reached for his gym bag beside the bed. He pulled out a condom package. She laughed. "Do you always travel so prepared?" she asked.

"This has probably been in there for years," he said. "From the days when I was either a little more active or maybe just more optimistic."

She was prepared to tease him more, but he ripped open the package and sheathed himself. Watching him made her mouth grow dry and she lost the power of speech. He arched over her, kneeling between her legs. "Are you ready?" he asked, caressing her hip.

"So ready," she breathed, and opened to welcome him in.

The intensity of his passion didn't surprise her, for it matched the power of her own need. But the tenderness with which he touched her moved her even more, as if he cherished as much as desired her. They began slowly, savoring the feel of each other's bodies, hands and mouths continuing to explore and excite.

But they could hold back only so long and soon they were moving in an urgent rhythm, one that was both familiar and brand-new. Her last nervousness vanished and she began a quick climb toward a climax that overwhelmed her with its intensity. The shock waves of her orgasm were still moving through her when he found his own release, and they clung to each other tightly for long moments afterward, until their heartbeats slowed and they came back to themselves.

He lay beside her, her head pillowed in the hollow of his shoulder. This, too, felt so right and comfortable. She had known Preston for over a year before she'd felt this comfortable with him. Was that only because she had been younger then, or was it because of Jack himself?

"What are you thinking?" he asked, gently squeezing her shoulder.

"Do you know why I agreed to go to lunch with you the other day?" she asked.

"Because of my good looks and charm?"

"Well, that may have had something to do with it, but it's not the main reason."

"What's the main reason, then?"

"You said you thought I would be good company." Did that confession make her sound pathetic? She plunged on. "You didn't try to flatter me by complimenting my looks or telling me what good company *you'd* be. You made me believe you thought I was worth listening to."

His arm tightened around her. "I do believe that," he said. "Do you know why I asked you to lunch?"

"You said it was because you were bored and lonely." She had to admit that had helped persuade her, too—nothing like a big, strong guy being a little vulnerable.

"I was. But it was more that in the hour we spent together in your office, I sensed a connection. Something that wasn't just about a doctor-patient relationship. I hadn't felt that with a woman before and I wanted to experience it a little longer and see where it went."

And they had ended up here, in bed together, though the route they had taken to get here was anything but conventional. "Being with you is easy for me," she said. "I can't say that about any other man I've met lately. Maybe it's because you're a good listener."

"Not always. But I like looking at you *and* listening to you."

She liked listening to him, too, and thought—maybe—he might be a man she never tired of listening to. That was a good start for a relationship, right? She'd have to see if she felt the same way when her and Ian's lives were no longer in danger, when Jack wasn't merely their best protection, but a man she wanted in her life as much as she needed him.

JACK WOKE BEFORE DAWN, the warm weight of Andrea curled beside him already familiar and right. In the midst of such a crazy, dangerous situation, he felt more at peace with her than he had in months. The soft sigh of her breathing was the only sound in the early-morning quiet. A glance toward the window showed a swath of pale blue sky, with no sign of storm clouds. Careful not to wake her, he eased out of bed and began to dress.

He slipped into the kitchen to make coffee, and when he returned from the bathroom to retrieve his shoes, she was sitting up in bed, the covers pulled up over her chest, a sleepy smile on her face. "Do you always get up this early?" she asked, her voice soft and quiet.

"The snow has stopped and plows should clear the road soon." He pulled on his shirt and began buttoning it. "I want to search the camp before we have to leave."

She drew up her knees and hugged them to her chest. "I thought you said the Bureau is sending in a team this afternoon to search."

"They are. But I want to see if I can find anything first." He knelt to tie the laces of his shoes. "I won't be long."

"Be careful," she said. "Preston used to tell stories about drug dealers and smugglers booby-trapping their hideouts. And that netting I was caught in may not be the worst trap Anderson and his buddies set."

"I will." He bent to kiss her. She slid her hand around his neck and pulled him close when he tried to move away. Desire heated his blood once more. "You're tempting me to stay," he murmured, nibbling at the side of her mouth.

"I just wanted to give you something to think about while you were gone." She smiled, then released him with a show of reluctance. "I know a little boy who's probably going to wake up soon, so I'd better be there for him when he does."

"I'll definitely be thinking about you." He rose and

left the room, stopping in the kitchen to pour the coffee. As he worked, he heard her come out of the bedroom.

"Hi, Mama," a sleepy voice greeted her.

"Did you sleep well, pumpkin?" she asked.

"Uh-huh. Is Jack still here?"

"I'm here, buddy." A cup of coffee in each hand, Jack moved into the living room. He handed one cup to Andrea and sipped from the other. "I'm going out to check on a few things," he told Ian. "I'll be back in a minute."

"Can I go with you?" Ian asked.

"Not right now. Somebody has to stay here with your mom." He ruffled the boy's hair. "I'll be back in time for breakfast."

Ian looked as if he wanted to argue, but Andrea said, "Let's go brush your teeth and then you can help me decide what to cook for breakfast."

Jack stepped out into sharp air, heavy with the scents of ponderosa pine and wood smoke. The sun was sending its first rays over the tops of the trees, revealing buildings shrouded in snow, their outlines softened and the drabness disguised by the cloak of winter white. He tried to imagine what the camp must have looked like in its heyday, with wader-clad fishermen gathering to cast their flies for the rainbow and brown trout that populated the river behind the cabins. He'd like to come back here to fish one day, maybe with Ian in tow. Jack would show the boy how to choose a fly and cast into the deep pools where the trout liked to linger. Andrea would be in the scene, too, perhaps with a younger child in her arms...

Where had that come from? He shook off the daydream and drained the coffee cup, then set it on the porch railing. He and Andrea and the boy needed to leave right after breakfast in case Anderson and his men elected to come back with reinforcements. He decided to start in the ruins of the office. The group appeared to have been using it as some kind of headquarters, and he hoped to find a safe or something in the ashes that might give a clue to their purpose here beyond holding Ian hostage.

Snow crunched under his boots as he made his way across the compound, and the bitter smell of char and ash stung his nose as he approached the ruins. He played the beam of his flashlight over the charred timbers and blackened plumbing. Careful not to disturb the scene, he moved to the front room, where Gravel Voice had been shot, but found no sign of a body. Springs from the sofa and the wheels of an office chair jutted up from the debris, but there was no sign of the dead man. If he had, indeed, died.

Had Anderson and Leo taken their boss with them when they left? Maybe the man's identity would provide a link to them that they didn't want authorities to discover. If so, he hadn't followed them out of the car when it stalled on the bridge. Jack would have to alert the team to look for it.

He didn't spot a safe or anything else useful in the burned-out ruins, so he moved on to the first cabin in the semicircle. Though he had briefly explored all the buildings yesterday after they had returned to camp, this morning he wanted to take a closer look to see if he could unearth more evidence. Special Agent in Charge Blessing would have lectured him on the need to wait for the professional evidence team, but Jack didn't want to lose his chance to be a vital part of the investigation again. Once he and Andrea left here, he had more weeks of medical leave that would put him further and further out of the loop. If he found important clues today, he'd have more leverage when it came to being included in updates about the investigation.

He worked his way down the row of cabins. All of them were unlocked, and the first two appeared to have been unoccupied for years, dust thick on the tops of tables and windowsills. A pack rat had built a nest in the bedroom of one, a massive, messy pile full of scraps of paper, bent silverware and old fishing lures. Definitely let the pros tackle that mess. For now, he wanted a better look at the cabin where Anderson had been staying.

Like the others in the camp, Anderson's cabin, in the middle of the semicircle, was a simple plank-sided structure with a small front porch and a bedroom, bathroom and kitchen lined up behind a larger front room. As Jack stepped into the front room, a mouse skittered away from an open bag of potato chips that lay on the floor by one of the armchairs.

The kitchen yielded only dirty dishes piled in the sink, the refrigerator stocked with cold cuts and cheap beer. The bathroom held only a towel and a used disposable razor. Jack moved on to the bedroom. Like the rest of the cabin, it was in disarray, bedclothes trailing to the floor, dresser drawers half-open to reveal a few T-shirts and some underwear and socks. Studying the scene, Jack felt the hair on the back of his neck stand on end. There was something important here, he sensed. Something he needed to see.

He tugged the blanket the rest of the way off the bed,

then pulled off the sheet and tossed it aside, too. Unlike the mattress on the floor in the cabin where he had spent the night, this room contained an iron bed frame with a mattress and box spring. Jack bent and shone his light beneath the frame. Something dark and bulky was shoved far back, against the wall.

He had to lie on his stomach to retrieve the item, which proved to be a backpack—the kind used by hikers and campers. It looked fairly new and unworn, so he doubted it had been forgotten by some long-ago visitor to the camp.

He deposited the pack on the mattress and unzipped the main compartment. His light revealed a handgun, a cigarette lighter, a spiral notebook and a sheaf of papers bound together with a rubber band. Definitely worth checking out. He slung the pack over one shoulder and left the building.

Andrea greeted him at the door of the end cabin when he worked his way back to it. "I was getting a little worried," she said.

"No worries." He kissed her cheek, surprised by how good it felt to have someone worry about him and welcome him back. He'd always dismissed such sentiments as unimportant, but now he saw he'd been wrong. Whereas before, the mission had been the most important thing in his mind, now coming home after the work was done was also a priority.

"Where did you get the backpack?" she asked as he moved past her into the cabin.

"I found it in the cabin where Anderson was staying. I didn't see it yesterday, because it was under the bed. I thought I'd bring it in here for a closer look."

"Breakfast is ready. Oatmeal and canned peaches. Ian insisted we wait for you before we ate." She started to lead the way to the kitchen, but he took her arm, stopping her.

"I checked the burned-out office," he said, keeping his voice low, not wanting the boy to overhear. "The man you shot isn't there."

Confusion clouded her eyes. "Did he…did he burn up in the fire?"

"I don't think so. Either he got out alive or Anderson and the others took his body with them when they left."

She pressed her lips together and nodded. "Okay. Thanks for letting me know. I was kind of dreading driving past there in daylight."

He squeezed her shoulder. "It's going to be okay," he said. "Let's go have some breakfast."

"There you are," Ian greeted Jack when he entered the room. "Let's eat. I'm hungry."

Jack set the backpack on the floor by his chair and ate the oatmeal and peaches without really tasting them. His mind was focused on the day ahead. He needed to get Ian and Andrea home and check in with his team to find out what they had learned about Anderson and his associates.

When they were finished eating and the table was cleared, Andrea sent Ian to wash up and Jack hefted the backpack onto the table and unpacked its contents. He set aside the lighter, the gun and a clip of ammunition and pulled out the spiral notebook and the sheaf of papers. Men's clothing, a pair of binoculars and half a dozen protein bars filled the rest of the bag.

Jack flipped through the notebook. Andrea moved

from the sink to look over his shoulder. "What's in it?" she asked.

"It looks like mathematical or scientific formulas or something." He passed it to her and she studied the rows of cramped handwriting, then returned it to him.

"It doesn't mean anything to me," she said.

"Maybe it's a code." He put the notebook back into the pack with the clothing, binoculars and the gun. Then he turned his attention to the sheaf of papers. He slipped off the rubber band and studied the first item in the pile.

"Is it a blueprint of some kind?" Andrea asked.

"I think it's a survey, or a plat for a piece of land." He studied the blue lines traced on the page and notations of longitude and latitude. "Somewhere called Center Line Gulch. Have you ever heard of it?"

"No."

He set the paper aside and selected the next page in the bundle, a legal-sized photocopy. This one was easier to decipher. "It's a map," he said. He studied the network of roads and waterways. "There's nothing to indicate where it's from and a lot of the roads aren't marked. It looks like it was photocopied from a larger map or a book."

She leaned forward to peer at the map upside down. "I think it has to be in Colorado," she said. "And this part of the state." She put her finger on a thin line running through the middle of the map. "Doesn't that say Pine River?"

"Yes. And this road has a number." He placed his finger an inch below hers on the map. "Four eighty-seven. I think that's the Forest Service number for the road we're on."

"Then that means we're about here." She tapped the intersection of the river and the road, then slid her finger to the inked circle at the top of the page. "So this has to be fairly nearby."

"Except none of these roads appear to have numbers or names," he said. "They might even be hiking trails, they're so small and faint. There's no legend or scale to indicate the mileage between points."

She squinted at the tiny print on the map. "Nothing on here looks familiar," she said. "I need more context."

He set the map aside. The next item in the pile wasn't a single sheet of paper, but a pamphlet.

"Is that...Russian?" Andrea squinted at the printing on the front of the booklet.

"I think it is." Jack flipped through the booklet but could make no sense of the Cyrillic lettering. He set it aside.

The last item in the pile appeared to be a laboratory report of some kind, detailing the percentage of different minerals found in a core sample. Jack's gaze zeroed in on the word *uranium*. Andrea noticed it, too. "They mine uranium in Colorado," she said. "Or at least, they used to."

He returned the papers to the backpack. "We'll have to dig deeper into this and see if we can figure out what it means. For now, let's hurry up and get out of here. I'll take you and Ian back to your home and coordinate with my team from there."

Ian skipped into the room. "Will you take me to see the creek, Jack?" he asked.

"No time for that, buddy." Jack clapped him on the back. "We're going back to your house."

"Are you coming with us?" Jack asked.

"Yes, I am."

It took only a few minutes to load into Jack's truck. Andrea wanted to straighten the cabin before they left, but he persuaded her not to bother. "The evidence techs are going to tear everything apart anyway," he said.

"I guess you're right," she said. "It just feels so wrong leaving dirty dishes in the sink and the bed unmade."

"Think of it as a good exercise in letting go," he said, steering her toward the truck.

Ian sat belted in the backseat this time, after Jack cleared out a space for him. None of them said anything as they left the camp, although Andrea averted her eyes when they passed the burned-out office building. No other traffic traveled the dirt road leading to the highway. "Do you think the car is still at the second bridge?" Andrea asked, her voice tense.

"If it is, we'll have to move it so we can cross," he said.

"Can you do that?" she asked.

"I have some tow chains in the back."

But there was no sign of the car as they approached the bridge. And little sign of the bridge, either. Snow filled it to the railings, and the road beyond was merely a faint depression in the drifts. "The plows haven't made it here yet," Andrea said.

"No." This wasn't good news. The more time passed, the more chance Anderson and the others had to get away.

"How are we gonna get across?" Ian asked.

Andrea looked at Jack, the same question unspoken in her eyes. He stared at the expanse of white. Even on his own, he wouldn't have wanted to attempt to hike out across that. "We have to go back to the camp," he said. "I'll call my office and see if they can send help."

Andrea said nothing as they returned to camp, though her face was pale and she gripped the edge of the seat, white-knuckled. Jack parked in front of the cabin they had just left and they filed inside. Andrea sank to the sofa and Ian crawled up beside her. "What are we going to do now, Mama?" he asked.

"We're going to sit here quietly while Jack makes a phone call," she said.

He punched in the special agent in charge's private number. "Blessing," the bass voice answered.

"Jack Prescott. I've got a problem."

"What's the problem? Where are you?"

"I'm still at the fishing camp. The snow has stopped but the road is still blocked. We need some help getting out of here."

"Are you or Dr. McNeil or her son hurt or in danger?"

"No." At least with the roads closed, Anderson and his crew weren't likely to return to cause trouble.

"I'll get in touch with local law enforcement," Agent Blessing said. "They should have a better idea of the plowing schedule. But it may be a few hours before they get out there."

"I understand. Give them this number. Any word on Anderson and the other two men I described?"

"We think one of them, the dead man, may be a con named Jerry Altenhaus. He's a small-time extortionist who celled with Anderson for a while about ten years ago. They've been spotted together a few times. No idea who the third man is."

"What about their link to Duane Braeswood?"

"The only one we can tie is Anderson."

"Any word on Braeswood?"

"Agent Prescott, you are still on medical leave."

"I'm still part of your team," Jack said.

Blessing made a sound that was a cross between a sigh and a groan. "We have a lead on Braeswood that we're investigating. At this point, we're pretty sure he's still alive and active."

"I did a brief search of the camp and found a backpack with some documents that may be relevant," Jack said. "I'll bring them with me when we get out of here and Forensics can see if they can make anything of them."

"Anything else I need to know?" Blessing asked.

Jack glanced toward the sofa, but Ian and Andrea were intent on a game of tic-tac-toe, scribbled on a scrap of paper she had found on the coffee table. He lowered his voice. "The man who we shot—his body isn't here. I don't know if Anderson and his companion carried it with them when they left or if he got up and walked out on his own. I don't think it likely. He was shot point-blank in the back with a .44-caliber pistol."

"In the back?" Blessing's voice was sharp.

"He was about to shoot me when Andrea—Dr. Mc-Neil—shot him."

"This will all be in your report."

"Yes, sir." Jack resisted the urge to argue that if he was well enough to write reports, he ought to be allowed to return to work.

"Jack?"

The strain in Andrea's voice, and the deathly pallor

of her face when he turned to look at her, put Jack on high alert. "Sir, I have to go," he said.

"Sit tight and stay out of trouble," Blessing said. "I'll be in touch."

Jack pocketed the phone and moved to Andrea's side. "What's wrong?" he asked, taking her hand.

With a warning glance toward Ian, who knelt at the coffee table, scribbling something on a scrap of paper, Andrea pulled Jack toward the kitchen. He could feel her trembling as they stepped into the room. "What is it?" he asked again. "You're shaking like a leaf."

"Someone was here while we were gone," she said. "Someone came into the cabin." Her eyes met his, a mixture of fear and anger reflected in their dark depths. "We're not alone anymore, Jack. And I've got a very bad feeling about this."

Chapter Nine

Jack reached inside his jacket to check the pistol in his shoulder holster. "Why do you think someone was in here?" he asked.

She pointed to the kitchen table, cluttered with the remains of their breakfast. "There was still some oatmeal in a pot on the stove when we left," she said. "It's gone. A can of milk and some crackers are missing from the cabinets, too. I came in here to make some cocoa and peanut butter crackers for Ian and I couldn't find them."

"Maybe some homeless person was looking for food." The words didn't even sound convincing to Jack.

"This isn't the city," she said. "This is the middle of nowhere. If a homeless person was around here, why not just move into one of the empty cabins? Why wait until we drove away and come into this one?" She gripped his hand, her fingernails digging into his palms. "Do you think it's the man I shot?"

"Andrea, there's no way he's still alive," Jack said. "You shot him at close range. I saw the exit wound."

"Then where is his body?"

"It's probably still in that car, buried in the snow on the bridge. Anderson and his partner probably took the body with them to delay having it identified and linked to them. Besides, if it was him, why wouldn't he have gone to the first cabin and retrieved the backpack? A weapon would be more use to him than oatmeal and canned milk." He stared at the clutter on the table. "None of this makes sense."

"What did your boss say about getting us out of here?" she asked.

"He's going to contact local law enforcement and see if they can get the plows out here to clear the road for us. He's going to call me back."

She rubbed her hands up and down her arms, as if she had a chill. "I hope they hurry. Whether this is a vagrant or one of the kidnappers on the loose, I don't want to be anywhere near those people."

"Neither do I." He walked to the window and checked the latch. "In the meantime, I'll find some nails and make sure no one can come in the windows. And we'll keep the door locked." That wouldn't be much defense against a high-powered rifle, but no sense worrying her further by mentioning that. Besides, he still wasn't convinced their thief had anything to do with the terrorists. "It was probably a kid thinking they were getting away with something," he said. "Try not to worry about it."

"I've always thought that was some of the most pointless advice in the English language," she said. She moved to the sink and began running water. "Considering the events of the last forty-eight hours, only a fool wouldn't worry."

"I know you're not a fool." He started to go to her but thought better of it. She didn't want comfort right now;

she wanted action. "I'll take care of those windows," he said. "And if anyone comes back, I'll be ready for them."

PUTTING THE KITCHEN in order helped Andrea feel a little calmer. Now that she had had time to process what had happened, it was hard to be afraid of someone who was desperate enough to steal cold oatmeal and canned milk. But the idea that someone else was out there, watching them, gave her the creeps.

The kitchen cabinets didn't contain much in the way of food beyond canned staples, but she unearthed a box of brownie mix and decided to mix it up. Baking would give her something to do with her hands, and after the stress of the last few days, she could use the chocolate.

She had just slid the pan into the oven when Jack returned to the kitchen, hammer and nails in hand. "Where did you find those?" she asked.

"I found a toolbox in the ruins of the office. It wasn't too badly damaged in the fire." He hammered a nail into the windowsill, then pulled it out. "Come here, Ian—I want to show you something," he called.

Ian came running and Jack dragged a kitchen chair over to the window for the boy to stand on. "See how this nail is sticking up from the windowsill?" Jack asked.

Ian nodded.

"Right now the nail keeps anyone from opening the window from the outside," he said. "Now pull on the nail for me. You'll have to tug hard."

The boy grasped the nail with both hands and pulled. "I got it out!" he crowed, and held up the nail.

Jack took it from him and slid it back into the hole.

"If you need to get out of the window—if there's a fire or your mom or I tell you to climb out the window—all you have to do is pull out the nail and push up on the sash. Can you remember that?"

Ian nodded. "Can we try now?"

Jack laughed. "I don't think so. I just wanted to make sure you knew what to do in an emergency." He handed the boy half a dozen nails. "Why don't we go find a chunk of wood and you can hammer these in for me."

"All right." The boy raced out of the room, clutching the nails.

Andrea looked after him. "Are you sure hammering nails is a good idea?" she asked. "He might smash his thumb."

"He might. But he'll be okay. It's good for their hand-eye coordination. And kids love to hammer things. At least, I did." He started to leave the room but stopped when his phone buzzed. "Hello?"

She studied his face as he listened to the call. The faint lines on his forehead deepened. "I guess all we can do is wait," he said, then hung up.

He turned to Andrea. "That was my boss. He says the local plowing crews are focused on clearing major roads and areas where people are living. This area is low priority. It's going to be a while before they get to us."

She tried not to show her disappointment. She wanted to be in her own home, with clean clothes and internet access and a good cup of tea. But Jack couldn't do anything to bring her those things any faster, so why waste breath complaining. "I guess it's a good thing I made brownies," she said.

"Jack! You said you'd help me nail things!" Ian called.

"Go," she said. "I appreciate you keeping him occupied."

"All right. Call me if you need anything."

I'm beginning to feel as if I need you all the time, she thought, but it was too soon to say so. When she returned to her normal life, she might feel differently. She didn't know yet if Jack was someone she could depend on not just to protect her in times of danger, but to stick with her when things were a lot less exciting.

JACK FOUND SOME shorter lengths of firewood and arranged them on the floor in front of the woodstove. The brick hearth made a good place for Ian to try out his carpentry skills. Jack showed the boy how to hold the hammer and helped guide the first few swings. After Jack let go, Ian missed the nail more often than he hit it, but he seemed to be having a ball.

Jack sat back and puzzled over their mysterious visitor. Was it possible an animal—maybe the pack rat from cabin two—had come into the house and taken the oatmeal and milk? But what animal was large enough to carry off the saucepan and the can?

If Gravel Voice had been wearing a ballistics vest, it was possible he had survived the shot, but then Jack wouldn't have seen blood on the front of his shirt. And surely the boss would have left in the car with the rest of his men. Even if for some reason he had stayed behind, he would have focused on obtaining a weapon, not leftover breakfast. So that left someone else for the thief. A stranded camper? A felon on the run? He'd ask

Blessing to check with local law enforcement for reports of other thefts in the area or recently escaped convicts or missing campers.

"I'm tired now." Ian laid aside the hammer and looked up at Jack.

"You did a good job." Jack admired the row of crooked nails. "Why don't you lie down on the sofa and rest up from your hard work."

"Okay." The boy crawled up onto the sofa.

Jack set aside the hammer and nails and went into the kitchen, where Andrea was just taking the brownies from the oven. "Smells good." He nuzzled the back of her neck. "The brownies, too."

She swatted him away, but her eyes shone. "Where's Ian?" she asked.

"He's on the sofa, taking a nap."

"He lay down without a fuss?"

"It was his idea. He said he was tired."

She switched off the oven. "That's not like him. I'd better go check on him."

She left the kitchen and Jack retrieved the backpack and spread the papers on the table once more. If he could figure out exactly where Center Line Gulch was located, he could relay the information to the team and they could go in and investigate. If it was another hideout, Anderson and his pal might have headed there, thinking they would be safe. The team might even get lucky and find the ringleader, Duane Braeswood, and wrap up this whole case.

Andrea returned to the kitchen. "He feels a little feverish," she said. "It might just be from all the excitement the past couple of days, but I'm worried he's coming down with something. I'll feel better when I can get him home."

"Do you want me to call my boss and tell him it's an emergency?" Jack asked.

"No. It's just a slight fever. He may feel better after his nap." She sat across from him. "Have you figured out anything from those papers?"

"No luck with the Russian pamphlet." Jack tapped the booklet. "It doesn't have illustrations, only a lot of words and what look like mathematical formulas. How's your calculus?"

"Nonexistent," she said. "One of the reasons I was attracted to psychology was that it doesn't require a lot of math."

"I took plenty of math for my robotics courses, but none of this makes sense to me." He set aside the pamphlet. "The map is a mystery, too. Did whoever owned this backpack have the map to help him find this place, or is the circled area the most important information?"

"It must be marked for a reason," she said.

"It could be another hideout or a meeting place, the home of one of the group members, or even a place they planned to rob or carry out an act of sabotage." He continued to stare at the network of black-and-white squiggles and lines until they blurred, then let out a frustrated breath. "I'll have to let the team figure it out. If we compare it to full-size maps of the area, we should be able to find a match."

"It's frightening not knowing what they were up to," she said. "Do you really think Ian's kidnapping was just a way to get back at you, or did they have something else planned?"

"I wouldn't put anything past these people. They don't hesitate to use or kill innocent people to further their agenda. The organization is like an octopus. Every time we cut off one arm, there's another arm wreaking havoc. It won't stop until we get to the leaders."

"Mama! Mo-om!" Ian's wail had them both on their feet and running toward the living room. They found the boy sitting up on the sofa, his hair mussed and his face flushed. Lip trembling, he held up his arms to his mother.

Andrea gathered him close. "Honey, what is it?" she asked, pushing his hair back from his forehead. "What happened? Did you have a bad dream?"

"The man. The man was here."

Andrea and Jack exchanged looks. "What man, honey?" she asked.

"The man at the window." Ian pointed to the window at the side of the house. "He was trying to get in." Ian buried his face against his mother's shoulder and began to sob.

Jack raced outside and leaped off the porch. He spotted no one at the side of the house or running away, but in the snow beneath the window were the fresh imprints of a man's shoes, distinct from the prints Jack had made when he had removed the plywood from the window earlier.

He scanned the area around the cabin. The footsteps faded out at the edge of the trees, where the ground was rougher and the snow less deep. Trees came to within a few feet of the building on two sides, but those at the back had been thinned, providing a clear view of the river. Sunlight glinted off the rushing current and a fish-cleaning station nearby. A snow-covered path led from where Jack stood to the water, but the snow showed no sign of tracks, and the riverbank provided no good hiding place for a man on the run.

To Jack's left, trees closed in. Though the dense underbrush would make movement difficult, someone standing only a few dozen yards away would be hidden from anyone in the camp. Jack started walking toward the river, then circled around and began moving, as quickly and quietly as possible, through the trees along the camp boundary.

A rabbit exploded from beneath a stand of scrub oak to Jack's left. Pistol drawn, he whirled toward the sound. Branches shook and a squirrel let out a furious chattering as something large and heavy moved away from Jack.

Jack plunged toward the movement. "FBI!" he shouted. "Stop, or I'll shoot." He ducked behind a large tree trunk, braced for a barrage of gunfire.

But only silence greeted his demand. The movement stopped, not a twig or tree branch moving. After a few seconds, the squirrel resumed fussing. Staying in the cover of tree trunks, Jack took one cautious step forward and then another. He couldn't see his quarry, but he knew he had to be close.

"P-please don't shoot me."

The voice wasn't what he expected. The words were quavery and high-pitched, more like the voice of a child than a grown man.

"I won't hurt you," Jack said. *Not if I don't have to.* "Put your hands up and move to where I can clearly see you."

The tall, slender figure stepped into the cleared space beneath a broad-trunked pine tree. Dirty-blond hair fell across a pale face, the cheeks fuzzed with a patchy, thin beard. The jeans and hoodie he wore were dirty and torn, and he had a blanket draped around his shoulders. Jack relaxed, though he held the gun steady on the boy. "What's your name?" he asked.

"Brian. Brian Keeslar. Who are you?"

Jack ignored the question. "What were you doing looking in the window of that cabin?" he asked.

"I was just trying to see if there was anybody in there."

"So you could break in again and steal something?"

"I just wanted food. I didn't want anything else. Please, mister. You're not going to shoot me, are you?" The boy began to cry—and Jack could see that he was a boy, though an almost grown one—shoulders shaking, tears flowing down his cheeks.

Jack lowered the gun slightly. "What are you doing here, kid?" he asked.

Brian sniffed. "It's a long story."

"Come on." Joe motioned toward the cabin. "Let's go back to the camp. You can get something to eat and tell me all about it."

Chapter Ten

"You promise you won't hurt me?" Brian asked.

Jack holstered the gun. "I won't hurt you," he said.

"Are you really with the FBI?"

"I really am."

The boy wiped his face with the back of his hand. "Maybe you can help me," he said.

"I probably can. Come on. Let's go inside." Jack took hold of the young man's arm, more to keep him from startling and running back into the woods than anything else. He looked scared half to death. Jack led him up onto the porch of the cabin and opened the front door. "Andrea, we've got a visitor," he called, and ushered Brian inside.

She was still holding Ian, rocking him in her arms. The boy turned his head to look at their visitor but said nothing. "Andrea, this is Brian," Jack said. "Brian, this is Andrea and Ian."

"Hello." Brian kept his eyes on the floor and shifted from foot to foot.

"Why don't we all go into the kitchen and sit down," Jack said. "I'll fix Brian something to eat and he can tell us his story."

Andrea and Brian sat at the table, Ian in her lap. Jack opened a can of chili and heated it, then served it to Brian with crackers and a glass of water. At the last minute, he cut two brownies from the pan on the counter and put them on a napkin beside the bowl of chili.

"Thanks," Brian muttered. He stared at the food.

"Go ahead and eat," Andrea said. "We'll wait until you're done to talk."

The boy ate quickly, as if he was afraid someone would take the food from him. When he was done, he pushed the plate away. "That was the best meal I've had in a while," he said.

Jack took the chair across from him. "It looks like you've been living rough for some time," he said. "What's your story?"

The young man shifted in his chair. "First would you tell me what you're doing here?" He glanced at Andrea. "I mean, you seem like a nice family, but this is a funny place for a vacation."

Jack glanced at Andrea. Ian had fallen asleep, his head on her shoulder. "We're not on vacation," he said. "We're here because the men who were living here kidnapped Andrea's son. We were able to rescue him, but they got away. Snow has blocked the roads, so we're stuck here until the plows get out this far."

"Oh, man." Brian buried his face in his hands and Jack thought he might start to cry again. After a few seconds, he looked up. "I can't believe they did that to a little kid. I wish you had shot them all."

"Did you know the men who were here?" Andrea asked.

"I guess you could say that." Brian made a face. "They weren't my friends, if that's what you think."

"What was your relationship to them?" Jack asked.

"They kidnapped me, too. About three months ago, as close as I can tell."

"Your poor parents," Andrea said. "They must be worried sick."

Brian rubbed his hands up and down his arms. "It's just my dad. I'm not sure he even knows I'm missing. Or still missing."

The kid was right. This was a complicated story. "Why don't you start at the beginning," Jack said.

"Yeah, okay." Brian stared off to the side for a long moment, saying nothing. Then he began.

"My dad is a physicist, Barry Keeslar. He does a lot of work with nuclear energy, enriching uranium, experimenting with fission and fusion and all that stuff. Right now he's in Russia, or maybe Iceland—it's hard to keep track of his schedule. He travels around consulting with different governments and stuff." He shrugged. "I'm not all that sure. I haven't seen him in like ten years and we only talk on the phone every few months. My parents divorced when I was a little kid, but he never remarried or had any other kids or anything. My mom died last year and since then I've kind of been on my own."

Andrea reached out and covered his hand with her own. "I'm very sorry. That must have been hard."

He hesitated a moment before moving his hand away. "I did okay," he said. "I was going to school in Boulder. I'm a freshman at the University of Colorado. My dad paid for that, at least. I had friends and a job and everything. Life was good. Then one day I'm closing up the pizza place where I work weekends and these two guys dressed in black come in. I figure they want to rob the place. My boss already told me if that happened, I'm supposed to cooperate. Shut up and give them what they want. But what these guys wanted was me. They knocked me out and the next thing I know, I wake up here, tied up and chained to a bed."

"Who kidnapped you?" Jack asked. "Do you know their names?"

"There were three main guys. The one in charge they called Chief, but he slipped a couple of times and I think his real name was Jerry. I never heard last names. The older guy who stayed in this cabin with me was Leo, and they called the other guy Andy, though he acted like he hated the name. Which only made the other two use it more. There were other people in and out of here a lot, but most of them, I never knew their names."

"And they held you here for three months?" Andrea looked stricken at the thought.

"They told me as soon as my dad 'cooperated,' they would let me go." He made air quotes around the word *cooperated*. "I didn't think it was money they were after, though I guess my dad has plenty of that. It might have had something to do with his job, but they wouldn't answer any of my questions, and they didn't like it if I asked."

"What did your father do when they contacted him?" Andrea asked.

"I don't know what my father did. From what little I overheard, I think at first this bunch was having a hard time getting ahold of him. He moves around a lot and he's kind of the absentminded-professor type. He doesn't always answer his phone or check his email, especially when he's involved in a project."

"The police must have been looking for you," she said. "Your friends and professors must have noticed when you didn't show up for class."

"I don't think so. They grabbed me just before a three-day weekend, so my friends probably thought I left town. When I didn't come back, they probably thought I'd quit school or transferred somewhere else. It happens."

"So they kept you here for three months," Jack said.

"Yeah. They kept me tied up a lot of the time, but after a while they'd untie me and let me walk around. They told me they'd kill me if I tried to get away and I believed them. They were mean. Sometimes they'd knock me around, not because they were angry or anything, just because they were bored. They fed me the same boring canned stuff they ate, but sometimes Leo would 'forget' to give me meals. The longer I stayed here, the more worried I got. I figured sooner or later they were going to kill me."

"How did you get away?" Jack asked.

"A couple of days ago, they left me alone. I couldn't believe it. I overheard them arguing and I guess Leo was pitching a fit about always having to stay here, guarding me, so they left me tied up and all drove away together. I couldn't believe it. I had a broken bottle I'd found in the trash a couple of weeks back. I'd stashed it under the mattress and as soon as they left, I got it out and used it to saw at the ropes. It took forever and I was terrified they would come back before I got done, but at last I was free. About that time they came back and

I ran into the woods. I thought I would hike to the road and hitch a ride, but it started snowing and then I got lost in the woods. By the time I ended up at the road, the bridge was blocked, so I came back here, only to find they were gone and you folks were here."

"Why didn't you come to us for help?" Andrea asked.

"I thought you might be part of their group," he said. "They've had all kinds of people in and out of here while I've been here. Some of them stay for a single night, some for a couple of weeks."

"You thought I was a terrorist?" Andrea's face betrayed her horror at this idea.

"There was a woman here once, about your age," Brian said. "Leo said she was the daughter of someone important. They didn't keep her tied up or anything, but I got the impression she didn't want to be here. They kept me out of sight while she was here. After a couple of days she left."

"I hate to think of you out in the snow, cold and hungry," Andrea said. She stroked Ian's sleeping head. "You're safe now."

"We'll locate your father and contact him as soon as we're back in Durango," Jack said. "I'll want you to give a statement to the FBI and look through some pictures to try to identify the men who held you. When we find them, we'll ask you to testify against them."

"I'll do it." He sat up straighter. The meal, and maybe talking about his ordeal, had vanquished the hunted look.

"For now, can you tell me anything about what the people here were up to?" Jack asked. "Anything you overheard about other people or locations or anything like that could help."

Brian shook his head. "I can't think of anything right now. Mostly they just groused to each other about being stuck here while their bosses got to live in some fancy house somewhere."

"Did they mention the boss's name?" Jack asked.

"No. They just called him Boss. When they weren't grousing about him, they liked to shoot off guns in the woods, and sometimes Leo went fishing. Jerry went on sometimes about the importance of their mission and how they were saving America, but the other two seemed to be in it for the money. They talked about what they were going to buy when they got their big payoff, but I never did figure out where the money was supposed to come from."

"You may remember more later," Jack said. "Whatever you can tell us will be helpful. Even details you think are unimportant could help us fill in another piece of the puzzle."

"I'll do whatever I can to help you nail these guys," Brian said. He turned to Andrea. "Is your little boy okay now?"

"The kidnappers didn't hurt him, if that's what you mean." She laid her hand protectively on Ian's head. "But he's running a fever and not feeling well. I think the stress of all this has made him sick."

"Do you know when the snowplows will be here?" Brian asked. "I don't want to stay around here any longer than I have to. I'm worried Jerry and his friends might come back."

"Jerry—" Andrea began.

"Jerry won't be bothering you anymore." Jack caught Andrea's eye and shook his head. No sense going into the whole story of Jerry and his shooting. There would be time enough for that once they had confirmed the man was dead. "I'll call my boss again and let him know we've found you and get an update on our rescuers."

He moved into the living room and took out his phone. The battery was getting low. As soon as he completed this call, he would have to dig out his charger.

"Blessing." As always, the special agent in charge barked the word like a command.

"Jack Prescott, sir. We've had a new development."

"What is it this time?"

"We've met up with a teenage boy who says Anderson and his group held him hostage for three months. He escaped right before they brought Ian McNeil here and has been hiding in the woods near the camp. His name is Brian Keeslar and he says his father is a nuclear physicist. He thinks the group was trying to force his dad into doing some work for them."

"Give me that name again?"

Jack gave him the boy's name and the name of his father. "Apparently, his dad is working overseas and hard to get ahold of. Brian doesn't know if the kidnappers succeeded in contacting him or not."

"If the kid spent three months with these people, maybe he can tell us more about them."

"That's what I'm hoping," Jack said. "It sounds like he had a pretty rough time of it, but he wants to cooperate. Any word on when we're getting out of here?"

"Not yet. I'll see what I can do to move you up the

priority list, but apparently, there are a lot of people ahead of you."

"Tell them we've got a sick kid here. Ian is running a fever and not feeling well. I think—" A loud noise vibrating the air cut off Jack's words. He raised his eyes toward the ceiling and the noise overhead.

"Is that a helicopter?" Brian stood in the kitchen doorway, Andrea behind him with Ian in her arms.

Jack opened the front door and looked out. "Sir, you didn't just send a helicopter to get us, did you?"

"Do you really think I have the budget to scramble a helicopter in a nonemergency situation?" Blessing asked.

"Then I think this just became an emergency situation," Jack said. He peered at the helicopter that was just clearing the treetops, preparing to set down in the middle of the camp. "I think Anderson has returned. And from the looks of things, he's brought reinforcements."

Chapter Eleven

Andrea clutched Ian so tightly he began to whimper. "It's okay, honey," she said. She smoothed the hair back from his feverish forehead, her heart hammering in time with the throbbing helicopter rotor. "What do we do?" she asked Jack.

"We've got to get out of here," he said. He ran past her into the kitchen and retrieved his coat and the pack. He turned to Brian. "We're going to run out of here straight to my truck. It's the black Ford parked out front. Andrea and Ian go in first, then you and me."

Brian's Adam's apple bobbed in his throat as he swallowed. "Can we get away from them?" he asked.

"We will." Jack slung the pack onto his back and drew his Glock. "Andrea, when I give the word, you make a run for it."

She woke Ian and helped him put on his coat, then shrugged into her own and retrieved the blanket from the bedroom and handed it to Brian. "Wrap up in this," she instructed. "Since you don't have a coat." She grabbed the other blanket from the sofa and draped it over Ian. Her instinct was to hide her baby from the men in that helicopter. "I'm ready," she said.

"Wait until I give the word." Jack eased open the door and peered out. Almost immediately, gunfire exploded from the helicopter, bullets slamming into the wood at his feet and beside him. Andrea screamed as he dived back into the room. Brian shoved the door shut, then retreated toward the kitchen.

"We'll have to go out the back window," Jack said, and led the way into the kitchen. By the time Andrea joined him, he had already removed the nails he'd driven into the windowsill earlier and pulled a kitchen chair over to the counter. "Brian, you go first," he instructed. "You can help Andrea with Ian. Andrea, as soon as you're out, head for the river. I'll be right behind you."

Brian's face had lost all color and his hands trembled as he clutched at the windowsill. But he didn't hesitate to crawl through the opening. His feet hit the ground below with a soft *thud*. No gunfire followed him.

"Take this." Jack passed the pack through the window, then reached for Ian.

Andrea clutched at the boy, reluctant to let him go. But Ian held his arms out to Jack and cuddled against his neck. Jack smoothed his hand down the boy's back. "It's going to be okay, buddy," he murmured.

Brian took Ian and held him while Andrea crawled through the window. She landed crookedly and fell but was immediately on her feet and taking her son.

"Go!" Jack commanded. "Run to the river. I'll meet you there."

Brian reached for her hand, his grip stronger than she had expected. "Come on," he said. "We have to hurry before they figure out what we're doing."

The race for the river felt like running in a dream, time slowing as she slogged through the heavy, wet snow. She carried Ian cradled against her chest, the blanket draped over him. His weight dragged at her. Brian, no longer holding her hand, moved farther and farther ahead of her. Her breath came in pants, lungs straining, ears attuned for the sound of the gunfire she feared would mow her down.

Then she was standing behind the fish-cleaning shelter with Brian. When Jack joined them a minute later, she almost sobbed with relief. "I shoved the chair away and closed the window behind me," he said. "Maybe that will delay them figuring out how we got out."

He took the pack from Brian and put it on, then reached for Ian. She surrendered the boy without protest. Jack would protect him, she was certain.

"Where do we go now?" Brian asked.

"If we stay in the woods, they won't be able to get a clear shot from overhead," Jack said. "We need to find a safe place to hide before they come after us on foot."

"I can't hear the helicopter anymore," Andrea said. Did that mean the kidnappers were already coming after them?

"They've probably landed," Jack said. "It will take them a few minutes to search the cabin and figure out we're not there. The faster we move, the more distance we can gain on them."

"I know a place we can hide," Brian said. "I spent the night there last night. It's an abandoned mine about a mile from here, maybe a little more. But we'll have to climb a pretty steep slope to get to it."

Jack clapped him on the back. "Let's go."

They jogged through the woods, maneuvering around downed trees and clots of underbrush too thick to push through. They stumbled through drifts and over hidden rocks, but beneath the sheltering trees the snow wasn't as deep. Jack broke trail and the others followed in his footsteps. No chance of hiding their path from anyone who might be searching behind them. Their best hope was to move as quickly as possible and find a good place to hide.

The scent of fresh pine and spruce washed over them, clean and bracing. Brian directed them west, the elevation gradually increasing.

Soon Andrea was out of breath. "I definitely have to get to the gym more often when this is over," she panted as she followed Jack and Brian up an ever-steeper slope. Jack stopped to wait for her. "How's your leg?" she asked when she caught up with him.

"It's okay." But his grimace of pain told her otherwise. He should be at home, resting and recovering, instead of climbing a steep slope with the burden of a child in his arms.

"Let me take Ian," she said.

"No. I've got him," he said.

"I want to stay with Jack," the boy said, as if he knew the man, even injured, was more capable of getting him safely up the slope than his mother.

They continued climbing, with Brian in the lead now, taking them to his hideout. "It's not much farther." Brian stopped and looked back over his shoulder to Jack. "Should we be doing something to cover our tracks?" he asked.

Jack shook his head. "There's no point in that now.

They know we're out here. Our best bet is to find a good hiding place and lie low until we can get help. When we're settled in, I'll call my boss and give him our location. He'll get help to us."

Andrea didn't ask how that help was going to cross a blocked road and get past the kidnappers to reach them. This was the FBI, after all. Maybe they would call in the National Guard or send in a SWAT team. She'd settle for the cavalry on horseback if it meant she and her son would be safe.

"I have to pee," Ian announced.

"Hold on a little longer, buddy," Jack said. "We're going to stop soon."

"I have to pee now!" He pounded his fists against Jack's shoulders and squirmed in his arms. "Put me down."

Jack looked at Andrea. "Tell him to hold on just a little longer," he said. "We need to put more distance between us and Anderson's bunch before we stop."

She took Ian from him. "You can hold it a little longer, can't you?" she asked.

"No, Mama. I have to go." He tried to get down, his face screwed up as if at any moment he might start screaming.

"It will be easier if we stop and let him go now," Andrea said. "It won't take a minute." She lowered the boy to the ground. "Okay, honey, you can go now."

"Not with everyone watching," he protested.

"We'll just, um, turn our backs," Jack said. He turned around and motioned for Brian to do the same.

"Hurry, honey," Andrea said.

Jack didn't like letting Andrea and the boy out of his

sight, but he hadn't heard any sounds of pursuit since they had left the camp, and Andrea wouldn't go far.

Her footsteps faded as she led Ian into the woods. He heard the soft tones of her voice as she reassured her son. The sound reassured Jack, too. As long as he could hear her, he knew she was all right.

"How much farther until we reach this mine?" he asked Brian.

"Maybe another twenty minutes." Brian wrinkled his forehead. "I kind of found it by accident, so I wasn't really keeping track of time."

"It is safe to go into?" Jack asked.

"I didn't go very far. But the entrance is pretty big and dry. It's just this cave carved out of rock. And you have a nice view of the valley from the entrance."

A good view of whatever was approaching them sounded safe to Jack. He turned around. "Andrea? Are you almost finished?"

No answer.

"Andrea!"

The sound of something moving very fast through the underbrush toward him had him resting a hand on his gun and looking for suitable cover. "Jack!" Ian's shout sent ice through Jack's veins. "The bad men took Mommy! She's gone!"

ANDREA FOUGHT BACK tears as a large man dressed all in black and armed with a semiautomatic rifle dragged her away from the others. She had let Ian run ahead of her as they made their way back toward the others, hoping that if he had a chance to stretch his legs now, he would be less restless later.

Her captor had stepped out from behind a tree, clamped a hand over her mouth and wrapped her in an iron-hard grip before she could so much as squeak. He had slipped the gun from her waistband and pinned her to him almost before she realized what was happening. Ian had stopped and looked back. His eyes widened when he saw her.

Run! She'd wished she could scream this silent plea. He must have seen the message in her eyes, however, since he'd whirled and raced away.

Her captor, who seemed to be alone, dragged her back through the woods. No way did she have the strength to fight him, so she made herself go limp in his arms. At least he seemed to be moving away from the others, not toward them. If Ian could get to Jack, her boy would be safe.

Her captor dragged her, with seemingly little effort, at least a quarter mile, to where four other men waited by the river. All were similarly dressed in black, with masks over their faces and weapons slung on their shoulders. She tried to memorize details about them, but their uniforms had clearly been designed to hide any distinguishing features. She was pretty sure none of these men were Anderson. They all looked bigger and more menacing than the man who had snatched her purse.

"Look what I found." Her captor shoved her toward the others. She landed on her knees in the snow at their feet—four pairs of identical black boots ranged around her.

"Where are the others?" The shortest and slightest of the group spoke, his voice slightly nasal.

"They're up the trail a little ways, near where I found her." Her captor jerked his head in the direction they had come. "The little boy and the first kid—Keeslar's son—and the fed."

"If you got close enough to see them, why didn't you just take them out and save us the trouble?" another of the group said.

"Grabbing the woman was better," her captor said. "We'll use her as bait to get the other three without any risk to us."

The shorter man nudged her with the toe of his boot. She'd been too afraid to move from her position on the ground. "Can you talk?" he asked.

"I don't have anything to say to you."

The reply earned her a sharp kick. "You want to see your kid or that fed again, you'd better cooperate," he said.

Her captor grabbed her arm and dragged her to her feet.

"What do you want me to do?" she asked, trying to sound stronger than she felt. She had always believed bullies played on weakness.

His smile sent a chill through her. "First we're going to tie you up," he said. "Then we're going to make you scream."

IAN CLUNG TO JACK, tears streaming down his face, breath coming in hiccuping gasps. Jack knelt and tried to calm the boy, even as his own heart hammered in his chest. "Tell me exactly what happened," he said, his hand firm on the boy's shoulder. "Who took your mother? How many people were there?"

"J-just one man. A big man, dressed all in black—
like a ninja!"

"He grabbed your mother, but you got away?" Jack
asked.

"She let me run ahead and when I looked back to
make sure she was coming, he was hugging her. He had
a big gun and a mask on his face."

His bottom lip quivered and Jack patted his shoulder, trying to hold off the tears. "Were there any other
people with the man?"

Ian sniffed. "No. It was just him. He started drag-
ging Mama away." He pulled on Jack's arm. "We have
to go find her."

"We will find her, buddy, I promise." He patted the
boy's shoulder again and stood, pulling his phone from
his pocket as he did so.

"Can you get someone here to help us?" Brian asked.

Jack shook his head. "No signal." He stowed the
phone, already shifting his focus to strategizing to free
Andrea. But first he had to see to his other obligations.
"You have to promise me something, too," he said.

"What?" Ian asked.

"You have to promise to stay with Brian while I go
and get your mom. Can you do that for me?"

Ian regarded the young man critically, then looked
back at Jack. "I want to go with you," he said.

"I know you do. But I don't want these men to try
to hurt you. Instead, I want you to go with Brian to a
hiding place he knows."

"Yeah." Brian straightened his shoulders and did his
best to look excited. "It's like a secret clubhouse I know
about. I'll take you with me."

Ian still looked doubtful.

Jack bent to put his face close to Ian's. "It's really, really important to me that you go with Brian," he said. "I'm going to fight these bad guys and get your mother and then we'll come to the clubhouse where you and Brian will be waiting."

Ian stuck out his lower lip but nodded. "All right."

Jack straightened and pulled Brian aside. "I want you to take this." He slipped the pack off his back. "Have you ever shot a gun?

Brian's eyes widened. "No."

Jack unzipped the pack and took out the pistol. "I hope you don't have to use this, but the people who are after us are armed, and I don't want to leave you help-less." He showed Brian how to operate the safety. "The rules are simple—don't put your finger on the trigger until you're ready to shoot, don't ever point it at any-thing you don't want to shoot, and when you do shoot, be aware of what is around and behind your target. Don't use it if you don't have to."

"No, sir, I won't."

Jack replaced the gun in the pack and adjusted the straps to better fit Brian. "How do I find this mine where you're headed?" he asked.

"Keep climbing up this mountain and above tree line you'll see the opening to the mine," Brian said. "It's kind of a scramble to get there, but there's sort of a trail."

Jack slipped his cell phone from his pocket and handed it to the boy. "I'm hoping you'll be able to get a signal when you get above tree line," he said. "When you're able to call out, call the number for Ted Blessing and tell him what happened. He'll send help."

"What about you?"

"Andrea and I will meet you either at the mine or wherever the FBI takes you. Don't worry about us. You take care of Ian and yourself." He clapped the young man's shoulders. "You've survived a tough ordeal for three months—you can get through this."

"Yes, sir."

Jack squatted down in front of Ian. "Everything's going to be okay," he said. "Now, tell me—which way did the man take your mother?"

Ian pointed in the direction he had run from. Was the kidnapper taking Andrea toward the river? Or back to the camp? Jack straightened. "Okay, guys. You'd better get going. I'll see you both soon." He hoped.

When he was satisfied Brian and Ian were headed away from him, he began searching the ground in the area where he had last seen Andrea and Ian. The recent snow made it easier to track movements. He found where Ian's small tennis shoes had scuffed through the drifts and, a few yards later, spotted a portion of a man's large boot print and drag marks, as if from someone—Andrea?—being pulled backward across the ground.

He moved forward slowly, trying to stay in cover, following the boot prints and drag marks. He hadn't gone far when a woman's terrified scream shattered the woodland silence. Jack straightened and began running toward the sound.

Chapter Twelve

The screaming continued, a ragged, piercing note that made the hair on the back of Jack's neck stand on end. He slowed as he neared the sound, every sense attuned to his surroundings, alert for danger. A flash of blue caught his attention and he turned toward it, tensing when he spotted Andrea, tied to a tree, her head thrown back, mouth open in a keening cry that echoed in the otherwise still air.

He moved to within a few dozen yards of her, using the trunk of an old-growth juniper for cover. His first instinct was to rush forward and free her from whatever was making her scream that way, but he took a deep breath and forced himself to assess the situation rationally. No one else was around her, but he sensed whoever had tied her up this way was close, probably watching. She appeared unhurt. He couldn't see any blood or obvious injuries or even torn clothing. The screaming continued, but he realized it had a mechanical quality, like an amateur actor performing on cue. Had her captor ordered her to scream in order to draw him in?

Movement to her right caught his attention and

he drew the Glock. But a man, wearing a mask and dressed in black, had already moved in beside Andrea and placed a knife to her throat. "You can come out now, Agent Prescott. I know you don't want to see this lovely lady bleed to death right in front of you."

Jack hesitated. The man in black brought the knife closer. Andrea cried out and a thin trickle of blood slid down her throat. Jack holstered the Glock and stepped into the clearing, his arms raised.

Four men, also masked and wearing black, moved out of the underbrush and surrounded him. One took the Glock and another bound his wrists behind his back. "Where is the backpack?" a shorter man with a nasal voice demanded.

"What backpack?"

The man slammed his fist into the side of Jack's head. His vision blurred and he struggled to remain upright. "What did you do with the pack you found in the cabin?" the man asked.

"I hid it."

"We're wasting our time with him." A different man spoke. "We should kill them both and go after the boy and the kid. They won't get far on their own."

"We need that pack," the short man said.

"He had it when I spotted them earlier." The man with the knife had moved away from Andrea and joined them. "He must have given it to the kid," he said.

"We'll go after the kids," the short man said. "But we won't kill them—yet. Tie him up with her."

Two of the men dragged Jack toward the tree. He resisted, earning another dizzying blow to the head. "Try that again and I will slit her throat," the first man growled, and shoved Jack hard against the same tree where Andrea was tied.

They bound Jack to the tree, his back to Andrea. Then four of them, including the man with the knife and the shorter man, left. One man stayed behind to guard the captives. He sat on a fallen log a short distance away, a rifle laid across his knees. "I'd love to have an excuse to shoot you, fed," he said. "So don't try anything."

The tips of Andrea's fingers brushed his. He curled his hands toward her, wishing he could reassure her. But the odds didn't appear to be in their favor. They would need a miracle to get out of this. Brian hadn't had time to reach tree line yet. Even if he had managed to call Agent Blessing right away, the team couldn't have mobilized quickly enough to get here, and they had no way of pinpointing Jack and Andrea's location.

"You shouldn't have come back for me," she whispered.

"You didn't really think I would abandon you, did you?"

"You should have stayed with Ian."

"Brian is with Ian. They'll be all right."

"Not with those four looking for them."

Jack studied their guard. He was heavier than the other men, though most of that bulk was probably muscle. He sat upright on the log, both hands on the rifle, his expression impossible to judge behind the black mask. "I'm not giving up yet," Jack said.

"You two stop blabbing over there," the guard ordered.

"What's with the ninja getup?" Jack asked.

The man grinned, revealing a crooked front tooth.

"We heard you guys could identify us from surveillance videos and stuff, so the boss decided we should dress like this to maintain our anonymity."

"In your case, it didn't work, Gordon Phillips," Jack said. "Or should I just call you Gordo? That's what your prison buds called you, isn't it?"

The comment earned him a blow to the side of the head but it was worth it to see Gordo squirm. He loomed over them, having sprung from his seat on the fallen tree. "Who told you my name?" he demanded. "I never saw you before in my life."

"We know all about you and your pals," Jack said. Though Gordo—thanks to his crooked tooth—was the only man Jack had recognized.

"I ought to shoot you now," he said.

"Then your boss wouldn't have the chance to find out what else I know," Jack said. "I'm guessing he wouldn't like that."

"I'd say you died trying to escape." Gordo hefted the rifle. "It happens."

"Then your boss would wonder why you weren't capable of looking after two tied-up prisoners on your own."

"Shut up!"

"Make me."

"Jack!" Andrea gasped.

Gordo took a step toward Jack. He raised the rifle butt-first over his head and Jack braced for the blow. But before Gordo could bring the weapon down on Jack's head, gunshots raked the clearing, bullets shredding bark from the tree where Jack and Andrea were tied and hitting the snow at Gordo's feet.

"What the—?" Gordo dived into the cover behind Jack and Andrea, but the bullets followed, the shots more focused on the man in black now. Gordo let out a scream and Andrea tensed.

The silence that followed rang in his ears. Jack tried to breathe normally, though his heart raced. "Gordo, are you okay?" he called.

Gordo swore. "I'm shot!"

"Come out with your hands up!" The voice that gave the order was strangely deep, with an echoing quality.

"Come in and get me!" Gordo shouted, and aimed a burst of gunfire toward the voice.

More gunfire peppered the bushes where Gordo sheltered. Not a rifle, Jack decided, but a pistol, of a large enough caliber to be effective at close range.

Gordo returned the fire but shot wildly, unable to see his enemy.

Jack couldn't see anything, either. The shots continued, first from one side of the clearing, then the other. The shooter was close but obviously moving around. Another cry rose from Gordo. "All right," he cried. "Don't kill me."

"Throw out your weapon!" the voice ordered.

The rifle landed in the dirt a few feet from Jack.

"Your handgun, too," the voice ordered.

Muttering under his breath, Gordo tossed out not one but two handguns.

"Come out with your hands up."

"I'm wounded. I can't walk!"

"Then crawl."

The bushes swayed and bent as Gordo crawled from

his cover. He had a black bandanna tied around his left thigh.

"Lay down with your face pressed to the ground," the voice ordered.

Gordo complied, his cheek nestled in the snow, arms stretched in front of him.

"Don't move or I'll kill you!" The voice was higher now—excited.

Gordo didn't move.

Silence followed, but Jack thought he detected movement through the bushes. After a tense moment, Brian, the pistol in one hand, a cone of paper in the other, stepped from the trees nearest Andrea. He stuffed the paper in his pocket and put a finger to his lips as he approached and knelt beside them. "I need something to cut you loose," he whispered.

"There's a knife in my pocket," Jack said.

Brian fished out the knife and freed Jack, then Andrea. "Where's Ian?" she asked. "Is Ian all right?"

"He's good," Brian said. "He's hiding somewhere safe."

Jack retrieved Gordo's discarded rifle and stood over the man. "Andrea, I need you to tie him up for me," he said.

Gordo had turned his head to watch them, but he hadn't moved. "You can't leave me here to bleed to death," he said.

Jack regarded the gunshot wounds to the man's thigh and forearm. "You're not going to bleed to death from those," he said. "Or would you rather I finished you off now?"

Gordo turned his head farther and glared at Brian. "You were the one shooting at me? You're just a kid."

Brian grinned. "Too bad I'm not a better shot, huh?" He gestured with the gun toward Gordo.

Jack gently took the gun from the young man. "Careful," he said, and slid the pistol into his pocket. Then he retrieved the two handguns Gordo had discarded.

Andrea finished knotting the rope around Gordo's ankles and stood. "I want to see Ian," she said.

"Take this." Jack handed her one of the guns. The other kidnappers probably had her handgun, along with his Glock. "Let's get out of here."

"This way," Brian said. He loped ahead of them, then stopped a few hundred yards down the river. He hooked two fingers in his mouth and let out a piercing whistle. "All clear!" he shouted.

"Look, Mama! I climbed a tree!"

Jack spotted Ian halfway up a leaning spruce. The boy scampered down the tree, climbing down the limbs as if he were climbing down a ladder. He ran to them and Andrea scooped him up in her arms. "I'm so glad to see you," she said.

"Brian and I came back to save you and Jack," Ian said.

Jack turned to Brian. "I told you to take Ian and keep yourselves safe," he said.

"I know what you told me, but I couldn't let you face those guys alone." Brian straightened his shoulders, as if bracing for a fight. "I knew there would be more than one of them. They always travel in packs. When they kidnapped me, there were four of them. Four of them against one teenager. I had to at least follow and make sure you were all right."

"And I'm glad you did." Jack clapped the young man on the back. "How many shots did you fire?"

"I don't know." He shrugged. "All of them. I used up all the ammunition, but I figured that guy back there didn't have to know that. It was pure luck that I hit him. I wasn't aiming or anything. I just wanted to scare him off."

Jack decided not to point out that the young man's wild shooting had come close to injuring Jack and Andrea. What mattered most was that they were safe, at least for now.

"Jack." Andrea moved closer to him, Ian on her hip. "Hadn't we better get out of here? The others might come back."

Jack nodded. "When you were headed back here, did you see the other four men who were here?" he asked Brian.

"We saw them. But they didn't see us. We climbed the tree." He pointed to the spruce that had sheltered Ian. "They never even thought to look up. That's why I thought it would be a safe place to leave Ian while I tried to help you two."

"Good job. But Andrea's right. We need to get moving. If we don't reach help or a good hiding place before nightfall, we could be in real trouble."

Chapter Thirteen

The climb became much steeper, so that they had to grab on to branches to pull themselves up the outcroppings of rock. The sun had melted the snow in places, but in others the ground was still hidden beneath foot-deep drifts. Soon they were all wet to the knees, breathing hard from the exertion. Eventually, the cover of trees gave way to snow-pocked rock, yellow mine waste spilling down the slope in places. Andrea tried to focus on carefully placing her feet and hands as she climbed, shaken by how close she had come to death. She hadn't wanted to scream—hadn't wanted to lure Jack into her captors' trap, but when the one with the knife had threatened to cut her throat, she had given in, ashamed of her cowardice yet wanting desperately to live.

She would need more time to sort out her tangled emotions about everything that had happened. For now, they weren't out of danger yet. She tried not to think of how exposed they were on this bare slope, though tension pulled at her shoulders as she braced for gunfire that never came.

"Not much farther now," Brian said. "You can see the entrance from here." He stopped and pointed up. Following his line of sight, she spotted the patch of black against the pale rock.

"How do we get up there?" she asked.

"There's a path. I can just make it out." Jack looked back at them. He had reclaimed the pack and his phone from Brian and taken Ian as well, the boy clinging to his neck. Andrea marveled at how well her son had weathered the ordeal so far—thanks in no small part to Jack's calm courage, which strengthened them all.

"Just a little farther." Brian turned to pull her up beside him. In the space of a few hours, the young man had transformed from trembling waif to almost-brash teen, brandishing the pistol and vaulting up the mountain slope. Andrea suspected Jack's example—and Jack's trust in him—had restored the young man's weakened confidence. She didn't think this quality to inspire others was something the FBI had trained him to do. It was part of Jack's nature, like his crooked smile and the gentle way he touched her.

"Here we are." Above her, Jack stopped on a narrow rock ledge. He reached down to pull her up alongside him. Instinctively, she moved to one side, into the shadows cast by the mountain that rose behind them.

"Here you go, buddy." Jack set Ian on the rock shelf.

The boy stood on his own, gaping at the scenery. "Wow. We're really high up," he said.

"Come over here, honey." Andrea beckoned him to her side. "How are you feeling?"

"Okay." He looked up at her. "Can we go home now?"

"Soon, honey." She hoped it was very soon. She needed to feel safe again and to feel in control once more.

"Is it safe?" Jack asked Brian as he joined them on the ledge.

"Like I said, I didn't go very far in," Brian said. "I didn't have a light and it was really dark. But I spent the night just inside the entrance. It's not that comfortable, but I was out of the snow and wind and hidden."

"Let's see what we've got." Jack pulled a flashlight from a side pocket of the pack and switched it on. The rest of them followed him inside.

The entrance to the mine wasn't as creepy as Andrea had feared. The space, approximately eight feet deep and six feet wide, was cut into the rock and was dry and appeared bug- and varmint-free. The only smell was that of dust and the dried leaves that littered the floor. A tunnel, shored up with square timbers, led farther into the mountain.

"You can use this to sit on." Jack handed Andrea the blanket and took off the pack. "I'm going to explore a little farther into the mine."

"I'll go with you," Brian said.

Andrea spread the blanket and settled down onto it. "I want to go with Jack," Ian said, and started after the men.

"You have to stay here with me," Andrea said.

"But I want to go with Jack." Ian stuck out his lower lip and his face clouded, the precursor to a storm.

"Do you want Mommy to have to stay here by myself?" She gently took his arm. "Jack and Brian will be right back. Stay here and I'll tell you a story."

"I don't want a story." But he let her pull him down into her lap.

"This is a good story," she said, wrapping her arms

around him, as much to reassure herself as to keep him warm. "It's about a brave little boy. He was an explorer."

"What did he explore?"

She looked around her, searching for inspiration. "He climbed mountains," she said. "And he explored caves."

"Did he find treasure?"

"Yes, he found treasure. Gold and jewels."

"And a spaceship," Ian said. "He found a spaceship and he flew it to the moon."

She smiled. "What did the spaceship look like?" she asked.

"Andrea! Come here!"

Jack's voice was urgent enough that she was on her feet immediately. "What is it?" she called. "What's wrong?"

"You've got to see what we've found," he said. "Evidence that could blow this case wide-open."

JACK STARED AT the contents of the metal trunk he'd discovered in an alcove just off the mine tunnel. Neat putty-colored bricks, each individually wrapped in plastic, almost filled the container. The trunk's stainless outer surface, covered with only a light coating of dust, stood out from the old tools and piles of rock around it. Though a padlock dangled from the trunk's hasp, it had been undone and Jack had no trouble lifting the top to reveal this treasure trove.

"What is it?" Brian asked. "Drugs or something?"

Jack lifted out one of the bricks and hefted it in his hand. "I'm pretty sure it's plastic explosives," he said. "Probably C-4."

Brian took a step back. "It's not going to blow up, is it?"

Jack tossed the brick back into the trunk. "No danger of that. It needs a detonator to explode." He moved aside another brick to reveal a small cardboard box filled with a row of white plastic tubes attached to insulated wire cords.

Andrea joined them, out of breath from her race down the tunnel with Ian. "What is it?" she asked. "What did you find?"

"Explosives," Brian said. "Lots of them."

Jack motioned to the trunk. "Plastic explosives. Probably stolen. I think it's the same stuff used in bombs set off at professional bicycle races around the country this past year. We caught a guy we think is connected to this group trying to sabotage the Colorado Pro Cycling Challenge in Denver in August."

"I remember hearing about that." Andrea shifted Ian to her hip and stared at the open trunk. "What's it doing here?"

"Good question." Jack closed the trunk. "It's not the sort of thing they use in mining."

"This place doesn't look like anyone has mined it in a hundred years." Brian picked up one of the chunks of rock piled beside the trunk. "What do you think these are? Geodes or something?" He examined the fist-sized specimen.

"Ore samples, maybe?" Jack shook his head. "They were probably here before the trunk was even brought in."

Andrea set Ian down and he immediately headed for the rocks and began picking them up. She glanced at the explosives. "I'm guessing that's enough to do a lot of damage," she said.

"That trunk is probably enough to level this mountain," he said. "At least, it would make a good-sized crater."

"Do you think Anderson and his bunch hid the trunk here?" she asked.

"We'll try to get fingerprints and DNA evidence off the trunk to be sure," Jack said. "But that would be my guess."

"I'm glad I'm not the one who had to haul that heavy trunk all the way up here," Brian said.

"They probably thought it was worth the effort because no one would ever find it up here," Jack said. "Before you found the place, probably no one had been here for decades."

"So this will help you connect Andy and the others to your Denver terrorists?" Brian asked.

"Yes. And it might even lead us to their ringleader— the man we've been trying to stop for the past year," Jack said. "He looks to be the money and the brains behind the operation."

"Somebody left their backpack," Ian said.

Jack whirled around and found the boy tugging at a black-and-orange backpack that had been covered by the pile of rocks. He knelt beside the boy and joined him in pulling the pack free. "Let's see what you've got there," he said.

"Maybe it will have a name or something," Brian said. "But I guess that would be too easy, huh?"

Jack hooked the end of his pocketknife into the ring attached to the zipper pull of the pack's main compartment and eased it open. He knelt and carefully upended the contents on the floor.

"No weapons in this one," Andrea observed.

"Candy!" Ian reached for the chocolate bar on top of the pile.

Andrea grabbed his hand and pulled him back. "You can't eat the evidence, dear," she said.

Jack slipped the candy back into the pack and fished out a man's wallet with the tips of his fingers. He flipped it open and stared at the driver's license, a cold chill sweeping over him.

"Mark Renfro." Andrea read the name over his shoulder. "He doesn't look like one of the men we saw at the camp."

"He's not." Jack closed the billfold and returned it to the pack, then stuffed everything else back inside.

"Who is he?" Brian asked.

"He's the brother of one of the agents in my unit. He disappeared on a hiking trip in Colorado over a year ago."

"Another kidnapping victim?" Andrea asked.

"Either that or a murder victim." He raised his eyes to meet hers. "We have to find these people and stop them."

"Yeah," Brian said. "As long as they don't find us first."

ANDREA SHIVERED AT Brian's reminder that they were far from out of danger yet. "What else is in the pack?" she asked. She didn't know what she was hoping for— something that could help them and get them out of this mess safely.

"Just clothing, some freeze-dried food and a first-aid kit," Jack said. "The kinds of things you would expect someone to take on a day hike in the mountains, which is what Mark was doing when he disappeared."

"Why would these guys want to kidnap him?" Brian asked. "Because they wanted to get back at his brother, the FBI agent?"

"I don't think so." Jack finished zipping up the pack and stood. "Like your dad, Mark Renfro is a nuclear physicist. The terrorists may want him to work for them."

Andrea wasn't willing to accept the conclusion her mind had leaped to. "Jack, you don't think these people are trying to build a nuclear bomb, do you?"

"I don't know what to think." He raked his hand through his hair. Like the rest of them, he was gray faced and weary, but anger sparked his words. "Judging by what they've done so far—the people they've killed and the lives they've disrupted—they'll stop at nothing to reach their twisted goals." He handed the pack to Brian. "This is important evidence," he said. "Can I trust you to keep it safe until I can turn it over to my team?"

Brian nodded and solemnly accepted the pack. "How are we going to get to your team from here?" he asked.

Brian took out his phone and studied the screen. "I'm not getting a signal in this tunnel. I may have to go outside. But I'll call my team leader and give him my coordinates. He can contact the people who can get us out of here and close in on this area and the camp while the others are still here."

"I don't like knowing those four are still out there looking for us," Andrea said.

"All we have to do is stay hidden until help arrives," Jack said. "Come on. Let's get back to the front entrance and I'll make the call."

He ushered them to the mine's entrance. "I'm bored," Ian announced.

"So am I." Brian sat cross-legged on the floor a few feet away from Andrea and Ian and began gathering pebbles. He used one of the pebbles to draw a circle in the dirt of the floor.

"What are you doing?" Ian asked.

"I'm going to have a battle with these rocks." He completed his circle, then put more rocks in the center of the circle. "See, I use this rock—" he chose a large roundish pebble "—to shoot the other rocks out of the circle." He demonstrated by flicking his thumb and forefinger against the pebble, sending it crashing into another rock, which shot out of the circle.

Ian inched closer. "Can I play?"

"Sure. It's better with two people anyway." He looked through the pile of pebbles and chose one for Ian to use as a shooter.

When Jack stepped out of the mine, Brian was showing Ian how to flick his thumb and forefinger in order to send his pebble crashing into others in the circle.

As he had hoped, his phone signal outside the cave was stronger. He called Ted Blessing's number and listened to it ring.

And ring. And ring. After five rings a mechanical voice informed him that he should leave a message. "This is Jack. We're in an abandoned mine about four miles east of the camp. Anderson and his group returned in a helicopter with reinforcements and—"

A long beep sounded, and then the phone went silent. Jack stared at the screen and pressed the button on the side of the phone to power it up again, but nothing happened. He swore under his breath and stared down at the woods below. In another hour or so the sun would set. If they were lucky, darkness would shut down the terrorists' search for them until the morning, but the prospect of a cold night without food or water wasn't one he looked forward to. He needed to find a way to get Andrea and Ian and Brian to safety, along with the evidence he had gathered. The sooner the team zeroed in on the camp and this mine, the sooner they could bring Duane Braeswood and his group to justice.

Andrea looked up when Jack stepped back into the mine. She had switched on his flashlight and arranged it in the center of the mine entrance, propped up with rocks, like a little candle sending its feeble glow on their gathered faces. "Did you talk to your boss?" she asked. "Is he sending someone to get us?"

"He didn't answer my call," Jack said. "I left a message with our location. Then the phone died." He looked away, not wanting to see the disappointment in her eyes. He should have charged the phone first thing this morning, when he saw the battery was low. His carelessness had put all their lives in jeopardy.

"Jack, come sit beside me."

Her voice was gentle, with no hint of judgment or reprimand. She patted the blanket beside her and he eased down next to her, trying to ignore the throbbing in his leg.

"This isn't your fault, you know," she said, with the same matter-of-fact tone he imagined she used when she talked to her patients.

"How did you know what I was thinking?"

Her smile—the fact that she could smile at all, considering the circumstances, and that she would smile at him—knocked him a little unsteady, as if the ground had shifted beneath his feet. "None of us would probably be alive right now without your help," she said.

"I'm betting you'd be alive," he said. "You're pretty resourceful and fearless."

"Not fearless. But it helps that I'm not just fighting for myself. Alone, I might give up, but I'll do anything to protect my son."

He followed her gaze to Ian, who was bent over the dirt circle, tongue protruding slightly as he concentrated on aiming his makeshift marble. "How is he doing?" Jack asked.

"He still has a fever, but he's not getting worse. We'll see what happens after nightfall."

Jack leaned his head back against the rough rock wall. "So you realize we'll probably have to spend the night here."

"Better to stay put than go stumbling through the woods at night." She nudged him. "You aren't really thinking you have to keep that chocolate bar as evidence, are you? I'll give you the wrapper, but that chocolate is going to be eaten if we stay here, along with that granola bar, and if you can figure out a way to get water and heat it, we'll eat that freeze-dried stew, too."

"If I was alone, I'd probably resist the urge to destroy potential evidence," he said.

"You're with a teenaged boy and a five-year-old—the very definition of eating machines," she said. "I don't care to listen to either one of them whine about being hungry if I can help it."

"What about you—aren't you hungry, too?" he asked.

"If I could get away with it, I'd claim that whole chocolate bar for myself."

Jack squeezed her hand, then glanced at Brian. "Brian doesn't strike me as much of a whiner."

"He's incredible. And what he's been through gives me nightmares. I want to wrap him up and feed him homemade cookies and then I want to find his lousy excuse for a father and box his ears and tell him exactly what I think of him."

"I love it when you're fierce." He kissed her cheek.

She closed her eyes. "Sometimes it's what keeps me going."

"I want to wrap you up in blankets and feed you cookies," he whispered. "I want to take care of you, the way you take care of others."

She opened her eyes and the soft look in them made him set aside, if only for a moment, the pain in his leg, worries about the men who were hunting them and the urgency of stopping a group of terrorists bent on destroying the country.

"This whole ordeal has given me a new perspective on the work you do," she said.

"What do you mean?"

"I don't think I realized before what a real threat the people you go after are. I mean, I knew it in the abstract, but now I've seen up close how ruthless and, well, evil, they are." She squeezed his hand. "What you and other men and women like you do is really important. I hate to think what the world would be like if people like Gordo and Anderson and the others were allowed to carry out their plans unchecked."

"Don't make me out to be some kind of hero," he said. "I have to live in this world, too. A lot of what I do is about self-preservation."

"You can pretend that, but I know different. Nothing you've done the last few days has been selfish. You didn't have to go to that fishing camp to rescue Ian, and you didn't have to come looking for me when those men grabbed me. You walked right in to what you had to know was a trap. You did it because you put our safety above your own."

"You and Ian are important to me. I thought you knew that by now."

She ducked her head, so that he could no longer read the expression in her eyes. "What I'm trying to say is that everything that has happened makes me realize I've been looking at some things wrong. With Preston—I used to think he chose his job over time with family because the work was so macho and exciting. He enjoyed the rush more than he enjoyed nights at home reading bedtime stories or talking to me."

"The job can be macho and exciting, and anyone who tells you they don't enjoy the rush is lying." Jack slid his hand up to caress her shoulder. "But none of that is more important to me than the world away from work. That everyday life, with the people I love, is the real world. The one that really matters. The one I'm working to protect."

"I guess it really is all a matter of perspective," she said.

"I didn't know your husband, or the kind of man he was." Jack chose his words carefully, aware that he was treading on sensitive ground where maybe he had no right to trespass. "But he loved you enough to marry you, and he gave you a great son. If he lost sight of his priorities sometimes—it can happen to the best of us."

She nodded. "I know. I forgot about what is really important, too. You've helped me remember that."

He wanted to ask her what he had done to change her thinking. Was she trying to tell him that his being a law enforcement officer wasn't such a black mark against him anymore? That she could see a future with the two of them together? But now, when they were still in so much danger, didn't seem the right time to press her.

"Mom, I'm hungry." Ian made Jack's decision for him by crawling into his mother's lap and giving her a mournful look.

"I'm sorry we don't have any dinner to give you." She rubbed his back.

"Jack has chocolate and he's not sharing."

Three pairs of eyes regarded Jack—two of them accusing, one sympathetic and maybe a bit amused. "All right, all right." He held up his hands. "We'll eat whatever is in that pack. But you have to let me unwrap everything so I can at least try to preserve the wrappers in case there are fingerprints."

"Great!" Brian shoved the pack over to Jack. "I'm starving."

Using his pocketknife and two fingers, Jack opened the pack and eased out the chocolate bar and two granola bars. He slit the wrapper from each, shook the contents into his lap, then passed them to Andrea. "You divide everything up," he said.

She broke each granola bar in half and distributed the pieces. "Give mine to the boys," Jack said.

She started to argue, but apparently, the look in his eyes or the set of his jaw made her think otherwise. "All right."

Brian accepted a chunk of granola bar and sat back. "You know what's funny?" he said.

"What?" Jack asked.

"There aren't any maps in there." He nodded to the pack. "You'd think a guy going hiking in the mountains would at least have at trail map."

"Maybe he knew the trail really well," Andrea said. She broke off another section of granola bar and handed it to Ian.

"That's not it," Jack said. "The man who owned this pack, Mark Renfro, had a photographic memory. He had probably memorized the map."

"Seriously?" Brian asked. "I thought that kind of stuff was only in movies."

"Jack remembers faces like that," Andrea said. "He truly never does forget a face."

"That would come in handy picking people out of a police lineup," Brian said.

"That it does," Jack said. If only he could remember the man who had murdered Gus. Pain pinched his heart at the thought, but it wasn't as sharp as before. He hadn't thought of his friend, or his own failure to remember the killer's face, in a few days. Was it because he had been preoccupied or, as Andrea had suggested, was he learning to live with that blank spot in his head?

"I guess you're pretty sure this is Mr. Renfro's pack," Brian said. "Since his wallet is in there. Too bad he didn't stash his phone in there, too."

"The phone would be dead after all this time," Andrea said.

"Not if he shut it off." Brian shrugged. "I guess we couldn't get that lucky, huh?"

"I don't know," Jack said, studying the pack. Back there in the mine tunnel, he had given the contents only a superficial look, reasoning he could examine it more thoroughly when he had it back at team headquarters. But now he noticed zipped pockets on the sides that he hadn't bothered to open before. He reached for the zipper on one of them now.

The cell phone was an older, no-frills model, not even a smartphone. But that meant no apps or Wi-Fi or Bluetooth to drain the battery as quickly.

"I don't believe it!" Brian whooped. "You found a phone."

Jack flipped open the phone. The screen was black. But when he pressed the on button, it glowed with life.

"Quick, call for help before it dies," Andrea urged.

Jack was already up and heading for the mine entrance.

Chapter Fourteen

Outside, dusk had descended and the first stars were visible in the clear sky overhead. Jack punched in the number for Ted Blessing. He groaned as it rang three times, then four. On the fifth ring, Blessing's clipped voice asked, "Who is this?"

"Jack Prescott."

"What are you doing calling on Mark Renfro's phone?"

"It's a long story. Did you get my message about our situation?"

"Yes, and we're trying to get someone in there to help you, but the only road in there is still blocked and we haven't gotten approval to hire a helicopter yet. Is Renfro there with you?"

"No. We found a backpack we think is his. At least, his wallet and ID and his phone were in the pack. We also found a box of plastic explosives we think Anderson and his bunch have stashed in the old mine where we're hiding. There may be more. We need to get a team up here to go over this place. This could link Anderson's bunch to Braeswood."

"What's your situation now?"

"The four of us are getting ready to spend the night in this abandoned mine. We had an altercation this afternoon with five men—not Anderson, but a man who is in our database, Gordon Phillips, and four others. They were wearing masks, so I couldn't see their faces to identify them, but Gordo's bad dental work gave him away."

"What kind of altercation?"

Jack gave a brief summary of the afternoon's events, glossing over Brian's wild shooting. "We left Gordo tied up by the river, but the other four are still out here, searching for us. They're bound to remember this mine sooner or later. I don't think it will be safe to stay here in the morning."

"Are you in a position to hold them off?"

Jack made a quick assessment—they had the two handguns he had taken from Gordo, plus Gordo's rifle, but extra ammunition for only one of the weapons, a pistol that used the same ammunition as Jack's Glock. The handgun Brian had fired had no more bullets. They had no more food or extra clothing, and their only source of water was melted snow. "We've got three weapons and a limited amount of ammunition. They have high-powered rifles, a helicopter and more men. We can hold them off a little while from our position, but we can't move farther back into the mine. We do that and they could easily close off the entrance and trap us."

"Is there another way out of the mine?" Blessing asked.

"I don't know and it's not safe to look. From what I could see of the mine tunnel past the point where we found the explosives and Renfro's pack, some of the timbers have fallen and there's a lot of rubble. My judgment is that the whole structure is very unstable."

"All right. Sit tight as long as you can and we'll find some way to get to you. The local authorities must know that area. Maybe they can help. Are there any landmarks or distinguishing geographic features they can use to find you?"

Jack studied the area around the mine, but the sun had set and the few exposed rocks looked like black smudges against a gray background. He tried to recall any features he had noticed on the way up. "It's a mine, so there's quite a bit of waste rock around the entrance—red and yellow rock that stands out where the snow has melted because it's a different color from the other soil."

"Anything else?" Blessing asked.

Jack peered down the slope and his gaze locked on a pinpoint of light. It was joined by three other lights, each bobbing gently, gradually moving toward him. Fear, sharp and hard as a bayonet, lanced through him as he realized what he was looking at, but he forced the emotion away. "You're sure there isn't a rescue team already out looking for us?" he asked.

"I spoke to Search and Rescue less than half an hour ago and they said it would be tomorrow morning before they could get anyone to that area. They've been swamped."

Jack nodded, even though he knew Blessing couldn't see him. "Then we're in a lot more trouble than I thought," he said. "I'm pretty sure the four men we met up with earlier are headed this way."

"You can see them?"

"I can see their headlamps. They're maybe a mile away but climbing fast."

"How did they find you?"

He studied the tight formation of lights moving up the slope. The steady, organized way they moved hinted at a disciplined, determined group. "Do you remember the men Braeswood had with him in the Weminuche Wilderness—the ones who were hunting Travis Steadman and Leah Carlisle?" Though Jack had been in the hospital by then, he had read the team's official report later.

"Yes. But we captured them all."

"But you remember the type of men they were—ex-military and mercenaries, trained trackers."

"Yes."

"I think these are the same type of men. Braeswood isn't trusting ordinary babysitters with this one. These guys probably have night-vision goggles and scoped weapons."

"Try to hold them off until I can get help to you."

"Yeah. I've got to go now."

Not waiting for a response, he ended the call and took a last look at the lights below. They were strung out in single file now, having reached a narrower, steeper section of trail. At the rate they were traveling, he estimated they would be here in fifteen minutes or less.

ANDREA SANG SOFTLY to Ian, running through every lullaby she could remember in an effort to both soothe him and take her mind off their situation. Ian rested with his head against her chest, either sleeping or merely being quiet. She cupped her hand over his forehead. It felt hot.

Jack rejoined them and she looked up, her spirits lifting with his presence. Having him to lean on made all of this bearable. After she'd been alone for so long, it felt good to have someone to stand beside her in times of trouble.

"We've got to leave," he said. He zipped up Renfro's pack and handed it to Brian, then opened the other pack and removed the smaller of the two handguns he had taken from Gordo. "Take this," he said, thrusting it at Andrea. "Use it if you have to."

Andrea eased Ian to the floor and stood. His grim expression sent a chill through her. "What's going on?" she asked. "Did you reach your boss on the phone? What did he say?"

"There are lights headed this way. Probably men coming for us." He thrust the gun at her again. "Take this."

She did as he asked, the weapon heavy and cold as she slid it into her waistband at the small of her back. The kidnappers had taken the weapon Jack had given her earlier. She hoped the same thing didn't happen again.

"Maybe it's a search party looking for us." Brian had risen also, though the pack still sat on the ground. "I mean, if they have lights and everything, they're not trying to hide."

"They're not trying to hide because they know we're trapped." He suspected the lights were also intended to intimidate, to let them know what was coming and paralyze them with fear. But he wasn't going to sit here and not act. "Put the pack on and get ready to leave."

Jack looked to Andrea. "Can you carry Ian? I need both my hands free."

In answer, she wrapped Ian in the blanket, then picked him up. "What did your boss say?"

"He can't get to us before these men do," Jack said.

"We outsmarted them once. We can do it again," Brian said. "They're bullies when there are more of them, but they're not smart or even particularly strong."

"These aren't Andy and Leo, or even Gordo by himself," Jack said. "These are trained hunters. Former soldiers. Mercenaries. They've probably got high-powered weapons. They've done this kind of thing before."

"How do you know?" Andrea asked.

"Because that's how these people operate. I've seen it before." He checked the load on the larger of the two confiscated pistols, which took the same .44-caliber bullet as his Glock. "We've only got a few minutes," he said. He plucked the flashlight from the floor and switched it off, plunging them into darkness. Ian began to whimper and he heard the rustle of fabric as Andrea shifted to comfort the boy.

"What are we going to do?" Brian asked. His voice shook. "How are we going to get away from them?"

"We've got to climb, up and around the side of the mountain until we're out of sight. Then we have to head back down before they realize what's happening." He couldn't see their faces in the darkness, but he could feel their fear, like a cloud surrounding them. The plan wasn't a good one. If the men below had infrared goggles, they might be able to track their movements or figure out what they were doing. If they had thermal-imaging scopes or goggles, they would be able to track them, even in pitch blackness. Climbing in the darkness, they could fall or be injured. But staying put only to be trapped and shot like rats in a bucket wasn't an option. "Come on." He reached out and found Andrea's hand. "Let's go."

While miners and others had worn a path to the mine over the years, the only trail leading up had probably been made by deer or mountain sheep. A quarter moon cast a silvery glow over the snow, allowing Jack to pick out the narrow line of the path that led almost straight up from the mine entrance. "Brian, you go first," he instructed. "Crawl if you feel more stable. Move as quickly as you can, but take the time to feel for good hand- and footholds. Andrea will be right behind you with Ian, and I'll bring up the rear."

Andrea clutched at his arm. "Do you really think this is better than staying and fighting?" she asked. "Or surrendering to them."

"Surrendering isn't an option," he said. "I don't think they're going to waste any more time holding us hostage."

She let out a small cry as his meaning sank in.

"Mom, you're squeezing me," Ian protested.

"I'm sorry, honey. Put your arms around my neck, okay? And your legs around my waist. Now hang on tight. When we get to the top, I'll let you off for a minute."

She squeezed Jack's hand, then began climbing up the rock in front of him.

He checked below them. Their pursuers were moving more slowly now as they reached the steepest section, but they were making steady progress. If only he had a better weapon than a pistol and a rifle with only one magazine, he could try to mow them down. As it was, he might take out one or two of them, but the others would figure out where he was about the time he ran out of ammunition. If the waste rock were bigger, he could have shoved boulders down onto them, maybe started an avalanche.

The image of boulders careening down into the men below sparked an idea. *There's enough explosives here to level this mountain.*

He ordered the others to go ahead, then ran back into the mine, pausing only to switch on his flashlight once he was in the tunnel. Thirty seconds later, he stood in front of the box of explosives. His hands shook as he tore open the cardboard box of detonators and he forced them to steady. *Focus. Remember your training.*

He'd had a crash course in explosives at Quantico, primarily in order to familiarize himself with those used by terrorists, from suicide bombs to infrastructure sabotage. But part of the training had involved learning how to build a bomb of his own. He switched off the flashlight and willed that training to come back to him as he carried the detonator and the brick of C-4 to the mine entrance.

Their pursuers were close enough now that he could hear their movements—boots scraping on rock, the soft percussion of a dislodged pebble bouncing from rock to rock as it descended. He moved to the side of the mine entrance, to the shelter of a boulder, and forced his own breathing to become quiet and deep. In the dim moonlight, he carefully unwrapped the brick of explosives and molded the puttylike material around the detonator.

He used only half of the brick, wary of taking out too much of the mountain and endangering himself and the others. He wanted to cause damage close to the kidnappers, but the destruction needed to be limited.

He forced himself to wait as long as possible. He wanted Andrea and the others to be as far from the mine entrance as possible when his homemade bomb went off. But he needed enough time to make his own getaway before the explosion.

He could make out faces beneath the headlamps the hunters wore—nothing recognizable, but the suggestion of chins and noses and human forms. They had removed their masks, probably to avoid hindering their peripheral vision. Their figures were bulky and dark, suggesting they wore packs and probably ballistics vests. The silhouettes of rifle barrels protruded from a couple of the packs.

When he judged that they were almost within firing distance from him, he took out the lighter and lit the end of the detonator cord. Then he stood and lobbed his makeshift bomb into the midst of the climbers.

Shards of rock exploded around him as bullets slammed into them. Jack scrambled up the slope, grabbing for handholds and hauling himself up, lurching from tree to boulder to depression—whatever he could find for cover. Bullets riddled the rock below him, but he had moved out of range. Not looking back, he made a mad dash for the top, propelled by a vision of the mountain collapsing beneath him.

"Jack, over here!" Brian's words, low and urgent, beckoned him. He moved toward them and found the teenager, Andrea and Ian huddled in the lee of the broken tower from an old mining tram.

"We've got to get out of here." Jack grabbed Andrea's arm and pulled her forward. "Move! Now!"

His lungs burned and the ache in his leg sent shock waves of pain through him with every step, but he ignored the pain, willing himself to focus on nothing but survival and protecting the people in his care. They had reached a false summit and were running along a high plateau when the ground shook beneath them. Brian stumbled and fell, and Andrea screamed. Jack launched himself on top of her and together they fell.

Chapter Fifteen

Andrea broke her fall with her hands and knees and rolled to bring Ian between her and Jack. The first shock wave was followed by a second. Then everything stilled, the silence like a roaring wind in her ears.

"What happened?" she asked, the words half-sobbed.

Brian crawled over to them. "Are you okay?" she asked.

"The snow cushioned our fall. I'm okay." He looked at Jack. "Was that a bomb?"

"I used some of the plastic explosives we found," he said.

"You built a bomb?" She gaped at him.

"Something like that," he said. "It was the only thing I could think of."

"That should slow them down," Brian said.

"Slow them down, but it may not stop them." Jack sat up. "We've got to get out of here."

"I don't even know where 'here' is," Andrea said. "Or where we can go that's safe."

"Now is when we need a smartphone," Brian said. "With GPS and a map. Do you think they have an app that would help us avoid crazed terrorist killers?"

"You mean like a video game?" Ian asked.

"Uh, yeah. Just like a video game." He reached into the pocket of his jeans. "I've got a little piece of chocolate left," he said. "Do you want it, Ian?"

"Yeah!" The boy reached for the treat.

"Thanks," Andrea said. Brian had a good head on his shoulders, and he was holding up pretty well, considering the circumstances.

"So what do we do now?" Brian asked.

Jack looked up at the tram tower. "Where do you think this goes?" he asked. "I mean, where do you think it went when it was in working order?"

"I guess down the mountain to the river or a road or a railroad, or to a mill or something where they processed the ore," Brian said.

Jack kicked at a rusted length of iron cable that lay at the base of the tower. "There are probably more of these towers, then," he said.

"Yeah," Brian said. "I see them all the time when I'm out hiking. And pieces of cable, too. When they abandoned the mines and mills, they left all this stuff up here. Some of the iron stuff was collected and sold as scrap during World War II, but most of it is still lying around."

"Then we'll follow the tramline as far as we can," Jack said. "When we get to the end, hopefully we'll find our way back to civilization."

Andrea suppressed a moan. Stumbling down a mountain in the darkness, carrying a child who grew heavier by the minute, seemed an impossible task. "I don't think I can do it," she said.

Jack knelt beside her. "You can do it," he said.

"You're strong. And the longer we stay on the move, the less the chance that those murderers will find us."

"Maybe none of them are left," she said. "After that explosion…"

"Duane Braeswood has the money and the resources to keep hunting us. If he doesn't hear from this bunch when they're supposed to check in, he'll send more men. Another helicopter. Weapons. We can't assume he's going to stop until we know we're safe."

She shuddered, remembering the masked faces and cruel voices of the five men who had captured her. Their casual talk of murdering Ian and Brian, not to mention Jack, made her sick to her stomach.

But the memory of their words also made her angry. She struggled to her feet. "All right," she said. "I'll keep going." If Jack wasn't ready to surrender, then neither was she.

AFTER THREE HOURS of walking steadily downhill, the group came to a plateau scattered with rusting metal ruins. Moonlight cast eerie shadows over twisted cables and rusting pulleys, broken timbers and the shell of an old boiler rising from the snow. "This must have been where they processed the ore from the mine," Jack said. He leaned on the tree branch he had cut several miles back to use as a crutch. The fact that he had resorted to using such an aid told Andrea how much his leg must be paining him.

Brian, a sleeping Ian in his arms, joined them. The two men had taken turns carrying Ian most of the way, after Andrea had almost dropped him from exhaustion. As it was, she was pretty sure she could have been perfectly cast as an extra in the latest zombie film. She'd willed herself for the last hour to stop thinking about anything but putting one foot in front of the other. "I took a geology course last semester and we visited a site like this," Brian said. "The professor said they hauled away most of the stamp mills to other locations when the mines played out. I guess they were worth enough money to make moving them a good idea." He looked around them. "But there should be a road around here somewhere. They would have hauled the processed ore by wagon or train to someplace else."

Andrea put her hand on Jack's arm. "We can look for the road in the morning," she said. "Right now we've got to stop and rest."

Brian lowered Ian to the ground, then sat beside him. "You could try to call for help again," he said. Several times during their trek down the mountain, Jack had tried to telephone his boss but had been unable to get a strong enough signal for the call to go through.

He took the phone from his pocket and switched it on. After a few seconds, he shook his head. "No signal," he said.

He looked exhausted, deep lines of weariness and pain etched on either side of his mouth and around his eyes. Andrea wanted to go to him and hold him, but she knew he would misinterpret the gesture as her needing comfort from him.

"Let's move to the woods over there." He gestured toward the thick growth of forest on the edge of the plateau. "I don't like being out in the open like this."

"You're right." Andrea hugged her arms across her

chest. She had a feeling it would be a long time before she could stand in the open without feeling like a target.

Once in the woods, they settled down with their backs against tree trunks or stretched on the ground. Though the cold seeped into them, they were out of the wind. If they stayed close together under the blankets, they should be all right. Andrea settled beside Jack. "There's probably ibuprofen in the first-aid kit in that pack." Until this moment, she had forgotten about the medical supplies in the pack Jack had found at the fishing camp.

"I took it a couple of hours ago," he said. "When we stopped at that creek to get water."

"Did it help?"

"Some."

"Liar."

The corners of his mouth tugged up and that attempt at a smile made her heart feel lighter. "What's going to happen when we get out of here?" she asked. She ought to try to sleep, and let him rest as well, but the question had been worrying at her for most of the last day. Exhaustion or the darkness or maybe simply desperation had given her the courage to ask it.

"I hope the evidence we've collected and whatever we find at the camp and the mine will help us to stop these people and bring them to justice," he said.

Of course. He had thought of his job first. Of the case. "I meant, what is going to happen with us?" she asked.

He turned his head toward her. "I want to keep seeing you," he said.

"If you solve the case, you won't stay in Durango."

"Maybe not. But they have these things called planes."

"I don't want a part-time relationship," she said. She had already had one of those, considering how much of Preston's focus had been on his work and not his home life. Even when he was with her and Ian, she could tell he was thinking about the job.

He let out a long breath. "I don't know what to tell you," he said. "I want to be with you and Ian. Can't you just have faith that we'll find a way to work this out?"

She needed more from him than wishful thinking and maybes. She needed—what—a commitment? From a man she had known only a few days? "You're right," she said. "This isn't the best time to be discussing this. We'll have plenty of time later." She patted his knee, then stood and joined Ian and Brian a few feet away. Ian still felt feverish and his lethargy during the hike down the mountain worried her. She needed to focus on her son instead of worrying about a man who could leave her life as quickly as he had entered it.

Andrea was sleeping when a low, throbbing noise entered her dreams. She pulled the blanket, which she was sharing with Ian, more tightly around her and willed herself back to dreamland. Maybe this was a dream, too, or the beginning of a nightmare.

Jack shook her. "Get up," he said. "Someone's coming."

"Is that another helicopter?" Brian asked. He sat up and looked around.

"Come on," Jack said. "Get up and bring everything with you. Whoever it is probably doesn't know we're here yet."

"How long have we been here?" she asked.

"A couple of hours," Jack said. "It will be dawn soon."

Andrea would have thought she was too exhausted to take another step, but fear propelled her forward once more. She didn't know if Ian even woke as she picked him up. She followed Jack and Brian farther into the woods.

"How did they find us?" Brian asked.

"They probably figured out we would follow the tramline," Jack said. "It was the most direct route off the mountain. I knew we were taking a risk using it, but any other course in the dark seemed too dangerous."

"Jack, I can't keep running through the woods like this," Andrea said. "I'm sorry, but I can't. And neither can Ian."

"Neither can any of us." He positioned himself behind a tree. "Do you still have the gun I gave you?" he asked.

"Yes." The hard pistol dug into the small of her back, though in her exhaustion, the discomfort hadn't been enough to keep her from sleeping.

"Do you think you can shoot it?"

"Yes, of course," she said. Hadn't they had this conversation once already?

"Would you kill a man to protect Ian?"

"Yes." She swallowed hard at the idea, but she knew she meant it. She would do anything to protect her son.

"Then find cover and be ready to shoot if anyone comes through the woods toward us. They won't be expecting us and if we're lucky and there aren't too many of them, we can pick them off before they get to us."

"What do you want me to do?" Brian asked.

"Take Ian and go about a hundred yards back. If we go down, you run, as far and as fast as you can. We'll try to distract them long enough for you to get away."

Andrea drew the gun and moved to stand behind a tree about twenty yards from Jack. She couldn't believe this was happening—that she was about to engage in a shoot-out in the woods, in the middle of the night, with killers. She was an ordinary woman—a mother and a psychologist. Nothing in her training had prepared her for this.

She heard Brian move away. She didn't look back, afraid she might cry if she saw Ian leaving her. Instead, she gripped the gun more tightly and tried to focus on the glow of light coming from the clearing they had just left. The throb of the helicopter rose until it was too loud to talk over. Light pierced the trees, and then the engine slowed but didn't die altogether. A door slammed. She imagined the killers piling out, in their battle gear, weapons ready. How many of them were there? Jack had said the helicopter would hold six people in addition to the pilot. How many men had died in the explosion on the mountain? Or had they brought in reinforcements, fresh troops who weren't exhausted by a trek up and down mountains?

"Agent Jack Prescott!" The words had the hollow, echoing sound of a command issued through a bullhorn.

Jack stiffened but made no response.

"This is Captain A. J. Lansing of the La Plata County Sheriff's Department SWAT. Special Agent Ted Blessing contacted us. We understand you have a woman and a child and another young man with you. If you can hear us, please acknowledge."

Jack relaxed. "We're here!" he shouted. "We're coming out!"

Andrea's first sight of their rescuers was of a man dressed in black-and-olive fatigues with a large German shepherd by his side. Ian gave an exclamation of surprise and leaned forward to gape at the dog. Andrea took her son from Brian and followed Jack into the clearing. The helicopter had shut down, making it easier to talk. "Dr. McNeil," the man greeted her. "I'm Alan Lansing. And this must be Ian."

"What's your dog's name?" Ian asked.

"This is Bella." At the sound of her name, Bella wagged her tail back and forth.

Two other SWAT team members joined them. "How did you find us?" Jack asked.

"We located you using the ping on your phone."

"Do we need to radio ahead for a medic?" one of the officers asked, eyeing Jack's makeshift crutch.

"I'm fine." Jack tossed the stick aside.

Andrea wanted to protest that he obviously wasn't fine—that none of them were. But Jack probably didn't need a medic right away, and he wouldn't appreciate her embarrassing him in front of another law enforcement officer.

"We've got food and water and blankets in the chopper," Lansing said. "Let's get loaded up and get you folks home."

They filed to the helicopter and were waiting to climb in when a burst of gunfire tore through the area.

Chapter Sixteen

Bullets rang against the side of the helicopter and one of the SWAT members collapsed. Andrea screamed. Then she and Ian were shoved to the ground. Jack slammed his body into theirs and rolled them beneath the chopper. He lay on top of them, his weight crushing yet reassuring. Ian began to cry. "Shh. It's going to be okay." Andrea tried to comfort him. The shooting had stopped, but the explosions still echoed in her ears. Her heart hammered as if she'd run up a mountain, and Jack's weight on top of her made it difficult to breathe.

"Where are the others?" she whispered, afraid the shooter might hear.

"Brian is inside the chopper with the pilot," Jack said. "Lansing and the dog took cover behind some rocks. I don't know where the third man is."

The sun was just breaking over the horizon and in the still-faint pinkish light, she could make out a narrow section of the clearing in front of the chopper. The officer who had been shot lay facedown in the snow, very still. Too still. She hoped Ian couldn't see him.

"Where is the shooter?" she asked.

"On the west side of the clearing. He must have been

following us. He came up the same trail we did." He shifted, taking some of his weight from her. "I'm going to try to get a better look at him."

"No." She clutched at his wrist. "It's too dangerous."

"I won't do anything stupid." He moved until he lay on the ground facing her. "I've got too much to live for to take foolish risks, but I've got to do whatever I can to end this." He kissed her, hard and fierce. She wanted to cling to him, to beg him not to leave her. But she knew he wasn't the type of man who would stand by and let others be hurt while he had the power to prevent it. That was one of the things she loved about him.

"Come back to me," she whispered, but he had already moved away.

JACK CROUCHED BEHIND the wheel strut of the helicopter and scanned the edge of the woods, searching for the shooter. The sun rising behind him cast a feeble light over the clearing, the shadow of the helicopter stretching out on the ground directly in front of him. Only one gun had fired on the group, so he thought it possible there was only one man—perhaps the only survivor of the bomb Jack had launched.

Movement to Jack's right distracted him. He shifted slightly and recognized Captain Lansing slumped behind a boulder. Blood stained the shoulder of his uniform, and the German shepherd, Bella, lay curled against him. The dog watched Jack, ears up and eyes alert, but didn't move.

Jack needed to draw out the shooter. He didn't want to give the man enough time to circle around behind them. Taking careful aim, he fired at the point he thought the shots had emanated from.

The shooter responded with another blast of gunfire, bullets blasting chunks of fiberglass from the side of the helicopter. Ian began to wail and the gunfire shifted, hitting the ground right in front of where Andrea and Ian lay. The thought of either one of them being hit was a physical pain gripping Jack's chest. "Come out where I can see you, you coward!" he shouted.

The only response was gunfire, but not from the shooter. Captain Lansing had raised himself up enough to fire his own weapon toward the shooter. A muffled cry indicated that—maybe—the captain had found his target.

Lansing caught Jack's eye and jerked his head toward the woods behind the chopper. Jack nodded. If he made the cover of the trees, he could slip around behind the shooter. If Lansing kept the man's attention focused on him, Jack would have a good chance of getting close without being detected.

Lansing opened fire again and Jack ran, keeping his body low and ignoring the pain in his thigh. He stopped a few yards into the trees to catch his breath and listen. The shooter had returned fire again. As far as Jack could tell, the man hadn't changed locations.

He shifted his gaze to the helicopter. The sun had almost completely risen now, light glinting off the chopper's drooping blades. He couldn't see Andrea and Ian from here, but he knew they were under there. As long as he and Lansing kept the shooter busy, the man wouldn't be able to move in closer and get a clear shot at Andrea and the others.

Slowly, stealthily, Jack crept from tree to tree. Every few minutes a fresh burst of gunfire alerted him to the gunman's location. Then, as he reached the west side of the clearing, a movement ahead caught his eye. A darker shadow shifted between the tree trunks. Jack took a step toward it and a twig snapped beneath his boot. The shadowy figure whirled, gun raised. Jack dived behind a tree.

The shooter shifted again, perhaps to get a better look at Jack. A shaft of light cut between the trees, spotlighting the side of the man's face before he ducked behind the tree trunk once more.

But that one glimpse had been enough to stop Jack's breath. A dizzying flood of emotion and memory washed over him: suddenly, he was standing on the front deck of the mountain home that had been rented by the suspected ringleader of the terrorist cell. Search Team Seven had a warrant to search the property and plant listening devices they would use to gather evidence to make their case against Duane Braeswood and the people with him in the house. Gus Mathers stood in the yard a few feet below Jack, tracing a phone line around the side of the house.

Then a man stepped out from behind a tree and shot Gus. Jack saw his friend fall, then turned to look at the shooter. Their eyes met, and the man raised his rifle to fire at Jack. Jack dived to the side so that, though the bullets put him in the hospital for weeks, he didn't die. The image of the man's face shimmered in his mind, as crystal clear and unforgettable as his own reflection.

"You!" Jack hadn't even realized he had spoken out loud, but the single word brought him back to the present—and to the people who needed his protection now. He stared at the man, who had peered from behind the tree at his shout. "You killed my friend," Jack said—a statement, not an accusation.

"And I will kill you," the man said, and raised his weapon.

But Jack had already raised his pistol. He fired once...twice...and the man slumped to the ground, his gun sliding across the snow and coming to rest against another tree a few feet away.

Jack didn't know how long he stood over the body, the pistol in his hand, before Andrea joined him. "Jack?" She spoke softly, concern and caution shaping her expression.

He holstered his weapon and turned to her. "He's the man who shot Gus," he said. "I remembered."

"I'm glad he didn't shoot you." She didn't quite smile, but it was enough to shatter the last brittle barrier of reserve within him. He held out his arms and she came to him. They comforted each other for a long moment as the sun rose higher in the sky and the helicopter's engines roared to life.

"Where's Ian?" he asked after a while.

"He's in the helicopter with Brian and the others. Captain Lansing is shot, but Corporal Scott thinks he's going to be okay." Her expression saddened. "Sergeant Rialto wasn't so lucky." She pressed her forehead to his chest. "Jack, I was so afraid."

"Yeah." He patted her back. "I was afraid, too. But we're okay now. We're all okay."

She looked up at him, some inner strength illuminating her face despite the weariness. "Let's go home now," she said.

He put his arm around her. "Yeah. Let's go home."

"I CAN'T BELIEVE you went through all of that and you still look so...so normal!" Chelsea pressed her hand against her chest and studied Andrea across the kitchen table, two days after her return home. "It's like something out of a movie or something."

"It's definitely not something I want to relive." Andrea sipped her coffee. "I'm glad it's over and I'm ready for life to get back to normal."

"Ian seems to be doing okay." Chelsea turned toward the living room and Andrea followed her gaze to where Ian was playing with baby Charlotte.

"He's doing great," she said. Though Ian had slept with her their first night home, that had been as much for her benefit as her son's and now he was back in his regular routine—although he had asked about Jack several times during the past two days.

"What about Jack?" Chelsea asked. "Have you heard from him?"

"He called and left a message while I was at work yesterday—just checking to see how we were doing." No great declarations of love or even an invitation to dinner. *I wanted to make sure you and Ian are okay. It's been crazy busy here, but you've been on my mind.* The kind of message any friend might leave.

"Are you going to see him again?" Chelsea asked.

"I don't know." She pushed the coffee cup away. "I'm not sure that's a good idea."

"What do you mean? Did something happen out there that changed your mind about him?"

"I wasn't aware that I'd made up my mind about him before," Andrea said. "If you recall, before this whole thing happened, we had only just met."

Chelsea waved this notion away. "Call me a romantic, but the first time I saw you two together, I could tell something clicked. You seemed perfect together. Did anything that happened to you while you were running around in the woods make you think otherwise?"

A kaleidoscope of memories played through her mind: Jack playing with Ian on the floor of the cabin, Jack making love to her with such exquisite tenderness and passion, Jack protecting her with his own body as a terrorist shot at them. Every image proved that he was a man of strength and character, capable of great emotion and caring.

"Jack has a very dangerous job," she said, choosing her words carefully. "One that requires a lot of his time and attention. The things that happened to us after those men kidnapped Ian—that kind of thing happens to Jack all the time. I think Ian and I need a little more stability in our lives."

"Maybe you do." Chelsea leaned forward and covered Andrea's hand with her own. "Or maybe you need a man who will go to the ends of the earth to protect you with everything he has. I know after what happened with Preston, getting anywhere near a law enforcement officer has to be scary, but tell the truth—in the three years you've been a widow, has any other man come even close to lighting you up the way Jack does?"

"Are you saying I have a thing for dangerous men?"

Chelsea sat back, smiling. "Maybe you do. Or maybe they have a thing for you."

The doorbell rang and Ian jumped up. "I'll get it!" he shouted.

"Ian, remember what I told you about opening the door to strangers." Andrea hurried after her son, Chelsea behind her.

"Hello, Andrea."

By the time the women made it to the door, Jack was standing just inside with Ian.

As a psychologist, Andrea was familiar with all the physical manifestations of attraction—pounding heart, wobbly knees and light-headedness, for example. Clearly, her body was determined to remind her of the attraction she felt for Jack by manifesting every symptom in the book. "Hello, Jack." Shaking, breathy voice—check.

"I'll just leave you two alone to talk." Chelsea took Ian's hand. "Come on, Ian. Let's take Charlotte outside to play for a little bit."

"But I want to see Jack," Ian wailed.

"I promise to come see you when I'm done talking to your mom," Jack said. "I brought that oil for your tricycle and I'll need you to help me work on it."

"We could work on it now," Ian said.

"Let me talk to your mom first."

"Okay," he relented.

By the time they were alone, Andrea felt in more

control of her emotions. "How are you doing, Jack?" she asked.

He took a step toward her, moving a little more stiffly than he had when they first met. "Are you asking as my therapist or as my friend?"

She fought the urge to back up. "Both," she said.

"My physical therapist lectured me on all the damage I've done by not staying off my leg and taking it easy, but she says I'll recover in time. My boss has agreed to give me a desk job for a while, since I managed to get into so much trouble while I was on leave. As for the rest…" He shrugged. "I'm grateful I remembered Gus's killer. I hated having that gap in my memory. It made me doubt myself—as a friend and as an agent with a job to do."

"So you have closure." She clasped her hands tightly in front of her to keep from reaching out to him. Did she and Ian and everything that had happened between them not count with "the rest"?

"His name was Roland Chambers. He was suspected of being Duane Braeswood's second in command. Taking him out put one more chink in the organization."

"He's out of your life for good now," she said. "You can move on with the work you love."

"I guess so. We've confirmed the backpack I found in the mine definitely belonged to Mark Renfro. We still don't know where he is or if he's even alive, but it gives us a lead to follow. We're still looking for the rest of the group, but we hope the evidence we've collected at the mine and at the fishing camp will eventually lead us to them."

"How's Brian?" she asked. "I want to get his contact information and keep in touch with him."

"He'd like that. He's back in Boulder right now. We were able to contact his dad and he flew in from Iceland yesterday. He hadn't taken the threats against his son seriously. He thought they were some kind of fraternity prank or something and was too engrossed in his work to pay attention. I think this was a real wake-up call for him. He's talking about taking Brian back to Iceland with him."

"I guess this is the kind of thing that would shake up anyone," she said.

"How are you and Ian doing?" he asked.

"Ian is great. I guess it's true about little kids— they're very resilient. Right now all he cares about is counting down the days until Christmas. But I've made an appointment for him with a friend of mine who specializes in children's therapy, just to make sure there's no lingering concerns."

"And you?"

She pressed her lips together, choosing her words carefully. "What happened shook me up a little," she said. "I…I know we wouldn't have made it without you."

He took another step toward her, until she could feel the heat of him and see the rise and fall of his chest as he breathed. "There's something you need to know," he said.

She forced herself to meet his eyes, and the searching look he gave her made her breath catch. She pressed her lips together, afraid to speak, to break the spell between them.

"When I faced that shooter in the woods, it wasn't about Gus or the job or protecting myself or anything like that. It wasn't even about revenge. All I wanted was to protect you. You and Ian. You were the only things that mattered. The only things that still matter."

"Oh, Jack." She pressed her fingers to her lips, a sob catching in her throat. He gathered her close and she relaxed against him, unable to hold back anymore.

He kissed the top of her head, his hands caressing her back. "I love you," he said. "You know that, don't you?"

She nodded. "Yes. I love you, too. I know we just met, but…"

"But it's right. I'm as certain of that as…as I am that I would never forget your face." He pulled back enough to smile at her and she returned the expression, happiness filling her up like light.

"What about your job?" she asked.

"What about it?"

"You won't be in Durango forever."

"I could be," he said. "The Bureau's resident agency here in Durango has an opening."

"What about your case?"

"I can stay with the team until they leave here, then transfer to the resident agency."

She clutched his shirt front. "You'd do that for me?"

"I told you. You and Ian are what matter most to me now." He cradled her head in his hand and kissed her. The kiss was as familiar and welcome as the taste of sweet chocolate and as intoxicating as an exotic liqueur. This was what life with Jack would bring her—his steadfast love and protection along with an electric dose of the unexpected. As much as she claimed to crave the ordinary and sedate, she knew Chelsea had been right. Jack's courage and willingness to face danger, to right wrongs, attracted her every bit as much as his muscular shoulders and tenderness toward Ian.

"Jack!"

Andrea's whole body hummed with the effect of that kiss when Jack raised his head to look at Ian. "What is it, Ian?"

"Are you staying?"

Jack looked at Andrea, who nodded. "I'm staying, buddy," Jack said.

"Then do you think, pretty soon, that you could teach me to ride a big bike? I asked Santa to bring me one for Christmas."

Jack released her and knelt in front of her son. "I hope I can teach you that, and a lot of other things," he said.

"Good." Ian threw his arms around Jack's neck and hugged him tightly. Andrea knelt to join in the embrace.

"The three of us are going to be a family now," she said. "Would you like that?"

"Uh-huh." He stepped back to regard them both solemnly. "Does this mean we can get a dog?"

"We'll have to talk about that later." Jack stood and helped Andrea up beside him. He put his arm around her and looked at Ian. "What do you think about me marrying your mother?"

Ian studied them a moment. "I guess that would be okay." He turned and headed out of the room. "I'll get my trike out of the garage. You can meet me out there."

Jack laughed. "I guess you're right," he said. "Nothing fazes him."

"Are you sure you're ready for this?" Andrea asked.

"More than ready." He began kissing her again and she wrapped herself around him. Ian and his trike would clearly have to wait a few minutes longer.

* * * * *

Cindi Myers's series
THE MEN OF SEARCH TEAM SEVEN
continues next month with P_HD_ PROTECTOR. *Look for it wherever*
Mills & Boon Intrigue books are sold!

MILLS & BOON®

Why shop at millsandboon.co.uk?

Each year, thousands of romance readers find their perfect read at millsandboon.co.uk. That's because we're passionate about bringing you the very best romantic fiction. Here are some of the advantages of shopping at www.millsandboon.co.uk:

* **Get new books first**—you'll be able to buy your favourite books one month before they hit the shops

* **Get exclusive discounts**—you'll also be able to buy our specially created monthly collections, with up to 50% off the RRP

* **Find your favourite authors**—latest news, interviews and new releases for all your favourite authors and series on our website, plus ideas for what to try next

* **Join in**—once you've bought your favourite books, don't forget to register with us to rate, review and join in the discussions

Visit **www.millsandboon.co.uk**
for all this and more today!